I0563120

The Rooks Parliament

Jenny Grover

Brushpanther Press

Copyright © 2010 by Jenny Grover

All rights reserved. No part of this book may be reproduced in any form by any means without express written permission from the author, except by a reviewer who may quote brief passages in a review.

Brushpanther Press
6 Woodridge Estates, Huntington, West Virginia 25704

Paperback first edition.

Author's note: This is a fictional work. Characters other than historical figures are not intended to represent any real persons, living or deceased.

Library of Congress Control Number: 2010911071

ISBN: 978-0-578-06383-6

Printed in the United States of America

To the memory of my mother, Melba Josephine Marshall,
whose love of music enriched and inspired those around her.

The Rooks Parliament

Chapter 1

"What *are* those things hanging from the ceiling? Pie plates?" Jules asked, leaning toward the TV screen for a closer look.

"Looks like it," Gina replied, crossing her ankles in the air as she stretched out on her stomach and propped herself up on her elbows.

"Who cares? Move!" Melissa said, legs crossed in front of her on the braided oval rug. "There's more interesting stuff than that to look at there!"

"You said it." Gina smacked her gum.

Jules reached out to turn up the sound just as the camera zoomed in on Mark Lindsay, inexplicably sitting in a rolling office chair to sing. Melissa let out a little shriek.

Jules grinned and sat back on her heels. "I love those tights." Paul Revere and the Raiders were singing "Hungry," clad in their pseudo-Revolutionary War outfits.

"You better hope your dad doesn't walk in," Melissa said.

"I'll just tell him they're being patriotic," Jules replied.

Gina sputtered. "You're gonna make me swallow my gum."

"What is that, a walrus?" Jules squinted at the furry hand puppet Mark was wearing.

"I guess," Gina shrugged. "It has tusks."

"Shh! Shut up," Melissa said, leaning closer to the screen, just as Mark took a hearty, full-face sniff of the puppet.

"I can almost taste it," he sang breathily.

"Taste what?" Gina whispered in Jules' ear.

Jules covered her mouth to hide her grin, both at Gina's remark and what she was seeing in front of her. Mark, sideways to the camera, had put his shiny black boots up on Paul Revere's keyboard. "Oh my God, look at those thighs."

"Very patriotic," Gina said. "I heard he recorded that song naked, to give it more feeling."

Jules laughed wickedly. "I'm sure Melissa would like to help with the feeling part."

"Shut up!" Melissa said.

"She's blushing," Gina observed.

The chorus came back around. "I can almost taste it," he sang again, having nuzzled the fuzzy puppet suggestively. They all shrieked.

Silly things began happening in the background with puppets and

4

someone hiding behind a wooden cut-out of a bush. "What's all that about?" Melissa puzzled.

"Who knows?" Jules shrugged.

"I think we should go to Kessler's Drugs, get a soda," Gina suggested. She poked Jules with her elbow and teased in a sing-song voice, "Bobby might be working."

Jules ducked her head and smiled, feeling the color rise in her cheeks. "Gina, I don't think he even knows I exist."

"Maybe it's time to change that," Gina said.

"Then I'd better change out of this." They went up to her room, where she took off last semester's blue, knee-length A-line skirt and put on her new navy mini-skirt and white tights.

"Jules, it's too hot for tights," Gina said.

"Daddy won't let me wear a mini-skirt without them," she replied. She paused at her dresser mirror to fix her hair. With a brush and a quick spray of White Rain she renewed the upward curl at the ends that sat just atop her shoulders, then smoothed her bangs.

"I'm thinking of getting a Pixie," Gina said, tousling the top of her dark hair. "Kind of a Twiggy look. Maybe you should cut yours short, too."

"I don't know, Gina." Jules considered her image in the mirror. "It would be a big change."

Melissa twisted one of her pale ringlets around her finger. "I'm tired of sleeping in rollers."

"I quit rolling anything but the ends a long time ago," Jules said, dabbing on just a touch of Jasmine cologne. "Mom!" she called out as they clattered down the stairs.

"Yes, dear?" Kate Greene's voice came from the small home office she had set up in the den, in which she tabulated her Tupperware sales.

"We're going to Kessler's, alright? Gina's driving."

"Alright, dear. Be home for supper."

"Thanks!" Jules picked up her purse from beside her books on the couch. "I want to go to the record store first," she told Gina.

They were barely out of the driveway when Jules reached up under her skirt and raised up from the seat. "What are you doing?" Melissa asked.

"You didn't think I was really going to wear these, did you?" she laughed, wriggling out of her tights.

"Just don't forget to put them back on before you get home," Gina admonished.

Jules' heart jumped when she looked through the front window of Kessler's Drugs. Bobby Lott was indeed working, jerking sodas behind the counter. He was a senior, and he was in a group, The Deep See. They were quite popular, not just in Midvale, Kentucky. They had played in Louisville and Lexington and even had a single out that had made the regional charts. Bobby played a sleek, red Farfisa Combo Compact organ.

Gina opened the door and the girls strode casually up to the soda fountain and sat on the high stools. Jules crossed her legs demurely, but her skirt was well up her thigh, a little higher than she had counted on. "What would you ladies like?" Bobby asked smoothly.

"A Coke float, please," Jules replied, though she really just wanted to say, "You."

"Chocolate soda for me," Gina said.

"I'll have a lemon phosphate," said Melissa.

"Coming right up," he said. As he turned to take the glassware down from the shelf, Gina tapped Jules' foot with her own.

Jules pulled her new records out of the bag to look at, or at least pretend to look at them, stealing frequent glances at Bobby preparing their drinks. His rich, dark brown hair fell below his collar, with longer, fuller sideburns than most of the boys had.

He brought Jules' float last. "The Animals," he observed her album.

"It has the full version of 'House of the Rising Sun.' I hate the way they cut the organ solo on the 45," Jules said. "I still can't believe Alan Price left."

Bobby leaned in closer. "What else you got there?"

She held up a 45. "'96 Tears.'"

"So, you like that Vox Continental sound, huh?" he pursed his lips.

"I do."

"Well, I may just have to save up for a Connie, then," he smiled, shook back overly long bangs, and looked straight into her eyes. She'd never been this close to him and it surprised her that his eyes weren't brown, as she'd thought, but dark grey. Her insides were tied in a terribly wonderful knot. "I saw you at the show the other night. With some blond guy."

"Oh, he's a neighbor," she replied. "He just gave me a ride." She took a long drink of her float, feeling the cold go straight to her head. She thought she saw Melissa twitch.

"We're playing that dance Wednesday night out at the park pavilion," he said.

"I know," she replied. "I wouldn't miss it."

"Riding with Mr. Blond?" he asked.

"I have other arrangements."

"I like your hair," he said, pinching up a golden strand.

"Stop flirting with the customers," Mrs. Kessler smirked and rolled her eyes, tugging him away by the apron tie around his neck. "If you're not busy, you can help me unpack this shipment."

They disappeared through the swinging double doors, but he poked his head back out just long enough to say, "I'll look for you."

Gina turned to Jules with raised eyebrows. "Well, now, somebody's been paying attention in class! You may be a babe in the woods, but you're sharp."

Jules had only been allowed to start dating the past spring, and she hadn't dated much. Mostly double dates, and mostly on little more than a friendly basis. Certainly no one in Bobby's league.

"Damn it, Gina," Melissa whispered. "Did you have to kick my shin like that?"

"You looked like you were gonna say something stupid," Gina replied.

"Well, I can't believe she said that about Chip," Melissa shook her head.

"I'm not that interested in Chip," Jules said, working on her float.

"Chip's nice, and he's cute. I think I'd be a little scared of that one," Melissa nodded toward the double doors.

"I'm not."

"You lie," Gina gently shoved her.

"Well, your dad might not be too keen," Melissa said.

"I'll worry about that if and when the time comes. I mean, he didn't exactly ask me out just now."

"Hasn't Chip asked you to the dance?" Melissa asked.

"He said he'd call tonight. He wasn't sure yet if he could go."

"So, what are you going to do if he does ask you?" Gina wondered.

"I'm going stag."

"Did Chip ask you to the dance?" Jules' mom asked as she wiped the kitchen counter top after supper.

"Yes, but I said I didn't want to go with him."

"I thought you wanted to go." Kate rinsed and wrung out the dish cloth.

"I do want to go, just not with him. Is it okay if I just get a ride with Gina and her date?"

Kate hung the cloth to dry and turned to Jules. "It's alright with me, as long as they get you home on time and whoever is driving isn't drinking or anything, but you'd better ask your father. Why don't you want to go with Chip?"

"I think Chip is getting too serious about me, and I'm not serious about him. School is just starting. I want to date other people. I don't want to miss the dance or seeing the groups who are playing, but I just don't feel like going with Chip. I hope his feelings aren't too hurt."

Kate smiled, drying her hands on her apron. "Well, that's what dating is all about, meeting different people, finding out who you like best. Some girls are too quick to just go steady with the first boy who asks them, just for the sake of having a boyfriend. Chip is a nice enough boy, but if you want to date other people, then you should. Maybe you'll even meet someone at the dance."

"Maybe," Jules shrugged. "Thanks, Mom."

Wednesday night after supper, Jules pulled on her lime green shift and matching hose with grey patent leather pumps. She grabbed a grey cardigan to toss in the car, just in case, and tucked her pale pink lipstick into her little, silvery satin wrist strap clutch. She checked her hair one last time in the mirror. She'd trimmed her bangs, but kept her same flip. All it had taken to make up her mind against a shorter cut was Bobby's having said he liked her hair. Hopefully it wouldn't wilt too much in the humid night air.

Gina drove, because Donnie, her date for tonight, didn't have a car. Jules sat in the back with Melissa, who was meeting Ed at the dance. "I'm so excited!" Jules announced. "I might finally be getting a car."

"What are you getting?" Melissa asked.

"A 1960 Dart 2-door. Cream. A guy Dad works with is selling it. Dad went and looked at it today after work and test drove it. He's going to take me over there Saturday when I get off work, and if I want it, he'll loan me the rest of the money." Jules had begun saving out of her summer earnings toward a car and decided to keep her job for the school year.

"Good! Then I won't have to drive you everywhere," Gina teased.

"And I won't need any 'just a ride' boys."

"I still can't believe you told Chip no for tonight," Melissa said.

"Jules has her sights set higher," Gina replied.

"And what if nothing comes of it?" Melissa said.

"Then nothing comes of it," Jules shrugged, hoping her nonchalant air was convincing. She didn't care if she didn't have a dance partner for tonight, or a date for a while, but she sure wanted Bobby to notice her, and notice her unattached.

The first band that night were called The Bottles. They played noisy, raw, tongue-in-cheek Beatles covers that teetered on the edge of parody. Jules and Gina thought them great fun, and fun to dance to.

They hadn't seen any of the Deep See members, but Jules recognized their gear set up behind The Bottles. Despite the fun she was having, that twenty minute Bottles set seemed to go on forever.

Chip was there with another girl, and he made a point of walking her right in front of Jules and her friends. He looked at Jules and nodded a hello as he passed, and she just smiled. She didn't care. She didn't even care that he could tell she was without a date.

"I'm going closer up," Jules said when The Bottles left the stage.

"We're right behind you," Gina said, dragging Donnie along.

"Where's Melissa and Ed?"

"They went to the concession stand. They'll find us if they want to."

Jules wanted to be all the way up front, not just to be seen, but because she really liked the group. Chip always wanted to hang back more, but Chip couldn't hold her back tonight. She was going to enjoy herself, and though her heart was in her throat as they took the stage, she was soon absorbed in their sound. Dwitty on the drums and Tyler on bass guitar set a fast beat. The reedy vibrato of Bobby's organ sneaked in subtly and expanded as he leaned into the knee lever, and then Terry stomped his fuzzbox and dived in with a loud, dirty sound from his old Telecaster and angry vocals about a girl doing him wrong. Jules forgot every care. Her body began moving to the music. She closed her eyes, lost in the song, and when she opened them again, Bobby was looking at her, smiling. She felt a flush rise through her face, and then something changed inside her. She wasn't nervous anymore. She wasn't self-conscious. She felt connected in some pure way, social artifice stripped away. Nothing else seemed to exist except the music, the group, that bright spot in the darkness they occupied that had admitted her.

The next song was slow and sad. Terry opted for clean, ringing guitar tones, and Bobby played a long, delicate, dexterous solo. There was little doubt he was the best garage band keyboardist for miles. Given the summer-like warmth, the group had opted for tee-shirts instead of suit coats. Bobby's was bright blue, but instead of drainpipe jeans, he wore flares in wide black and white stripes, and black Chelsea boots. He was one step ahead of the rest of the Midvale crowd in more ways than one.

The Deep See crashed or crooned their way through several more songs, including some covers, but most of what they played they had written themselves. When the set was over and the applause and cheers had died down, Jules sank back with her friends as the group removed their gear from the stage and the last band hastily set theirs up.

"That," Gina declared, "Was seriously fab."

"Yeah," Jules drifted slowly down, watching Bobby fold his organ up and latch the case. "They just get better all the time."

"And did you hear Terry say that one song is going to be their next single?"

"You bet I did."

Melissa and Ed waved to them from farther back, so they went to join them. Records were played in between bands to please the dancers. Someone put on a scratchy copy of "I Wanna Hold Your Hand." Overflowing with the energy of what she'd just experienced, Jules began bopping and singing along with Gina and Melissa, shaking their heads Beatles style on the "Ooooooh."

"You're on fire, girl," Gina said to her after the song. Jules just smiled.

The next band was The Fire Escapes, another local teen group, who took their inspiration largely from The Rolling Stones, spitting out jumpy, fast Rhythm & Blues. Jules danced beside her friends and their dates. Suddenly, someone grabbed her hand and tugged her away. "Come and dance with *me*, girl," Bobby grinned.

They danced for the rest of the song, and then the singer announced, "This one's for lovers." They began playing Wilson Pickett's "If You Need Me." Jules started to step back, but Bobby took her hands and pulled her closer.

"I never asked your name," he said.

"Julia. My friends call me Jules."

"Jules. I like that." He pulled her yet closer. "You go to Midvale High?"

"Mmm-hmm," she nodded.

"So do I."

"I know."

He let go of her hands and slipped his arms around her waist. She took the luxury of resting her face against his chest, acutely aware of every place his warmth touched her, every brush of his legs against hers as they shuffled their feet slowly to the music.

When the song ended and they moved apart, he took her hand again. "Take a walk with me? I need to make sure someone's watching the gear."

"Alright." As he led her through the crowd, past her friends, she caught a glimpse of Melissa's uncertain face.

The park pavilion was little more than a large pole barn with electricity and two small restrooms. Along either side of the stage, at the outer edges of the roof, ran a walkway to a backstage parking area. Only a couple of park rangers patrolled the venue and they didn't know what belonged to whom. Jules followed Bobby out into the gravel lot to a shabby, old blue station wagon parked under a light. He cupped his hand to peer inside the back window, then looked toward the building. "Hey!" he called out to someone and whistled through his fingers, then waved his hand while sliding the other around Jules' waist. Tyler emerged from the shadows behind the stage and walked toward them, running a hand through his short, blond hair. "Where the hell's Terry?" Bobby asked. "He's supposed to be watching."

"Probably went to take a piss. You go on. I'll watch."

"Thanks, man." He walked Jules slowly back toward the walkway, pulling her close to his side. "Did you like the show?" he asked her.

"I loved it."

"You looked like you were enjoying yourself."

"I was." She was tempted to say, "I still am," but instead she asked, "When is the new record coming out?"

"We're supposed to go to Lexington Saturday to record it."

"So, then how long after that?"

"Don't know yet. Soon, I hope."

"I'll be looking for it." She gingerly put her arm around him.

As they neared the walkway, he stopped just before the edge of the light and leaned back against a cement block partition that shielded the electrical system, turning her to face him. He looked into her eyes a moment, and then he kissed her. One soft, brief kiss. Then another, longer. She sank into his warmth, the scent of his cologne and his skin, a hint of citrus, a hint of sweat, and something uniquely male. He smiled, shook back his hair and slid a few inches down the wall, more at her level, drawing her between his legs, tight against him, undeniably aroused. Her body tingled with craving as his hands caressed the small of her back. She reached up to touch his hair and their lips met again.

"Jules!" came a hoarse whisper. "There you are." She turned to see Gina tapping her watch. "We've got to go!" Gina nodded to Bobby. "Sorry."

"I've got to go," Jules said softly, running her fingertips down his cheek.

Melissa grabbed her other hand and tugged her away. "Jules, come on, it's late."

"I've got to go," she said again.

"I'll see you around," he gave a little laugh.

Chapter 2

"I didn't want to say anything in the car last night in front of the boys," Gina began as Jules switched out books in her locker, "but, Mustang Julie, I think you better slow your Mustang down."

"Yeah, you're probably right." Jules probed for her English homework.

"You should have seen yourselves last night. I think you genuinely shocked Melissa," Gina laughed, then grew serious again. "He's got a little bit of a reputation, so just be careful."

"Half the boys in this school have a little bit of a reputation," Jules chuckled.

"I just don't want to see you get hurt, is all."

"I know. Thanks. But, you know, he still hasn't even asked me out." She straightened the books and notebooks on her arm.

"Um, well, don't turn around, but– I've gotta go get something out of my locker." Gina fought a smile and quickly left.

Jules puzzled a moment, then closed her locker and spun the dial on the lock.

"Jules?"

Warmth rose in her chest at the sound of his voice. She turned to face him. "Hi."

"Hi," he smiled. "I'm glad I found you."

"So am I," she smiled in return. He glowed in his red polo shirt and navy pants. In the watery light of the hallway, his hair was the color of black coffee.

"You never told me your last name, but Dwitty knew who you were."

"Oh. I'm sorry. It's Greene."

"Yeah, I found that out," he laughed. "Wanna go to a movie or something?"

"Sure. I'd like that."

"Say, Friday night?"

"Should be fine."

"We can get something to eat first.' He tucked his book under his arm and reached for her books. "Where's your class?"

"104." They began walking that way, slowly, and he stayed close at her shoulder.

"I'll call you tonight. That is, if you'll give me your number."

"I'll write it down for you."

"Good. Wouldn't want to have to hold Mr. William Blake here hostage." He lifted the edge of her report teasingly.

God, he was smooth. She suppressed a smile. "He's dead anyway. He might start to stink."

He laughed. As they neared her classroom doorway, she stopped, tore a scrap of paper out of her notebook, wrote her number, and handed it to him. He stole a quick kiss and walked away. She hadn't expected that.

Jules worked at Shearer's Books till 6:15 on Tuesdays and Thursdays and a full day shift on Saturdays. Her dad, as was his custom, had already eaten by the time she got home, and was watching the national news from his brown recliner. Sometimes her mother ate with him, sometimes with Jules. Tonight she had eaten with him, and went to work in her office as soon as Jules sat down to her pork chops, Tater Tots, and green beans at the woodgrain-print Formica table. Jules was about to be glad of the little bit of extra privacy.

Bobby called at 7:00. Jules was just finishing her supper. "Hey," he said, his voice over the phone sending a thrill through her.

"Hey," she responded.

"I just got off work and I've got a rehearsal with the guys tonight. We go pretty late sometimes, so I thought I'd better call you now. You wanna go to the 7:30 or the 9:30 tomorrow?"

"It'll have to be the 7:30. I'll have to be home by 10:30."

"Wow. Okay. Can you hang on a second?"

"Sure."

He covered the receiver and she heard him call out to someone, then a brief, muffled discussion. "Sorry about that," he came back on. "Had to see if I could take off work a little early, so we'll have time to get something to eat."

"I hate for you to have to do that. I can eat here."

"No, it's okay. I gotta eat too, ya know," he laughed. "How's 6:30?"

"That would be fine." She gave him directions to her house.

"See you tomorrow," he said, "if not at school, then tomorrow night."

She saw him just briefly at school. He met her near her locker and walked her the rest of the way to her class, but he was running late and the bell rang before they had time for much more than hellos and confirmation that things were still on as planned. He sprinted away down the hall, keys clinking in his pocket, soles slapping the black and white tile floor.

After class Gina rushed up to Jules. "You will not believe this," she panted. "Your old friend Chip just asked me out."

"You're kidding."

"I can only figure he's trying to make you jealous."

"What did you say?"

"I told him I don't go out on my friends," she laughed. "He said you broke up with him, so it was okay. I said, just the same, no thanks."

"He was glaring at me in Math yesterday. He's probably seen me with Bobby."

"Probably saw you dancing with him, at least."

"Well, even if things don't work out with Bobby, I'd never go back to Chip. He was starting to act like he thought he owned me, and we weren't even going steady."

At 6:30 sharp, Bobby pulled up in his dented, 9-year-old, blue Pontiac Safari wagon. Jules peeked through the avocado green curtains to watch him walk up to the front door. He wore a blue and white striped sport shirt, black flares, and those black boots. When he rang the bell, she invited him in.

"You look nice," he eyed her in her peach shift and ivory herringbone hose.

"Thank you. So do you."

Her father came into the living room to meet and scrutinize him, eying him coolly. "I expect you to behave honorably, and to have her home by 10:30 at the latest," Dan Greene stated firmly.

"Yes, sir," Bobby nodded.

"Can't any of your friends afford haircuts?" Dan muttered to his daughter.

"Oh, Dad," she gave a little laugh and rolled her eyes.

Bobby played it well, soft-spoken, deferent, yet confident. He shook hands like a gentleman, complimented Jules' mother, opened the car door for Jules. "I'd say you passed muster," Jules smiled.

He took her to Rick's Diner, one of the favorite hang-outs of Midvale teens. The burgers and malts were good and the jukebox was never idle. He put his arm around her waist as he walked her to their booth, acknowledging a few friends Jules didn't know. He held her hand across the table as they waited for their food. As they talked, she looked down at his hand, lithe and strong, long fingered, his onyx and gold class ring shining.

"I'm sorry I had to dash off the other night. Dad's strict about curfew. My friends were just looking out for me."

"Understood," he nodded, stroking the back of her hand with his thumb.

"I really like that second song you played."

"'Time Tonight.' I wrote that one," he said. "Except the lyrics. Terry wrote those. I'm no good at lyrics."

"I write poetry," she said. "I guess that's similar. I'd like to learn how to do it better. That's what I want to study in college."

"Going to college, huh?"

"Probably. I'd like to, and everyone seems to think I should. What about you?"

"I don't see myself going."

"Why not?"

He shrugged. "I've about done my time. I'd rather not add onto it. I want to be able to put as much time as I can into my music. We don't have the money, anyway."

"I'm hoping to get a scholarship."

"I'm guessing you get good grades."

"Mostly A's. I'm a little weak in Math."

"I do okay with it. I don't make too many A's, though. I guess you have to study to do that," he laughed. "Or maybe you just have to care."

"There's times I don't care," she admitted, "but if I don't keep my grades up, my dad gets on my case, won't let me do things."

"Yeah. Well, you'll have to show me some of your poetry."

"I don't promise it's any good," she laughed.

"I'm sure it's at least as good as my lyrics," he grinned.

Just outside Rick's they passed Terry, his arm around a girl with big, brown eyes. "Don't forget," Bobby hailed him. "10:00."

"I'll be ready."

Bobby and Jules walked a few blocks to Castle Cinema to see a Michael Caine comedy, *The Wrong Box*. Sitting in the dark, shoulder to shoulder, sharing popcorn, Jules was comfortable and content. She liked Bobby's laugh, neither loud nor long. A simple, sincere, understated sort of laugh. She loved the feel of that strong hand enveloping hers, and the way that during the most complex parts of the plot, when she was most intent on the screen, he would gently start tickling her ribs to distract her. He was warm and fun and sensuous. He was everything Chip was not.

When the movie was over and they stepped out into the warm night, he looked at his watch. "We've got some time. You wanna go for a drive?"

"Where?"

"Anywhere."

"Alright."

They rolled down the windows and sped into the dark at the edge of town. Crickets shrilled in the grass along the roadside and the radio played The Yardbirds, "For Your Love." Jules wished they could just keep going, just keep feeling that rush of air, that taste of adventure.

He turned down a gravel road and pulled over, under a canopy of dense trees, killing the engine and the lights, even the radio, so all they heard were the sounds of the night insects and the breeze rustling the drying leaves. He turned toward her, reached out to touch her hair, twining it gently and pulling his finger through it, then sinking his fingers to her scalp as he pulled her into a kiss. She'd never been kissed as artfully as Bobby kissed. He enticed, keeping her hungry for that next little satisfaction, and the next, then sealing her in a warm, sweet, deep involvement.

The fingers of his other hand began slowly creeping up from her knee, up under the hem of her skirt. She could feel their warmth through the open weave of her stockings, and it was maddeningly wonderful. But she had to stop it. It was too soon for this. She reached down and grasped the back of his hand through her skirt fabric, pulled her mouth back from his. "I think you should slow down," she said.

He withdrew his hand, as a stroke, meant, she was sure, to make a point, then sat back against the seat, looking straight ahead, silent, chilly. She might not have had much experience, but she recognized a game when she saw one. "It's our first date. We barely know each other yet," she said. He huffed a petulant sigh and it got her ire up. "Look, if you think I'm going to hop in the back seat with you just because you're in a band–"

"No, it's not like that," he pleaded, turning back toward her.

It was her turn to be chilly now. "What is it like, then?"

"I just want to be with you," he said softly. "I like you."

"I don't do it for 'like'," she replied.

"Fair enough." He considered the dark ceiling of the car a moment.

Even if she wouldn't have believed him, given the situation, she wished he would say he loved her. She began to doubt all his intentions, back to day 1, and that doubt began to hurt, a hurt that grew with every second of new silence as she looked down at her hands folded in her lap.

"Ah, shit," he finally said. "Is there anything I could say right now you wouldn't take wrong?"

"That you want to actually get to know me?" she ventured.

He reached out to smooth her hair. "Of course I want to get to know you. And not just in that way."

"Thank you," she said softly and let him draw her into a kiss

16

again, lingering and warm, but he was keeping his tongue to himself now.

"I'd better take you home," he said, consulting the phosphorescent numbers on his watch dial. "It's after 10."

By 10:20 the next morning the band was on the road to Lexington, Bobby driving the station wagon. Their gear was crammed in the back. Dwitty and Terry shared the back seat with Terry's guitar case. Tyler rode shotgun.

"So, did you get some last night, Bobby?" Terry asked.

"That's personal," he replied flatly.

"I'd say," Dwitty chimed, "that that means 'no.' Wait, you didn't take her to see *Alfie*, did you? Tricia wouldn't touch me for a week after that. I thought she was gonna swear off men."

"Yeah, well, that's probably just the effect of going out with you," Tyler said.

Dwitty reached up to punch Tyler's arm, and Tyler reached back to scruff up Dwitty's head.

"Kids, don't make me have to stop this car," Bobby said. "No, we didn't see *Alfie*, we saw *The Wrong Box*."

"Now there's a title," Dwitty snickered.

"Not losing your touch, are you, Bobby?" Terry teased.

"Shut up, alright?" Bobby said. "Jules is a nice girl."

"That's a switch for you," Terry laughed.

"Well maybe she won't go putting it around town," Bobby muttered.

"Maybe she's just a tease," Dwitty said. "Or maybe she's a cherry." He and Terry chuckled roguishly.

"Heard Cindy took up with Dave Slater," Terry said.

"I don't want to hear about Cindy, alright?" Bobby raised his voice. "I don't give a damn what she does with who anymore."

"Knock it off, guys," Tyler said. "Leave him alone." He grasped Bobby's shoulder. "Just ignore them, man."

"Yeah, well maybe we should be talking about something else, like *you*, Dwitty. Like that fill in the second verse of 'Mean Girl.' You were half a beat early again Wednesday night. We might not get more than a couple of takes today."

"Relax, man. I worked on it last night. I won't miss."

Dwitty's uncle Tony was already at the studio when the band arrived. Two years past, at the age of 14, Dwight Haye had lost both his parents in a car accident. Tony was his father's brother. He and his wife took Dwitty in. Uncle Tony managed The Deep See.

They were all a little early and had to wait for the previous session to finish. Bobby paced up and down the linoleum floor of the small lobby, drinking bad coffee out of a Styrofoam cup, then finally sat down in a folding chair next to Tyler. Dwitty and Terry were outside smoking cigarettes.

"Like you need that right now," Tyler flicked at Bobby's cup.

"They just pissed me off back there, is all. Why do they have to talk shit about the girls first thing in the morning?"

"Because they always talk shit about the girls," Tyler laughed.

Bobby kept looking at the clock.

"You nervous?" Tyler asked.

"Yeah, a little. I just want to get this one right, man."

"We will. We're well rehearsed, and Dwitty has been working hard."

"I don't just mean the record." Bobby stared at the undissolved powdered creamer swirling in his coffee.

"The girl you were with, out at the park pavilion?"

"Yeah."

Dwitty and Terry came back in, chuckling over something. Another group of young musicians filed out, carrying electric guitars. A man stuck his head out of a door. "You boys The Deep See?"

Tyler bumped Bobby's arm. "Put your war paint on." Tyler always said that to Bobby as they went on stage, to encourage him and help assuage his stage fright.

Jules didn't hear from Bobby over the weekend. She wasn't sure what to think. She didn't tell Gina what had happened, nor anyone, just about dinner and the movie. "Do you think he'll ask you out again?" Gina asked.

"I don't know. We'll have to wait and see," she replied. "He's tied up with the band right now." It seemed as good an excuse to give as any.

But she had the excitement of her first car to take her mind off things. She fell in love with the old Dart, so they bought it. She drove Gina and Melissa around Sunday afternoon, then proudly washed it so it would be clean and shiny for the next day. For the first time, she would be driving Gina to school.

She didn't see Bobby at school Monday and it left a grey feeling in her chest, even as she showed off her car. She tried not to acknowledge the ache, lest it grow. Tuesday passed in like manner. Even Gina was beginning to feel the chill. "Maybe he's come down sick," she offered to try to pacify Jules.

Wednesday, before her English Lit class, he showed up at her locker. "Will you go out with me again? I won't try anything, I promise." He braced his hand against the metal frame, over her shoulder. "I do want to get to know you, and I do want to be with you."

"Alright."

"Tonight?"

"I have a big History test tomorrow. I have to study."

"I could help you study."

"You serious?"

"Of course I'm serious." With his free hand he twisted a strand of her hair around his finger. She was aware of the attention this drew from passersby, and she liked it, even the jealous glare that redhead Cindy just threw her. She'd heard enough about that one, even that she'd been with Bobby at one point, but she didn't care. He wasn't with her now.

"I'd like that. How about 8?"

"8 is good. See you then." He bent to give her a quick kiss and strode off just before the bell rang.

"He seems like a nice young man," Kate Greene said as she handed Jules a plate to dry. "And he's handsome. I can see why you like him."

Jules smiled, tried not to blush as she ran the towel around the border of silver starbursts.

"I hope he's treating you right. Boys will take advantage if they can."

"Yes, Mom, I know. Everything's fine."

When they'd finished the dishes, Jules went upstairs to check her appearance one last time and brought her books down to the kitchen. She'd finished her other homework, but while she waited for Bobby, she carefully copied a page from her notebook onto a sheet of pale blue stationery, the top edge scalloped, pierced, and accented with white to resemble lace. She folded it and tucked it into the back of her textbook, just as the doorbell rang.

"Come in, Bobby," she heard her mother say. "Julia's in the kitchen."

In a moment he walked in, dressed in blue jeans and a wide-striped black and blue polo shirt. "Hi," he smiled.

"Hi, have a seat," she said, getting up. "Would you like a Coke or something?"

"Sure. Thanks."

She opened a bottle for each of them.

"I see you got your car," he said.

"Yes," she grinned, handing him his drink. "I love it. No more hitching rides to work."

"Congratulations." He shook her hand, holding onto it a moment, stroking the back of it with his thumb.

"How did the session go?"

"I think it went alright."

"You know I want a copy as soon as it comes out."

"I'll get you one, don't worry."

"Thanks. We'll have to study in here," she said quietly, as she sat down. "I'm not allowed to have boys in my room."

"Right." He tipped his chair back on two legs. "Let's get started, then."

"Here are my notes. Just ask me questions."

He flipped through them quickly. "That's a lot of notes. No wonder you get good grades." He read awhile, then asked, "What English document from 1215 helped inspire the Constitution of the United States?"

"The Magna Carta."

"Okay, what state is known as The Constitution State?"

"Connecticut?"

"Connecticut it is. Where was the Western Reserve?"

"Northeast Ohio."

"Would you like to go out Saturday night?"

"I'd love to."

"That is the correct answer. What act of Parliament in 1765 inspired the rallying cry, 'No taxation without representation?'"

"The Stamp Act. What did you have in mind?"

"We're playing the Fall Festival dance. Who were the Carolinas named after?"

"King Charles I."

"And what was he king of?"

"England. What time does it start?"

"7:00."

"I don't get off work till 6:15."

"I don't get off till 7," he laughed. "We don't have to start playing till 7:30. Tyler's gonna set up for me. Still, it means he'll have to take my car to get the gear there. I'll have to find a ride over there."

"I'll take you."

"Alright. Thanks. Now, back to work. What state is known as the Old Dominion?"

"Um... Virginia?"

"Ding-ding. You win the grand prize."

She leaned closer. "What do I win?"

"One of these." He kissed her hand. "If you want something grander, you can collect it later. What British social reformer founded the colony of Georgia?"

She closed her eyes. "Wait, it will come to me. Oglethorpe. James Oglethorpe?"

Bobby put on a Georgia accent. "Gen'ral Oglethawp thanks you fo' rememberin' him."

Jules laughed, and knew she would have no trouble remembering that answer ever again.

At 10:00 her dad leaned in and tapped his watch. "Okay, Dad," Jules acknowledged. Bobby handed her back her notebook and stood up. "Thanks for helping me study," she said.

"You're welcome."

"I'll come out with you," she said softly, her dad having returned to the living room. "And here," she handed him the blue paper. "You can read it later." He tucked it in his shirt pocket.

"Don t be long, it's late," her dad said sternly as she went out the door with Bobby.

"Is he like that with everybody, or just me?" Bobby asked quietly as they walked toward his car.

"He's like that with everybody, and I try to stay on his good side."

She walked around to the driver's side with him, away from the glare of the porch light. He leaned against the door and pulled her close. She ran her hands up his arms, strong from hefting that 65 pound keyboard around. "We'll have some fun Saturday night," he said. He kissed her sweetly, squeezed her tight a moment, then released her. "You better go back in, baby. I'll see you tomorrow. And good luck on your test."

"Thanks," she whispered, and he watched as she went inside the house.

In his room, he unfolded the paper she had given him. He figured it might be a fairytale romance poem. Girls seemed to like writing that sort of thing. Longing for some godlike perfect man to sweep them off their feet. Just what did Jules expect him to be, he wondered. He read.

I hold a shell within my hand,
shake from it tiny grains of sand.
Inside lined with sunrise peach.
Outside, color of the beach.

I hear the waves within its folds.
I feel the sunshine, warm and gold.
Whisper to me of the sea,
ever my favorite place to be.

Delicate, soft. Peach and gold. Like Jules herself. It eased him to read it, soothed his cares. So, she loved the sea. Like him. It pleased him to know. It made him want to know more. He taped her poem up on the wall over his bed, so he could read it when he woke.

He met her at her locker the next day. "How did your test go?"
"I think it went well."
"Was General Oglethorpe there?"
"No, he stood me up."
"That's his loss." He took her books to carry. "I love your poem," he said.
She smiled and looked down. "It's not much, I know."
"Don't put yourself down. It's perfect."
She stopped and turned to him. "Be honest."
He drew his fingertips down her cheek. "It's perfect," he repeated.
"Thank you," she said softly.
"Someday," he said, "I want to take you to the sea."
She smiled, looked down, then back up into his eyes. The bell rang.

"I hope you don't mind," Melissa said to Jules at school on Friday, "but Chip asked me to go to the Fall Festival dance with him, and I accepted."
"I don't mind in the least. I hope you have a nice time," she smiled.
"Is Bobby taking you?"
"Sort of. Actually, I'm taking him." She explained the complicated arrangement. "I hope we have time to dance together."
"It must feel odd, having a date that's up on stage, and you just waiting."

"I wouldn't call it just waiting. I love to watch him play."

Saturday evening Jules went straight from work to Rick's Diner, where she got a couple of take-out burgers and a fried apple pie. Then she went to Kessler's Drugs to wait for Bobby to finish work. Shearer's Books preferred female employees to dress "modestly," so Jules was wearing an autumn print A-line dress, the hem just below her knees. "Hi, baby," Bobby said as she took a seat at the counter. "You look nice."

"Thank you."

"Do you want anything?"

"Just a Coke. I got us some supper."

"Ah, good. I'm starved. Thanks." He drew her a Coke, then waited on customers until his replacement, Jimmy, came in and tied his apron on. Bobby took his off, put it in the laundry bin, and Jules met him at the open end of the counter.

"Break a leg," Mrs. Kessler said, "or whatever you say to musicians."

"I'd rather not," Bobby laughed.

Bobby ate while Jules drove. "That pie is for you," she said.

"Thanks, baby. You're a sweet girl."

When they got to the armory he dashed off to change clothes. She quickly ate her burger in the car before going inside. Bobby had given her a ticket.

An Everly Brothers record was playing. Ladies ladled up paper cups of punch and sold cookies cut in leaf shapes. Children competed in a bean bag toss and bobbed for apples. The Deep See would be toning down their set for this varied crowd, playing more covers, some old pop tunes, some slow dance songs. There would be some fun for their peers, but something for everyone else, as well. Dwitty hated playing such gigs. He wanted to rock, and the louder and wilder the better. "I hate playing for squares," he grumbled.

"It pays," Tyler reminded him. "We'll get our kicks next week."

Melissa and Chip, dressed to the nines, said hi to Jules as she waited near the stage, and stood a little ways behind her. Gina, sporting her new Pixie cut, came bouncing up with Donnie. The lights dimmed a little and people gathered loosely on the open concrete floor. The Deep See took the stage. They wore dark chocolate brown, chalk stripe suits and pastel pumpkin orange shirts with ivory ties. "They look good in those," Gina said.

Bobby exchanged a smile with Jules before focusing on his playing. They only played a couple of originals, due to the raucous nature of most of their songs, but they played "Time Tonight," and Jules was just as enchanted as she had been at the park pavilion dance. Every time he played it, Bobby improvised his solo a little differently. Tonight it twined like Morning Glory vines.

"This is our last song," Terry announced afterwards, and he and Tyler took up the familiar opening riff of "Gloria," a staple cover song for most of the young bands. The hipper kids quickly took over the dance floor and began jumping and shaking. Bobby's organ faded in, a single backing chord swelling with vibrato, and then he began doubling Terry's riff. Dwitty hit the snare and Tyler came in with the first beat of the kick drum. Jules looked to Terry, anticipating the start of the vocals.

"Let me tell ya 'bout my baby..." But it wasn't Terry singing, it was Bobby. Bobby never sang lead. Jules and Gina exchanged a surprised look. His voice was thin and plain compared to Terry's, but he carried the tune, and he wasn't holding back. "She comes around here, just about midnight. She makes me feel so good. Makes me feel alright. And her name is J-U-L-" He paused a bar, then threw his head back and let fly. "I-yi-yi-yi-yi-yi-yi... J-U---L-I-A!"

"Julia." The band took the alternate lines.

"J-U---L-I-A!"

"Julia."

"J-U---L-I-A!"

"Julia."

"J-U---L-I-A!"

"Julia."

"I love you."

"Julia."

"I want you."

With that he jumped off the stage, put his hands around her waist, and as the band played the closing staccato riff a few extra times, he whirled her around and around, the room spinning behind them as he grinned and she smiled breathless, open-mouthed. With a last crash of the cymbal, the song ended. The crowd was cheering. "Wait for me right here, baby," he said, kissed her, and climbed back on the stage to take down his gear.

Jules was speechless, just standing there thunderstruck, a little dizzy. Gina was hopping up and down, saying, "Oh my God!" She gave Jules a hug.

Jules felt like every eye on the dance floor was on her. The disc jockey put on "Time is on My Side" by the Rolling Stones, and the Jimmy

Court Trio set up their gear.

"Where did Melissa go?" Gina looked around, then elbowed Jules and nodded to the back of the room. Melissa was sipping punch, and when Jules looked in his direction, Chip quickly turned his back to her. "I think someone is feeling out-classed," Gina observed.

"Who cares?" Jules said, as if from a dream.

Bobby came out from beside the stage just as Jimmy Court and his group began their set. They sang old favorites and romantic, danceable pop songs in three-part harmony. Bobby took Jules' hand, put his other hand around her waist, and danced her slowly toward the side of the room where it was a little less crowded, a little darker. "I meant what I sang," he said. "I do love you."

"I love you, too," she smiled up at him.

"Do you, baby? Really?"

"Really."

He stopped dancing. "Go steady with me."

"You're the only one I want," she said.

He pulled off his class ring and slipped it onto her index finger. It was still a little loose, so she curled her finger tight. He kissed her, discreetly, then held her close, and they danced. With each slow step, each gradual turn, they carved a space that was theirs alone.

"You should sing more," she said.

He just laughed.

Jules found herself something of a hot topic in school on Monday. "I think our little Julia is famous," Gina joked.

Jules stroked the side of Bobby's ring with her thumb. She had wrapped the back of the band with navy blue yarn to tighten the fit.

"You're really going steady with him?" Melissa asked. "You haven't even gone out much yet."

"I'm sure we will now," she laughed. "How was your date with Chip?"

"I like him," Melissa said. "He's a real gentleman. I can't believe you let him go."

"Maybe y'all are more suited to each other."

Then Cindy came waltzing down the hall. When she reached Jules at her locker, she paused. "Enjoy it while it lasts," she sneered, and walked on. Jules gave her a nasty/nice smile, then made an obscene gesture behind her back.

Melissa shook her head. "Do you really think it's real, Jules?"

"I don't know," Jules said. "But I think it is."

"And if it's not," Gina said, "do like that bitch says and enjoy it while it lasts."

Jules slapped Gina's arm and laughed, but Melissa turned and walked away.

Gina grew serious. "Do you think it's real?"

"I hope so. If it's not, it's gonna hurt like nothing's ever hurt before."

Chapter 3

"I think it's time we met this boy's parents," Dan Greene said to his wife.

"You're right, dear. Let's invite them over for coffee."

So, Wednesday evening found the Lotts at the Greenes' house, sitting in their living room, drinking coffee and eating pecan pie. Though Kate had declared the event "casual," she wore a pink linen sheath and a long string of white beads, her tawny hair in an up-do.

Nora Lott was a quiet, practical woman, neither ahead of her time, nor behind it. She wore little make-up beyond fairly natural shades of lipstick, and kept her dark hair in a simple bob. In her lavender gingham shirtwaist dress, she sat up straight on the couch beside her husband, Rob, who leaned back into the cushions a little more comfortably. "Does Bobby have any brothers or sisters?" Kate asked her.

"Two sisters. Maggie is 21. She and her husband live in Columbus, Ohio. Susan is 11."

"How nice. I might have had another, but the doctor advised against it."

"I'm sorry. My children are a great joy to me, as I'm sure Julia must be to you. Bobby said she's an honor student. You must be very proud."

"We are."

"We're proud of our son. Well, all our kids, of course. He's very talented. I'm pleased he's doing something with that talent. If he so chooses, I think he has a good chance of making a living with his music."

"Julia played me his record. I must confess, it's not really my thing, but I suppose they're good at what they do."

"He can play other styles of music. Maybe you can come over sometime and hear him play the piano."

"That would be nice," Kate smiled.

The men, in their dark trousers and white, short-sleeved shirts, regarded each other as they discussed their work. "I've been a civil engineer for the county for 18 years now," Dan was saying. "There are a lot of old bridges over the creeks around here that need replacing. It's just a hassle getting the funds. I understand you work at Chatt's Printing." Dan had asked around at work to learn that piece of information.

"Yes. I'm a typesetter."

"A typesetter," Dan repeated, rubbing his chin.

"You're quite welcome to join the Women's Circle," Kate invited Nora. "We get together twice a month to socialize, and we do service projects in the community. We're doing a Christmas bazaar this year to raise money for the public library. But it's not all work. We share books, sometimes we have a speaker. A lady from the garden society spoke to us last month about taking cuttings from rose bushes."

"I think I might like something like that," Nora said.

Jules and Bobby sat side by side on the front porch steps, eating pie and drinking Cokes, listening to Jules' transistor radio. They were more than happy to be excused from the conversation indoors. The air was warm. Moths swooped and circled the porch light. "We're playing the Harvest Dance out at the fairgrounds at the end of the month. Should be a good time. They're having fireworks after. I don't know how many bands are playing. Several."

"I sure won't want to miss that," she smiled.

"Only problem is your curfew. I don't know how late things will go, and I can't run you home if we're in the middle of band stuff. I'd hate for you to drive home all that way by yourself."

"We'll figure something out. Maybe I'll just spend the night with Gina and ride with her." Jules stacked Bobby's empty plate atop her own and set them aside. "How do you think they're getting on in there?"

"Well, nobody's kicked anybody out yet," he laughed.

When the parents all emerged from the house, exchanging thank-yous and reminders, Nora clutching a Tupperware brochure, Jules and Bobby were sitting hand in hand, talking quietly, the radio low so they could listen to the insects buzzing. Bobby stood, keeping hold of Jules' hand to help her up. "Mom, Dad," Jules asked, "Is it alright if we go out Friday night?"

Everyone looked at everyone else a moment. "What are your plans?" Dan asked.

Bobby spoke. "There's a show at the community center, a couple of bands. Thought we'd get something to eat first. Sir."

Dan raised his eyebrows at Bobby.

"Julia, you and Bobby could eat at our place," Nora put in. "We'd love to have you over. That is," she looked to Dan, "if it's alright with you."

Dan ran his hand over his short, sandy hair, then nodded. "Alright. 10:30, no later."

The Lott house was a ranch with a carport, a few years older than the Greenes', and considerably more worn from nurturing kids and pets, but Nora kept it as clean as she could. To Jules it felt like a favorite sweater, comfortable and worn in. The air was rich with the smell of spaghetti sauce. Bobby's old dog, a black and white collie mix named Lady, nudged Jules to be petted. An old upright piano took up one wall of the living room. A spunky girl with long, wavy, brown hair bounced in. "This is Sissy," Bobby said.

"My real name is Susan," she said, "but he's always called me Sissy."

"Nice to meet you," Jules smiled, looking for resemblance to Bobby. Something about her eyes, though they were bluer. The high cheek bones.

Sissy plunked down on the piano bench and began pounding out "Heart and Soul." Bobby laughed and shook his head. "We're here," he said to Nora as they reached the kitchen doorway. The long, wooden table was already set.

Nora wiped her hands on her pink and green plaid apron. "Hello, dear," she smiled at Jules. "We're just waiting for your father," she said to Bobby.

Lady followed as Bobby led Jules into the hall. "Who are we seeing tonight?" Jules asked.

"Johnny and the Spots, and Grave Concerns."

"Are they good?"

"Don't know about Johnny. We've opened for Grave. They're from Indianapolis. Hypnotic stuff, lots of fuzz guitar. I think you'll dig them." He led her through a doorway near the end of the hall. "This is my room." To one side of the door was his bed, to the other the Farfisa, near the window. On the far wall a dark chest of drawers rubbed shoulders with a small desk, at the foot of which leaned a stack of record albums and 45s. Above the organ and the desk and at the head of the bed, pieces of music, hand-notated, some on printed staves, some completely hand constructed, were taped or tacked to the walls, interspersed with a few snapshots, a letter or two, hand-written lyrics. "Have a seat," he motioned to the bed. She sat down on the edge as he pulled a Seeds album from the stack and put it on the turntable atop the chest of drawers.

"You hung up my poem?" she noticed and laughed.

"I like it," he said. "I like to read it when I wake up." He sat down on the bed beside her. Lady jumped up behind them and lay down in the middle of the green and white chenille bedspread. Jules played with a small tuft of the soft fabric.

"This alright?" he nodded to the stereo.

Sky Saxon was whining, "I can't seem to make you mine."

"It's fine, but I'd rather hear you play," she smiled.

He kissed her. "If there's time after supper." As he drew her into another kiss, he reached behind them and pushed Lady's rump out of the way, then lay back on the bed, taking Jules with him, their legs still bent over the edge. It excited her, halfway horizontal with him, on his bed, even with a dog pressing up against her back. His kiss deepened, fingers sunk into her hair. She flinched at the sound of Rob's voice, his footsteps on the hardwood floors, but Bobby just tightened his hold on her head.

A few moments later three small knocks sounded on the open door, followed by an exaggerated, "Ahem." Bobby casually relinquished Jules, lying on his back and turning his face toward Sissy, who stood in the doorway, rolling her eyes. "Mom says it's time to eat."

"Leave room for dessert," Nora advised, which Jules found difficult, given how good the spaghetti and crusty Italian bread were, but the effort was rewarded with rich chocolate cake and vanilla ice cream. She felt at ease with his family, even while they questioned her about her life and aims.

Seated across the table from Bobby, she could compare his features with his parents'. She decided he looked about equally like them both. He had Nora's dark hair and eyes and high cheekbones, his father's straight nose, pleasant mouth, and strong chin. Rob had light brown hair, and tall though he was, Bobby had slightly surpassed him.

"Sissy, please help me clear the table," Nora said when they had all finished eating.

"Mom," she protested, "I did it last night."

"Your brother has company," she said. Sissy heaved a sigh and set to work.

Bobby led Jules to the living room and sat down at the piano. "What do you want to hear?"

"Anything you want to play." She sat in the nearest armchair, royal blue fabric ticked with tiny, gold fleurs-de-lys. She had never heard him play a piano before.

He began with Debussy's "Claire De Lune," and Jules was enchanted by the dreamlike delicacy with which he played it. "Mom's favorite," he commented. He opened a book of Chopin nocturnes and began to play. "Here, come turn pages for me." She sat beside him on the bench, trying to follow along. "Turn," he would say gently if she missed it. He would laugh at his mistakes, pleading that he was out of practice on a particular song. He dismissed a couple of difficult passages. "We'll just skip that part." Still, she was impressed. He closed the book and began playing a pretty, haunting melody, and her eyes, no longer occupied with following printed notes, could watch the grace of his fingers on the keys. And then he just suddenly stopped.

"Why did you stop?"

He shrugged. "Ran out of ideas."

"What was that you were playing? I like it."

"Nothing. Just making stuff up as I went."

"You just made that up just now?"

He nodded.

"Wow."

He laughed and squeezed her knee. "We should go."

They had both opted for the ease of blue jeans that night, Bobby in a red t-shirt, Jules in a candy stripe blouse. The air was warm, but the breeze smelled like rain. They heard thunder as they got in the car, and by the time they reached the community center it had begun to sprinkle. He parked as close as he could to the door and they dashed inside.

Gina and her family had left right after she got home from school, to visit relatives for the weekend. Melissa and Chip were nowhere to be seen. Terry was there with a pale-skinned, dark-haired beauty he introduced as Elise. She made an interesting contrast to his tanned skin and mouse brown hair. Tyler was with a tall red-head named Vicky. Terry produced a flask and discreetly tipped whiskey into their soft drinks. With Bobby's arm around her, as she sipped her drink and the music began, Jules felt all her cares melt away.

Johnny and the Spots jumped and jived their way through Bo Diddly covers and jittery originals, inspiring many in the audience to dance or clap their hands. Their harmonica player was on fire.

Grave Concerns were quite different. Fuzz guitar, yes, but they had added a sitar, something Midvale had never seen, and while the fellow who played it wasn't adept, his simple accompaniments added to the mystical, snaking character of the music and esoteric lyrics filled with flowers and bones and moons. Jules couldn't help moving to the slow groove. Bobby slipped his arms around her from behind, journeying with her as colored lights splashed across the ceiling and onto the band.

After the show, encapsulated with him in his car, parked at the side of a darkened road, as heavy rain poured steadily down the windows, Jules put her head back as Bobby's lips strayed from her mouth and traveled down her throat. As his kisses followed her collarbone, she barely noticed the quick flick of his fingers unbuttoning the next button of her blouse, and the next. Her lips parted, but not to protest, as his fingertips traced along the edges of her bra. He nestled his face between her breasts, the heat of his breath flashing across her skin as she stroked his hair. Then he took her hand and placed it against the front of his jeans, leading her in a slow, gentle stroke. A flush of heat washed through her as her fingers began to outline his shape, and then he stopped her, lifting her hand and squeezing it tight as he kissed her chest one last time and raised his head. "I'd better get you home," he whispered.

Schoolwork, work, and band business kept them apart the next week, except for brief encounters between classes or when Jules and her friends took refreshment at Kessler's. She couldn't look at him anymore without thinking of how he had felt under her hand, under that thick cloth she just didn't want in the way. Her eyes would stray down his body. He caught her looking once and laughed, then their eyes locked and everything and everybody else, all the noise and traffic in the school hallway, just disappeared for a luxurious moment. Their attraction was so obvious Gina nicknamed them The Magnets.

Saturday night was the Harvest Dance. Jules had arranged to spend the night with Gina in case Bobby had to stay too late or take the other guys home. With a carload of gear and Tyler in the back seat, Bobby picked Jules up at 6:30. She had barely had time to change out of her work clothes and grab her overnight bag. Tyler and Bobby were dressed for the show, in black suits with the pumpkin-colored shirts they had worn for the Fall Festival. Jules wore a short, black skirt, just long enough to evade the tights mandate, and a lightweight lavender sweater. "How many bands are there?" Jules asked as they rode.

"Six," Bobby said. "We're on fourth." He leaned his head back and asked Tyler, "Did you ever find tubes for that old Carvin amp?"

"Yeah, finally. Had to go to Louisville to get them. We need a better music store. Trainor takes too long to get stuff in."

"Yeah, tell me about it. Terry said he asked for Rotosound strings and they looked at him like he was from Mars."

"Terry is from Mars," Tyler laughed.

"I'll stay with the car for the first band," Bobby said. "That okay with you, baby?" he asked Jules. "You can go on in, if you want. Then I'll meet you later."

"That's fine," she consented.

He put his arm around her and hugged her close. "You're a good sport."

"I'll take the second band and up to set-up," Tyler volunteered.

Bobby parked in the gravel lot behind the open exhibit hall where the dance was being held. Tyler left them and went in the back entrance. The first band was just starting, a group of junior high boys playing simplified, but enthusiastic covers of old Merseybeat hits. "I'll go get you something to eat," Jules said.

"Thanks, baby," he smiled and climbed up onto the hood to sit and read from *The Odyssey* for school.

She returned with hot dogs and lemonade and stayed to eat with him, then went in to look for friends and watch the second band, The Rebble Rowzers, who seemed to think they were more rebellious and up-to-the-minute than they were. "I should have stayed out there with Bobby," Jules commented to Gina.

"Yeah, they're not much," Art, Gina's date, said.

Terry and Elise stood nearby. After a couple songs, Bobby walked in from the front and joined them. Terry took a long draw off his cigarette and blew the smoke toward the ceiling. "I swear, if I hear one more cover of 'Who Do You Love?' I'm going on a killing spree."

"Better keep your gun clean in this town, then," Bobby replied.

Dwitty and Tricia appeared at the side entrance, looking, pointing, then sighting the others. They were a cute couple. Dwitty was short, so they were about the same height, both brown-haired, Tricia's shoulder length and as naturally straight as if she had ironed it. They hurried in. "Did we miss anything good?"

"No," the others replied in unison.

"Oh, not these guys," Dwitty twisted his nose.

"Dwitty, you're taking the last shift," Terry informed him.

"Yeah, alright," he shrugged.

The Fire Escapes were up next, but halfway through their set the girls were on their own, as The Deep See left to fetch their gear and get ready. Jules spotted the nicely dressed Melissa and Chip near the back and waved them over. "Did you just get here?" Jules asked.

"Yes, we went out to eat first," Melissa said.

"Where'd you go?" Gina asked.

"The Terrace," Chip said. He seemed to be growing his sideburns a little longer.

"The Terrace," Gina commented. "Pretty uptown!"

"It's really nice," Melissa smiled.

Jules introduced Elise, then said, "The guys are up next."

Chip led Melissa away to dance. Art and Gina joined them. Tricia joked, "The Band Girlfriend Club meeting will now come to order."

"Any new business?" Jules played along.

"Nah," Tricia replied. "Just the same old business." She poked Elise in the arm. "Get used to it."

When The Fire Escapes left the stage and the crowd fell back during the changeover, Jules said, "I'm moving up front."

"Sometimes the sound is better back here," Tricia said.

"Yeah," Jules shrugged, "but I want to be up there."

"Worshiping at your man's feet?" Tricia teased.

"Something like that," she laughed. "I just feel more a part of it up there."

The Deep See won the crowd's attention with their professionalism and progressive sound. Jules heard some girls screaming after the first number, and turned to see that it was Tricia and Elise. She laughed. Terry smiled and pointed at Elise. 'You, baby. I want to see you after the show." He quickly tuned a string. "This one isn't about you. This is our new single, coming out soon, we hope, 'Mean Girl.'"

Bobby didn't sing that night, but he played with more energy than the stylistic confines of the Fall Festival had allowed, at times just closing his eyes, head back in abandon. Here the band could throw themselves into what they wanted to play, how they wanted to play it. Jules thought Dwitty's drumming had never sounded so crisp or tight. The crowd rewarded their efforts with the loudest applause of the night so far.

When the set was over, Jules saw Elise and Tricia head for the sliding metal door to the side of the stage, so she followed them out into the dusky parking lot, passing the next band as they hurried to set up. The Deep See came out presently, smiles and sweat, but not fully back to earth yet. The girls knew to give them space while they loaded the car and caught their breath. Bobby pulled off his suit jacket and grabbed a worn, sage green sweater from the back seat, tying the sleeves around his waist. Terry took the next watch, with Elise at his side. Dwitty and Tricia hurried back into the dance hall, smiling and effervescent. Tyler clapped Bobby on the back and said, "See ya later, old man."

"I need something to drink," Bobby said to Jules as he took her hand. At a table near the concession stand he drank two lemonades to her one, a few fans coming up to him to compliment him on the show. Two girls about Sissy's age asked him to sign their autograph books. He laughed and asked their names so he could personalize the pages.

The Four Sooths were playing when he led Jules out on the dance floor. They were from Lexington, label mates of The Deep See, a few years older, and veterans of the fraternity circuit. Their set was geared to young couples dancing, nothing too fast, but not everything slow, mostly covers of well-known songs. Bobby and Jules danced their way to the side of the crowd where the air was a little cooler. He held her close as they danced in half time to a Beat version of "Kisses Sweeter Than Wine," and she rested her cheek against his warm shirt front. "Let's go for a walk," he said quietly. "I just want to be alone with you."

"Alright," she said. As the song came to an end, he kept an arm around her waist and they left the dance floor. They walked the sawdust paths between the empty livestock buildings, passing other couples walking, kissing, giggling from dark nooks. They passed a group of laughing drunk boys, smelled marijuana smoke from a small, shadowy circle of figures. They kept walking, out by the demolition derby track. He led her through a gap in the fence and they ascended the rise behind the track, waist deep in tall broom sedge, feathery and golden in the bright moonlight. The music from the dance floated up to them softly.

"I think we're finally alone," he said, squatting down to pat the ground. "Seems dry." He pulled off his sweater and spread it on the ground for her.

"It's so beautiful," she said, as they lay on their backs and looked up at the moon. "So bright. I can see colors." She turned on her side and stroked down the front of his shirt. "Your shirt just glows."

He turned toward her, picked a dry leaf from her hair. "You glow."

They kissed, slow, lingering, deep, and she eased onto her back. His hand wandered down the front of her sweater, and she didn't stop him. She felt his fingers work their way under the hem, stroking warmth along her ribs. He slid his palm up to cup her breast through her bra. "Touch me," she whispered, arching up to let him unhook her strap. He pushed her clothes up out of the way, looking as he touched. She didn't feel shy. Tingling sensations shimmered up the insides of her thighs. She reached up to run her fingers through his hair and he brought his head down to kiss her breasts. Her breath quickened, her whole body craving closeness. As he brought his mouth up to meet hers again, she stretched her hand down to touch the front of his trousers, not the tentative touch he had led her in before. She traced the shape of him through the cloth, full and firm, and then she pressed her palm against him and stroked, fingers closing around him.

"I don't want to stop," he said.

"I don't want you to," she breathed, unbuckling his belt.

In a blur of heat they were kissing, touching, moving clothing out of the way. They laughed together as he tucked her panties in his shirt pocket. "Let's not forget they're there," she said.

His pants were down around his thighs as he took his wallet from his back pocket and flipped it open to pull out a condom. "Don't want to get you in trouble," he said.

Her skirt fell back as she brought her knees up around him, breathless at the feel of his body moving against hers, his finger teasing until she thought she would die from want. With one hand braced at her shoulder, he positioned himself against her with the other, slid that hand behind her hip and pushed. She cried out. Sharp, searing pain. It startled her. He eased back, moved more slowly, but she couldn't stifle her voice. She gripped his shoulders. God, it hurt. She hadn't counted on it hurting so much. She wanted to curse the tears filling her eyes.

He stopped, crouched on his elbows, cradling her head in his hands. "Oh, baby, am I your first?"

"Yeah," she whispered.

"I'll stop if you want. I don't want to hurt you."

"No, it's okay. It's okay."

"Are you sure?"

She caressed his face. "I'm sure."

"Try to relax," he said softly.

She tried, and she knew he was trying to be gentle. She could sense him fighting the impulses of nature as long as he could. Though pain had eclipsed pleasure for her, she wanted to see this through, feel him reach his release, hear his breath catch in that moment when he closed his eyes and threw his head back, his face silvered by moonlight.

He rolled onto his back, pulling her close, and she rested her head against the soft folds of his shirt, reaching inside it to run her hand slowly up his breastbone. "You okay, baby?" he asked.

"I'm okay," she said, but she felt shaky, couldn't prevent a tear slipping out and onto his shirt. It wasn't pain now, but some new emotion, beautiful and glowing, yet terribly needy. They lay silent awhile, the breeze rustling the last dry leaves in the oak trees up the hill. A song thumped up from the dance as the last band began playing, a jangling guitar piercing the air like pins. She wanted the quiet back.

He turned onto his side to face her, stroking back her hair, picking straw out of it. "I've made you cry," he said, wiping the damp remnants of her tears away with his thumb. "I never wanted to make you cry."

"It's okay," she said. Then she laughed. "Someone had to make me cry. I'm glad it was you."

He laughed and shook his head. "I do love you, Jules. I really mean that. You're my only girl. I want to be your only man."

"I want you to. I love you." She kissed him, then slowly sat up. "We should be getting back."

He sat up with her. "I guess so, but God knows I'd rather just stay here with you all night."

They began putting their appearance back in order. "I'm guessing you want these?" He took her panties out of his pocket. She reached for them, but he stuffed them back in, leaving them hanging partway out.

"Actually, I think they look good there," he grinned. She snatched them back out, laughing.

He shook his sweater out and draped it around her shoulders as they walked back. She slipped her arms into the sleeves, rolling up the cuffs. Her legs felt weak. "I need to stop at the rest room," she said as they neared the dance hall.

"I'll meet you right out here," he said, and they split up.

Gina walked into the grey, painted cement block ladies' room just as Jules was pounding her fist against the out-of-order Kotex machine. "Shit!"

"Relax," Gina said, "I've got a Tampax in my purse."

"I don't think that's going to help," Jules said. "I'll just have to make do with toilet paper." She started to go back into a stall.

"Why wouldn't it help?"

Jules turned to look at her through the doorway of the stall. "Because I'm not–" Her voice dropped quiet. "That's not why I'm bleeding."

Gina's eyes widened as she covered her mouth. "Jules," she said behind her hand, "Do you mean–"

"We went all the–" She stopped, as another girl was walking in.

"Wait for me, okay?" Gina said, ducking into the next stall to pee. Jules closed her door, wrapping a length of toilet paper around and around the crotch of her bloodstained panties. She smirked at the thought that they would have been safer in his shirt pocket.

Jules washed her hands while waiting for Gina, and for the other girl to leave. When Gina came out, Jules turned to face her and leaned back against the wall by the sink. She smiled, gave a quiet laugh, felt her eyes pooling again. "God, I love him, Gina."

"You okay, honey? He wasn't rough with you, was he? Didn't take advantage of you?"

"No," she shook her head. "No, I wanted him to, and he was sweet. Oh, Gina, what have I done? I'm happy, a little scared, I want to laugh one minute and cry the next."

"You're in love, honey." Gina reached out to brush dried grass from the sleeve of Bobby's sweater. "That's what being in love is like."

Jules chewed her bottom lip, then laughed softly again. "Good thing I wore a black skirt."

Gina gave her a hug. "We'll talk more later. He's waiting for you outside. I would say it's almost time for the fireworks," she smiled, "but I think some people already had theirs."

"Just don't tell Melissa, alright?"

"I won't tell anybody, I promise." She patted Jules on the back and they went out. "We'll go to the car when the fireworks are over. You just meet us there and let us know if you need to ride with us or not, okay?"

"Okay," she said.

Bobby turned and she saw a look pass between him and Gina. He reached for Jules and drew her close, touching his forehead to hers. The music had stopped and people were filing past them, into the rest rooms or on toward the grandstands. "I don't want to be with all these people," he said.

"Neither do I."

"Let's just go sit on the car, okay?" He put his arm around her and they walked away from the crowd. When they were alone he said quietly, "I made you bleed, didn't I?"

"Yeah. I think it's mostly stopped now."

He clutched her tighter. "I'm so sorry."

"Don't be. Rite of passage," she said. "I'm just glad I don't have to go home tonight."

"I'm glad you don't either. I sure as hell wouldn't want to walk in there tonight with your dad waiting in his chair."

"Let's not even think about that."

As they neared the Safari, Bobby craned his neck to look for signs of life. He stopped, held up a finger. "Wait here a second." He crept closer, peered in the window, then backed off. He turned to Jules, a finger over his lips, and motioned her closer. In the pale light from the back of the dance hall she saw a grin spread over his face, then he swung himself up onto the hood of the car with a great bounce, banging loudly on the metal with his hands.

Doors sprang open and out clambered a startled Tricia from one side and a cursing, befuddled Dwitty from the other. Bobby was laughing harder than Jules had ever heard him laugh before, and she couldn't suppress a giggle. "Goddamn it, Bobby!" Dwitty slammed the door. "You scared the shit outta me."

"What?" Bobby played innocent. "Can't I sit on my own car?"

"I'll get you for this, Lott."

"Ah, go on," Bobby grinned. "You can go neck in your own car now."

"You just wait..." Dwitty threatened as he escorted Tricia away.

"Yeah, yeah," Bobby waved him off. "Just remember, I've got your drums."

"You're mean," Jules said as he hopped back down and reached for her.

"Nah, you have no idea some of the history of this band. Anyway, they were just kissing." The first skyrocket flew up into the night, cracking into a cascade of blue. He lifted her up in his arms and laid her gently on the hood of the car, her back against the windshield, then climbed up beside her. She nestled up against his side and rested in his warmth as the sky split into colors above them.

"What do you want to do?" he asked. "Do you want to ride with Gina and her guy, or with me and Tyler?"

"With you, but I have to call home from Gina's and check in, and it must be getting late."

"You don't get any peace, do you?" He kissed the top of her head.

They met Gina and Art at Gina's car, and Bobby hailed Tyler as he was crossing the parking lot. Bobby would take Jules to Gina's house first, then drop the gear off with Tyler at his house, as they were going to practice there the next day. There simply wasn't time to go to Tyler's first.

Tyler sat in the back seat. Bobby drove with one hand, his other arm around Jules, who rested her head on his shoulder. They kept the radio down low. No one spoke.

They got to Gina's before Gina did. Tyler waited in the car. Bobby let Jules out and waited with her for Gina. He leaned against the side of the car, heels resting on the curb to straddle her at her eye level, and held her close. "When do you go home tomorrow?" he asked.

"After lunch, I guess. I can't stay too long. I have to finish writing a paper."

"I can come and take you home."

"I'm not sure that's a good idea," she shook her head. "I know how my dad's mind works."

"Goddamn it." He pounded his fist back against the metal.

"It's okay," she whispered, stroking his cheek.

"I want to see you tomorrow."

Headlights splashed over them. "That's Gina," she said.

Art pulled into the driveway and let Gina out.

"Wait here," she said, and went to confer with Gina, then rushed back as Art walked Gina to her front door. "I'll call you from here tomorrow. We may be able to go to the library. You could meet me there."

"Okay," he nodded.

She took his face in both her hands and kissed him. "I have to go, baby. I have to call home." She walked quickly to the house and he watched until she and Gina were inside. Art got back in his car and pulled away. Tyler moved to Bobby's front seat.

"Everything okay, man?" Tyler asked.

"Yeah, except for her old man and his rules."

"You two have got it bad for each other, don't you?"

"Yeah," Bobby said, putting the car in drive. "I hate to leave her tonight."

"Special night?" Tyler cocked an eyebrow.

"Yeah," Bobby gave a little laugh. 'You're starting to sound like Terry and Dwitty."

"God forbid. Sorry, man."

"Nah, it's okay."

"I figure Dwitty just pesters us 'cause Tricia won't put out."

Bobby laughed, then grew serious again. "Don't say anything to the guys, alright? I wouldn't want anybody to embarrass her."

"I won't."

Bobby rested his elbow on the window frame, cool air flapping his sleeve. "Why don't you find a steady girl?"

Tyler laughed. "I'm not ready for that yet. I want to see the world."

"Midvale not good enough for you?" Bobby joked. "You think there's something better out there?"

"I'm damn sure of it!"

They laughed, then grew quiet. At a stoplight Bobby leaned his head back against the seat and looked up at the ceiling. "I was her first," he said. "I've never been anybody's first."

Jules, in her nightgown, dumped her dirty clothes on the floor beside the cot set up at the foot of Gina's twin bed, except for what she had washed out in the shower and hung to dry. Gina's mom always offered Jules the guest room, but Jules always declined. How could she and Gina talk each other to sleep if they weren't in the same room? "I forgot I had this on," she hugged Bobby's sweater. "I guess I can give it back to him tomorrow." She put it on over her gown and sat next to Gina on the bed. They had the radio on, as much to mask their conversation as to listen.

"Please tell me you took precautions," Gina said quietly.

"We used a rubber."

"Thank heavens. Rubbers are kinda scary, though. You should get on The Pill."

Jules laughed. "Just how do you think I could get away with that?"

"Same way I do," Gina whispered. "There's a doctor, Dr. Aikens. Carol's the one who told me about him. He won't tell your parents."

"Oh, Gina, I don't know."

"Think about it. If you want to, I'll take you. We can say we're going shopping."

Jules smoothed wrinkles out of the skirt of her gown. Where was Bobby now? Was he at Tyler's house? Was he home? Sleeping? Was he lying awake thinking of her, in the dark, in his room with pieces of music all over the walls, her poem over his head? "I don't feel like I sinned," she said softly. "I would never take tonight back."

"I would never take my first time back, either," Gina said. She smiled, clasped her hands in her lap and looked up at the ceiling. "It was last Valentine's Day. We went to the dance. It was so cold."

"I remember!"

"But we were determined," she laughed. "We went way out Quarry Road. His mom's car. And he left the engine running so we'd have heat, and because he was afraid if he shut it off it might not start again. It was his first time too, so we weren't exactly the smoothest performers."

"Did it hurt?"

"A little. I didn't bleed like you. I must have lost it horseback riding or something. She's still got that car. Whenever I drive by and see it–" She clasped her hands together until her knuckles whitened, and turned to Jules, tears filling her eyes. "I miss him so much."

"Oh, Gina." Jules put her arms around her friend, who covered her face and sobbed. "Just let it out. I'm here."

Gina had been a sophomore, and Tim a junior. They fell hard for each other and were quickly inseparable. Melissa called them the Siamese twins. It seemed nothing would ever part them, until that cold March morning his father went out to the garage to go to work, and found Tim hanging by a rope from the garage door track. The blue dress Gina had bought to wear to his junior prom she ended up wearing to his funeral. She put on a brave face, remained the jokester she had always been, became a sort of Dear Abby to her friends, started dating again by summer, but Jules knew the hurt was never far below the surface.

Jules reached for the Kleenex box from the night stand and pulled a couple tissues out. "Here," she touched one to the back of Gina's hands. Gina took them and pressed them hard against her eyes. Jules stroked her hair until she calmed.

"I'm sorry," Gina said raggedly.

"Hey, it's okay."

"When they closed that lid on him, they closed my heart in there. But I want it back. I want to fall in love again. But I'm scared. Every time I start to feel it, I run. I can't help it."

"Is that what happened with Donnie?"

"Oh, I don't know," she shook her head. "I like Donnie, but I don't think he's the one. Art's probably not the one either."

"I hope you find him. And I hope you don't run again."

"Thanks." Gina squeezed Jules' hand. "Cherish every second with him, Jules. You never know what's going to happen. I sound like some old lady dishing out the wisdom," she tried to laugh.

"No. You just know the hard truth. I don't take him for granted, Gina. And I really do believe he loves me."

Jules slept in Bobby's sweater that night, wrapped in its warmth and softness, comforted by his scent in the collar.

Chapter 4

At the library, after lunch the next day, she found him flipping through the record albums. He pulled *Thelonious Monk with John Coltrane* out of its sleeve. "Look at that," he said. "Scratched to hell." He slid it back in and left it in the rack. "Do you like Monk?"

"I confess I don't really know much about jazz," she said quietly.

"I've got some things you should listen to sometime."

"I'd like that. Here's your sweater," she held it out to him. "I'm sorry, I kinda forgot I had it on last night."

"It doesn't matter," he smiled.

"I slept in it."

His smile widened. He took it from her and put it on.

She took his hand. "T.S. Eliot," she said, leading him down an aisle. She pulled a couple volumes and set them in an empty space on a shelf, and then, deep in the stacks, they kissed and clasped. Memories of the previous night flooded over her.

Someone rapped on the end of the shelves. They turned to see Mrs. Dern, the librarian, staring sternly at them. "This," she said, "is not the place for that."

They separated reluctantly.

"Want to go to a movie or something?" he asked.

"When?"

"Tuesday? We've got a gig tomorrow. Private party, or I'd take you there."

"Tuesday should be fine. Let me take one more look here and then we can find Gina and check out. We can go sit in the park."

While she browsed, he picked up a book and flipped through it. He began snickering. She turned to look and could see he was trying hard not to laugh out loud. "What have you got there?"

He sidled up to her to point out the passage. "This the kind of stuff you read in class?"

She read the immortal words of Percy Bysshe Shelley:

> Suck on, suck on. I glow, I glow!
> Tides of maddening passion roll,
> And streams of rapture flood my soul.

She covered her mouth, but couldn't contain her laughter, and that set Bobby laughing. Gina poked her head around the corner. "I could hear y'all all the way down there," she whispered loudly.

"Gina, you've got to read this," Jules croaked.

"Must be good, your face is red." Gina read, sputtered, and then all three of them were laughing through their noses. Mrs. Dern paused on her return trip and cast a warning eye.

"We should go," Jules said. "Gina, are you ready?"

"Yeah."

They checked out and went across the street to the small park in front of the court house. A modest fountain, a few benches, a row of tall, spreading oaks along the sidewalk. Fall was in the air, despite the warmth, the light already slanting. Gina poked around the fountain. Bobby leaned against a wide tree trunk, holding Jules. "I really can't stay long," she said, caressing his chest through his shirt. "I do have to write that paper. I've been putting it off. Obviously, I didn't get anything done on it yesterday."

"It's okay. I've got practice in an hour. I just wanted to see you."

Monday was Halloween. Near the end of the school day, when pep rallies were often held, 30 minutes had been set aside for a costume contest. Students could dress up in the locker rooms and go to the basketball court to dance to a few records while the teachers circulated and judged the costumes. The winner got dinner for two at Rick's diner. Terry Wallace, in a dowdy house dress and polka dot kerchief, was a big hit. "You look like Aunt Jemima," Dwitty giggled. Dwitty was dressed like a bug, with green grease-paint on his face, a pair of swimming goggles, and aluminum foil forming antennae and an extra set of legs sticking out of his pants pockets.

"That suits you," Bobby said to Terry. "Wanna go out?"

"Sure, baby," Terry batted his eyelashes and rubbed shoulders with him. They laughed and shoved each other away.

Bobby simply wore red devil horns. "I plan on wearing these tonight," he said. "You wearing that? It is pretty damn scary."

"Think people will give me drinks?'

"I think they'll *need* drinks."

Gina, Jules, and Melissa sauntered up, laughing at Terry and Dwitty. Melissa was dressed like Dorothy from *The Wizard of Oz*, with red patent leather shoes, and a stuffed toy dog in her basket. "Hey, that's pretty good!" Dwitty commented.

"What did Chip dress up as?" Gina asked.

"He wouldn't dress up," Melissa shrugged.

"I see you didn't either," Gina teased Bobby. "You just look like your natural self."

Terry was eying Gina in her gypsy costume when Elise came up, dressed in a man's suit, her hair tucked up in a man's hat, a mustache painted on, to complement Terry's outfit.

"You look good, baby," Bobby said to Jules. She wore all black – soft sweater, tight-fitting pants, flat shoes – and a headband with fuzzy black cat ears. Her eyes were outlined in heavy, black eyeliner, with which she'd also painted whiskers on her cheeks. She had pinned on a length of black satin drapery cord as a tail, which Bobby was twirling.

"Where's *your* tail?" She looked behind him.

He leaned closer to her ear. "I don't show my tail to just anybody."

"Don't you?" she teased.

He lunged at her, tickling her sides, and she shrieked. He stole a quick kiss to silence her, just as Gina punched his arm playfully and said, "God! Knock it off, you two!"

With a piercing whine of feedback, Principal Sammons picked up a microphone and announced the start of the contest. One of the teachers turned on the portable record player set up behind a second microphone, and set the needle down on "Wooly Bully." Terry in a dress, doing the Twist, was just too much, but Bobby was concentrating on matching Jules' gyrations in an understated Frug, close but not touching, eyes locked on each other's.

After "Monster Mash" the winner was declared, a theatre club member named Barry, who had constructed an elaborate Pharoah headdress encrusted with rhinestones and dusted with gold glitter.

When the assembly broke up, Jules left her costume on. "I'll wear it tonight to hand out candy to the trick or treaters," she told Bobby as she got her things out of her locker.

"I wish you could come with us tonight," he said.

Bobby, still wearing his devil horns, hadn't been at the party that night very long before he was glad Jules wasn't with him. He didn't want her exposed to this sort of scene. The Modern house, on a hill overlooking Midvale, sported Space Age décor – bubble chairs, a Lucite coffee table, hanging globe lights. The hosts and their guests were well into their twenties, even their thirties, and they were getting lit and loose. Women in slinky cocktail dresses were dancing barefoot in the furry carpet, an odd collection of stiletto heel shoes scattered around. "Midvale has swingers?" Dwitty said, adjusting the black mask over his eyes. Terry had, thankfully, not worn his dress, but opted instead for a cowboy hat. Tyler sported a skeleton print shirt. Any guests' costumes consisted of fake fur animal prints, Mardi Gras masks, or funny hats.

The band set up outside on the patio. "Do not," Uncle Tony said, "drink anything. I wouldn't even trust the tap water."

"Come on," Bobby protested. "We can't go all night without anything."

"If you want something, you make sure it's sealed, you open it yourself, and you don't take your eyes off it for a second," Tony warned.

Bobby had nearly dismissed this advice as overly cautious, until halfway into their first set he could see that some of the ladies who had spilled out the patio door to dance to the band were obviously in the throes of something besides alcohol. Tyler leaned over to Bobby and laughed, "Those chicks are fucking tripping!" One little red-dressed minx tried to sidle up to Terry while he was playing, until a man scooped her up and flung her over his shoulder, bare thighs and red lace panties in the air. Terry was laughing too hard to finish the verse.

When the band took a break, Bobby slithered through the revelers to the kitchen. The only sealed beverages he saw were bottles of beer in an ice chest, so he nabbed a couple. When he straightened and turned to leave he came face to face with a very attractive woman in a dress of black plastic discs, probably ten years his senior, who reached up and began stroking his horns. "Um, excuse me," he said, trying to sidestep her. "My horns are taken."

She shrugged. "Pity." A man stumbled past them to retch in the waste basket.

Back on the patio, Bobby handed Tyler a beer and they prised the caps off with their keys. Dwitty came out of the house looking a bit white. "Man, this woman tried to follow me into the bathroom."

"Come on, Dwitty, you're always wanting some," Terry teased.

"No, man, she was old. It was creepy."

"Two more songs," Uncle Tony put in their ear as they reassembled. "Then just discreetly pack up."

They figured it didn't really matter what they played at this point, so they took an easy route. A man lay on his back, passed out in the middle of the patio. It sounded like a riot was going on in the house. Bobby looked up at an upstairs window. The light was on and behind the sheer curtains a woman was doing a striptease. He nudged Tyler and they snickered, watching the action as they played. Dwitty turned to look and dropped the beat. Tony made a cutting motion across his throat, so they made a quick conclusion of the song, just as a punch-up started out in the garden. "Carry what you can and stay out by the cars," Tony instructed. "I'll bring the rest. Let's just get the hell out of here." As they packed up the Safari, it was hard to ignore the man in the front yard trying to swim up a tree trunk. When they were ready to go, Tony slapped a $10 bill in each of their hands. "Thank God I made this guy pre-pay."

"How was the party last night?" Jules asked Bobby over burgers at Rick's.

"Bunch of drunk and drugged up swingers. We cut out early. It was too crazy," he shook his head. "Tony made sure we got paid, so it was worth it, and I got a beer out of it. You never know what you're getting into sometimes, though."

"You didn't get anything thrown at you, did you?"

"Not this time," he laughed. "Terry got hit with a bottle once. He put his arm up to keep it from hitting him in the chest." Bobby re-enacted. "It left a huge bruise. He almost couldn't play."

"That's scary," Jules said.

"Speaking of scary," he looked at his watch.

"I'm almost done. I hope things go better for you this weekend."

"So do I. Tony's supposed to pick up the singles Friday. I probably won't be able to get one to you till after we get back."

"That's okay," she said. "I guess a couple of days won't kill me. I sure wish I could go down there and see you play."

Tony had gotten the band booked in Nashville for Friday night, and a pick-up gig in Knoxville for Saturday, taking the place of a band who had canceled. He planned to deliver the single to some radio stations in both towns and see if any record stores would be willing to carry it. Bruce Cotton, the Lexcot label owner in Lexington, for whom The Deep See recorded, was as anxious as Tony to break the band outside the confines of Kentucky. Bruce really thought they had hit potential, if they could be heard.

Jules and Bobby finished eating and walked to the theatre to see *The Blood Drinkers*, hoping for a good scare, but the rubber bouncy bat on a string just made them laugh out loud, and they were puzzled by the film changing between color and magenta at odd times. "Do you care how this ends?" he asked.

"Not really."

"Let's go, then."

They drove out into the night, down a dirt road, and pulled off behind a grove of trees where the moonlight glinting off the car wouldn't be so obvious from the road. He folded down the back seat and spread out the old blanket Dwitty used to pad his drums, and they climbed in through the tailgate. They loved and touched to a fever pitch. And then he tried to take her, and she stifled a cry, clenched up. "Still hurt?" he asked.

"Some."

"We'd better give you more time to heal."

"I'm sorry."

"It's okay, baby." He kissed her. "There are other ways."

Jules picked up Gina for school the next morning. She couldn't stop smiling, couldn't get her head out of the clouds. "Well, don't you look like the cat that ate the canary," Gina observed.

"Um..." Jules felt her face flush. "It wasn't a canary."

Gina's jaw dropped. "No!"

Jules grinned, "Well, I owed him."

"Aren't you two something! So, how was it?"

Jules nibbled her grinning bottom lip. "Nice," she said. "Really, really nice."

"You're blushing."

"Let's just say... I didn't know my body could do things like that."

"Ah, lucky girl! So, how was it doing him?"

"I liked it," she beamed. "I liked it a lot."

"Oooh, you naughty thing. You didn't think it was, you know, kinda gross?"

Jules laughed, "No. It just seems... natural. You don't like it?"

"Honey, I've never done that."

Jules covered her mouth, laughed through her nose. "I've done something you haven't?"

"You are red as a beet!"

"Well, Gina, maybe you need to catch up."

"Maybe I will someday, based on your glowing recommendation, because you, my dear, are definitely glowing. I'm curious, though. What does it taste like?"

"Gina!" Jules laughed.

"No, I'm serious. I heard it tastes kinda bad."

"I wouldn't say it tastes particularly good. I mean, it's not exactly ice cream. But I didn't mind it. It's hard to describe, but a little like the ocean."

Friday afternoon, right after school, found Bobby flying down the highway in the Safari, Tyler in front, Terry and Dwitty in back, following Uncle Tony to Nashville.

"I hope it's not a bunch of drunk Country & Western fans," Dwitty said.

"It's a fraternity dance," Tyler said.

"So? They can be as mean as their daddies. Probably throw harder, too," Dwitty said. "I knew I should have added another cymbal."

"Yeah, you're too chicken to stand up front like me," Terry said and poked him in the ribs. "Brawk! Brawk!"

"Too smart, more like," Dwitty laughed, fending him off.

Terry pushed up his sleeve and rubbed a finger into his forearm. "I still got a fucking dent in the bone."

"Next time let it hit you in the head," Bobby grinned. "It won't do any damage there."

"Oh yeah?" Terry sat forward. "I'll hit *you* in the head." He delivered a play punch above Bobby's ear.

Bobby laughed. "Hey, not while I'm driving, man, unless you like the looks of that ditch." He jerked the wheel toward it just a twitch, throwing everyone off balance, and laughed harder.

"Alright, that's enough of that," Tyler said, seriously.

"Yes, Mom," Bobby sighed.

The dance was a more sedate affair than they had expected, alumni as well as student brothers and their dates or wives. Still, they seemed in a mood for some rock and roll, and while the response was initially lukewarm, the band did get most of them up and dancing. They broke out a new cover they had prepared for the trip, "These Boots Are Made for Walkin'," and it went over well, some of the girls strutting Nancy Sinatra style.

After a night in a cheap motel, all of them in two rooms with all the gear, since they couldn't risk leaving it in the cars, they made the rounds with Uncle Tony to several record stores and radio stations, most of whom seemed indifferent. One disc jockey gave it a spin off the air and seemed excited, but couldn't guarantee his program director would approve it.

As they walked to a lunch counter, Terry, distracted by a window display, dashed into a Western wear store to buy a pair of cowboy boots. Poking around in the store, waiting while Terry tried on a couple pair, Bobby saw a little, white, fringed buckskin vest. He bought it for Jules.

The Knoxville gig was at a bar near the University of Tennessee campus, a hang-out for the older students. The atmosphere was loud and rowdy before the band went on, and the place was filling up. "This is either gonna be a lot of fun," Terry said, "or a fucking nightmare."

Bobby fretted and fidgeted. Tyler punched his arm. "Put your war paint on."

They took their places and Terry adjusted his microphone. "Hi, we're The Deep See and we're from another place that starts with a K." They jumped right in with "Mean Girl." The sound of live music seemed to fuel the party spirit, and the floor at the foot of the low stage soon filled. Some bounced, some yelled, some stumbled into each other. Three coeds in mini-skirts danced and wiggled teasingly in front of Bobby and he couldn't help smiling. He just hoped they didn't have jealous boyfriends on their way back from the bar.

This crowd pretty obviously didn't want anything slow or cerebral, so the band kept the energy levels up and threw in several covers, including "Gloria." But what really got the revelers going was a rocked up version of the old Bluegrass murder ballad "Knoxville Girl" that they'd worked up as a closer just for the occasion. The guys up front demanded an encore of it, and since they were hoisting beer bottles, the band figured they'd better oblige. At the conclusion, instead of throwing a bottle at Terry's head, they thrust one into his hand. He lifted it in salute and they all yelled and did the same. Beers quickly worked their way into the other bandmembers' hands. Terry turned around to them as they all took a long drink. "'Boots'?"

They looked at each other, shrugged, nodded. "Sure," Bobby said. Tyler struck up those downward sliding bass notes and the crowd whooped. When it got to the outro, instead of faithfully reproducing the horn section part, as he had the previous night, Bobby flew into a wild, manic solo that had the crowd jumping up and down and the trio of girls kicking up their boots. He finished with a flourish, swiping his hands up and down the keys while Dwitty crashed away on the cymbal. It was a fine moment and a fine ending.

The trio of girls followed them out to the cars. One of them, an alluring blonde in a grass green dress and black boots, leaned against the side of the Safari as Bobby slid his Farfisa into the back. "Do you really have to go right away?" she asked.

"I'm afraid so," he said.

"Right right away?" She drew a glossy pink nail down his sleeve.

He took a deep breath, fighting what she made him feel. "You're a pretty lady," he said, "but I've already got a pretty lady."

"Well, I won't tell on you," she grinned.

He shook his head. "No, thanks."

She shrugged and sashayed back inside, and he was thankful she hadn't been more persistent.

Spirits were high as Bobby tossed Tyler the keys and they set out for home. Out of the records the cautious stores wouldn't take, they had sold twenty after the show. But the drive was long and monotonous and dark. "Why the hell didn't Tony get us a room for tonight?" Terry grumbled, drawing hard on a cigarette.

"I don't know, man. I'm beat," Tyler said, fooling with the radio, trying to tune in something to help him stay awake. They weren't even halfway home.

"I'll take over if you want," Dwitty offered. Tyler flashed the headlights at Tony to signal they were going to make a stop. Tyler and Dwitty switched out, and Terry got into Tony's car to sleep in his back seat.

"Go ahead," Bobby nodded to the back seat of the Safari, letting Tyler have it for a nap. "You tell me if you need a break," he told Dwitty, then dozed off in the passenger seat.

Sunday afternoon Jules got a phone call. "Hey, baby," he said.
"You home?"

"Yeah. I just got up. We didn't get home till after 5. We were ready to kick Tony's ass, but we were all too fucking tired. I don't think he was thinking it was that long a drive."

"How did things go?"

"Real well, I think. Knoxville was fun. You would have liked it. We sold some records there. Speaking of which, I've got yours. I thought I'd bring it over, if you want."

"I'll be here."

"I want to get something to eat first."

He showed up at her door an hour later and handed her the single. "It won't hit the shelves till tomorrow, so you're the first in town to have it. Well, besides the band."

"Thanks. I can't wait to play it. Come on in. We'll put it on now."

"I can't stay. Dad's got stuff he wants me to do."

"What's the flip?" She turned it over. The label read, "Time Tonight." She grinned and bounced excitedly.

"It was almost 'Vicky Vain,' but Bruce decided to hold that one back for later."

"I'd much rather have this," she smiled.

"I brought you this, too." He handed her a paper bag, the top tucked under and taped. "Sorry it's not wrapped fancy."

She opened it to find the fringed vest. "Oh, wow. Thank you." She slipped her arms into it and straightened it across her chest.

"Does it fit alright?"

"It's perfect," she smiled. "I love it."

"Your souvenir from Nashville."

"Wait here." She set the record in on the coffee table, then stepped back outside and closed the door. She reached up to stroke his unshaven face. "You look so tired."

"I'll be okay." He bent to kiss her.

Monday he met her at her locker and handed her a manila envelope, his right hand swaddled in gauze. "Here, I thought you might like one of these." She was wearing the vest he'd bought her, over a blue and white striped blouse. "That looks real cute on you." He reached out to toy with the fringe.

"What did you do?" she lifted his bandaged hand.

"I was helping Dad fix the stove last night. There was some sharp piece of metal in there."

"How bad is it?"

"Wanna see?" He pulled back the edge of the gauze to show her. She winced. It had sliced into the heel of his hand. A line sealed with dark, dried blood was closed by an X of black thread at either end. "It's not bad. Couple of stitches," he dismissed it. "Wanna go out?"

"Of course, but I can't. Not for a while. I mean, I can still go to the play Friday, but other than that, well, Dad's leaning on me right now. He thinks I'm going out too much, that I need to stay home more, concentrate on schoolwork, spend more time with the family."

Bobby bit his lip, bounced his heel. Then he held out his left hand for her books. "Well, you'd better appease him, I guess."

"I think after exams he'll ease up, and I think we can still go out some, maybe once a week." She ferociously kicked a stray paper wad from her path. "I hate when he's like this."

Bobby shifted her books to one arm and put his other around her. "It's okay, baby. I understand. I'll have to spend some extra time with the band for a while, too. We've got a lot of gigs coming up. I'm guessing he would never let you come up to Louisville with us."

"No," she shook her head. "I hate to miss seeing you play anywhere, but TV! That's so exciting."

He smiled and kissed her cheek. "My biggest fan."

She reached inside the envelope and pulled out a black and white promotional photo of the band dressed in dark suits, standing on the shore of a small lake. "This is good of you."

He had signed it, "To Jules, my only girl."

"That's sweet of you," she smiled.

"Can you get that channel to tune in?" he asked.

"Sometimes. I sure hope I can Saturday. I'll just die if I can't."

"Don't die," he kissed the top of her head. "I don't want to lose you over a TV show."

"Are you sure you don't want to go?" Jules asked her mother Friday evening. "It's supposed to be really funny. Gina plays a crabby old grandma, and she wrote most of her lines."

"Honey, I've got a Tupperware party. And your dad won't go if I don't. He said it would be different if you were in it. But you just go enjoy yourselves."

The play was a comedy the drama club had written themselves, about a Thanksgiving Day family reunion. Gina Romano's parents sat in the front row. Jules and Bobby said hi to them before taking their seats farther back. "It's fine with me," Jules said as the house lights went down, "that Mom and Dad didn't come, but I had to act like they were welcome to."

"I wouldn't want to be sitting next to your dad right now," he said. "I wouldn't be able to do this." His hand crept teasingly up her thigh.

"Behave," she whispered. "For now."

The play was very funny, and Gina in a white wig, crocheted shawl, and fake glasses was in fine form, complaining about everything, bossing everyone around, and beating them with her gnarled cane. "I bet she's really like that in 50 years," Jules laughed. Their friend Carol played the baby, sitting on the stage floor in footed pajamas, shaking a giant rattle and screaming at particularly startling or irritating moments. At one point she used her rattle to engage in a fencing match against Gina's cane.

The play was over earlier than they had expected. As they left the auditorium and walked out into the parking lot, Bobby slipped his arm around Jules. "We've got time to burn, girl," he said as they neared his car. "What do you want to do?"

"I want to be with you," she said quietly. "I want to try again."

He let her in the car, then got in his side and shut the door. "You sure?"

She nodded. "I want to get it right this time."

He gave a little laugh and stroked back her hair. "Baby, it's not like you've been getting it wrong."

"You know what I mean."

He kissed her, then stuck his key in the ignition. "I think I've got just what the doctor ordered."

Once away from the school, they roared down the two-lane

highway to the country, parking in a secluded spot on a creek bank, behind a row of trees. He took something out of the glove box and slipped it into his shirt pocket before they got into the back of the car. "This should help." Stretching out on his back, he took her hands and led her down over him. "We're gonna put you in the driver's seat tonight," he said. "You know better than I do how much you can take, and when."

"I'm not sure I'll know what to do," she said.

"Just do what feels natural."

The next morning found the band on the road to Louisville to play "Mean Girl" on *Lou's Louisville Dance Party*, a Saturday afternoon teen show. Bobby was driving the Safari. "Terry, hand me the map, will ya? It's in the glove box."

Terry pulled it out and gave it to Bobby, who shook it open and laid it out on the dash.

"Whoa-ho! What have we here?" Terry took something else out of the compartment. "Surgical lubricant. Been doing some surgery, Bobby?"

"Just put it back," Bobby smirked.

"How'd you score that, man?" Dwitty asked.

Bobby held up his hand and wiggled his fingers. "Light fingers in the doctor's office."

"Good man!" Tyler clapped his shoulder.

"Ordinary Vaseline not good enough for our man?" Terry teased.

"Vaseline eats rubbers, you dumb shit," Bobby said.

Terry went quiet, put the tube back in the glove box and shut the lid. "I knew that."

Everyone else burst out laughing. "Living dangerously, Terry?" Tyler reached up to punch his arm.

"Guess that means you are getting some, Bobby," Dwitty chirped.

Bobby sighed annoyance. "Yes, Dwitty, I am getting some. Now shut up."

"When do you get your stitches out?" Tyler asked.

"Supposed to go Wednesday, but I might just take them out myself."

"Don't risk your hand, man," Tyler said. "Get it checked out right."

Gina and Melissa sat on the living room floor while Jules fussed with the aerial. "Is that any better?"

"Maybe a little," Gina said.

"That's clearer," Melissa said, "But the color dropped out."

"Oh, I *knew* this was gonna happen," Jules pounded on the top of the set.

"Wait! That helped," Gina said.

"Should I smack it again?"

"No, you might make it worse," Melissa advised. "Just leave it."

Jules backed off and sat with her friends.

"If you squint your eyes it looks clearer," Gina said.

"I know. That's so weird," Jules said. "Kinda gives me a headache, though. I'll just wait till they come on."

"What are you doing for Thanksgiving?" Melissa asked.

"Going to Grandma's," Gina said. "And no, she's not as bad as in the play."

They all laughed. "We're going to my grandparents' too," Jules said.

"We're having both sets of mine come here," Melissa said.

Kate came in with a big bowl of potato chips and handed it down to the girls, as the last of the new records was rated for danceability by the teen audience. She was about to leave, but Jules stopped her. "Wait, Mom, they're on next!"

The camera panned from Lou to the stage, and there they were. The three girls shrieked and Kate laughed. "They do look dashing," Kate commented.

Jules squinted her eyes, her heart racing, her mind trying to will the cameraman. *Please zoom in on Bobby. Please. Just one good, solid close-up.* And he did, once, during Bobby's solo, and Jules felt brief satisfaction wash over her.

"Yes," Kate said, "I can see that Bobby does know how to play." As soon as the song was over, she returned to the kitchen.

Jules lay back on the carpet and smiled. "There," Gina said to Melissa, "lies one happy woman."

They watched to the end, just in case there was another shot of them or another mention, which there wasn't, except for Lou expressing thanks for their being on the show, and then Jules turned off the set.

Melissa said goodbye and walked off toward Chip's house for their date that evening. As they stood at the screen door watching her leave, waving one last time, Jules turned to Gina and said quietly, "I think maybe we should go shopping soon, you know, like we talked about the other night."

Chapter 5

"Mr. Lott?"

The sound came from somewhere above the surface as satiny, tepid water rushed through his hair and over his skin.

"Mr. Lott?"

He felt no need to breathe as he stretched his body for another stroke through the sparkling turquoise depths.

"Mr. Lott!"

He startled, lifted his head in the glaring light, heard laughter. Where the hell was he?

"Mr. Lott, perhaps you would care to tell us what a participle is."

He stared blankly at Mrs. Welsh in her blue plaid dress.

She heaved a sigh. "Mr. Lott, this is the second time this week you have fallen asleep in this class."

"Sorry, Mrs. Welsh. I have trouble staying awake after lunch."

"Perhaps, Mr. Lott, rather than lunch being the culprit, it is your lifestyle catching up to you. Or perhaps all that hair makes your head too heavy." More laughter. "Please move to the front. Miss Bell, please change seats."

Bobby gathered his books and papers and, still foggy, moved forward, while the perky Miss Bell flounced past on the other side of the row.

"From now on, I want you at the front of the class every day. Maybe that way you can manage to remain upright, perhaps even conscious."

Snickering all around.

Fighting to stay awake right now was painful and what few thoughts he had were rude. He was going to have to start bringing a Thermos of coffee to school with him.

That afternoon Jules quickly scanned the public library stacks for the book numbers she had scribbled down out of the card catalogue. She flipped through each book, choosing the four best suited for the paper on Antarctica she had to write over Christmas break. Why did they always insist on homework over the holidays? She glanced at her watch, grabbed one last book as an afterthought, and headed for the circulation desk. She figured she had half an hour before she needed to go home.

As she opened the door of Kessler's Drugs she saw Bobby at the far end of the counter, bent over an open book, elbows on the counter top. As the door closed behind her, he looked up. She walked down to the empty stool nearest him. "Hi, baby," he smiled. "The usual?"

"Please."

As he fixed her Coke float, she leaned to see what he was reading. *The Rules of Grammar.* Beside it was a dark cup of coffee.

When he set her drink in front of her he glanced behind him. "On the house," he said.

"Thanks."

"Baby, I need a favor," he said.

"I knew there was a catch," she teased, looking up at him from under the fringe of her bangs as she took a sip through her straw.

"With all the gigs and stuff lately, I can't seem to keep up in this class. Hell, I can't seem to stay awake in there. I need this class to graduate. I've got to do well on the exam. I was hoping you could help me study."

"I'll ask. I don't think it will be a problem."

"Thanks, baby." He kissed her hand. A group of customers walked in and he had to wait on them. Then another. Then he had to clear up and wipe down the counter as earlier patrons left. He looked tired and stressed, but still managed to work quickly and remain pleasant.

"When's your exam?" she asked when he was momentarily free.

"Monday." He took a gulp of coffee.

"When do you want to study?"

"Sunday, if you can. We've got to play a party Saturday night after I get off work here."

"I'll call you tonight, okay? I've got to get home."

"Okay, baby." He stifled a yawn.

"Get some sleep tonight. You look like you're going to fall over any minute. You can't live on coffee."

"Yes, Mom," he smirked. As she got up he squeezed her hand.

"Mom loves you, is all," she replied.

That night after supper, she called him. "I can help you study Sunday," she said, "but you'll have to come to my place. Dad doesn't trust there to be anyone home to 'properly supervise' us at your house."

"For Christ's sake! This is about studying!"

"I know, I know. I'm sorry."

"It's not your fault, baby. It's just– God!"

"How do you think I feel?" she said.

"I don't know how you stand it."

"I don't have much choice, do I?"

"What time?" he asked more quietly.

"Whatever time is good for you."

"We're not having practice, so if afternoon is okay... "

"That should be fine. Just come over when you're ready. I'll be home."

At lunch the next day, in the school cafeteria, Jules scribbled in a notebook as she ate an apple. Bobby had a different lunch period, so she never saw him then.

"What are you writing?" Gina asked.

"A poem for Bobby," she said.

"Can I see?"

Jules blushed.

"What, is it X-rated?"

"No." She showed it to Gina.

"Jules, this could be a song. Hang onto this, don't give it to him yet. I've got an idea."

"What?"

"Carol's party. You are coming, aren't you?"

"I hope so."

"And Bobby will be there, right?"

"Yeah."

"Carol thinks it's time to reprise The Rebelles. I think we should do something with this."

"Are you serious?"

"Dead serious." They found Carol at the next table.

Carol tucked her copper hair behind her ear and looked over what Jules had written. "Yeah," she grinned. "I think we can do something with this. It's got kind of a Phil Spector girl group meter, don't you think? Like a Ronettes or a Blossoms song. Can you come over after school?"

"I have to work today," Jules said. "I could come over tomorrow."

"Tell you what. I'll see if I can get the girls together today, work something up. Then you come over tomorrow and tell us what you think. Okay?"

"Okay," Jules smiled.

When Jules showed up at Carol's house, The Rebelles were in full swing in the basement rec room. Carol's mom answered the door. "They'll never hear the doorbell down there with all that racket," she laughed, and showed Jules the stairwell.

"Hey! There you are!" Carol grinned, wielding a cherry red Fender Mustang guitar. "We came up with a tune for your song. I hope you like it."

Gina was there. "Wait till you hear."

Jules only knew Carol, and not very well, so Gina introduced them all. Nita, the dark-haired, elfin drummer, counted off and the girls started playing a mid-tempo, Motown girl group beat. Nita and Carol sang back-up vocal harmonies to Alene, the bassist's, lead. It was more pert and perky than Jules had felt writing it, but catchy. They had repeated a few lines after each verse, sung in harmony, to serve as a chorus.

"What do you think?" Carol asked when they were done.

"I like it. It's great." Jules clapped her hands. "It's kinda different than I imagined, faster, but it works."

"Want us to run through it again?"

"Sure."

Jules caught the tune and it stuck in her head. She was nodding to the beat as she listened. "Yeah," she smiled when they finished. "It's good. It's fun."

"Do you think it should be slower?" Nita asked.

"No, it's fine. I like it this way," Jules approved.

"So, you ready to try it, then?" Alene asked, raking her fingers through her long, loose, dark wine curls. "Come on, I'll help you with the tune till you've got it."

"Um… what do you mean?" Jules puzzled.

"You wrote it for your boy," Alene said, "you gotta sing it for your boy."

"Sing it? Me?" Jules' eyes widened in horror. "I can't sing."

"Sure you can, girl," Carol said.

"I– I don't know."

"You don't have to be perfect," Nita said. "When you get up and start singing to him, he's gonna love it. Trust me."

"And you'll have us backing you up," Carol encouraged. "Come on, what do you say?"

"Remember," Gina said, "he never sings lead, but he sang for you."

Jules sighed, nodded.

"And you loved it, didn't you?" Gina asked. "Even though he doesn't have the greatest voice?"

"Yeah."

"Because it was him and he was doing it for you."

"Yeah," she nodded. "Alright, but promise you won't laugh, and that if it's too bad you won't make me do any more."

"We promise," Alene said. "Right girls?"

"Right," they replied in unison.

"Alright, we'll take it slow," Carol directed.

Shaky at first, fighting a constricting throat, once Alene had led her through the first verse, Jules found it started to come easier. "Nobody can hear you but us right now," Alene said, "so don't be shy. Just let go."

They did the second verse, and Jules tried to relax. "It's a little high," she said, rubbing her throat.

"Let's try dropping it down a tone," Carol suggested. She and Alene ran through it, working out the transposition. "Try it now."

Jules tried a verse. "That's much better. I think I can do that." They took it from the top. Jules closed her eyes, concentrating, breathing, feeling the song happen around her. It wasn't till the middle of the second verse that she realized Alene had stopped singing the lead along with her and had taken a harmony part. She felt a momentary panic, but finished the song.

"Bravo!" Carol applauded.

Jules blushed, laughed.

"You're gonna do just fine," Alene assured her. They took a break to rest Jules' voice, since she was unaccustomed to singing, and Carol gave her a 7-Up with a twist of lemon to drink.

"That's a sweet little song," Nita said to Jules. "Who's your boy?"

"Bobby Lott."

"Bobby Lott?" she raised her eyebrows. "Woo, honey, he is *fine*. You're a lucky girl."

"I think," Gina said, "that he's a lucky boy!"

"Hear, hear!" Carol raised her bottle of Tab.

Bobby showed up at Jules' house about 4 p.m. on Sunday, books and notebooks in the crook of his arm. She kissed him as she let him in the door. "Come in, baby."

She led him to the kitchen and got them Cokes and a bag of potato chips. They sat down at the table, side by side. "I know this is a year ahead, but maybe you can make some sense of it for me," he said. "If you can't, it's okay."

"Let's have a look," she said. He opened it to a relevant chapter and she flipped through it. "Sure, I can help you with this stuff." He didn't have much in the way of notes, but he had written down a few terms.

"This what you need to know?"

"At least," he said.

"Subject/verb agreement," she said. "That just means that if you have a singular subject, you need a singular verb to go with it. If you have a plural subject, you need a plural verb."

"Okay," he said.

"You don't sound too sure. You know what a subject is, right?"

"Yeah."

"And you know what a verb is?"

He nodded.

"Here," she pointed to a sentence in the text. "See anything wrong with this sentence?"

"Yeah," he said. "Shouldn't that be 'have' instead of 'has'?"

"Right, because 'they' is plural, so it needs a plural verb. 'Has' is a singular verb."

"That's not so hard, then. But please tell me what the hell a participle is."

"You know what a verb is. Do you know what an adjective is?"

"Like red," he said. "Or beautiful." He quickly kissed her cheek.

"Right," she smiled. "Something that describes a noun. Now, imagine you take a verb and use it like an adjective, by adding -ing or -ed to it. Like this sentence here," she pointed. "'The chirping robin heralds spring.' See how 'chirping' is made from a verb, but it's describing the robin, like an adjective would? That's a participle."

He heaved a sigh. "Thank you. You make this stuff sound almost easy."

Kate came in and started working on supper at the counter, mixing and shaping a meatloaf and putting it in the oven, peeling potatoes and setting them on to boil, then leaving. Jules and Bobby continued studying.

Jules worked with him through three chapters. "You understand how things work," she concluded. "You're just tripping over the terms. Here, tell me if this helps." She took his notebook, began writing, taking each term he needed to know and writing out an example of it, underlining the relevant words.

"That's exactly what I need."

Kate returned to the kitchen to make a salad. "Honey, it's almost time for supper."

Bobby began gathering his papers. "I guess I should go."

"Why don't you stay for supper with us?" Kate invited.

"Thank you, Mrs. Greene. I'd like that. Do you mind if I call my mom and let her know?"

"Go right ahead," Kate smiled.

Bobby saw this as an opportunity to look serious and responsible in Dan's presence. What better way to prove Dan's suspicions wrong than to spend a couple hours diligently studying right under his nose and then share a pleasant, ordinary meal before returning home on his own? Quiet, respectful, and mild-mannered, he could tell he was winning Kate over. She even commented favorably on his television performance. Dan didn't say much, but at least he seemed relatively relaxed and wasn't looking at his watch.

"How did it go?" Jules asked Bobby after school the next day.

"I think it went alright. I guess I'll find out when I get the test back. Gerunds are verbs with -ing on them, right?"

"Right."

"I sure owe you, baby."

The Sunday afternoon before Christmas found Jules sitting beside Bobby on the piano bench, but she wasn't turning pages. She had been, a few minutes earlier, as he entertained his family's guests with an assortment of Christmas songs, but now he was placing her fingers on the keys, slowly walking her through the monophonic melody line of the chorus of "Jingle Bells." As she blushed through a couple of mistake-laden tries, two of Bobby's young, boy cousins wrestled on the floor in front of the Christmas tree, while Sissy and a couple of her girlfriends whispered and giggled in the far corner. A chorus of adult laughter erupted in the kitchen, then faded. Jules tried again, with more success. "That's good, baby. You learn quick," he said. "We'll go slow. You play that while I play this." He sang it very quietly, just to help her keep her place, as he added a simple ostinato bass accompaniment with one hand.

She missed a note and stopped. "Sorry."

"It's okay. We'll start again, but if you miss, don't worry about it, just keep going."

"Assuming I know where I'm going," she laughed.

They recommenced and got through it with only one stumble. "Good. You just do the same thing again." This time he accompanied her with both hands, and before she could stop at the end, he said, "Faster." This time he started really rocking it up, Boogie Woogie style. "Once more," he grinned, and they were both laughing at the end when he reached around her to finish it off with some fancy fingerwork in the high treble. Applause came from the doorway nearest the kitchen and they turned to the audience she hadn't noticed in her concentration. She covered her mouth, embarrassed, but he hugged her close to his side and smiled, "Couldn't have done it without her."

Even Dan nodded approval.

"You do play wonderfully," Kate said.

"Thank you," he said humbly.

"He always had a natural talent," his aunt Dorothy said.

Nora put her hands on his and Jules' backs, and said, "Come in and get some more goodies before they're all gone."

Since Bobby's family would be away visiting relatives Christmas weekend, Jules and Bobby had decided to exchange gifts at the party. With a relatively private moment to themselves, the boy cousins facing the other way, lying on their bellies, noisily battling with tiny, green plastic army men, and Sissy and her friends off in her bedroom, Jules and Bobby sat on the couch. "I hope you like it," he said, handing her a present that, though wrapped, was obviously a record album. "If you really don't, I'll get you something else." He bent to kiss her cheek. She stripped the paper off to reveal The Bill Evans Trio, *Explorations.*

"Thanks," she smiled. "I look forward to hearing this." She nodded toward the beribboned box on his lap. "Well, go on, open yours."

He took the bow off and stuck it on top of her head. "I'd rather unwrap you," he whispered in her ear.

"Behave," she grinned.

He peeled off the paper, opened the box, and pulled out a luxuriously soft, slate grey sweater. "Ah, thank you, baby," he smiled. Laying it back on top of the box, he grabbed the hem of the cranberry sweater he was wearing and peeled it off from over his white dress shirt, laying it aside.

"You're not stopping there, are you?" she teased quietly.

He raised his eyebrows and wagged his finger at her. "You're on Santa's 'naughty' list."

"Right under you."

He leaned close to her ear. "Not always."

She snickered. He pulled the new sweater on and she tried to be serious. "Does it fit alright?"

His eyes twinkled and he tried to suppress a smile. "You tell me."

"Stop," she mouthed.

"What?" he acted innocent. "What did you think I meant?"

"I know very well what you meant." She cleared her throat. "Does the sweater fit alright?"

"Yes," he said, straightening the sleeves, then running his hand down one. "It feels nice."

"It's part angora."

"You'll spoil me," he said, lifting her chin as he bent closer.

"You're already rotten," she said as his mouth came down over hers.

Giggles fluttered past in the hall.

"Ew!" A small duet from near the tree.

Bobby turned to look, flicked a dismissive hand toward their wide eyes. "Just– get back to your war there."

"I must admit," Dan said in the car on the way home, "The boy can play. Real music. I'm impressed."

"He'd be pleased to know that," Jules said. "He takes his music seriously."

In her room after supper that night, she put on the jazz album and let its quiet complexities transport her spirit and open her mind. She liked it very much.

The Christmas sleepover at Carol's house took place the evening of the last day of school before the holidays. Boys were welcome to the party, but would have to leave by 11:00. Jules had never been to a party at Carol's house, having not known her very long. She was a little surprised how willing Carol's parents were to just shoo everyone down to the rec room and shut the door, to let them be loud, but also leaving them largely unsupervised. The room was dimly lit, just a couple of lamps in the far corners. A rotating, color-changing Christmas tree light was trained on the ceiling for a psychedelic effect. The Rebelles had set up their plywood and pallet stage in front of the laundry nook. A Mod print sheet hung from the ceiling to create both a backdrop and a backstage curtain. A Zombies record was playing and people were dancing. Jules guessed there were at least a couple dozen people there and she suddenly felt there was no way she would be able to perform, especially seeing Terry among them. Gina handed Bobby and Jules each a cup of Coke, leaning close to Jules' ear. "You might need this." Upon taking a sip, Jules realized it was spiked with rum.

Even feeling gradually numbed by the drink, as she danced with Bobby she was still contemplating chickening out. When she heard the pops and buzzes of amps coming to life, guitars being plugged in, a finger tapping a microphone, her stomach seized. Someone turned a flood lamp on to light the stage, and The Rebelles counted off and dived into their first

64

number, a ferocious cover of "(I'm Not Your) Steppin' Stone." During the first verse, Gina came up to Bobby and shouted, "Excuse me, I need to borrow her for a couple minutes," grabbed Jules' hand, and dragged her back behind the curtain.

"Oh, God, Gina, I can't do this. I just can't."

"Oh, yes you can," said Patty, Carol's cousin, unzipping Jules' dress and tugging it down over her arms.

"Take a slug of this," Gina pushed the mostly empty rum bottle into her hand. Jules obeyed as Patty tugged her tights down. The Rebelles started singing their cover of "I Saw Her Standing There," changed to "I Saw Him Standing There."

Jules wriggled into the pink sequined, sleeveless mini-dress they had found at the second-hand store and slipped into candy pink pumps, while Gina quickly teased her hair at the crown and smoothed the top, setting it with a few quick bursts of hair spray. Gina examined her from the front, then turned her for Patty's approval. Jules felt like a race car about to leave the pit. Alcohol and adrenalin were burning a hole in her stomach. Alene took a quick glance behind the curtain and Patty gave her a thumbs up.

"And now," Carol announced, "The Rebelles would like to present a very special guest, here to perform her brand new song, the lovely Miss Julia Greene!" She froze. Gina lifted the corner of the curtain while Patty gave her a shove from behind, and she teetered up onto the stage. Alene put a microphone in her hand and she stepped timidly forward. She could barely see anything with the flood light shining in her eyes, could just hear a few hands clapping, and then the intro, just as that swig of rum mercifully kicked in. She trembled through the first couple of lines, but then she just let go and let it happen. It was too late now to turn back, so she might as well give it all she had.

In the harvest moonlight
You took me by the hand.
In the harvest moonlight
We danced to the band.
You led me to a new beat,
Your kiss so warm and so sweet
In the harvest moonlight that night.

(In the harvest moonlight)
(In the harvest moon-li-i-i-ight)
(In the harvest moonlight)
(In the harvest moon-li-i-i-ight)

In the harvest moonlight
I held you in my arms.
In the harvest moonlight
You showed me all your charms.
We stole the night together,
We saw the light together
In the harvest moonlight that night.

(In the harvest moonlight)
(In the harvest moon-li-i-i-ight)
(In the harvest moonlight)
(In the harvest moon-li-i-i-ight)

In the harvest moonlight
You stayed right by my side.
In the harvest moonlight
You held me as I cried.
I don't want any other.
Don't dance with any other
In the harvest moonlight tonight.

(In the harvest moonlight)
(In the harvest moon-li-i-i-ight)
(In the harvest moonlight)
(In the harvest moonlight tonight)

She took a quick bow and handed the microphone back to Alene, grinning from the unexpected rush, but determined to get the hell off that stage as quick as she could.

"Julia Greene!" Alene grabbed her hand and held it up a moment as if she were a winning prize fighter.

"You were great!" Carol beamed, and it sank in that people were clapping, a few even cheering.

Jules turned to step off the side of the platform and Bobby caught her in his arms. "Baby, that was wonderful!"

She was blushing, trembling. "Well, they wrote the tune," she said. The Rebelles began thundering through a song Carol had written, too loud to talk above. Someone patted her shoulder, and she turned her head to see Patty smiling.

"I knew you could do it!" Gina shouted at her ear as she and Patty returned to the middle of the room and their dates. Bobby hugged her from behind as they watched The Rebelles play the next song, but soon they were dancing with the rest of the room to the girls' fun mix of covers and originals. Finally, after a stomping version of "Wild Thing," Alene, her voice grown hoarse, said, "That's all the songs we know!" They switched off their amps, switched off the flood light, and someone put on the Love album.

"I'm so proud of you," Bobby told Jules, toying with a stiffened strand of her hair. "That was real pretty."

"I was petrified."

"If it's any consolation, sometimes I'm petrified on stage, too."

"You shouldn't be."

"Neither should you. I guess we just can't help it."

"I just wrote that as a poem. I was just going to give it to you. They talked me into all this."

"I'm glad they did." He bent to kiss her. "And I like this," he smiled and flicked at a few sequins.

Someone patted her rear and she jumped. "Good job," Terry said as he passed behind her.

"Hey!" Bobby smirked. "Hands off the merchandise."

A lamp snapped off and the room grew darker. Jules felt a cold draft on her arms. Someone had opened a basement window and a few people had gathered around. Curious, holding Bobby's hand, Jules led him closer, saw a puff of smoke vent to the outdoors. Patty handed her a joint. It wasn't the first time she'd tried it, and since she didn't have to go home tonight, she took a hit and passed it to Bobby, who did the same and passed it back to the group. He turned to her and French inhaled, which made her burst out laughing. "I didn't know you smoked," he grinned.

"I'm sure there are still a few things you don't know about me," she smiled. Someone nudged her and she took another turn, handing it again to Bobby, who took a deep draw and passed the dwindling roach along.

"I seem to be learning a few tonight," he said, scooping her up against him and slow dancing her back to the warmth.

She reached up to caress his face and look into his eyes. "If I'd done it with you that first night, would you be here tonight, still learning about me?"

"I don't know," he said, something almost sad creeping into his eyes. "I like to think I would, but honestly, I don't know." He'd stopped moving his feet. He looked up at the ceiling, gave his head a little shake. "God! Did they put truth serum in that stuff?"

"Did you think I didn't already know the answer?"

"Does it matter now?" he pleaded softly. "I'm so in love with you."

"I don't want any other," she said gently. "Don't dance with any other."

"Jules, you'e my only girl."

She laid her head against his chest and he slowly rocked her. Arthur Lee was singing, "I could love you more and more each day for a million years." As the full effect of the drug came on, everything became a soft, warm dream, just Bobby, his arms, his chest, the sound of his heart during a quiet song. Whether by accident or deliberately, she wasn't sure, she had opened the next button on his shirt and her fingertips were touching his skin, tracing the arc of his collarbone. His hands were on her hips. He kissed her hair and she kissed his throat and then they were sitting on the battered couch, slowly stretching out and down to lie facing each other, Bobby scrunched against the cushions, Jules hanging on the edge. They were laced together, kissing. "Gawd, where's a bucket of ice water when you need one?" Gina's voice came from behind Jules.

Chapter 6

A mid-January Sunday, Jules was filling the bird feeder at the side of the house when Bobby drove up for their afternoon date. He parked and walked toward her. "Ready to go?"

"Yeah, just let me grab my purse and tell Mom and Dad." She emptied the rest of the seed from the scoop into the feeder.

He followed her to the garage where she put the scoop into the pail of seed and fastened the lid. He was jittery, fidgety, shifting his feet. "What's the matter, baby?" she asked as he followed her back out into the sun. Then she looked in his eyes. His pupils were huge.

He raised his eyebrows. "What?" he smirked, lifting his palm. His hands were shaking. Not just quivering, really shaking.

"What are you not telling me?"

He looked away and huffed. "Alright, so I did some speed."

"Speed."

"Look, I had to work yesterday, then we played last night, we had a long drive, and I've got this paper due tomorrow for Kentucky History that I completely forgot about, so I went ahead and wrote it when I got home, since I was up anyway."

"You were up all night."

"Yeah."

"How many times have you done this?"

"A couple. Three," he shrugged.

"Baby, don't do this. This is not the way. You need to slow down."

"Slow down?" he laughed. "I don't have time to slow down. I have a band, I have a job, I have school. I can't quit work, and if I quit school I have to move out of the house. That's the rule."

"If you ever show up at school like this, you're liable to get expelled. What you need is not speed. What you need is sleep." She reached out to take hold of his arm. He shook her off. "You'll end up hooked," she warned.

He met her stern look with a set jaw and an obstinate stare.

"I'm going to a movie," he said flatly. "You can come if you want to, but I just want to come down in peace."

She heaved a sigh and shook her head. "Wait out here."

He drove to Fourth Street and parked. They were nowhere near the Castle Cinema. He let her out of the car and led her down the sidewalk. "Where are we going?" she asked.

"I want to see this movie. Terry said it's good."

They rounded the corner. The Phoenix. A small, aging theatre that showed mostly adult and foreign films. "*Blowup*, that's the one," he said.

"I'm not old enough to get in."

"They won't bother us," he assured her.

He bought their tickets, without incident, and they went inside. Hardly anyone was there. They sat in the middle, and once the film started, Bobby finally settled deep into his seat, still twitchy, but focusing on the movie. The plot engrossed them both, the mystery, the sensuality, and they were pleased to see The Yardbirds perform in a club scene, Jeff Beck smashing his guitar. Word of that scene is what had drawn Terry to see the film. Jules had never seen nudity in a film before, or such overt sexuality. She'd never been to anything that wasn't rated G. She was a little shocked at first, but it so suited the film and was so artfully handled that those feelings faded quickly. Another rite of passage, another step out of naiveté.

Bobby was gradually relaxing, his body starting to slow down. She held his hand in one hand, stroking the back of it with the other. He leaned his head against hers. "I'm sorry," he said softly.

She squeezed his hand and said quietly, "I love you. I care about you."

"I know."

"Come with me to my place," he said as they left the theatre.

Nora was at the kitchen table when they arrived, pasting S&H Green Stamps into a saving book. Rob was watching TV. Bobby and Jules said quick hellos and he led her to his room. "Leave the door open," Rob called after them.

They took off their coats and laid them on a chair. Bobby put on The Byrds *Fifth Dimension*, Side Two. "Eight Miles High." He sat down on the bed beside Jules, still a little tight, a little tetchy, but fatigue was creeping into his bones, into his head. He pulled her back on the bed with him, lying on his back beside her, feet on the floor, looking at the ceiling while the song played, jittery guitar over the smooth, deep vocals. He felt bad that he'd been sharp with her. The drug made him that way. And he hated how it made his hands shake. It made playing more difficult. "I'll try not to do this anymore," he said.

She rested on her side, stroking back his hair, running her cool fingers down his face. He closed his eyes and felt her fingertips soft and smooth against his eyelids. He turned and pulled her close, sealing his mouth on hers, reaching up under her sweater, under her bra to touch her breast, to feel her warmth and her womanliness. Her small hand slipped under the waistband of his jeans, just rested on his hip bone. He was thankful for her grace.

They heard the soft slap of Nora's slippers in the hall and quickly sat up, withdrawing their hands. She knocked gently on the door before leaning in. "Would you like some hot cocoa?" she offered. "It's starting to snow a little out there."

"Yes, please," Jules said. Bobby nodded. He hadn't eaten all day and something warm now appealed to him.

"Marshmallows?" Nora asked.

"Yes, please," Jules smiled.

When the record had finished, they went to the kitchen, sitting across from each other as they sipped their rich, sweet drinks. The heat washed through him, soothing his nerves, though his stomach tightened at first. Nora set out homemade banana nut bread. Yes, he felt ready to eat something now. Hunger and tiredness had begun gnawing at him simultaneously. When they'd eaten, they returned to his room with their mugs.

He turned the record over and finished his cocoa, setting the mug on the night stand. Jules was still warming her hands on hers. He lay back on the bed while she finished it, and then she joined him, snug against him, resting her head on his chest. "I just want to go to sleep now," he said.

"Then you should take me home now and come back and do just that."

"You sure you wouldn't mind?"

"Baby, you've got to get some rest. I can give you up early for that."

"Home already?" Kate smiled when Jules walked into the living room, quickly tucking something between the arm of her chair and the seat cushion. A book, Jules imagined. This wasn't the first time. Jules had discovered one by accident a year ago, and since then she occasionally took a peek to see if any others had made their way there. Kate always had an acceptable book prominently displayed on the lamp table by her chair, one she would read when Dan was present. The ones she hid often had Janice Deal's name written inside the cover. Janice, who was in the Women's Circle club, was a stylish, charmingly off-beat woman with long, straight, auburn hair and a penchant for maxi skirts. Kate and Janice liked to go shopping together and have lunches out. Kate always seemed a bit brighter and more confident after a day out with Janice, bringing home clothes that were a little more daring or fashion forward, or experimenting with some eye-catching new hors d'oeuvre for her Tupperware parties. And then there were the books. First it was *The Feminine Mystique*. Later volumes included *Lolita*, *Spy in the House of Love*, *Mrs. Dalloway*, and *The Second Sex*. Jules had never read any of them, though Gina had read *Lolita*, deeming it, by turns, "fascinating" and "disgusting." But she would read the reviews or synopses on the covers, glance through them and read a page or two. She often wondered what her mother thought of them.

"Bobby's really tired," she answered Kate. "He had long day and night yesterday, between work, homework, and playing a show," she explained.

"Did you have a nice time at the movie?"

"Yes, we did, and then his mom fixed hot cocoa for us. It's snowing out now. It doesn't seem to be sticking, though." She wanted to divert the conversation before her mother asked what movie they had seen. She was trying to remember just what was showing at the Castle that she could substitute if asked.

"I think that boy's gotten under your skin," Kate said. Jules felt a moment of panic, thinking she was going to say "under your skirt."

"I guess he has," she played it down with an innocent tone. She wasn't going to say "love" and have to endure the "maybe you're just infatuated" talk. Jules knew infatuation. It had never felt like this. "Well, I have some homework to finish," she excused herself.

At school the next day Bobby looked worn and didn't have much to say. "You okay?" she asked.

"I've been better, but yeah, I'll be alright. I'm just tired." He caught both her hands and squeezed them. "Sorry about yesterday," he said quietly.

"It's okay," she said. "Did you get some sleep?"

"I tried to take a nap after I took you home, but I couldn't get much rest. But last night I slept like I was dead. It was really hard to get up this morning, but I had to turn that damn paper in. Good thing I got it written when I did. There's no way I could have done it last night."

"You think your parents know?"

"I don't think so. They knew I was out late Saturday. They were asleep when I got home. When they got up for church I played possum. Mom likes for me to go, but she doesn't make me. I go some just to make her happy. I skipped out before they got home, just went for a drive until I picked you up."

"Mom has to needle Dad to go, so then he makes me go," she said. "I don't mind. I like the singing, and when the sermon gets boring I look at the windows, and the way they color the light coming through them. It's mostly peaceful."

"We can all use some peace," he said.

Tuesday found Bobby in better spirits. "Good news," he said. "Tony called last night. Knoxville loves us. They want us to come back. People who were at the show started calling the radio station, requesting our record. It's made the Top 20 there. The store that didn't want to carry it called up Bruce and ordered 50 copies."

"That's terrific!" Jules beamed.

"And a promoter in Midvale, Ohio wants to do some sort of Midvale/Midvale thing, pairing us up with one of their bands to play there and then here."

"That could be fun."

"And I'm so fucking glad we don't have any gigs this week. I never thought I'd say that," he laughed. "Four more months of school and I'll have that off my back. Seems like forever."

With a local hit on their hands and a lot of gigging under their belts, The Deep See were even more the school celebrities than they had been, eclipsing any other Midvale High garage bands and striking fear in the hearts of any fellow Battle of the Bands contestants. Sally Perkins, a reporter for the *Jaguar Journal*, the school newspaper, had talked Bobby and Terry into an interview during their lunch period one day. "So, how did you guys meet?" was her first question.

Terry laughed. "Well, obviously we all go to school together."

She jotted down his answer in shorthand. "And what made you all start a band?"

Terry said, "We like a lot of the same music. We always talked a lot about music. Bobby and I had already been playing on our own for a while, so we started jamming together. That was what, 9th grade?" He looked to Bobby.

"Yeah, that summer," Bobby said.

"Tyler decided to take up bass so he could play with us, and then Dwitty came along. He's a year behind us in school. He was already pretty good. We'd all, except Tyler, been in some kind of little band or other at some point."

"How did you get started playing live?"

Again, Terry took the question. "We played friends' parties, neighborhood cook-outs, that sort of thing. Word got around and people started hiring us. Dwitty's uncle became our manager, and he's been able to get us all kinds of gigs, and he got us started recording."

"So, how do you write your songs? Do the words come first, or the music, or what?"

Terry took the lead. "Sometimes the words, sometimes the music. It just depends. I might just be playing and come up with a riff I like and build a song from there. Or maybe I see something or someone says something and I come up with some words from that."

"How about you?" she turned to Bobby. "You're awful quiet over there."

He laughed. "Well, I don't much write words. I just like to sit down at the keyboard, fool around till I get a sound I like, or a set of sounds, and just play, let those sounds lead me where they want to go. It's like I become a part of the sounds, like I can feel them, like the keyboard becomes an extension of my thoughts, or me an extension of its thoughts. It's hard to describe."

"I think what Bobby's saying," Terry broke in, "is that he's always thinking with his organ."

They snickered, Bobby shoved Terry, and they all broke out laughing.

"I can't print that!" Sally blushed.

Spring came slowly to Midvale that year. After a warm spell in mid-February, a snowstorm hit, closing school for a day. When school reopened, the front lawn of the building became a snowball battlefield, before and after the school day. Bobby and Tyler were going at it after the final bell, laughing, mostly dodging each other's missiles, when Jules and Gina came down the sidewalk. "Hold these." Jules said, setting her books atop the ones Gina carried. She made a snowball, sneaked up behind Bobby, and fired it right between his shoulder blades. Snow flew out from the impact, and she ran, giggling. Unluckily for her, he was already armed. He wheeled and threw, hitting her in the back, and ran after her. As he closed the gap, she hastily made a lopsided snowball and hit him in the chest, but it hardly slowed him down. She shrieked as he reached out to grab her, and then she slipped in some slush and they both went down in a flop of wet white. Laughing, she scooped up a handful of snow and flung it at him. As clumps of it slid down his hair he caught her wrists and pinned her down. "I should just stuff a handful right down your shirt," he grinned.

"No, don't, please," she shook her head.

"No?"

"No, please."

"Bribe me," he said, bringing his mouth down on hers in a kiss both cold and warm. But it didn't last long before she felt a jolt, then another, as Tyler and Terry began pelting Bobby with snowballs. "Excuse me," he said against her lips, got up, turned and took off after them, leaving her sitting on the wet ground. Gina offered her a hand up, and as she dusted herself off, she watched the boys tangling, throwing gobs of snow, laughing and threatening each other. He trotted back to her, puffing white breaths, nose red, snow melting in his hair, and stooped to throw his arms around her thighs and hoist her over his shoulder.

"Put me down," she laughed.

"So, Gina," he said, starting down the sidewalk alongside her, as though carrying a gunny sack, "How's life treating you these days?"

"Well, let me tell you," she played along. "I get tired of working in the dress shop sometimes. Some of the women who shop there are real snobs. And then there's other things, like carrying people's books that aren't mine," she directed at Jules.

He put Jules down, manhandling her into an ardent kiss, then let her go, taking her books from Gina. Jules reached for his free hand and he put his arm around her.

"You two," Gina shook her head.

March 1st, Bobby brought Jules astounding news. "Baby, you won't believe this, but we're going to play London. You have to come with us."

"But that's 100 miles."

He threw his head back and laughed. "Not London, Kentucky. *The* London. London, England."

Her eyes widened. "For real?"

"For real."

"How? I mean–"

"Uncle Tony set it up. You knew Dwitty's real mom was English, didn't you?"

Jules shook her head.

"That's why he talks kinda weird. She was a war bride. Tony and Lynette have been going over there for years, even before they adopted Dwitty. They take Dwitty every year now so he can see his gran and some of his other relatives over there. Anyway, Dwitty's English uncle has some kind of connections, so he got us on the bill for some all-day outdoor concert in June, after school's out. Oh, Jules, you've got to come with us. Tricia's coming. I don't know who all else yet."

"How the hell? You know my dad!"

He tapped her head. "Use that brain of yours. Start thinking. Maybe you should work on your mom. I've got some ideas, too, for whatever they're worth. But you sure don't stand a chance if you don't try."

The following Sunday, Tony and Lynette Haye, conservatively dressed and dignified in manner, relaxed on the Greenes' couch, sipping coffee as they addressed Dan and Kate in their armchairs. "It's a wonderful opportunity for these young people. As a junior high school history teacher, I can tell you there's nothing like going abroad to stimulate a child's interest in history and culture, to let them see firsthand the places they read about in school, to see how people in other countries live. It's given Dwight an edge in school, and a deeper understanding of his heritage."

"That's all well and good," Dan said, "but what's to keep these kids from getting into all sorts of wildness and trouble over there?"

"As you know, my wife and I will chaperon," Tony replied, "and we'll take the same care in supervising their activities that we take with Dwight. My brother-in-law and his wife will be vacationing on the Continent, so we will stay at their house. We will put the boys up there, and the girls will stay with Dwight's grandmother. There will be no coed sleepovers or anything of that sort, I can assure you. They'll be quite busy for the short time we're there. If there is free time the day we arrive, there will be sightseeing. The next day the band will need to prepare for their show. My boys, as I call them, are all very serious about their music. This will give them a real opportunity to see if they are up to the rigors of a professional music career, so they will be applying themselves toward putting on the best performance they can. Lynnette can shepherd the others on some nice outings. We'll check the schedule for the Royal Shakespeare Company. They might be able to see a play. The following day is the band's performance, and that festival is an all-day event. The following day will give them some last sightseeing and shopping opportunities, and time to prepare for the return trip."

Dan and Kate looked at each other. "I think it would be good for her, dear," Kate said.

"How much will it cost?" Dan asked.

"She'll need her plane ticket, and we're working on a charter group discount for that. Other than that, since she won't be paying for room and board, she would just need money for some of her meals and for admissions to events or museums, and any shopping she might want to do. Dwight's grandmother has offered to cook the girls a substantial breakfast each morning. Oh, and if she doesn't have a passport already, she'll need to get one. It's best to start on that soon."

"She's already applied for one," Kate said.

Dan frowned surprise at his wife. "She has?"

"I thought it best, just in case. It doesn't do any harm for her to have one, even if she doesn't go."

Dan heaved a sigh and thought things over. "I still have my misgivings," he said.

"Maybe I could go over with her," Kate offered. "I've always wanted to see England. Or anywhere over there, really."

"I can't take the time and money for us all to go, and you're not going and leaving me here to deal with everything," he asserted.

"I do think it would be good for her, and you know she's a good girl, Dan. She never gets in trouble here, why should she there?"

"Julia!" he called out.

"Did you call?" she asked as she came down the stairs, as if she hadn't been listening in the whole time.

"Julia, I've decided you can go, on one condition," he said sternly.

"Yes, Daddy?" Her face brightened.

"You finish off the school year with straight A+s. That means A+ in every subject, no just plain As. You do that and stay out of trouble and you can go on the trip."

"Oh, thank you," she kissed his cheek, then kissed her mother. "Oh, think of it, Mom! All those famous places. Big Ben and the Tower of London and Buckingham Palace and everything."

The Greenes and the Hayes shook hands and exchanged good-byes. Once they had pulled out of the driveway, Tony turned to Lynnette. "Jesus, he's a tough customer. I see what Bobby means now."

"You said it. I have to hand it to you, honey, you did quite a job back there, though."

"Yeah, well, I know this is important to Bobby, and that poor girl could use a break. Phew! Straight A+s, though. I hope she's got it in her." He wrested his tie loose and unbuttoned his top button. "Bobby said she's a good student. I just hope she's good enough." He reached down past Lynette's knee and tugged at her dress hem. "Where did you find that old thing?"

"It's Mom's," she laughed.

April brought the senior prom. Jules was like spring, all flowers and soft breezes. Pinning a corsage on her seemed almost too much, too heavy, even this white gardenia, but it seemed to please her with its sweet scent. She fastened a white chrysanthemum to the lapel of Bobby's grey suit coat, the lightest color suit he owned, and getting a bit short in the pantlegs for his liking, even after his mom had dropped the hems. Kate snapped photos in the living room, then outside in front of a white dogwood blooming in the front yard. When the breeze gusted up, he could feel Jules' skirt wrap around his leg. He just wanted to whisk her away somewhere, on their own, far from Midvale. He prayed she would be able to go to London.

They danced, and danced. Any excuse to hold her, to move with her. No one even tried to cut in. They had become sacred.

"How are your grades?" he asked.

"Mostly fine. Physics, though," she shook her head. "I don't know. If anything will keep me from going, it's that one. I understand the concepts, but the math is hard. Can you help me with it?"

"I don't know, baby. I took the easy math. I can have a look at it with you, but I don't promise."

"Thanks. Oh, I'm so worn out with studying. I just don't want to think about school at all tonight."

"Then we won't," he kissed her ear.

Gina was back with Donnie, at least for the prom. Tyler had taken Carol. Terry and Elise were acting so stately it was amusing. "She's sure got her hooks in him," Carol commented to Gina.

"They always struck me as kind of an unlikely pair," Gina replied. "Ah, but look at The Magnets! They look like they're dancing at their own wedding."

"I think they will be someday," Carol said.

"I hope so," Gina sighed.

Bobby shook his head when he looked at Jules' Physics textbook. "I don't know, baby. I think I'm doing it right, but I can't be sure. I don't want to risk telling you wrong. I'm sorry."

"It's okay. I'll see if I can find someone else to help me. If not, I'll see about staying after school, if Mr. McComas will stay and help me."

"I'll ask around, too," he said.

Chapter 7

Dwitty turned out to be quite good at Physics. "I took it last year," he told Jules, leaning over her kitchen tabletop to check the equation she had worked in her notebook. "I made an A. I loved it. I mean, music is all about physics. Sound waves pushing through the air, or through wood or whatever makes up an instrument. Electrical energy amplifying sounds, being altered by components in the circuitry. Music is all forces and impulses, actions and reactions. It's physical." He tapped her results with his pencil. "This looks good, Jules."

"You sure Tricia doesn't mind this?" Jules asked.

"Come on. Trish knows me better than that, and like everybody doesn't know how devoted you and Bobby are? She wants you to be able to go to England, too. So let's not get distracted here. Okay, if v is a vibrating string, that's equal to the square root of T over μ. So, what's T?"

"The tension of the string."

"Right. And what's μ?"

"The string's mass?"

"Per unit length. Yes."

As the semester neared the end, Jules talked to Mr. McComas. "I need to know how my grades are in this class. I really need an A+ in here. I have a trip to England riding on it, and I really, really want to go. Am I going to make it?"

"Let's have a look," he said, opening his grade book. He did some quick mental calculations. "I'm afraid that even if you make 100% on your exam, you'd be 1 point shy."

"Oh, no." She felt sick. All that studying, all that work, and still it was unattainable, and by one lousy point! "Oh, please, no. Oh, I can't believe it." She felt the beginnings of tears burning her eyes.

"However," he said, "Since you're so close and you've worked so hard to improve, I'll give you a break. Of course, to be fair, now I'll have to give everyone that same break, but I'll devise an extra credit project, worth 5 points. But it's up to you to make that 5 points be enough."

"Oh, thank you. Thank you. You don't know how much this means to me." She clasped her books to her chest.

"Five points maximum. I can't give you any more," he warned.

Jules studied and fretted and studied some more. She felt like a hermit. She didn't even see Bobby outside school. The extra credit project had been fairly easy for her, a set of 20 logic puzzles to solve. She got her full 5 points. But there was still the exam to conquer, and she had to be near perfect to make her goal. Dwitty couldn't help her much now. He had his own exams to study for. Her parents didn't like for her to drink coffee, so she doubled up on Cokes to try to stay awake late the night before the exam.

When the day of the exam arrived, she just wanted to take it, to not have to wait till 3rd Period. She was afraid to talk to or listen to anyone, lest she forget something important. And then, when the time came, she trembled all through the exam, close to tears on a couple of difficult questions. "When will they be graded?" she asked Mr. McComas as she turned her test in.

"Tonight," he said.

Couldn't he just grade it right now? Did she really have to wait till tomorrow? When she saw Bobby after class, her nerves were shot.

"How did you do?" he asked.

"I don't know," she shook her head. "I don't know, and I won't know till tomorrow, and I can't stand it!"

"Shh-hh–" He took her in his arms and rocked her. "It's done now, it's over." He kissed the top of her head. "If it's not enough, there's nothing more you can do. You did all you could, and way more than I could have. So, let it go. Whatever happens, it will be alright." He flinched and turned his head, thumped hard on the crown with a pencil.

"I don't know who you're smothering under there, Lott," Principal Sammons said flatly, "but not at school."

Gently, reluctantly, Bobby released Jules, waiting until Sammons had passed to smooth her hair and soften his scowl.

She tossed all night, even cried into her pillow briefly. She tried so hard, like Bobby said, to let it go, but she just wanted to know, either way. Oh, she needed him now to hold her and soothe her and tell her it would be alright.

When she got to school the next morning, she rushed straight to Mr. McComas' classroom. He looked up from his desk, diagrams of atoms swirling dizzily on the wall behind him. "Ah. I thought you might stop by," he looked over the top of his reading glasses at her.

"How did I do? Did I make it? Please don't make me wait."

He shuffled through his papers and stoically handed her her exam.

When she saw Bobby in the hall she ran to him. "I did it!" she panted. "I did it. With 1 point to spare."

June 2nd, Jules sat proudly between Bobby's parents and her own in the auditorium, watching Bobby, Tyler, Terry, and Elise graduate. Nora's parents had come, too. Dwitty, Tricia, and Uncle Tony sat nearby. After the ceremony, Jules, the Lott clan, and the Greenes all met for a celebratory dinner out. Then Bobby left with his family and Jules with hers. In only a week they would be leaving for London. In her room, Jules put on the new Beatles album, *Sgt. Pepper's Lonely Hearts Club Band*, and tried to figure out who all the people on the cover were.

"Oh, Gina, I wish you could go," Jules said as she laid a modest nightie in her suitcase on top of her jeans.

"Yeah, me too, but Dad said no. Funny, huh? Your dad saying yes and mine saying no? Just goes to show... something." She shrugged.

"One for the books, for sure," Jules shook her head and patted down the contents of her bag. "Tricia said be sure and leave room so we can buy clothes over there. I hope we find some really far out things. I promise I'll bring you back something fab."

"So, who all is going?"

"Tricia and her little sister, Stella. She's either 14 or about to turn 14. She starts high school next fall. Two of Dwitty's American cousins are going, Mandy and Caroline. I think they're 15 and 17. And the guys, of course."

"Elise isn't going?"

"She's started work as a candy striper. She wants to see if she's really interested in becoming a nurse."

"You think Terry has nurse fantasies?" Gina joked.

"I'm betting Terry has all kinds of fantasies," Jules laughed.

Few of the gang going to London had ever flown in an airplane. Jules had once flown to Florida and back with her parents, when she was 8. Bobby had ridden a few times in small private planes with a friend of Rob's who was a recreational pilot. Dwitty, of course, had flown to England and back several times. For the rest, it was a new and exciting experience. O'Hare airport in itself was an experience, none of them but the Hayes having been inside such a large, busy building. Already the Instamatics were snapping.

For veterans of interminably long family vacation car rides, the 8 hour flight to London didn't seem so awful, and whenever one needed a rest room, there was no need to beg one's dad to make a stop. They flew from sunset into the morning. Some slept. Most were too excited to get much rest.

Jules and Bobby looked out the window, fascinated by Atlantic Canada, how it changed from land full of bodies of water, to water filled with islands, like an Escher painting of birds going one way gradually changing into fish going the other way. And then it was all sea. Mile upon mile, hour upon hour of sea, with only the rugged mass of Greenland to break it up. Hand in hand, shoulder to shoulder, they dozed off together, happy, free, so far from Midvale they had yet to believe it. Even when they touched down, when every voice on an intercom, every airport employee and customs official spoke with a British accent, it had scarcely started to sink in.

Harry Beecham, the son of Dwitty's English aunt and uncle, was a 20-year-old with brown hair down to his shoulders. Sporting wide-striped black and white trousers and an orange vest lined with white fake fur, over a pink floral, silk shirt, he came to collect the luggage and take it back to his parents' house. Lynette decided to go with him, desiring a nap. "Pretty birds," he smiled, eying the girls up and down. He and his 18-year-old sister Anne had their own flats. Their younger brother was staying with friends in Surrey while their parents took their holiday in France.

Tony took his dazed young American flock out for lunch. Jules found it startlingly disconcerting with everyone driving on the left. Terry found it confusing that everyone held their forks "upside down and in the wrong hand." Tricia couldn't believe the restaurant didn't have hamburgers. Bobby was already wondering how he would deal with the apparent scarcity of coffee, but three strong cups of tea later he guessed he could manage. Tony made sure everyone had timetables for the buses and the Underground. None of the kids but Dwitty had ever ridden a subway train, anywhere, so Tony took them on the Tube to get them familiar with it.

The girls were deposited at Gran's house, a charming two-story semi-detached. Gran rushed out to give Dwitty a hug. "You look more like my Iris every time I see you," she beamed. Iris had been Dwitty's mom. "And this must be your Tricia." Everyone was introduced and then Tony took the boys with him to the Beechams' house to settle them in.

The Beecham house had been handed down for generations, an

imposing, grey stone two-story with a steeply pitched slate roof and roses in the back garden. It wasn't long before the phones were ringing back and forth between the two houses. While some of the group were too tired to do anything but nap, others wanted to do something more exciting.

"You'll have time for stuff in the city later," Dwitty told Bobby. "I'm taking Tricia to see some of the country. Y'all are welcome to come along."

So Bobby called Jules, and the four of them set out in a borrowed car. Dwitty seemed quite adept at driving on the left. "I'd crash head-on in two minutes," Tricia laughed.

"Nah, you'll get used to it," Dwitty said.

Out of the city, he drove them deep into Kent, down narrow, winding lanes through rolling green hills, past centuries old houses growing sparser and larger behind mouldering stone walls. They stopped a few times to take pictures, and toured a manor that was open to visitors. Big, black birds called down from the roof in mysterious, grating tones. "Those are rooks," Dwitty said.

"Look like big crows to me," Tricia shrugged.

"They're related," Dwitty said.

Something about them captured Bobby's imagination, he wasn't sure why. He took a couple photos, though he knew the birds would appear as little more than black dots on the prints.

"What are those bushes with yellow flowers all along the road?" Jules asked when they resumed their drive.

"Gorse," Dwitty said. "And you don't want to land in them," he laughed. "Had that experience once. They're thorny."

They ended up in Canterbury. There wasn't much time to tour the cathedral, but Jules was awed, not just by its beauty and history, but by its sheer age. She kept touching things. The stone and wood themselves seemed alive. In a souvenir shop she bought a paperback copy of *The Canterbury Tales*.

Dwitty confessed he was getting tired, so after a quick supper in a pub, they headed back to London. In the back seat, Jules dozed off under Bobby's arm, more than ready to make an early night of it.

In the morning the girls breakfasted with Gran while the boys ate with Tony and Lynette and went over plans for the show. Jules was surprised and rather pleased to discover that English bacon was more like ham than what she was used to. Bobby wished he had some sort of keyboard to practice on, but the house didn't even have a piano. Tyler and Terry had brought just their guitars. All the rest of the gear was being rented or borrowed, and would be waiting at the venue the day of the show, no chance for them to try it out beforehand. They had put in a good, hard rehearsal session the day before the trip. Tony assured them they were plenty ready.

By early afternoon Dwitty and Tricia had taken Stella and Mandy out sightseeing. Tricia kept Stella protectively close, since she was so young. Mandy, though only a year older, was more independent, but she liked Stella and they became fast friends. Terry had gone with Tony to see about details for the show. Lynette was out shopping.

The rest of the gang were lounging around the Beecham house. Anne had brought her friend Mimi over. Harry had latched onto Caroline. After all, they weren't blood relatives.

"As you know, The Pink Floyd are playing tonight," Anne announced. "In the meantime, if anyone would like to take a little *trip*, we'll be your tour guides." She held up a sugar lump and raised her eyebrow.

Jules looked at Bobby. Bobby looked at Jules. "We've got to," she smiled.

"Count us in," he said. He was certainly curious as to what all the fuss was about.

Tyler nodded and raised a finger.

"The bus leaves now," Anne slipped a cube into each traveler's hand. "Here's your ticket."

They didn't take a bus, but a couple of cars. Nothing extraordinary happened until they'd arrived at a park and spread out on a lawn. Bobby felt a slight tingling sensation, a bit of a nervous flutter in his stomach. Things began to shimmer, then recede continuously. He looked at Jules, who looked a bit ashen.

"I feel sick," she said. He helped her to her feet, toward a hedge, where she lurched forward and retched. She sank to her knees and he squatted behind her to steady her, rubbing her back to soothe her until she sat back on her heels.

"You okay now?"

"Yeah, I think so."

"Let's go sit down." He helped her up and walked her back to the group, his arm around her.

"I need some water," she said.

"There's a fountain over there," Anne pointed. Bobby walked her to it.

She rinsed her mouth and spat on the ground before drinking, and Bobby laughed. "That wasn't very ladylike."

"Neither is puking in the bushes," she replied.

"Yeah, but you couldn't help that."

As they walked back, the grass writhed and swayed like thousands of lime sea anemones. Bobby was grinning. He couldn't look at it for very long.

"She okay now?" Anne asked.

"Yeah." Bobby failed to suppress a laugh as he and Jules sat back down on the grass.

"Here, take a sip," Mimi handed Jules a bottle of wine. Jules took a sip and passed it to Bobby.

Over his tongue it rolled, dark and sweet, a hint of salt. He tasted its color. Black cherry. He passed the bottle on, somehow seeing the inside of his own mouth.

"Look. Look at the clouds," Jules nudged him and pointed. He looked up to see them billowing and rolling rapidly, constantly toward them, yet somehow staying in place. He laughed again, couldn't stop grinning. He looked at Jules, and she was grinning, too. They lay back on the grass, gazing up at the crazy clouds, then at each other. The grass tentacles were tickling his arms. Jules plucked a tiny blue flower from between them and turned it, studying it, then drew its petals down his nose. When it reached his lips, he bit it, the stem hanging out between his lips. This seemed to distress Jules, so he stuck his tongue out under the stem to pull it all into his mouth and hide it.

"Oh my God!" she laughed and covered her eyes. "Your tongue is green."

He pulled the flower out of his mouth and tossed it aside. "No, it's not."

"Yes, it is."

"Look. I swear it's not."

She peeked out from under her fingers and he stuck his tongue out. She flopped back on the grass, laughing, the sound rippling back off the surface of the sky. Her hair was swimming in the sun. He plunged his fingers into it, silky around his tingling skin. He kissed her, and it was all warm, pulsating sun, flowers of wine. "It's like apples," she said softly.

"Come on, you two," Tyler smiled, tugging at Bobby's shirt.

"Where are we going?" Jules asked.

"To get something to eat before the show," Harry said.

As they walked through that crazy grass toward the street, Bobby ducked and drew Jules closer as they passed beneath the wriggling branch-arms of a menacing oak tree. Then the street crashed upon them with noise and glare. "Look at the bus!" Jules pointed, and it growled past them, two decks of bulbous red shine, window panes like grinning teeth.

Bobby laughed through his nose.

"We need one of those in Midvale," she said.

He quickly lost any sense of direction or place. He just knew they were moving, always moving. Everything was always moving. And then he stopped. Flowers spread before him, explosions of color, each hue a tiny voice in an ethereal choir. Jules tugged his little finger. "Come on, baby."

"No, wait. Wait." He pulled out his wallet, made his choice, and put a bouquet of fireworks in Jules' hands.

Harry led them into a café, where they were seated around a table of dark, deep-grained wood that looked as alive as the tree in the park. No wonder that tree was angry. Its relatives were ending up in places like this. Bobby stared at the bright yellow menu, which seemed riddled with strangely shaped, receding beige holes. What exactly were they supposed to be? He probed one with his fingertip and it snapped to flat, colorful attention. It was food, or a picture of food, though he wasn't sure just what it was supposed to be. "What you want, then, mate?" Harry poked him and nodded to the waitress.

"Umm... I don't know."

"Fish and chips, maybe?"

"Yeah. Fish and chips."

"You, miss?" the waitress asked Jules.

"I don't think I want anything, thanks."

Mimi nudged her. "Have a little of something. It will help."

"Can I just try a little of yours?" she asked Bobby.

"Sure," he said, turning to look at her. She was holding her flowers protectively in her lap. Someone slipped the menu out of Bobby's fingers and he moved to touch Jules' eyebrow, tracing it slowly, over and over, each tiny, glinting bronze hair increasingly magnified. She closed her eyes, as though concentrating, then suddenly opened them, startled, and stifled a laugh.

Crunchy food. It was marvelous! Tickling his teeth, and up through his jawbones into his ears, satisfying little crackles and roars. Jules ate a few bites as she leaned against his arm. "You feel okay?" he asked before putting a softly melting flake of fish meat in his mouth.

"I feel fi-i-i-ne," she smiled. "There's a lot of blue things in here," she said, and Bobby saw them all emerge in high relief. "And red," she said, and those came forward instead.

Bobby let his eyes, his mind, drift around the cacophonous café, its colors and shapes, disembodied voices. A laugh hung in the air, dancing over the booths, and he suddenly felt claustrophobic, shifting his feet under the table, stretching his knees this way and that. He was relieved when everyone at the table seemed to suddenly rise as one and clatter out onto the street.

Eventually they ended up in some dark, cavernous place amidst a motley assortment of astonishingly dressed people, even a woman in a see-through blouse. At least, he was pretty sure it was, and not just in his mind. Jules had tucked a flower behind each of his ears. Somehow he had acquired a scarf of colorful, swirled chiffon, knotted loosely around his neck over his t-shirt. Colored lights pulsed and flashed. Slides were projected onto the stage, wrapping The Pink Floyd in shapes and shadows. Soap bubbles floated everywhere. Syd Barrett slumped over his guitar, sliding and scraping some object over the strings, building swirls and wails, ever denser and louder. Roger Waters screamed and the whole room became one huge, screaming mouth. Rick Wright's keyboards slithered sinuous into the air, then floated like lavender smoke, swirling, dispersing. Even in his current state, Bobby could tell Rick was using some kind of device to throw the sound of the Farfisa to different parts of the hall. Nick Mason's cymbals shivered cold starshine on an interstellar journey through an expanding universe. No one back home sounded anything like these guys. If they ever put an album out, Bobby was determined to buy it.

Coming down was gentle, spacious, and long. The hallucinations faded, thoughts gradually became more normal, but he still felt softly high, and tired. Sitting on the floor in Gran's living room, resting their backs against the wall, he and Jules nestled close. As others talked and played Radio London quietly, he floated off to sleep, resting his cheek against the top of her head. A few stray patterns spun out of the darkness behind his eyes, and then nothingness.

He woke to noises in the kitchen and the hot smell of a stove. Thinking it must be late, he turned his head to stretch the stiffness out of his neck, and opened his eyes, only it wasn't lamps providing the light, it was sun. Somewhere a clock methodically ticked, but he couldn't see it. Jules slept soundly against his side, a few wilted flowers in her lap. He was trying to decide if he should wake her or let her dream, when Gran walked in, hand on her hip, shaking her head.

"Sorry," he said, "I guess I–"

"Well, at least you've both got all your clothes on."

Jules startled awake, pushing herself bolt upright.

"Julia, is it?"

"Yes, ma'am."

"When you've pulled yourself together, you might warn the other girls that there's a young man here."

"Maybe I should leave now," Bobby said, bracing himself with his hands, ready to get up.

"Nonsense, not without something in you first," Gran said and returned to the kitchen.

He and Jules looked at each other in the sun filtering between the chintz drapes, shared a quiet laugh, a kiss. She ran the backs of her fingers over his cheek, smiling. She seemed to enjoy the feel of his whiskers. "You're beautiful," he said, and she kissed him.

While Jules went upstairs to freshen up and change clothes, and warn the girls of his presence in case they didn't want him to see them in their nighties, Bobby helped Gran in the kitchen and they had a nice chat. After breakfast, he and Jules walked to the bus stop and rode back to the Beechams', where she waited downstairs while he got a quick bath and a shave. He could hear Tyler on the phone in the upstairs hall as he toweled off, and when he'd dressed and opened the door, Tyler was just hanging up. He looked troubled.

"Who was that?" Bobby asked.

"Brenda." She was Tyler's sister.

"Something wrong at home?"

"No, just– family business," he shrugged and walked away.

When Bobby went downstairs, the rest of the band and the girls were assembling. "The prodigal son has returned," Terry announced as Bobby walked into the kitchen. "I understand a certain keyboard player was tripping his brains out yesterday and didn't come home last night."

Bobby pursed his lips to squelch a smile and the others laughed.

Today was the festival. The Deep See would be one of the first bands on, so they needed to get there by noon. Bobby was anxious about the "hired" gear that would be waiting for them. They would have little time to set up, borrowing another band's amps, and they wouldn't get a sound check. At times like this, Bobby's stage fright kicked in. Terry offered him a hit off a joint, but Bobby didn't like to play high. Instead he shared a bottle of wine with Jules, just enough to soothe him, to take the edge off. "Hey," Tyler punched his arm, "Put your war paint on." They took the stage in a sun-splashed park speckled with concert-goers, lounging or standing in groups on the lawn, the spaces between them ever filling.

They only got to play four short songs, but they seemed to go down well. Tripping girls were dancing in front of the stage like a harem in colorful frocks and scarves. A shirtless, long-haired man had chosen a lamp post for his vantage point. Bobby dealt with a couple of keys that wouldn't sound, improvising to make up for the missing notes. Tyler gave him a puzzled look once, but Bobby just gave him a reassuring nod to convey, "Just play your part straight and I'll work with it."

It seemed ludicrous to fly all the way across the Atlantic to play four songs, but he was really enjoying the experience, and having Jules with him to share it all. As they finished their set and he came offstage, he took Jules under his arm, energized now. They found a spot in the growing crowd and settled down on the grass, finishing the wine as they watched the next band. "I'm so, so proud of you," she said.

"'Dodgy gear' and all?"

"Especially with 'dodgy gear.' You're good enough to take those things in stride."

There were twelve bands on the bill, and as they increased in importance and popularity, their sets got longer respectively. Bobby noted that all the bands had a more psychedelic bent than the common fare in Midvale, both the lyrics and the music more fanciful and playful, more experimental, less dance-oriented, though certainly people could dance to it and were dancing to it, but in a more free-form way. He felt that The Deep See needed to absorb this as a lesson, use what they heard here as a template for moving forward. The final band, The Move, even incorporated bits of Classical music into some of their pop songs. When they sang "I Can Hear the Grass Grow," Bobby laughed. "No question what they're singing about," he remarked to Jules. Their set culminated with their taking an ax to a TV set.

"Toto, we're definitely not in Kentucky anymore," Jules said.

Darkness had settled over the littered park. "I'm starved," Bobby said. "Let's go find something to eat."

In a nice pub, Bobby enjoyed a pint of stout and a hearty roast beef sandwich, while Jules dined on huge, succulent prawns in butter sauce, and drank a glass of shandy, a mix of beer and lemon soda. Jules had never been particularly fond of beer, but this she liked.

A party atmosphere reigned at the Beecham house, as most of the group gathered to chat noisily about the show. The band members were in high spirits. Tony had passed a few singles around, hoping to get some airplay or a review out of it. No one was terribly optimistic, but it seemed worth a try.

Monday was their last full day in England, the last chance for sight-seeing or anything else they wanted to try to do before packing for home. The girls had come over to the Beechams' and everyone was pairing off or grouping up to go out. "Jules and I are gonna see some sights, hit the shops. You wanna come?" Bobby invited Tyler, who seemed unattached.

"No thanks. I've got some other stuff I want to do."

"Something's bugging you, man, isn't it? Anything you want to tell me?"

"Nah, it's okay. Some shit back home, is all. Don't worry about it."

Bobby punched his shoulder. "War paint, man. And you know I'm here."

Tyler nodded, and went out the door. Everything was suddenly quiet. Jules was finishing up a cup of tea, putting some things in order in her purse. "Enough money left to have some fun with," she smiled as she zipped it shut. She got up to rinse out her cup and Bobby came up behind her, putting his arms around her waist.

"Did you notice?" he said at her ear.

"Notice what?"

"We're alone in the house." He kissed her ear.

She laughed, "Yeah, and what if someone comes back?"

He released her, then reached for her hand to lead her. "Come here. I want to show you something."

She gave him a teasing poke in the side. "That's the worst come on line I've ever heard."

He led her up the stairs, down to the end of the hall, and opened a door to another set of stairs, dim and smelling of old wood. "Terry and I came up here last night to smoke a joint." A sharp turn at the top of the stairs opened into a sloped attic room, rough beams framing the ceiling, the dark wood floors smoothed by centuries of use. Birds twittered outside, somewhere near the window, its wavy diamond panes admitting watery, grey light. For the first time since their arrival, the famed English rain had made an appearance.

He closed the upper door and shot the bolt. Wings fluttered as he walked toward her to the center of the room. As much as they had loved, he had never seen all of her naked all at once, much less in daylight. The luxury of such privacy had never been afforded them. They undressed each other, completely, daring to linger in the light. "You're so beautiful," he whispered, his eyes trailing his fingers across her skin.

They lingered at love, birds cooing under the eaves as the rain pattered on the roof, Jules making soft, shuddering sounds.

As they sat on the floor, Jules in his lap, facing him, her arms and legs wrapped around him as she rested her head against his neck, he pulled his sweater around her, against the coolness that had begun settling around them. "We really should go," she said, "but I wish we didn't have to. I wish we didn't even have to go home. I've been so happy here."

"I have too, baby. Maybe we can come back someday."

On a bus to King's Road, Jules stroked the back of Bobby's hand. "Saturday, when we were in the park, I was looking at your hands, and suddenly it was like I could see right through your skin. I could see your bones, and it scared me."

"Well, I got scared by a tree," he laughed.

"So, would you ever try it again?" she asked.

"Oh, hell yes," he grinned.

"Me too."

In the boutiques they shopped for outrageous, trendy clothes. Bobby picked out a hunter green velvet suit with flared trousers and tried it on. "What do you think?" he asked her.

"That's beautiful! Oh, it looks so good on you. You have to get that. Nobody in Midvale has anything like that."

"Hell, half the bands in Midvale are still in drainpipes and winklepickers."

Jules found a pale yellow mini-dress with rectangular cutouts down the long sleeves and a tidy bow at each cuff. She tried it on and modeled it for Bobby. "That looks real sweet on you," he said, so she bought it. She bought Gina an extravagant red feather boa.

At another shop she found a pearl grey dress with a sweater-knit top and a silvery, satiny skirt with bands of grey fake fur around it, and metallic silver boots to go with it. "This will about clean me out, but I've got to have them."

Bobby got a lavender satin shirt and a hyacinth blue brocade jacket with metallic gold embroidery on the lapels and cuffs. "I hope Terry makes it down here. His style is looking kinda dated for a front man."

"Listen to you," she thumped his shoulder. "You sound like a girl."

In a record shop, Bobby found a single by The Pink Floyd, "Arnold Layne" backed with "Candy and a Currant Bun." He and Jules each bought a copy. "There's a new one out next week," the clerk told him.

"Just my luck. I won't be here then," Bobby sighed. He would have to see if someone in the Midvale area could order it for him.

Many of the group, including Jules and Bobby, had dinner together at a pub that night. Jules wanted to pack and change clothes, so Bobby saw her back to Gran's, and then went to pack what he could of his own things. Harry and Caroline were on their way to a party some friend of Mimi's was throwing and invited everyone else along. Bobby decided to go just for a while until it was time to pick up Jules for an evening out on the town to investigate some of the public entertainment options.

The party was noisy and crowded, but there were few people there that even Harry or Anne knew, so they didn't stay long, nor did Terry, Dwitty, or Tricia. Tyler was in a far corner, talking to a girl, when Bobby left.

Bobby and Jules went to a couple discotheques, but didn't stay out very late. Jules was tired, her body clock confused. Bobby took her back to Gran's. Harry was dropping Caroline back at the same time, so he offered Bobby a ride, inviting him over to his flat for a few beers, if he wished. So, Bobby went. It wasn't a party, as such, just a few friends having a few drinks and talking. They were full of questions for Bobby, such as what a tornado is like, what American football is like, and what American girls want.

It was dawn when Bobby got back to the Beecham house. Terry had the kettle on. Dwitty sat resting his head on his folded arms on the tabletop. Water ran through the pipes to another part of the house. "Well, look what the fucking cat dragged in," Terry teased.

"Fix me a cup, will ya? I gotta go change and finish packing," Bobby replied and headed up the stairs. It didn't strike him right away that Tyler's things were gone. Everyone was packing and assembling downstairs, so maybe Tyler was just in the bathroom down there or something. Bobby changed into a reasonably clean pair of jeans and his last fresh shirt. All his socks were dirty now, so he decided to just go barefoot in his sneakers. As he slipped his foot into one, he crunched something stiff. Paper. Neatly folded, or at least it had been, it looked like a small note. He opened it.

> When you get this, I'll already be gone.
> Don't look for me, but if you can, buy me some time.
> Destroy this and don't tell anyone.
> I'm sorry I can't tell you more.
> > Ty
>
> Take care, brother.
> Maybe someday–

What the hell? What was he saying? Gone? Gone where? He read the note again, searching for something he might have missed. Was he supposed to understand this? Was there something he should know? His first impulse was to run downstairs with it, ask the others about it. But no. This had to be something important. Tyler wouldn't pull a prank like this. "Goddamn it, Tyler, what have you done? What's happened?" he whispered. He thought back to yesterday, how odd, how distant Tyler had been, even at that party. Ever since that call from Brenda... What had she told him? Bobby took a risk, tearing the bottom two lines from the note and tucking them into his wallet. The top portion he flushed. He was shaking all over, distraught. He nearly cut himself shaving. He splashed his face with cold water, tried to steel himself, to calm himself, to act as if he knew nothing, expected nothing unusual. Tyler was trusting in him. He couldn't let him down, no matter how much he wished he could stop him.

He felt a little sick as he sipped a strong cup of tea. "Looking kinda rough today, Bobby," Terry teased.

"Yeah. Bit of a hangover. You got an aspirin?" He did feel an ache organizing itself between his eyes, but it had little to do with the aftereffects of alcohol.

"There's a bottle in the cupboard over there, or at least there was," Dwitty nodded.

"Thanks." He got up, found the bottle, took two with a last gulp of tea, and rinsed his cup.

"You seen Tyler?" Terry asked while Bobby still had his back to them.

Bobby felt a stab of pain through his stomach. "Nope," he said. "I figured he was down here already. His stuff is gone."

"We haven't seen him at all," Dwitty said.

A look of confusion, of growing agitation passed between them. "Maybe he went on to the airport," Bobby ventured.

"Why would he do that?" Terry wondered.

"Maybe he's with that girl," Bobby said.

"What girl?" Dwitty asked.

"That blonde at the party. In the white dress with the fuzzy stuff."

"They ended up together?" Terry said.

"I guess," Bobby shrugged. "They looked pretty tight when I left to go dancing with Jules. That's the last I saw him." This was all true, and the gears were turning in his head now.

"You with Jules all night, then?" Terry asked.

"No, I took her back to Gran's about midnight. She was tired and I wanted her to get some rest and not have to rush this morning. I went with Harry over to his place. He had some other guys over. We had some beers, just sat up talking all night."

Dwitty looked at his watch. "Well, shit, we gotta go soon or we're all gonna be late. I hope he's got sense enough to be watching the clock."

Tony and Lynette came out then and the boys apprised them of the situation. Tony made some hasty phone calls, but no one knew where

Tyler was. They waited at the house as long as they could, then drove to the airport.

Tyler was nowhere to be seen, and he hadn't checked in at the desk. The girls were well ahead in the customs line, Anne and Gran having driven them. Jules saw Bobby and gave up her place to stand with him. "Have you seen Tyler?" he asked her.

"No, why?"

"He wasn't at the house. We don't know where he is," Terry said.

Tony strode up. "No sign of him?"

"No. No one's seen him," Dwitty said.

Tony looked at his watch. If he's not here in five minutes I'll alert the police. Honey," he addressed Lynette, "You and the kids go on and get to the plane. I'll handle things."

Two uniformed men came with Tony to the gate. They pulled Terry and Bobby aside to talk to them. Terry returned to the group, but they were still questioning Bobby. Jules grew very nervous. "Bobby was the last of us to see him," Terry explained. "They're just trying to get any information they can."

Boarding began, and still the men were talking to Bobby. Jules walked up to them and slipped her hand through Bobby's arm. "It's okay, baby," he said. "Go ahead and get on."

"Go on, miss," one of the policemen said.

She stepped back a bit and Tricia took her hand. "Come on, Jules, we've got to go."

"Why won't they let him go? What if they don't let him go? What if he misses the plane?"

"Then he'll get a later one. Come on, now. It will be alright, I'm sure."

Jules looked over her shoulder as long as she could at Bobby, saw him solemnly nod at something being said. In the cabin, she stashed her tote bag and sat down by his empty seat, leaning against the window, frightened, near tears, watching the cabin door. A woman she didn't know took the aisle seat. Soon no one else was boarding and the stewardesses began making final preparations.

Bobby stepped onto the plane. They immediately shut the door behind him. The woman in the aisle seat got up. He hurriedly took the middle seat, beside Jules, and buckled his seat belt with shaky hands.

"What happened? What did they say?"

"They just wanted to know whatever I could tell them, if he'd said anything to me, if he was planning something, what time I got in, what time I saw that he was gone, what that girl he was with looked like. I told them all I could. I told them he'd been acting strange every since Brenda called him. He wouldn't tell me what they talked about, but they're going to get in touch with her, and they're going to talk to Mimi. Tony is going to stay behind and try to help." Jules took his cold, damp hand as the plane began to taxi and the stewardess gave the safety instructions. "Jules, I swear to God I don't know where he went or why."

"Maybe he overslept somewhere or got caught in traffic or something."

"I don't know, baby. I just don't know, but I have a bad, bad feeling." He braced himself for take-off, and Jules watched out the window as they left the ground. She watched London slip away beneath them, then the countryside. Bobby was silent. The whole group was subdued, talking quietly, no rowdiness or laughter.

Land turned to sea beneath them. Here and there people pulled down window shades for a nap. From the row behind them, Terry stood and leaned over Bobby, reaching down to clasp his shoulder reassuringly before slipping out to the lavatory. Bobby closed his eyes, so Jules took out her book of *The Canterbury Tales*, but she couldn't concentrate on what she was reading. She tucked it into the seat pocket and looked at Bobby. He was sitting back, eyes still closed, but tears were streaming down his cheeks.

"Bobby?" she said softly. He opened his eyes and she reached up to wipe away his tears. "You okay, baby?"

"He's my best friend, Jules, and this really scares me."

She tucked his hair back behind his ear, tried to ease him. "He missed the plane. I'm sure there's a good reason. He's bound to turn up. He can't have just disappeared." The look of pain that shot through his face worried her. "Bobby, is there something you're not telling me?"

He shook his head, then covered his face with his hands and leaned forward, resting his elbows on his thighs. The woman in the aisle seat got up and walked away.

Jules stroked Bobby's back. "You're tired, baby. You shouldn't have stayed up all night."

Terry sat down in the vacant seat, clapped Bobby's shoulder, and slipped Jules a pilfered miniature bottle of whiskey. "This is what he needs. Hair of the dog." Terry returned to his own seat. Bobby rubbed his eyes, downed the whiskey, and rested against Jules.

"Everything's going to be alright," she soothed.

Chapter 8

"I never should have let you talk me into letting her go," Dan leveled at Kate. "I knew no good would come of it. I never should have let her go out with him in the first place. Rock and roll bands. It's trouble, that's all it is. Well, I'm putting a stop to it right now."

Jules quivered at her desk, hearing every word. She heard her father's heavy footsteps on the stairs, heard him approach her room. She stiffened. He walked up to the desk, towering over her like a thunderhead. "From now on, you are not to see, or talk to, or communicate in any way with Bobby Lott, or anybody in that band, or anyone who was on that trip. At all. Do you understand?"

Nausea crept over her. "Yes, sir," she said weakly.

"You are grounded for the rest of the summer. You can keep your job, I suppose, but that's it. No parties, no visiting, no rock and roll shows, no dances. After school starts, we'll see. You keep your grades up and we'll see. But the rest still stands. From now on you are through with him and his friends. Period. I'm going over to his house right now and make sure he and his parents understand, as well." Dan held out his palm. "Give me his ring. I'll take it back with me."

"No, please," she covered it with her other hand.

He snapped his fingers and reopened his palm. "You're not keeping it."

"Please let me go with you. Let me give it back to him."

"No. You're staying here. I don't want you seeing him again. It's over, here and now. Give me the ring."

Slowly she twisted it off her finger and handed it to her father. For a few moments, it left its impression in her skin, and then even that was gone. She heard him tromp down the stairs, heard the front door shut. She closed her door.

In the Lotts' kitchen, Dan Greene paced and proclaimed like a sheriff laying down his law. Rob and Nora stood solidly, civilly affirmed their understanding of his terms, but Bobby, seated at the foot of the table, would not rise and would not reply. He sat like a rock, hands folded on the table in front of him, watching the heat rise in Dan's face. When Dan approached him, Bobby would not look at him directly, not a cowering gesture, but a refusal of acknowledgment.

"Here's your ring back." He dropped it just above the tabletop so it clattered and rocked back and forth a few inches in front of Bobby's hands. Bobby didn't pick it up. He just stared beyond Dan, off to the side, at the wall behind him, jaw set hard. "You give me your word, young man."

Bobby didn't speak, didn't look at him, but every muscle in his body tightened like a coiled spring.

Dan took a step closer, took a dominating stance over him, and waited. "I want your word," he said through his teeth and pounded his fist on the table. Bobby didn't flinch.

"Please leave our house," Nora said firmly.

Without moving his head, Bobby turned his eyes on Dan. Nora had never seen such pure hate in her son's eyes. And still, Bobby did not speak.

Rob strode up and took hold of Dan's collar. "It's high time you went. You are not welcome in this house."

He jerked Dan's collar and Dan pushed his arm away. "I'm going." Dan turned and stamped out the front door. Bobby didn't move until he could no longer hear Dan's car driving away. Then he stood and walked to the kitchen door, pulling his keys from his pocket.

"Where are you going, honey?" Nora asked. She reached out to touch his shoulder, but he eluded her.

"For a drive."

Minutes later Terry answered the knock on his door. He looked Bobby up and down. "Hey, what's up, man? You look like you wanna kick somebody's ass."

"I need a drink or ten."

"Alright, give me a minute." Terry put on a pair of sneakers and went to the kitchen. Bobby heard cupboard doors, glass clinking. Terry returned with half a bottle of whiskey. "He probably won't miss this," he said. "And if he does, fuck him. He's got enough stashed around. Let's go."

A creek, more like a large drainage ditch, ran through Terry's neighborhood, a couple blocks away. Terry lit up a cigarette, and they walked in long strides down the street, past the last streetlight and into the dark, into the small trees that crowded the top of the creek bank. On a boulder near the water, they sat down. Terry pulled the bottle from the waistband of his jeans and handed it to Bobby, who took a long drink before handing it back. Terry took a swig and passed the bottle back to his friend. "Now, tell me what's going on," Terry said.

Jules had locked the door to her room, something she had rarely done, mostly as a young child, trying to escape a spanking when she'd pushed things a little too far. And once when Gina had filched a dirty magazine from her cousin's house. But this was different. Now she just wanted to shut them out. She wanted to be left alone. She didn't even turn the radio on. She just sat on the floor by her bed, staring at the design of scattered pink roses in her rug, stroking tangles out of the magenta fringe. Her emotions, her thoughts were such a jumble she just wanted to blank them out, too. She had cried till she gagged. Tears now were just occasional, fleeting things. Snowflakes melting.

There was a gentle knock. "Can I come in, honey?" Kate asked "I just want to talk to you."

"I don't want to talk," Jules replied.

"Julia, honey…"

"How could you let him do this? Bobby told the truth. Everything he said was true."

"Your father thinks he's a bad influence, that you've been running with the wrong crowd."

"He gossips like an old woman and he wants to believe the worst about everybody."

"Julia!"

"Go away."

A week had passed since their somber return from London, and still there was no sign of Tyler. Uncle Tony had returned home. The only new clue had come when the focus shifted from Bobby to Brenda, and she revealed what her phone call to Tyler had been about. She had found his draft notice in the mail.

Dan had grounded Jules as soon as he learned Tyler was missing, the very night of her return home. Regardless of what had happened or what might come to pass, he was determined to keep her away from these wild, dangerous, irresponsible people.

When Bobby had called the day after their return, to tell her what Brenda had revealed, she had dropped to her knees beside her parents' bed, clutching the receiver. "My God," she breathed. "He barely even got out of school. Oh, God, Bobby I'm so scared. What if it was you? What if you were next?" Her heart pounded. She felt dizzy. "What would you do? What would we do?"

"I don't know, baby. I just don't know."

"Promise me. Promise me you wouldn't disappear. Promise you'd take me with you."

"Shh-hh... I promise, baby. Aw... don't cry, honey," he soothed, but she could hear the strain in his own voice. "He was free. He didn't have anyone like you."

And now this. Nothing Jules had said or could say was going to change Dan's mind or his resolve. In the morning, Jules pushed pieces of scrambled egg around her plate. "I see you come down for food," Dan remarked coldly. "You show your mother more respect."

Jules wanted to say, "Why?" but she nibbled her toast instead, to swallow the word down.

"Do you hear me?"

"Yes, Daddy," she mumbled.

He tossed down the rest of his coffee, kissed Kate on the cheek, and left for work.

June 30th, a lazy Thursday afternoon, Gina got a letter in the mail. A pink envelope, no return address. It looked like Jules' handwriting. She sat on the porch steps and opened it. Inside was a smaller envelope, sealed. There was a note with it. "Please take this to Bobby. Don't mail it, put it in his hand. I want to make sure he gets it and that no one else sees it."

Bobby was back working at Kessler's, so Gina went the next day. He was there, behind the counter, but he was different. She didn't expect him to be jovial, but his general ease of manner was gone. She didn't see him smile at anyone, and Bobby had always had a ready smile. "How are you doing?" she asked.

"How do you think?" he tossed back.

"I have something for you, from Jules."

She saw just a spark in those dark eyes. He took the envelope and slipped it into his shirt pocket, pressing it against his chest. "Thanks. Please tell her I love her. Tell her I don't blame her for anything."

"I will," Gina promised.

Home from work, alone in his room, except for Lady stretched out beside the air conditioning vent, he sat against the headboard, stretching his legs out on the bed, and opened the shell pink envelope from Jules. There were two sheets of paper, the same color as the envelope, folded separately. He caught a suggestion of her perfume and sniffed the paper. Yes, she had scented it, and he was thankful for that little extra bit of her.

The first page was a letter.

> My only love,
>
> I want you to know that I did not want to return your ring. He insisted. I asked to return it to you myself, but he wouldn't let me. I don't know how much he told you. I'm grounded for the summer. I can only go out to go to work. I can't have anyone over. Even my phone use is monitored. I don't know what things will be like once school starts. It seems it will depend on my grades, but you know that's no problem. I'm forbidden to have anything to do with any of the band, or anyone who went on the trip. I told him I still have to go to school with Dwitty and Tricia, and that they might be in my classes. I'm still supposed to avoid them as much as possible.
>
> Somehow, some way, once I'm not grounded, maybe we can devise some way to see each other, but we'll have to be careful. He probably has his little spies everywhere. In the meantime, don't forget me. I will always be your girl, as long as you want me to be. If you decide you don't, make it quick and clean. The sword, not the ax.
>
> I love you with everything I have to love you with,
>
> Jules

He unfolded the second piece of paper and began reading. It was a poem. It read like music, like lyrics. Already the inklings of a tune began to form in his head.

> My world is torn apart now that I've lost you.
> I look up at the sky and it just makes me blue.
> I've cried so many lonely days
> Thinking of the many ways
> we loved.
>
> The birds on my windowsill have stopped trying to sing.
> They know that they can't cheer me now I've lost
> everything.
> I walk out through the sunny park
> Wishing it would just be dark
> above.

All I want now is to get back to you.
No matter what they say I will always be true.
Till then I'll spend the lonely days
Just thinking of the many ways
we loved.

"I will get you back, Jules," he said to the air. "I swear to God I will get you back. I give you my word on that, Dan Greene."

When Nora Lott walked through the door at the Women's Circle meeting, the room hushed. "My son," she said, "had nothing to do with Tyler Leighton's disappearance. Everything he told the police checked out. It's the sister caused all this."

"We heard about that," Janice said.

"Yes, I'm sure you've heard all sorts of things, and passed them on. And you, Kate Greene, you can tell that husband of yours to keep his mouth shut and quit spreading lies. He has no right to treat my son the way he has."

"I can't go against him, Nora. And Bobby was drinking that night."

"He's legal age over there."

"Julia is not," Kate asserted.

"He had already taken your daughter back to the house. He said she was not drinking with him, and I believe him. My son is not a liar. He is not a 'dirty hippie', a 'draft dodger', a 'drug addict', or an 'instigator.' He's never gotten a girl in trouble," she leveled at impromptu grandmother Dreama, who stiffened in her chair, face reddening. "He was never even held back a grade," she flung at Annette, whose son, at 19, still hadn't graduated. "I'm fed up with all of you, you gossiping hypocrites. Call yourselves Christians. And you, Kate Greene, you need to grow a backbone." With that, Nora turned on her heel and walked out.

"Well!" Lauren huffed to break the stunned silence. "I guess we've seen the last of her!"

Nora wanted no more to do with any of them. Night after night her wounded son paced his room, torn from his girl, from his best friend, from his band. She divorced herself from anyone who had brought this upon him.

They had returned from England to a country where people of different races could finally legally marry, yet all over the country vicious race riots raged. Every evening images of hate and death from around the world seared the TV screen. Hippies and demonstrators, crying for peace and love, were portrayed as agents of chaos, while the daily body counts from the Vietnam War had become as normal a part of the news as the weather report. Too many shots of fly-covered, dead war victims. Too many protesters beaten bloody by police batons. Jules had to stop watching the news, even in passing her father's chair.

But June 25th she tuned in the TV to watch *Our World*, the first live, internationally broadcast satellite TV show. The whole world watching the same thing at the same time, as it was really happening. Performers from all over the world taking part in the same TV show. That in itself was an exciting thing. Jules thought of Dwitty's gran, of Harry and Anne and Mimi. Maybe they were watching. She thought of Dwitty and Tricia, of Terry, of Tyler, wherever he was. And Bobby. *Oh, Bobby, please be watching. Please, let's be doing this together, at least.* She particularly hoped so when the show switched to England, and there were the Beatles and their musical friends, decked in flowers, singing "All You Need Is Love." *If only the whole world would believe that. If only my own parents would believe that.* As happy and hopeful as the song was, she was blinking back tears.

June slid into July, hot and bright, the air thick with moisture and cicada song. On her days off work, Jules, with her radio, lay sweating in her swimsuit in the sun, or reading in the shade. Anything to get out of the house. She and her mother had reached a truce. Kate enlisted her help with a Tupperware party. "It's not that I need your help so much," Kate said in the car on the way to the event. "I wanted you to have a chance to get out and have a little fun, and there are things I want to say to you. These decisions were your father's, not mine. I told him I thought he was being too severe, but he didn't want to listen. Your father is the head of the house. There's only so much I can do. That being said, that is kind of a wild crowd you were running with."

"They were good to me," Jules defended.

"Maybe so, but maybe they dance a little too close to the edge." She sighed. "Oh, honey, I know this is hurting you, and I feel sorry for that. Time will heal."

But time was what kept picking open the wounds. A rare moment in the house alone, Jules had called Gina. Yes, she had given Bobby the letter, and she conveyed his sentiments. Jules felt relief wash over her. Once she was back in school, she would have a network. She could get word to him, and from him, with more ease, she hoped. "Gina, I thank God now that you didn't get to go to London. If you had, I wouldn't be allowed to speak to you anymore. I couldn't bear that."

"I couldn't either. As awful as everything is for you, still, I do want to hear all about the trip. I want to see your pictures."

"You will, and I have some things for you, too."

And there it was again on the radio, a black shadow under all that sun, a song by The Deep See, and the DJ announcing, as he had yesterday, "That was Midvale's own The Deep See. Or they were. With bassist Tyler Leighton still missing, the group have called it quits."

Jules knew there was another component. Gina had told her that Elise wasn't happy about Terry going to England without her. In fact, she just didn't want him in a band anymore. She wanted him to settle down, and she had given him an ultimatum, to choose between her and the band. With Tyler gone and Bobby, as he had worded it, "difficult to deal with anymore," he had chosen Elise.

A glaring morning, the last Saturday of July, Jules left for work. She was a little early. That was the norm anymore, as though she couldn't wait to get away from the house, even just to go to work. She parked and walked up the side of the block that held Shearer's.

"Jules."

Her heart jumped. She turned. Bobby stood in the shadows by a loading dock, in the alleyway behind the buildings. She nearly ran to him.

He clutched her, kissed her, basked in her smile. He hated to dim that smile, felt the pain rising up in his throat.

"I've missed you so much," she said, breathless, glancing around. A man walked down the sidewalk, but didn't seem to notice them.

"Baby, I have some news," Bobby began gently. "I've joined a band, The Late Knights. It looks like a good deal. They have a following and their single has done well for them. They were getting ready to record again, and their keyboard player quit, so they approached me. I auditioned, and I got the gig."

"That's terrific!" He felt hope radiating out of her fingers as she stroked his ribs.

"There's one catch," he said, pausing to bite his bottom lip. "They're in Cincinnati." He smoothed back her hair, caressing the side of her head. "I've got to do it, baby. I'm packed and on my way out now. I'm doing this for us, do you understand? I've got to take this chance."

"Take me with you," she interrupted. "Oh God, please take me with you. Don't leave me behind." Tears were falling from her lashes.

"Shhhh– Baby, I can't. Not yet. I don't even have a place to live yet." He held her close and rocked her, could feel her tears soaking into his shirt front. "I know it's hard. It's hard on me, too. But please be strong for me. I need you to stay here for now. Stay in school, save what money you can. I'll go up there, work, get us a place, and I'll send for you. I promise. It's just for a while." He fought it and fought it, but his eyes burned and filled. He felt a tear fall into her hair. He drew a hard breath, then held her back from him, tracing her cheek. "I'll get news to you somehow. Just be patient."

Her tears bathed his fingertips and he knew he would never forget how that felt, that warm, liquid pain flowing right out of her body. He kissed her again, slowly, deep into her mouth, tasting past the mint flavors, tasting *her*, feeling her ease a bit in his arms, her trembling quieting as she focused on him, her breath evening out. He tried to memorize the contours of her back with his fingers, the spacing of her ribs, the curve of her waist, of her hips. Breathless at the feel of her body sinking into his, he drew back. "Baby, I have to go now, and you need to get to work before someone sees us. It's like you said in your letter: I love you with everything I have to love you with. But if you can't take this, if you find it's just too much, I'll understand. But in any case, take this." He pulled off his class ring and pressed it into her palm, closing her fingers over it and holding tight. "Even if you can't wear it, even if you have to hide it, keep it. Now go," he whispered.

She backed slowly from him, a long, tortured look, then turned and walked toward the sidewalk. She wiped her eyes, stepped into the sun, turned once more, a vision in gold, mouthing, "I love you," and then she disappeared behind the side of the building.

In his car, the taste of her mouth mingling on his lips with the taste of her tears, he turned onto the highway and hit the gas, leaving Midvale behind.

Jules picked at her supper that night, thankful her father had eaten before she got home and was enthroned in his chair in front of the TV. "Honey, you've hardly eaten a thing," Kate said.

"Sorry, Mom. I don't feel very good. I think I just want to go lie down."

Jules took her remaining Coke with her and went upstairs. She turned on the radio and lay down on the bed, waiting. Waiting for her parents' bedtime. Waiting for privacy. Waiting for blackness. Waiting to take out his ring and slip it on her finger, press its cool contours against her lip. Waiting to bury her face in her pillow and release some of the pain.

Kate tapped on the half-open door. "Come in," Jules said.

"How are you feeling? You're not coming down with something, are you?" Kate sat on the edge of the bed, reached out and laid the backs of her fingers against her daughter's forehead. "You do feel a little warm."

"I'm not sick, Mom," she said.

"Then, what is it, honey?"

"I heard some news today," she said. "Bobby moved to Ohio to join a band there." She purposely would not say where, nor the band name. If asked, she would say she didn't know.

Kate took one of Jules' hands between both of hers. "Oh, sweetheart, I'm so sorry things had to turn out this way."

They didn't fucking have to, she thought, but she just nodded.

"I guess it just wasn't meant to be," Kate said, sounding far too pat, and Jules screwed down her anger.

"I just want some time alone now," she said.

Throughout August she worked, she read, she bided her time. If there was any sort of silver lining to being grounded, it was that it saved her money. She made her car payments to her father, and the rest of her money she saved, with few exceptions. On breaks at work she sometimes walked down to Record Tree for a record, a music magazine, or just to chat with the clerks. She was sad to learn that Radio London had been shut down. She would never forget the fun of sharing Gran's upstairs with the other girls, on their odd assortment of beds and cots and an old divan, listening to pirate radio while recounting each day's events, or dressing for new adventures.

As Jules dressed for the first day of school, she put on the new Jimi Hendrix Experience album, *Are You Experienced?*, drawing strength and resolve from the title track, its otherworldly blend of backwards and forwards guitars, its worldliness, its difference. She knew she would be entering those familiar halls more experienced, and more isolated. She put on the yellow dress she'd bought in London. She would hold her head high, no matter how difficult, no matter how painful.

Dwitty walked up to her at her locker. "Hey," he said softly and patted her arm. "I know you're not supposed to talk to me, but I'll be close by. Me and Tricia. If you need us…"

"Thanks," she said.

"These are from Trish," he said, putting a small envelope in her hand. He squeezed her shoulder and moved on.

She opened it. Snapshots from England. Jules and Bobby, arms around each other, in front of Canterbury Cathedral, some of the girls lounging at Gran's, Bobby on stage at the festival, Bobby and Tyler at the Beechams' house. She slid them back in and turned toward her locker to hide her face.

Gina came up beside her. "You okay?"

"Not really."

"Look at me," Gina coaxed. A tear had spilled down Jules' cheek. "Hey, is this any way to start the school year?" She tried to cheer her. "Just remember," she produced a Kleenex out of her purse, "You're doing this for him. It's what he wants you to do."

Jules nodded and began composing herself.

"It's like singing your song for him, except you don't have to sing," Gina smiled. "So, buck up, and let's go get those A's, or else your dad will never let us have any fun."

Chapter 9

The Late Knights had gathered in their drummer Frankie's basement to rehearse and decide just what they wanted to record on their single. They had had an A-side in mind when their former keyboardist quit, and Bobby was up to the task on that one, but they needed to make sure that song was the best option, and they needed a B-side.

"We need new songs," Hank, the bassist, said.

"Well, who's got any?" asked "Thorny" Rosario, their robust vocalist, who also played a mean harmonica.

"Stickboy's got songs. He's got songs stuck all over his walls, they just don't got words," Randy said, combing his fingers through his stringy brown hair. They had nicknamed Bobby "Stickboy" because he was from the sticks and was tall and thin.

"One has words," Bobby said.

"Well, let's hear it, then," Thorny said.

Bobby led them through the melody slowly, calling out the chords. "Alright, Frankie, pick it up to mid-tempo." Bobby sang it for Thorny while Randy started fishing for a lead riff. "Yeah?" Bobby sought their assessment.

"Yeah, I like it," Hank said. "Sad song. That would be a change for us."

"I like it too," Randy said. "Yeah, different for us, but maybe different would be good."

"Write me out the words," Thorny said. "We'll see what we can do with it."

Bobby scrounged up a paper napkin and a pen and wrote them down, just as they were written on his heart. "I don't know what to call it, though," he said. "I would call it 'We Loved,' but I think there is one already."

"So? There's other songs with the same name that ain't the same song," Randy said.

"Hell, there's bands with the same name that aren't the same band," Hank laughed.

They opened up some beers and got to work on Bobby's song, as he tried to coach them. There were problems, the same problems he heard every time they rehearsed. "Let's work on some other stuff and come back to this. I think we're overworking it right now," Bobby suggested.

They worked on another song, then just jammed a bit to try to loosen up and find some common thread. When they took a break, Bobby spoke up. "I know I'm just the new guy, but coming from the outside, I've gotta say, as a band, I don't know who you are, and by that I mean I don't know what you want to be. Even as a player I don't. Even without me in the mix, you've got four people bringing in their own favorite styles, and that's a good thing, but it's not meshing. It's bumping heads. That's why we're not getting prime gigs, because people don't know what we're supposed to be. They don't know if we're gonna fit their event."

"Stickboy's right," Hank said. "We need a sound, not a buncha sounds."

"Variety's good, though," Frankie said.

"Variety is good," Bobby replied, "but it needs an overall sound to hold it all together. Everything we play, we've gotta make it our own. Randy, you've got a good surfing sound going, and that's big right now. Thorny, you've got a good voice, man, but your vocals are kinda... I don't know... aloof?"

"Aloof? What do you mean aloof?" Thorny puffed up.

"Put some soul into it, man," Bobby said.

"I'm not into Soul music," Thorny smirked.

"I'm not talking about Soul music. Give it some passion. Give it some pain. Make us feel it."

"I think he's right, Thorny," Randy said.

"Why did you hire me? What did you hear that you wanted?" Bobby asked.

"Those wild solos. Phew! You play hard for a keyboard man," Thorny said.

"I put whatever I'm feeling into it. Love, pain, anger. I put it all in there. I don't hold it back. I don't try to be all cool and tough. Cool and tough went out with the 50s."

Thorny pursed his lips and tapped his foot, thinking.

"I'm not picking on you, man," Bobby held up his hands. "But look at our audiences. Too many guys, not enough girls. Girls buy records, too. Girls like to dance."

"Yeah, and I just like having them around," Randy laughed.

"Look at the charts," Bobby said. "I know you don't wanna go teeny-bopper, and I sure as hell don't, but what are those guys doing that makes the little girls wet? It's not just the looks. It's the vocals, it's the tempos. Put some pain in it, and the girls want to comfort you. Put some passion in it, then go a little soft, and they just want you."

"Tempos," Frankie realized. "Yeah, we should bring it down a little. Foot stomping's good, but maybe a little more..." He swayed his hips.

"Exactly," Bobby smiled. He clapped Thorny on the shoulder. "Never be too tough for the ladies."

"I hear that," Hank said.

"Yeah, well how come I don't see you with these ladies?" Thorny thrust his jaw out at Bobby.

Bobby took a deep breath and let it out slowly, looking down at his shoes. "Just because you don't see her–" he said quietly. "Excuse me. I'm gonna get another beer."

Randy grabbed Thorny's shoulder as Bobby walked upstairs to the kitchen. "Shh– Man, don't you know?"

"Know what?"

"It's like Romeo and Julia," Randy said just above a whisper.

"That's Juliet," Thorny corrected him.

"No, man. Her name's Julia," Randy said, "and she's back in Midvale. I guess I know him better 'cause I room with him, but look in his eyes sometime. He's all tore up inside."

Jules watched the summer sun soften and fade, the leaves turn and fall. Soon she'd need coats instead of sweaters. Soon she would be able to turn the kitchen calendar page, not have to see that little circle representing the full October moon, not have to hear people at school talking about the dance she couldn't go to at a place she longed, and yet was almost afraid, to revisit. For the first time since she could remember, the county fair had come and gone without her, and all she really wanted to see was that clearing above the dirt track. She pulled her pictures from England out of the back of her desk drawer, found the picture of Bobby she had taken on Carnaby Street, his expression between a smirk and a smile, his eyes mischievous, but gentle, looking directly at her. She ran the backs of her fingers over the image of his face. "I'd do it all again," she whispered to him. "Every single minute."

At least she had Gina and Carol. Melissa mostly kept her distance. Jules figured she just didn't know what to say anymore, and who knew what Chip was feeding her? With Jules' usual straight A report cards, she wasn't grounded anymore, but beyond visits and phone calls with Gina and hassle free trips to the library, it didn't mean a whole lot. She still wasn't allowed to go to rock shows or any dances that weren't school dances. She went to one school dance, just to see a band, any band, but they weren't very good. Gina had a date, some guy named Tommy. Jules felt like an exhibit. She would turn and see people quickly look away, feel eyes following her back as she walked. What did they say in their hushed tones when she had passed? Pity? Criticism? Judgment? She didn't want to be a martyr in their eyes. St. Jules, patron saint of hanging-onto-a-desperate-dream-while-everyone-else-was-having-fun. But enduring an evening like this wasn't fun. She went home early. Melissa's friend Cora told Jules in gym class, "Some of the boys are calling you Sister Julia, because you live like a nun." What did she care? She didn't want any of them. She felt removed from the Midvale High world. She was part of a larger world now, a world that increasingly concerned her.

"What the fuck is he doing?" Jules thumped the newspaper. "He's making them all look like flakes, like idiots!" Jules had just read about Abbie Hoffman leading protesters to sing and chant in an attempt to levitate the Pentagon and make it turn orange, as part of an anti-war protest. She tossed the newspaper on the floor.

Gina picked it up to see what Jules was talking about. "That does sound pretty stupid."

Jules turned the record over. Pink Floyd, *Piper at the Gates of Dawn.*

"And you saw these guys?" Gina marveled, looking at the album cover, images of the band members refracted in a kaleidoscope swirl. "This stuff is pretty far out."

"It is." She leaned close to Gina's ear. "And so were we when we saw them."

Gina laughed and handed the album cover back to Jules, then grew serious. "You heard about Terry and Elise, didn't you?"

"No. What about them?"

"They broke up."

"You're kidding."

"Nope."

Jules clenched her fists and looked up at the ceiling. "I can't fucking believe this!" she whispered.

"I know. I never thought they were right for each other. I wish they'd figured that out before—" She waved a hand, not wanting to say it, that Terry had broken up the band for nothing, that Bobby might not have had to leave town.

Jules heaved a sigh. "Yeah, tell me about it. Oh, Gina, I haven't heard a thing. Not a word. I don't know what to think anymore."

It was a slow business day the Tuesday after Thanksgiving when Jules was re-stocking a shelf at Shearer's Books. She heard someone come in the door, the little bells on the handle jangling. She caught a glimpse of a girl between the gaps in the shelves, and turned to greet her, then stopped short. "Sissy?"

"Shh!" Sissy put a finger to her lips, eyes stern as she whispered harshly, "You don't know me!" As she passed behind Jules, pretending to browse the opposite rack, she handed her a flat paper bag, as deftly as a spy making a delivery. Jules opened it enough to look inside. A 45 and a photo. Her heart jumped. Before she could say anything to her, Sissy was slipping out the door to the sound of clinking bells. Jules took the bag to the back room and put it with her purse. She would quickly stop by Gina's after work. She didn't want to play it at home the first time.

In Gina's room, Jules pulled out what Sissy had brought her. Gina started the A-side on the record player, "Drivin' with My Baby," a nice enough, groovy pop song, Bobby's playing confined to a simple back-up role except for a short solo break at the bridge. The singer was smooth and masculine, but Jules missed Terry's energy. She sat on the edge of the bed and pored over the photo, hands trembling. There was nothing written on it, no note inside the bag. Discretion, she guessed, but still, she would have welcomed the risk. Anything, any word. Had he come down to visit for Thanksgiving? Had he tried somehow to see her while she was feasting at her grandparents' house, filling herself with comforting food to try to fill the hole in her heart?

It felt odd to see him posed with a band full of strangers. He was wearing the brocade jacket he'd bought in London. There was only a band name on the photo. She didn't know who the other guys were or what they played. The only other information was a record label contact.

"Turn it over," Jules said stoically when the A-side had finished. Her stoicism was about to go out the window. That reedy Farfisa came right in with the drums in the intro, the guitar and bass joining soon after, mid-tempo, but sad, building up to the vocals, and then– the lyrics. She felt the blood drain from her face.

"My world is torn apart now that I've lost you. I look up at the sky and it just makes me blue… "

She covered her mouth with her hands and the trembling spread through her whole body. He had to have written the music. The melody, the chord progression – they were so… *him*. "The words," she said. "Gina, I wrote those words." Damn those tears, she would not let them out. She had to go home in a few minutes.

"You did? Jules, they're wonderful." Gina sat down beside her.

"You know he still loves you. He did this for you."

"I know," she whispered.

Bobby's solo, though short, was heart-twisting, full of longing, but with just a glimmer of hope, that one turn to a major key before falling back into the minor for the final verse. She closed her eyes and fought, and fought, and fought. It would be easier next time she played it, she told herself. "What does it say? Let me see what it says," she said, going to the turntable as the song faded out. She lifted it off the spindle and read the songwriting credits. "(Lott, Greene)" On the A-side it was a list of unfamiliar names. She slid it back into its paper sleeve. "It's our turn now," she said. "I'll go to Record Tree on Thursday. You talk to Dwitty. Carol can help us spread the word. We need to start calling the radio station and requesting it."

On December 15th, the Silver Bridge linking Point Pleasant, West Virginia and Kanauga, Ohio collapsed into the frigid Ohio River, at the peak of rush hour. Jules didn't likely know any of the victims, but hearing the story on the TV news as she passed her father's chair, it still hit her hard. Sometimes it felt like the whole world was collapsing, that no one anywhere was safe. She heard the phone ring as she walked upstairs to study, but paid it no mind.

Chapter 10

When Bobby opened the door, he couldn't believe his eyes, but there she stood, in a white sweater, black slacks, and her long, grey tweed coat, her honey hair still in the shoulder-length flip with bangs that he liked so much. "Jules, what are you doing here?"

"I couldn't stand it. I had to come and see you."

He enfolded her in his arms, pressed his cheek into her hair as her head touched the nook between his shoulder and chest. "You drove up here yourself?"

"Mmm-hmm."

He turned her slowly, into the room, and closed the door against the sharp steel air. He hadn't wanted her to see this place, didn't want her to see how he lived now. Dirty clothes, a couple of empty beer bottles, and other clutter were scattered around the floor of the front room, sheets a twisted wad on the mattress in the corner. One corner of the psychedelic poster had come un-taped and lopped over heavily. He saw the unsettled look in her eyes, noted her quietude. "My room's through here," he steered her. "Sorry about Randy's mess. He's not much of a housekeeper," he chuckled softly. He was glad he'd felt like straightening up his own space today. "Sit down," he gestured toward his own mattress and the tired blue blanket spread over the sheets. "I'll take your coat, if you like, but if you want to leave it on, I understand."

"It is kinda cold in here."

"Yeah. Sorry." He didn't offer an explanation as he closed the door and sat down beside her, didn't want to tell her the heat was cut off because they couldn't pay the gas bill, didn't want her to know how hard he'd shivered some nights under that blanket, fully clothed, hugging himself to conserve his own warmth, or how he'd warm his hands over the electric hot plate to limber up his fingers so he could practice. "I've missed you so much," he said as he slid his hands around her waist, inside her coat. She lifted her chin, leaned her lips toward his, slightly parted. Her kiss sent a surge of warmth through his core that at once soothed and hurt. They kissed with the hunger and joy of the moment. They kissed for all the days apart. Her tongue seemed fascinated with the edges of his teeth, and that made him smile, but despite this delight, as he laid her back on the bed he felt as though he could cry. What could he possibly offer her? How could he hope to hold onto her? He couldn't even support himself.

All he'd eaten that day was a can of thin soup, its meager noodles more like little decorations than substance. He tried to pull the edge of the blanket up over them, but it didn't reach far. She was unbuttoning his shirt, running cool hands up his breastbone. "Here," he sat up, pulling her with him, pulled her to her feet, slipped her coat down off her shoulders and arms. He peeled back the bedding and tucked her up inside it with himself, feeling the growing glow of warmth that two bodies made, that one alone could never manage to radiate.

Their coupling now felt different, more relaxed and focused. It didn't feel like sneaking around, though it surely was. Desperate, nervous haste had matured into something like a place, a nest, constructed with their own rhythms, a space where he could almost forget his circumstances. Almost. For a moment, at least.

As he rested on his back, she lay against him, stroking his chest with her small, delicate fingers. "Your chest is getting hairy," she commented, and he laughed as she ran the tip of her tongue up his sternum. "I like it." Smiling, he brushed back her hair and moved to kiss her, but when they drew apart, he could not meet her eyes. "What's wrong?" she asked, her voice like a wisp of spring breeze across his heart. He shook his head, just barely, more a twitch, or a wince. "I've been true to you," she said, cupping his cheek with her hand. "If you haven't been, I guess I understand."

"Jules, you're my only girl," he smiled, gathering her half-clothed body against his, nestling his face into the warmth of her neck. An evasive reply, but in his mind and in his heart, she was his only girl. No need to tell her about the backstage girls who were more attracted to the idea of a rock and roll band, any band, than the actual people in it. No need to tell her about the orange-fringed, orange-haired siren who had slinked up to him, up against him, cooing, "Sock it to me, baby," and to whom, in his inebriation and deep loneliness, he had done just that, feeling very special, until she approached Randy the same way. Such encounters had quickly lost their appeal in the wake of their emptiness. All he wanted now was to be able to keep his promise, and he couldn't.

"Something's troubling you, I can tell." Jules' fingers combing through his hair sent little shivers down his lower spine. Again he felt the pressure of unshed tears behind his eyes.

"I'm tired," he said. "Tired of being poor, tired of being cold and lonely." He pulled back from her, now staring straight into her eyes. "We're not making it, Jules. Yeah, we cut a record. The local stations are playing it. A little. But no one else is playing it. We play our guts out in any place that will have us, and we can't pay the fucking bills. And I lost my job because the fucking place burned down. I can't do this, not like this."

"Don't give up. You're too good. You'll get a break, I know it."

"Well, I don't know it." He sat up abruptly, pulling his shirt together against the chill in the room.

"It's a new sound," she offered, and he detected a slight quaver in her voice. "Maybe people just aren't used to it yet, but they'll catch on."

He pulled his pants up as he stood, buckled his belt with his back to her. "We failed, Jules," he stated. "We failed, and I'm fucking broke and I just want to go home." He shook the last of a can of coffee into the basket of the dented aluminum percolator and plugged it in. As he stared at the little red light on the front, he could hear her rustling behind him, gathering herself, clothing herself. And then she was at his back, draping one side of the blanket around his shoulders, keeping the other around her own. He turned and pulled her close against his chest, cocooning them. "I'm sorry," he said quietly at her ear. "I'm so, so sorry."

"It's okay."

"Oh, Jules, I'm worried. I'm worried about us. I'm worried about you! How is it that you're here? How did you even find me?"

"I called the record label."

"You did get it, then. Was it okay, your song?"

"It's beautiful. I couldn't believe it when I heard it. Thank you."

"I wish to God I had more to give you than that."

"It means a lot to me. It keeps me going. And now," she leaned back and took his face in both her hands, "I can't believe I'm really here with you."

"Baby, how are you going to get home in time? Does anyone even know where you are?"

"Don't worry. I'm up here visiting my cousin, Sonya. She got the part of Clara in *The Nutcracker*. Tonight is opening night and she really wanted me to see her dance. Daddy has to work this weekend. Mom convinced him it would be okay for me to drive up by myself. She's got a Tupperware party tomorrow."

"*Your* dad?" he laughed. "I can't believe it."

"I couldn't either. I don't think he would have, but my aunt – she's my mom's sister – talked to him on the phone about how important it is to Sonya, and with it Christmastime, I guess she managed to get his sympathy. See, my uncle died from a brain tumor five years ago."

"Wow. That's heavy. I'm sorry to hear that."

"It's okay. Anyway, this *is* important to Sonya, but I think Mom and Aunt Nat wanted to give me a chance to get away for a little while, too."

The pot began gurgling and the scent of coffee began to bloom. It reawakened the gnawing in his stomach. Upstairs a door slammed. Muffled voices. The tinny sound of a transistor radio began scratching through the ceiling. He rocked Jules gently back and forth, staring over her head at the battle-scarred Farfisa tucked into the corner, out of sight of the window and the eyes of thieves. The thermostat on the coffee pot clicked. He relinquished the blanket as they pulled apart and she sat back down on the edge of the mattress as he poured coffee into a mug. Without a fridge, there was no way to keep cream, so all he had was Coffee Mate. He tipped the powder into the coffee and added two packets of sugar, purloined from a diner, then sat beside her. "Here, warm yourself up."

"Aren't you having any?"

"There's only enough for one cup." He hadn't meant to say that. It had just slipped out.

"I can't take your last cup. Here," she offered it back.

"No, no. I made it for you. I'm fine." The truth was he wanted a cup very badly, but he would never have told her so. As it was, it killed him that he had nothing more to offer her.

"We'll share it," she said.

He gratefully accepted a few sips.

"Is there a phone?" she asked when the cup was empty.

"There's one in the hall. Just let me check first..." He got up and tapped on the door that separated his room from Randy's. The last thing he wanted now was for Jules to blunder in on Randy in some liaison, or enjoying himself with his stash of porn. Hearing no reply, he cracked open the door. No one there. Good.

"And where's the bathroom?"

"I'll show you." He led her through a door near the back of Randy's room, into a dingy hall that, while chilly, was decidedly warmer than his and Randy's quarters. A black phone hung on the wall, shared by all the tenants of the old house. A few odd phone numbers were scrawled on the wall in pen or pencil, and someone had drawn a peace sign. There was one bathroom for each of the two floors. "Bathroom's through there," he directed her to the beige door, gloss paint covering unevenly scraped multiple layers beneath. He returned to his room to wait, leaving the doors open for her.

"It's decided," she announced with a determined smile when she returned. "You're coming with us tonight."

"What?"

She flung back the faded orange curtain that hung over his closet, the door gone long before he had taken up residence, and he heard the hangers scrape across the rail. "These," she said, flopping his hunter green velvet flares and matching jacket onto the bed, the ones he had bought in London and often wore on stage. "With this," she pulled his camel beige sweater down off the shelf.

He laughed. "Jules, seriously, we can't. I don't want to get you in trouble, not now. Not yet." He couldn't suppress a grin at that last statement, but it quickly faded. "I can't take care of you right now, baby. If anything goes wrong…"

"Don't worry. Aunt Nat already knows about you. She won't give us away. That's who I called on the phone. She wants you to come tonight. And Sonya's dying to meet you."

He laughed again and looked down at his sock feet. He didn't have to ask what footwear Jules wanted him to wear. His black Chelsea boots. "Okay, if you're sure."

"I'm sure. Now, get changed, we've got to stop by the florist. That's the errand Aunt Nat sent me on in the first place." She pulled her coat back on and reached deep into a pocket. "But first– I hope you don't mind that it's not wrapped. I bought it on the way up here. I don't know if I'll see you again before Christmas, so here."

She handed him a small, flat paper bag, the top folded over. He opened it, and out slithered a satiny, purple paisley tie. "Aw, thanks, Jules. This is groovy!" But in his mind, he saw himself wearing it on stage, not with The Late Knights, but some fantasy band that didn't exist. He tried to keep the defeat from creeping into his face and bent to kiss her, the touch of her lips sending tendrils of flame through his chest and down his thighs.

She fingered the points of his collar. "I couldn't just get you a tie, though. That's too much like you're my dad or something." He gave a little laugh. She drew back from him to reach into her pocket again. "Hold out your hand." He did, but instead of her putting something in his palm, she reached for his wrist.

Cool metal touched his skin as she fastened a chain around it, and he turned his hand over to see the plate of the I.D. bracelet, engraved not with his name, but just the word LOVE. He clasped her to himself and kissed the top of her head. "Thank you, baby. I'll wear it always."

"Good," she said, gently pushing him away, "Now get changed. We really have to go soon."

He rode with Jules, carried the roses to the car for her. Two white bouquets for Sonya, one from Aunt Nat and one from Jules and her mom, to hand up to Sonya on stage when she took her curtain call. Jules pinched a rose flower off its stem and slipped it into the buttonhole of Bobby's jacket lapel.

"Jules!"

"She'll never miss it. And if she does, she won't mind. She'll be getting some after every show. Now, just lay those on the back seat. I'll be right back. I just need to run into the market and get one thing." She dashed off, leaving him holding an armload of flowers. He reached over the front seat, laid them out carefully, then pulled his overcoat tightly around himself, got in and closed his door against the increasing cold. In a moment Jules came hurrying back, white puffs of breath rising from her smile. "Here," she handed him the paper sack as she got in. He dutifully held it on his lap. "It's for you," she clarified as she started the engine. He opened it to find a can of Maxwell House.

He didn't know why he had envisioned Sonya as a little girl, but when she strode up to him in Aunt Nat's living room, smiling confidently, he was taken aback. She wasn't much younger than Jules, tall, dark-haired, dark-eyed and quite pretty.

"We saw you! On *Johnny's Jumpin' Jukebox*. You wore that suit," she grinned and poked his sleeve.

"You saw that?" he laughed.

"Of course!"

"Sonya always watches Johnny, every Monday afternoon after school," Aunt Nat smiled and nodded.

"Jules and I write to each other. She told me you were in the Knights, so when that came on, boy, was I thrilled!"

"I wish I could have seen it," Jules said. Johnny's was just a local show, so Jules didn't get it.

"It was far out," Sonya declared.

"It was alright," he smiled softly. He hated that twisting sensation inside at the mention of the band, that braiding of hunger and regret and anxiety. "Put on your war paint," Tyler used to say, and punch him in the arm. Tyler. Where was he now? Bobby tried to muster up some war paint inside. The girls were all happy to see him. For tonight, he should just let it all go, take their comforts and their praise, and keep his dear Jules as close as he could.

A car horn honked. "That's Linda," Aunt Nat said. "We'll see you after the show."

Sonya grabbed a small, pink duffel bag, exchanged a quick kiss on the cheek with her mother, and one with Jules, then looked to Bobby, who just gave her his best "thanks, but I don't think so" smile and said, "Best of luck."

When she had gone, Aunt Nat said to him, "That was Sonya, if you hadn't guessed."

He nodded. Natalie Manning was a handsome woman, and he could see the resemblance to Jules' mom, to Jules a little. Something around the eyes. She was sturdy, but not plump, her brown hair cut in a Pixie.

"Would you like something before we go? There's time. Coffee? Tea? Coke?"

"Thanks, Mrs. Manning. Coffee would be great."

"Call me Aunt Nat. Jules, take his coat." She breezed into the kitchen.

He slipped out of his coat, though he still felt so cold he would just as soon have left it on, and Jules laid it with her own over the back of an armchair. "Come in by the fire." She led him through to the dark paneled family room. He sat down on the brick hearth, luxuriating in the heat of mature coals, holding his hands open to let it seep into his fingers, leaning close until his face felt like it might cook. Jules sat beside him, stroking his back, straightening his hair. She didn't speak, and he didn't want to dispel the simplicity and comfort of the moment.

The whistling of the kettle roused his mind as if from a dream. "Jules, can you come here a moment?" Aunt Nat spoke from the doorway, and Jules got up. "Bobby, what do you take in your coffee?"

"Cream and sugar, please. Just a little."

He started to get up, but Jules pressed gently down on the top of his head, ending the gesture with a stroke. "Stay here, baby," she said softly.

He could hear their voices, but not their words, heard cupboard doors and clinking and running water. Drowsy from warmth, he moved to a chair near the hearth and closed his eyes.

"How long before we need to leave?" Jules' voice, somewhere near, woke him. He must only have been asleep a minute or two, but he felt disoriented at first.

"About a half an hour," Aunt Nat replied.

"I'll run and change, then," Jules replied, handing Bobby his coffee.

"Dinner's a long ways off yet," Aunt Nat said, setting a tray of Christmas cookies on the coffee table, then handing Bobby a plate with a generous ham sandwich on it. "I thought you might be hungry."

"Thank you," he said. He truly was grateful.

"When you're done eating, if you could just poke down that fire and close the glass doors," she requested.

"Sure," he nodded, and she left the room. He tried not to wolf down his food too fast.

He was deadening the fire when Jules came in, wearing a long-sleeved, green and purple floral mini-dress, green tights, and white go-go boots. "Like my dress?" She twirled around and the air lifted her skirt a little higher.

"I'd like to take it off," he whispered by her ear.

"You bad boy," she grinned and stole a quick kiss from his lips.

"You look beautiful."

"Thanks. I'm not exactly embarrassed to be seen with you, either." She snugged up the rose in his lapel. "Look." She held up her index finger with his ring on it. "I figured I could get away with it tonight."

It didn't take a follower of ballet to see that Sonya was a very good dancer, or that her red-headed boyfriend Tad was completely enthralled. Introducing himself to Bobby, and declaring his suit "neato," he sat beside him, complaining that boys in the school he and Sonya attended weren't allowed to have hair longer than the tops of their collars. Tad unbuttoned his double-breasted, navy coat, and Bobby noted the burgundy brocade vest underneath.

When the house lights went down, Tad's mouth closed and his head turned straight toward the stage, and never turned aside until intermission. Aunt Nat turned her attention away from Jules, and in the new darkness Bobby could feel Jules' soul shift toward him, as well as her body. Her upper arm came to rest against his. Though her left leg crossed over her right, away from him, her right foot on the floor nudged up against his. He wrapped her left hand in both of his, and though their eyes were on the stage, all he could think about was how incredible it had felt to make love to her today, and how bad it was going to hurt to give her up tomorrow. That and the cruel absurdity of thinly clad characters lingering in enjoyment of a wintry night with benign dancing snowflakes, considering what he faced later tonight on what was sure to be the coldest night of the year so far. Maybe he could crash at Hank's pad.

Backstage after the performance was a flurry of rustling skirts, sweet-scented bouquets, and giggling girls, Sonya holding court like a teen princess. Bobby hung back by the curtains, feeling too conspicuous and out of place, waiting with Tad while Jules and Aunt Nat followed Sonya into the dressing room to help her change out of her costume and gather her effects and flowers. "You been to Antonio's?" Tad asked Bobby. Bobby shook his head. "I think you'll like it. Their meatballs are the most." Bobby felt like someone had just hit him in the stomach.

"There you are," Jules' voice came from behind him and he turned to see her smile.

"Jules, baby," he said softly, pulling her aside as Sonya bounced up to Tad, all a-bubble. "We're going out to dinner?"

"Mmm-hmm."

"Baby, I can't. Honestly, I have 50 cents to my name."

"Shhh–" She stroked his arm. "It's okay. I'll take care of it."

"You've spent so much on me already. I don't want–"

"Sh–sh–sh." She reached up to press her fingertip to his lips. "Mom gave me some money. Just enjoy it."

"You two coming?" Aunt Nat called back to them, as the rest of the group had begun walking away.

After putting Sonya's bag and flowers in the trunk ("They'll keep just fine in this cold," her mother assured her), they began climbing into the car. "You're all going to squeeze into the back?" Aunt Nat laughed. "Bobby, your legs are so long, why don't you sit up front?"

"No, it's okay, Mrs. Manning," Tad spoke up. "I'll sit up front."

"Tad!" Sonya protested.

He leaned closer to Sonya, and Bobby heard him whisper firmly, "No. Let them." Bobby felt he owed the kid one now. As they rode to the restaurant, Sonya leaning over the front seat to be closer to Tad, commenting to her mother on what various dancers had done well or done wrong, Jules laid her head against Bobby's chest in silence while he stroked her hair. He hurt already, so much so that involuntarily his head went back against the seat and a deep sigh escaped his mouth.

As Natalie watched Bobby polish off a very large serving of lasagna, she wondered how long it had been since he'd had a decent meal. Even in the soft light of the candles dripping their wax down the necks of old chianti bottles, he looked old and tired for 18. Julia was obviously miles away from the conversation she was trying to participate in. What had Dan Greene wrought? She saw Julia shuffle some money into Bobby's hand under the table so he could look like he was paying when the check came. Natalie made sure the waiter understood that she intended to pay for them all. Somehow she knew Bobby would protest. "Tell you what," she granted him, "You can leave the tip."

At the car she saw Bobby and Tad both heading for the front passenger door, overheard Tad saying, "Thanks, man, but no. I get to see Sonya every day. Now, go on." Bobby got in the back again with Julia.

Back at the house, Tad and Bobby got the fire going again and the girls were playing records. Natalie left them in the family room to go clean up the kitchen. "How can I be sure in a world that's constantly changing?" the Young Rascals were singing as she put the last plate in the draining rack. "Whenever I... whenever I'm away from you, my alibi is tellin' people I don't care for you." That line had never struck her the way it did now.

Headlights flashed up the driveway as she dried her hands. "Tad, your mom's here!" she called out on her way to the family room.

"I'll see you tomorrow night," Sonya snatched a last quick kiss.

"Three weeks," Tad gestured to Bobby with the appropriate number of fingers as he passed. "Three weeks and I get my license."

"Goodnight, man. Good meeting you," Bobby nodded from his seat on the couch, Jules lounging in his lap.

Natalie looked at her watch. "Girls, it's getting late."

"I guess I need a ride home, baby," Bobby said to Jules as he straightened her up.

"I'll take you home tomorrow," Natalie said. "You can sleep on the couch tonight. Jules, you've got a long drive tomorrow and it gets dark early. Sonya, you've got to dance at 2." She nodded toward the hall doorway, a gesture meant to get the girls moving. He gave Natalie a puzzled look. "Well you can't go back there tonight. Not without heat. It's going down to zero. Besides, I want to talk to you tomorrow."

"Thanks," he looked at her with those soulful eyes. "Good night, baby," he kissed Jules' hands.

When the girls had gone, Natalie addressed him. "I'm responsible for her tonight. I don't know what you two get up to on your own," she said, though she was rather certain she did, "but don't try your luck. I really do have insomnia." She led him to the master bathroom, handed him a washcloth and the last unopened toothbrush, and got out a sleeping bag and a pillow.

It was midnight before the strip of light under Sonya's door snapped to darkness, and some time later before the girls grew silent. It had occurred to Natalie that Julia might need keeping an eye on at least as much as Bobby, so she'd issued her a warning as well, then sat up reading in her room with the door open until all had been quiet for some time. It must have been 2 when she went to the kitchen for a glass of water. No sounds. The hall door to the family room was closed, but she hazarded a look from the living room. Bobby was sound asleep, alone, in the firelight.

At 8 Natalie got up to start breakfast. Not a peep out of anyone else. She went to check on Bobby. He was out like a light, lying on his back, one bare muscular shoulder and half his chest exposed where he had pushed back the top of the sleeping bag, evidently too warm at some point in the night, though the fire had died out now. It was easy enough to see what Jules saw in him – good-looking, hip, polite, and not quite safe. He was no boy anymore, not with that overnight growth of whiskers, and he definitely had a mind of his own. Taciturn though he was, she'd heard his records, seen just that flicker of abandon when he'd played on Johnny's show that one afternoon. Still waters, indeed. *Someone like you must scare Dan Greene to death.* Gingerly she brought the edge of the sleeping bag up to cover him before she spoke. "Bobby?" He woke suddenly, glanced around quickly, as though unsure at first where he was. "If you'd like a shower before breakfast, you can take one in my bathroom while I get the girls up."

"Thanks," he said softly, stretched his neck to one side, then moved to sit up, keeping the covers around him.

"Would you like a change of clothes?"

"Not if it's a dress," he snickered.

She laughed. "No, not a dress, though with those long legs of yours..." She saw just a twinkle in his eye to go with the smirk. "Seriously, I suppose I should get rid of them, but I still have some of my late husband's clothes. You're welcome to borrow them."

He looked down, away. "If it wouldn't... I mean–"

"No, it's okay. Maybe it's time I put it behind me anyway."

He looked back up, straight into her eyes in the most comforting, yet unnerving way. "I'm so sorry."

"Thank you." She fought the lump in her throat as she turned and left the room.

"Daddy's old shirt?" Sonya pinched a loose bit of worn blue Oxford cloth at one sleeve as she passed Bobby, who sat at the kitchen table, his long fingers wrapped around a cup of hot coffee. "Doesn't look too bad on you."

Jules straggled in, suppressing a yawn, just as Natalie handed Bobby a plate of fried eggs and toast. "Jules, do you want eggs?"

"Maybe one."

Natalie turned back to the skillet to crack "maybe one" egg into it.

"Hi, baby," she heard Bobby say quietly.

"Honey, put this on the table." She handed Sonya a plate heaped with bacon and sausage links. "Anyone else want toast?"

"Me, please," Sonya answered.

"Did you sleep alright?" Jules was asking.

"Yeah, I really crashed," Bobby answered.

When she'd finished cooking for everyone else, Natalie sat down to eat. Bobby was really tucking it in, even by teenage boy standards. "Jules said you lost your job."

He huffed a little mirthless laugh. "Which one?"

Jules turned to him with an inquisitive look.

"I started out at the Queen City Café. Four days a week I'd go in on the biscuit shift, 4:00 in the morning. On nights we had a gig, I'd just stay up. A few times we played so late I didn't have much time to get my gear in, get a shower, and get back out the door. I don't think old man Foley much liked me anyway. One morning – we'd played some crazy house party that went all night – he decided I was drunk and he fired me. And I wasn't, I swear. I was just dead tired, but he wouldn't listen. So I went to work at Kowalski's, flipping burgers in the afternoons, and then the damn place burned down."

"And you haven't found anything else?" Natalie asked.

"I'm trying. Staying up all night for a morning job obviously didn't work. I can't go long on just three or four hours of sleep, either. Nights are out. Afternoons I'm competing with the school kids, and they've grabbed up the extra holiday jobs."

"Well, I can't exactly hire you on permanently," Natalie said, "But I can give you a job for today, if you want. I need a man's help with a few things around here."

"Alright," he accepted. "I've got a gig tonight, though, and I'll need some practice time."

"Sonya dances at 2 this afternoon. I'll drop you home on the way to take her."

Jules gave Natalie an appreciative, but conflicted look.

"I suppose your parents don't know your situation," Natalie guessed.

"No," he shook his head. "I don't want them to worry. I'll figure something out."

"Well, maybe you should worry them."

"Julia, honey, you'd best get going soon," Natalie said when everyone had finished eating.

"It's okay. I can wait and take Bobby home after lunch."

"No, you need to get home before dark. You need to get home early, help your mother with her Tupperware party. Maybe it will get your dad off your back. Maybe he'll let you come up by yourself again." Sternly, Natalie stared down Jules' pleading eyes.

"I'll get my things," she said solemnly.

Through the kitchen window, Sonya and Natalie watched as Bobby put Jules' suitcase in the trunk of her car, closed the trunk, and held out his arms to her.

"He's so fine, wish he were mine," Sonya dreamed.

"Do-lang do-lang," Natalie filled in dryly. "Well, he's not."

"Those old pants are a little short, though," she snickered, rinsed a plate, and set it in the rack. "They're so in love, Mom. It's not right what Uncle Dan did."

"It's not your place to say."

"Oh, come on, Mom. Do you think it's right?"

"I don't know. I don't know what all has happened. But I can't see that what he's done has done anyone any good." Natalie watched how Bobby rocked Jules in his arms, tucking her inside his coat, how he held her head in his beautiful hands as he kissed her, as he talked to her, looking into her eyes. His long thumbs brushed tears from her cheeks, and he kissed her again, lingeringly, and Natalie wanted to cry. Sonya walked away, shaking her head. Jules got in the car and drove away. Bobby just stood in the driveway, in the cold, coat open to the wind.

He came back in, chewing his bottom lip, avoiding anyone's eyes. Natalie reached out and stroked his upper arm, grasped it. He threw his head back, squeezed his eyes shut, and drew a ragged breath. Then he looked down at Natalie through watery eyes and said, "What do you need me to do?"

"Let's start with the attic. I need some boxes brought down."

After lunch, Sonya limbered up at the barre in the family room. Bobby had toted boxes, cleaned out a bathtub drain, brought in more firewood, and reattached a loose downspout. "You don't owe me anything," he told Aunt Nat when she tried to pay him.

"Take it," she insisted, pressing a $10 bill into his palm and squeezing his hand shut. "And I'll get your heat turned back on, but I can't call the gas company till tomorrow. No one answers on Sunday."

"You won't need to," he said. "I won't be there anymore."

"If you want to sleep here tonight—"

"No," he shook his head. "I have some things I need to take care of."

"Then take that space heater in the bathroom with you tonight. It's going to be damn cold again."

"Thanks."

In the car, he spoke with Sonya. "When you write to Jules, be very careful. You never know who might read it. Do you understand?"

"Yes, I understand."

"Good. And take care of that boyfriend of yours. He's a good guy."

"I will. I wish you could come and see me dance today."

"You're good," he said. "But you know that already."
She laughed.

The next morning came brittle and grey. Natalie made sure Sonya bundled up before going out to meet the school bus. As she opened the back door for Sonya, whose arms were full of books, she noticed something on the porch. There stood the space heater, and beside it a paper bag containing her late husband's clothes. On top of them was a note in a fluid, mature hand. "Thank you," it said. "Don't bother about the heat." On her way to work she drove to his apartment. It was vacant.

Chapter 11

Jules sat on her bed Sunday afternoon, reading *A Tale of Two Cities*, her Literature class reading assignment for over the holidays, when her mother came in. "Julia, I need to talk to you about something."

"Yes, Mom?"

"Julia, did you go meet Bobby when you went up to see Sonya?" Kate asked.

"Mom, I don't even know where Bobby is anymore. I heard he moved," she replied. That part was true and she hoped her genuine gravity was enough to deflect Kate from realizing she hadn't really answered the question.

"Oh, honey." She sat down beside Jules, who closed her book in one hand, keeping her place with her finger. "I know how upsetting this all has been."

No, Mom, she thought, *You really have no fucking idea.*

"I can't agree with what your father did, but maybe it's worked out for the best. Maybe it's time you put it all behind you now. There are lots of nice boys out there. You're pretty, you're smart, you're going to college." Kate took Jules' free hand, patted it, managed a weak smile. "There are parties and dances before you graduate. You don't have to get serious about anyone. Just have some fun. You deserve it. I'm sure once your dad knows Bobby's out of the picture he'll ease up on you, as long as you keep your grades up."

Jules swallowed hard. "Maybe you're right, Mom."

"That's my girl," she gave her a hug. "I'm going to start supper now. Your father will be home soon."

Once she heard her mother's footsteps on the stairs, Jules drew a deep, hard breath, letting it out slowly through her mouth, hoping at least some of the pain would go with it.

Sonya had called Wednesday night, under the guise of thanking her for coming up to visit. "Jules, your cousin's on the phone," Kate had called to her up the stairs.

"I'll take it in the bedroom," Jules answered.

Once Jules' mom had said goodbye and they'd heard a click, Sonya had dropped the happy, charming tone. "Jules, I've got a big secret to tell you about this guy I met. I hope nobody's listening." Jules' heart jumped.

This was code.

"Hang on a minute." Jules, in her sock feet, crept down the stairs and peered into the living room, then quietly returned to her parents' bedroom. "They're watching TV downstairs."

"Okay. Maybe you know this already, maybe you don't, but I got a friend to take me by his place. I overheard him tell Mom not to bother having the heat turned back on, because he wouldn't be there anymore. I knew where he lived, because I was with Mom when she took him home Sunday."

The blood coursed hot through Jules' face, but she was shaking.

"He's gone. He moved out."

Jules clapped her hand over her mouth, tried to breathe.

"You there? You okay?"

"Was there anyone else there, a Randy?"

"No, he was gone, too. The landlady didn't know where they'd moved to. She couldn't hardly speak English anyway. She was Chinese or something, and kinda rude."

"Maybe they just found a better place," Jules tried to soothe herself.

"I hope so. It sure didn't look very nice there. But here's the other thing. I had seen this ad that The Knights were supposed to play some dive tomorrow night, so I called, and the guy said no, it was canceled because they broke up!"

"Oh my God. Oh my God."

"Jules, is there anything at all I can do?"

"Just let me know if you hear anything, or if your mom knows anything. I'm sure he'll get word to me as soon as he can."

"You let me know, too, okay? Write me, if you can't call."

When Sonya hung up, Jules quickly dialed Gina. "Gina, you've got to help me. You have to help me find Bobby."

That was the last she'd heard from Sonya or Gina, and she'd gotten no message from Bobby. She had to get ahold of someone, had to find out what had happened, where he was, but with school out for the holidays and some of her friends out of town, this was proving difficult. At the same time, she would have to be careful who she asked, lest word get around and back to her parents. It had been a week now since her visit to Cincinnati. Every day she'd act indifferent, and every night the tears spilled into her pillow as she caressed it. Tonight would be no different. No, it would be different. It would be worse.

Late Monday morning the phone rang. Jules answered it in the kitchen. It was Gina. "Jules, come Christmas shopping with me now. You won't believe the sale Hancock's is having."

"Gina, I just don't feel like Christmas shopping today."

"Jules, I mean it. Meet me at Hancock's. Now!"

Suddenly it sunk in. Gina knew something. "Hang on a second," she told Gina, then covered the mouthpiece with her hand. "Mom!"

"Yes, dear," her mother called from the den.

"I'm going shopping with Gina, okay?"

"Okay, dear. Don't forget you have to work this afternoon."

"I won't. If I run out of time I'll just go right there from shopping."

"Be careful, the roads might be slick."

"I will." She uncovered the mouthpiece and said, "I'm on my way."

"Menswear," Gina said.

Jules' heart was pounding as she passed the kids in line for Santa, wound through hosiery and jewelry to the escalator, and up. Why would Gina choose menswear? She had no sooner reached the top and turned than Gina appeared and grabbed her hand, pulling her down an aisle and past a rack of suit coats. She grinned, dropped Jules' hand, and Jules stopped dead, suddenly unable to move or breathe.

"Hi, baby," he smiled and reached out to her. She could only cover her mouth with her hands as the tears filled her eyes. He stepped toward her, laid his hands on her shoulders, and she sank against his chest. "Shh– don't cry." He stroked her back, rocked her ever so slightly. "It's okay."

"I'll just go look at the ties," she heard Gina say.

Jules clutched at his crisp shirt, unable to contain a quiet sob. "It's okay, baby, I'm here. I'm home." He eased her back from him, pulled a handkerchief from a pocket of his smart charcoal suit and handed it to her.

She dabbed her eyes. "I didn't know where you were," she said, struggling for composure.

"I know. I'm sorry. I had to work some things out, make sure I could stay. Here, come and sit down." He led her to a chair near the fitting room.

"Everything okay, Bobby?" another well-dressed young man inquired.

"Yeah, it's alright, man. The lady just needs to sit down here awhile." Bobby squatted down in front of her chair. "I'll be back, okay? Just stay here. I need to go wait on someone."

While he was gone, Gina came back to Jules. "Hey, you're pretty shook up."

"Yeah. It's just been hard, that's all. I'm sorry. I must look like an idiot," she tried to laugh.

"Nah, you're okay. At least you weren't wearing mascara. When do you take lunch?" she asked Bobby as he walked back to them.

"Around 1, give or take, depending on how busy it is."

"Look for us in the coffee shop. Come on, Jules, no one will ever believe you've been shopping with me if you go home empty-handed."

Jules choked out a little laugh as she stood. Bobby cupped her cheek in his hand and she saw the glint of the bracelet she had given him. "I'll see you in a little while, okay?" She nodded. "I love you," he whispered as she passed.

Gina took Jules to the ladies room so she could blow her nose and freshen up a bit. "I just wanted to surprise you, I didn't want to make you cry," Gina said as she smoothed on a fresh layer of mauve lipstick.

Jules clapped a hand over her heart and smiled. "I just–" How could she possibly describe all she was feeling? "How did you–"

"I ran into Terry last night. Bingo."

"Last night?" she snapped her purse shut. "And you didn't fucking call me?"

"Hey, be cool. You think your dad would have dug me calling you at 11:00 last night?"

"Sorry."

"It's cool." She laid a hand on Jules' shoulder.

"Gina, I didn't dare tell you on the phone, but I was with Bobby last weekend."

"I guessed as much."

"This week has been pure hell."

Gina hugged her friend. "Well, that's over now. Come on, let's do some shopping. We've got an hour to kill."

Jules' mom was right in one respect – she did deserve some fun. Shopping with Gina had always been fun, so Jules just let go and enjoyed that long, hungry hour as much as she could. She found an enameled yellow flower brooch for her mom, a far out pair of flower-print tights for Sonya, a crocheted hat for Aunt Nat. She laughed at Gina's goofy, affected modeling of various scarves and hats and prim, white gloves.

A little before 1 they made their way to the store coffee shop, Jules' stomach all aflutter. It was just a small café with a limited menu, and more crowded than usual with holiday shoppers, mostly women with small, testy children, and a few store employees on their breaks. Gina grabbed the most discreet table she could, even though it needed a wipe-down.

"Eat," Gina commanded.

"I can't."

"Come on. You can't go to work empty, you'll pass out."

"Okay, okay. I'll try." She ordered a Coke float. Not food, exactly, but enough to shut Gina up.

"Stop looking at the door. Act casual," Gina cautioned between bites of sandwich. "And quit fidgeting."

"What time is it?"

"Five after. Relax."

Jules leaned forward and took a long, creamy drink of her float. As she straightened she thought she saw a flicker of suppressed smile on Gina's lips, and then suddenly a pair of warm hands covered her eyes from behind. She didn't have to guess who. Even if she hadn't recognized his touch, she knew his scent. She leaned her head back against his stomach, looking up at his teasing smile as his forearm slipped down to her collar bone and hugged her tight against him. He slid into the chair beside hers. "Feeling better?"

"Yeah."

He hailed a waitress, ordered coffee and an egg salad sandwich.

"You look so respectable," Gina teased, tugging his wide striped navy and silver-grey tie.

"Yeah, well I owe Dad for the suit. We have to wear clothes from the store. At least we get a discount."

"Oh my, Jules," Gina batted her lashes. "You're dating a male model."

"Oh, shut up," she laughed and turned to Bobby. "You do look good." She dared to reach up and touch his hair, just trimmed up a little, but still over his collar.

"I got lucky. Dad knows the department manager. I don't know if this will last or if they'll let me go after Christmas, but for now… well, if nothing else, I get a nice suit out of it."

"You're back to stay?" Jules needed confirmation.

He nodded. "Living with Mom and Dad for now."

"How are they?" Jules asked. "It seems like forever since I've seen them."

"They're fine. Can you believe Sissy starts 9th grade next year?"

The waitress brought Bobby's order and Jules took a casual sip of her float. "I used to make those for you," he nodded toward her glass as he pulled a sugar packet from the rack and tore it open. "That seems like a long time ago."

"Gawd, you sound like an old man," Gina teased.

He shrugged. "Maybe sometimes I feel like one."

"Terry said you're starting a new band," Gina said.

"He's the first person I've asked, but he's game." He tipped cream into his coffee and gave it a quick stir.

"What happened with The Knights?" Jules asked.

"We played our gig Sunday night," he said, stopping to take a bite of his sandwich, "I took my cut, we loaded our gear, and I quit." He ate some more. "Randy said he was quitting too, and that was it. I went home, packed, and was out before dawn." Jules said nothing while he finished his sandwich. "I know you believed in us, baby, but it was never gonna work." He plucked a napkin from the holder, wiped his hands, and took a sip of coffee. "That band couldn't decide what it wanted to be. They all had their ideas, but nobody wanted to give up any ground to anybody else. I tried. I honestly tried. But it was time to cut my losses."

"We tried to get the single going here," Gina said. "They played it a little. I guess Record Tree sold a few."

"That was sweet of you," he smiled.

"You've been back since Monday," Jules said.

"Yeah."

She glared at him. "Why the *hell* didn't you tell me?" she breathed through her teeth.

His eyes were stern, not breaking contact with hers as he took her hand and squeezed it for emphasis. "I wasn't sure how," he said evenly. "You know, it's not like I can just call you up."

"You could have called someone else, told them to call me."

"Jules, I don't even know who you can talk to or see anymore," he kept his voice low, but his frustration was evident. "If your situation wasn't so *fucked up*," he dropped to a whisper. She looked away, fighting the tears that tried to return. "Jules, look at me." His eyes had softened, as had his tone. "I've been trying to lay low, for your sake. I don't know what's going to happen yet. God only knows who could be watching us right now, even. Your dad can't touch me. I'd as soon deck him as look at him. But he could sure as hell make life more miserable for you."

"I know," she whispered. "I know. It's just– it scared me."

He raised her hand to his lips and kissed it. "I didn't mean to." She saw him steal a glance at the clock over the lunch counter.

"Bobby," Gina interjected quietly, "Anytime you need to get a message to Jules..."

"Thanks," he nodded. "Baby, I've got to get back to work soon." He kept hold of her hand, but reached for his coffee with the other.

"Do you work tomorrow?"

"I know what you're thinking. I really don't want you risking it. We'll figure something out, baby, but it may take a little time. Trust me, okay?"

She took a deep breath. "Okay."

"In the meantime," he reached inside his suit coat, pulled a small, black velvet bag from an inner pocket, and tucked it in her hand. "Merry Christmas."

She loosened the drawstring and poured the contents into her palm, a delicate gold chain, and punctuated by a tiny ruby, a small gold heart.

"You've already got my real one," he smiled.

She fastened it around her neck, pressed the heart against her chest where it came to rest at the top of her breastbone. "Thank you."

They held each other's gaze a moment and she drew strength and courage from his eyes.

"I've got to go," he said, taking his last sip of coffee, and Gina got to her feet. She and Jules gathered their bags, and Gina snatched up the checks to take to the cashier, teasing Bobby like a toreador as he tried to snatch his back. It made Jules laugh.

They all walked back to menswear together. When they arrived at the tie table, Jules cleared her throat. "Excuse me, sir. I need a gift for my father. Do you have something less… hip?"

They all burst out laughing.

When she'd selected an innocuous burgundy tie, Bobby rang up the sale. "Would you like that gift wrapped, miss?" He tried to hold a straight face as he laid the tie in a box.

"Yes, please."

He pulled a sheet of gold-dotted navy paper from under the counter and laid it out, pulled the edges up around the box and taped them together, leaving the ends to be finished. "Fuck," he whispered. "I still don't really know how to do this very well."

"Let me show you," she said seductively, and began guiding his hands, surreptitiously caressing his fingers.

"Um… I'll be in shoes," Gina ducked out.

When she found Gina downstairs, fondling a pair of red patent leather pumps, Jules could still feel that quick kiss on her lips.

"My God, Jules, he's a goddamn prince," Gina quietly declared. "I can see now why you've hung on through all this."

"Gina," she said, "We've got to talk. We need to plan."

"Coming from you," she grinned, "that means 'we need to plot.'"

Christmas Day, once the guests had gone home and he and Sissy had helped Nora clean up the kitchen, Bobby went right back to the keyboard, like every night, headphones on, practicing, composing, notating. "Son, it's late. Knock off and go to bed," Rob would say as they turned in for the night. Bobby would shut his door and keep working, trying to play with a lighter touch so the clicking of the keys wouldn't keep Nora awake. Scraggs would rub against his legs or curl up at his feet. Scraggs was a scraggly, brown striped stray cat that had hung around Bobby's apartment in Cincinnati, so he fed him. He couldn't leave him behind. Now Scraggs was fluffy and filled out.

Bobby had called Dwitty to invite him to join the band, but Dwitty declined. "Thanks, man, but I can't. I started night school. Electronics. TV and radio repair, stuff like that. Tricia and I want to get married as soon as we graduate. I need to be able to get a good job."

"Congratulations, then," Bobby said, and he did mean it. "We'll sure miss having you on board." As much as he wanted to stay underground, he was going to have to start casting about for band members, aggressively. He had to get this ball rolling.

"Carol's having a little New Year's Day hen party," Jules approached her mother. "Just a few of us girls, tea and cakes kind of thing. May I go?"

"It's fine with me, honey," Kate replied, "But you'd probably better ask your father."

"Thanks, Mom." To her relief, Dad gave permission, but took note of the starting and ending times on the invitation.

New Year's Eve passed innocently. Jules stayed home, watched the ball drop on TV to the strains of Guy Lombardo and his Royal Canadians, and shared kisses and a small glass of wine with her parents as they sang along to "Auld Lang Syne." Then she and her dad went outside to set off a few bottle rockets in the driveway, and Melissa and Chip stopped by to watch and extend their wishes. Kate invited them in and made hot cocoa. Chip was making a point of holding Melissa's hand and snuggling up to her shoulder, as if to say, "See, you could have been with me now instead of on your own." But Jules held her head high. She wasn't as "on her own" as most people assumed. Melissa and Chip were still unaware that Bobby was back in town. Jules had told no one.

New Year's afternoon, Jules parked her car conspicuously right in front of Carol's house and joined the party of half a dozen chattering girls munching on cookies and finger foods, sipping tea from china cups and eating little sandwiches. Carol's mother helped set out the trays in the living room, then retreated to another room. Her father was gone duck hunting with some buddies.

"You did know, didn't you, Jules?" Nita said in hushed tones. "Bobby's come back!"

"Yes, I'd heard," Jules said solemnly. "I'm still forbidden to see him, and my mom wants me to start dating other people."

"Well, I think you should," Melissa said. "It's pointless you sitting around alone, and there's the prom coming up in the spring."

"That's right," Cora, said. "You sure don't want to miss that!"

"Yeah," Jules nodded. "Well, nobody's asked me out in a while."

"Because you keep saying no," Melissa said.

"Well, we'll see what the new semester brings," Jules sighed.

"I'll keep an ear out," Gina put in. "I'm sure someone hasn't given up yet."

"I can't believe school starts tomorrow," Beth grumbled.

Jules was relieved when the conversation turned. For two hours she tried not to squirm in her seat, to pay attention to stories and gossip, laugh at the right times, or show appropriate shock. Eventually the party began to break up. "I'll stay and help you clean up." Jules made a point of her offer being heard by some departing guests. As Carol saw the last of them, save Gina and Jules, to the door, Gina ducked into the kitchen to make a quick phone call.

Carol closed the front door. Jules slipped her coat on and had barely reached the kitchen when Gina hung up the phone and said, "Go!"

"Good luck!" Carol whispered.

"Thanks. I'll be back in a while." She quietly closed the back door, looked around, and hugged the neighbors' fence line to the back of the yard, then quickly cut through a tall forsythia hedge to the back yard behind and one over from Carol's. Her heart pounded painfully, her stomach a knot as she knocked on the back door.

Terry opened it and let her in. A huge, dark German shepherd approached her. "Bruno, sit." The dog obeyed. "He won't hurt you." Terry's parents were gone for the weekend. The tea party had all been set up just to cover for this one moment. Even her invitation had an ending time of 4:30 written in, instead of 4:00. Sounds of screeching cars and gunshots came from a TV. "Have fun," Terry smiled and gave a quick sideways nod down the hall.

In Terry's room Jules was swept into Bobby's warmth, his scent, his kiss. He pushed the door shut and she let her coat slip to the floor. "We don't have much time," she said.

Chapter 12

Dan Greene announced his arrival by shutting the front door forcefully and stamping his boots on the mat. "Kate," he called.

"Yes, dear?" she answered from her office.

"Come here, I need to talk to you."

Jules was in the kitchen, fixing herself a snack. It was Monday afternoon, the 8th of January.

Kate emerged.

"I was just at the hardware store, and who do you think I saw?"

"Who?" Kate asked.

He lowered his voice, but kept the grim tone. "Rob Lott and that son of his. I don't know if he's back or visiting or what, but we better keep on our toes."

"I don't think Julia knows," Kate said just above a whisper. "But Janice bumped into Claire and she said he is back, that he's been taking piano lessons from her again."

Jules put on her innocent face, picked up her plate, and blundered into the living room to turn on the TV. Her father shook a menacing finger at her. "You just remember, young lady."

"What?" She threw her mother a look of confused surprise.

"Oh, I'm sure you know, missy," he continued. "You are still forbidden to see him or talk to him, or anything, and don't think you can put anything over on me." He strode through the house to the garage and slammed the door.

"I guess you know now. Bobby's back," Kate said softly. "You'd better not cross your father."

Jules didn't have to pretend to tremble. She had dreaded this day. Things were going to be much more difficult now.

"I'm sorry, honey," Kate reached out to smooth Jules' hair. "I know you still have feelings for him, but you just have to accept things and move on."

"Yes, Mom," she quietly conceded. "I think I'll just go to my room now."

Bobby thought back on England, sight-seeing with Jules, rooks calling down from atop a building, their rasping voices more haunting than crows', making him think of winter, even in the midst of summer. And yet, they were reputed to bring good luck. Rooks. He looked them up in a bird book, discovered that a group of them is called a parliament. A parliament of rooks. A rooks parliament. It stuck with him, that combination of words. It sounded English, sounded Gothic, mysterious. The Rooks Parliament. A name for his new band.

By mid-January the new players were in place. Stephen Segrest, the drummer, was green as grass, but he kept good time and could play complicated changes. He'd played in the drum corps of the school marching band before dropping out of school at age 16 a year ago. Miles Peterson, the bassist, who had graduated with Terry and Bobby, was a veteran of the The Bottles. His approach was different from Tyler's, and at first Terry had problems meshing with him, but they worked it out, practicing together apart from full band meetings.

"Music is changing," Bobby told them. "Second rate R&B covers won't get you anywhere anymore. We need a more psychedelic sound, and I need more room to stretch out as a player. We shouldn't confine all our songs to what will fit on a 45. We can always edit if it comes to that, but live we should expand our ideas." He and Terry began taking turns at solos, sometimes switching back and forth in long, instrumental midsections. When it was flowing between the two of them, Bobby felt that old spark, that old magic that he'd felt with The Deep See. He and Terry would exchange a knowing smile. But the other two weren't quite waist-deep in the stream yet. Bobby tried to be patient, but some days he felt frustratingly held back. Sometimes Terry would just bring practice to a close. "I think that's enough for tonight. Tomorrow night after work?" he'd ask Bobby.

"Yeah, alright," Bobby would capitulate.

"Ease up on them a little," Terry would say when they'd gone. "You tire them out too much sometimes. They start resisting. I can feel it. I can hear it."

"We can't afford to ease up."

"It's coming, man. It is. They don't have your stamina yet. They have to build up to that."

It was like a drug with Bobby. Terry could see that. Bobby might have been working out the technical aspects of the music with his brain, but he was playing from the gut. He was clearly a haunted man and sometimes it worried Terry. He understood that Bobby wanted to take a fast track as part of being able to provide for Jules, but there had to be more to it than that. Tyler, perhaps. Terry couldn't help feeling sometimes like Bobby knew more about that than he was saying.

By the end of January they began playing a few gigs. Along with a few new numbers, they had reworked some Deep See songs. Bobby called up Uncle Tony. "We need a manager."

"I'm not managing anymore," Tony said. "Since Dwitty isn't playing professionally now, I'm not really interested in doing it. I'll tell you who you need, and that's Jerry Simms. He's a hotshot young lawyer with an interest in entertainment. I'll call him and set it up for you to meet him, if you want."

"You know him? Is he good?"

"He could sell milk to a cow, and he can see through the crap in a contract."

"Set it up."

On February 2nd, Bobby's 19th birthday, Gina stopped by Hancock's menswear department and delivered a pale yellow envelope to him. It seemed to emanate warmth in his hand. "I think you know who this is from. I didn't know if you'd be out tonight, so I figured I'd better look for you here."

"Nah, I've got no special plans. Terry might come over and jam." He slipped the envelope into the inner breast pocket of his suit coat.

"Well, Happy Birthday from me." She stood on tiptoe and slipped her hand around his neck to pull his head closer and deliver a kiss to his cheek. "And that's from Jules."

"Tell her I love her. Please."

"I will." She patted his shoulder, and as she walked away, she said, "Stay tuned to this channel."

Bobby waited till he got home to open the envelope, alone in his room except for Scraggs rubbing against his legs. Jules had made the card herself, a little bouquet of four-leaf clovers drawn with colored pencils on pale yellow paper. In careful script it read, "For your birthday, here's a little luck..." He opened it. "...and all my love. To my only man. I miss you so much. Jules." Inside were a folded piece of the same butter-colored paper and a tiny white envelope. He sat down on the floor by his Farfisa, leaning against the wall, happy to hold these things in his hands, despite the terrible ache of separation. He unfolded the page and read her gentle cursive.

Vanilla snow to wrap me in.
A blanket blue for all our sin.

Orange dawn claims all her dead.
The sisters whisper in my head.

Vibrating sun will shake the land.
A tiny flower in your hand.
Licorice wind from night to day,
Black velvet wings for purple ray.

Trembling summer, dream of god
to sweep away the numbers odd.
Sinking stars of man no more,
Vanilla dust upon the floor.

He read it again, and again. Sadness, loss, hope, the turn of seasons. His old blue blanket that had covered them that cold afternoon in Cincinnati. Images from their time together in London. It was exactly the gift he needed. He reached up to spread it out on the keyboard.

The little envelope read, "I have so much, no one will ever notice it's gone." He opened it to find a lock of her hair, a curve of pale gold silk in his hand. He stroked it with a fingertip, pressed it against his cheek. He pulled it across his lips, strands of cool satin clinging, searched it for any trace of scent, finding just the barest hint of her. He wound it tightly around his finger and just sat awhile, running his thumb over it, feeling it, thinking, but not in words.

Then he got up. He curled the lock back into its envelope and tucked it in his wallet. He sat down at the keys.

"You haven't seen Bobby since New Year's, have you?" Gina asked Jules.

"No. Not at all. Not even in the distance somewhere."

"I'm not too surprised. Terry says he puts all his spare time into the band. He's like a hermit. And a slave driver. But you've been a good girl, right? Stayed on your dad's good side?"

"I think so, yeah."

"We've got the Sweetheart Dance coming up. I may have found you a cover. A 'ride,' shall we say."

"Who? "

"Do you know Mark Jacoby?"

"Not really, no. He's in my Math class."

"Jules, you've always struck me as open-minded."

"I try to be."

"Mark is in a situation sorta like yours. He's– involved with– someone he's not supposed to be. For different reasons, but– he needs a cover, too."

"Oh, God, I don't know Gina. Sounds like double trouble."

"Yeah, but let me put it this way. He's got an awful lot at stake, so he's very careful. He's not going to talk and give you away. And it's bound to look just fine on the outside to most people, even better for him than for you, and you won't have to worry about him getting the wrong idea, or Bobby, either. I'll make sure of that."

"What exactly are you saying, Gina?"

"Mark is queer."

Jules was stunned.

"You can't ride with me or be around me at the dance," Gina said. "In fact, I may be kinda dangerous for you to hang around with in general these days."

"Why?"

"Terry and I are... well, we're getting pretty serious."

Jules' mouth fell open. "Should I have seen this coming?"

"I don't know. Probably not. I know you're not allowed to be around him, so... "

"Well, now, isn't this a complicated picture?"

"I know. Sorry to make things weirder, but, Jules, I just might have found a way to– get on with life."

Valentine's Day, as they sneaked away from the dance and slipped out the Science Department door, coatless into the cold, Jules turned one direction and Mark disappeared in the other. Bobby stepped out of deep shadows and enveloped her in his coat. "You're fucking crazy," he whispered.

"About you."

"Oh, God, I love you, Jules, but you can't keep doing things like this. I mean it." He held her head tight against his heart. "I need you. It kills me not to see you, but this scares me. It's dangerous, not just for you. If you get caught, what do you think is going to happen to him?"

"It scares me too," she admitted.

"I know it seems like time is going too slow, but we're getting close now. We're so close. Don't make things worse."

He felt a catch in her breath, felt her hand tighten around a slack fold of his sweater. "Shh– don't cry." He closed his eyes and gently rocked her. Everywhere she touched him was a beautiful torture. "Wait for word from me, okay?"

"Okay."

"Promise me."

"I promise."

He kissed her, so hungry for her, so sorry for her. He could taste her tears and that hurt him worse than anything. He dried her cheek with the backs of his fingers. "Be strong for me." He squeezed her one last time, then let go. "Go inside before you catch your death."

He couldn't sleep that night for worrying, couldn't even lie quietly in bed. Was she okay? Did she get home alright? He never should have agreed to it, never should have let her take that kind of risk. He could see now just how foolish and degraded things had become. She deserved so much better. He paced around his room in the dark in his pajama bottoms until he was cold, then pulled the blanket around his shoulders and sank to the floor beside the bed, back against the wall, knees pulled up under the ends of the blanket. *All I ever seem to do is make you cry.*

3 a.m. found him back in his clothes, sitting at the Farfisa, power off, picking out the fingering to the melody in his head. He didn't have to hear it sound. He could hear the intervals in his head, could see them on the keys. Didn't even need to see them. His fingers knew their positions on the keyboard. He didn't have perfect pitch. He might be playing from a different root note than the one in his head, but it rarely mattered, and if it did, like if it didn't quite fit Terry's vocal range, he could transpose it later. For tonight he just needed to impress upon his brain a visual image of how the tune in his mind could be played.

Still dressed, he finally lay down on the bed, exhausted, but never managed to get beyond the shallowest stages of sleep. At 7 a.m. there was a knock on his door. "Who is it?" he said half into his pillow, as he lay on his stomach.

"It's Sissy. Mom wanted me to wake you up in case you want to go to church."

"I have an alarm clock," he replied flatly.

"You going with us?"

"No."

"Well, do you want something to eat before we go?"

"No. I can feed myself."

"Are you okay?"

"No."

"Are you sick?"

"No."

"You want me to leave you alone?"

"Yes!"

Lady began pawing at the door to get in.

"Sissy, you still there?"

"Yeah."

"You can let Lady in."

He heard the door creak open and the dog panting as she approached. He rolled onto his back and opened his eyes to see Sissy through the half open door, dressed nice for church, staring at him. "You don't look so good," she said.

"Thank you."

The dog jumped up on the bed and lay down next to his legs.

"You hung over?"

"No," he managed a laugh. "I just couldn't sleep. Now my head hurts."

"You want some aspirin?"

"Yes, actually, and a glass of water."

She disappeared from the doorway. He felt the bed bounce, as Scraggs jumped up and curled, purring, against his side. He felt like an animal sandwich. When his sister returned with the aspirin, he turned on his side and raised up enough to shake out four tablets and swallow them. "Sitting with Jamie today?" he asked, setting the glass on the night stand.

"Yeah, if he's there."

"You look sweet."

"Thanks." She took her leave.

"Close the door."

He heard it shut, her footsteps in the hall. His baby sister, already 13, interested in boys, not valuing her naiveté. *God, give her an easy road, please.*

He heard them all leaving, and then the house was mercifully quiet. As his headache eased, he slept, sinking straight from his sunlit room into deep black.

He didn't hear them return, didn't wake until he heard banging and clinking in the kitchen and smelled sausage. Nora always fixed a big lunch after church. Bobby extricated himself from his pets and got a quick shower. He didn't bother to shave.

"There you are." Nora looked concerned as he walked into the kitchen. "Feeling any better, honey?"

"Yeah, I'm fine, Mom. I'm just tired." He headed for the coffee pot.

Rob was already seated and filling his plate with sausage links, scrambled eggs, biscuits, and fried apples. Sissy set out a hot casserole dish of baked cheese grits, Bobby's favorite. Bobby sat down and spread out a generous portion on his plate to cool. "Bad night?" Rob asked.

"Couldn't sleep. Couldn't turn my brain off."

"Got things bothering you?"

He sighed. "We've got this session. Some new ideas. I don't know, just 'things.'"

"You drive yourself too hard, son," Rob said, spooning sorghum onto his biscuits. "You need to back off."

"Yeah," he said, just to end the conversation. He couldn't back off yet. There was too much happening too fast. Terry would be over later, and he had work to do beforehand. Sissy and Nora sat down, Rob said the blessing, and they turned their attentions toward food. Sissy was bright and cheery. Jamie must have been at church. Nora seemed happy just to see him eating.

Bobby took the time to help Nora clear the table, kissed her on the cheek. She reached up to pat his bristly face, and laughed. "I do worry about you. You may be 6 foot 2, but you're still my baby."

With another cup of coffee, Bobby was at the keys, calling up last night's melody, and something else, something he hadn't expected. His pulse quickened as feather thoughts pulled together and took flight.

"Terry, I've got an idea. I really want to try to do this."

"Yeah? What?"

"I've got a song. I really want to make it the B-side."

"I thought 'Stray Boy' was gonna be the B." "Stray Boy" was a Deep See song. It would have been their next single. The Rooks Parliament had reworked it and been playing it live to fill out their set.

"Why use something old if I've got something new? It's really not our style anymore anyway."

"Bobby, this is Sunday. We're recording Tuesday. That gives us one practice, tomorrow night. One. And I don't think I can write lyrics for it that fast."

"I've got the lyrics."

"From Jules?"

"No. They're mine. They're mine and I want to use them." He handed Terry a handwritten sheet.

"Just so you're not planning to sing them," Terry smirked.

"No," Bobby laughed. "That's your job."

"Alright, let's hear what you've got."

"I wrote it for your range," he said, "so, bear with me." He played it, sang it, voice cracking on the higher notes.

"Again." Terry started picking out chords on his guitar, feeling out the timing, the slow end of mid-tempo.

"That's good, that's good. I like that." But he saw the uncertainty in Terry's expression. "Terry, we can do this. You know we can."

Terry sighed. "Maybe we can. Can they?"

"Yes. They've got the talent, or they wouldn't be in the band."

"What if Bruce says no?"

"If we can sell it to Jerry, I think he'll make it happen. We have to try, Terry. I just have a feeling about this."

"Yeah, I know what that feeling is, just from the lyrics." He shook his head. Bobby could tell Terry was implying it was all about personal agenda.

"It's more than that. Trust me, Terry. This will do more for us than 'Stray Boy.' We shouldn't lean on the past any more than we have to."

"Alright, man. I'll give it a go. You got a piece of tape or something?"

Bobby scrounged in a desk drawer and tossed him a thumb tack. Terry tacked the lyric sheet up on the wall. "Sing it from the gut, man," Bobby directed. "Give it some pain."

The next night at practice, Bobby's song took shape. He called Jerry. "I can't get over there tonight," Jerry said. "You guys really have a conviction about this one?"

"We do." Bobby had given him all the logical reasons to use it instead of "Stray Boy."

"I'll work on Bruce. You just show up on time. We'll record 'Sidewalk Girl' and 'Stray Boy' as planned, and we'll do this one, too. If it works, we'll use it."

In the studio Tuesday, they gave it all they had, and it did sound good. Bruce was sold. He liked the idea of new material, and something that wasn't as lengthy or experimental as "Vanilla Snow" and some of the other new songs. It sounded more like single material to him. "It needs a fuller sound, though," he said. "I've got an idea. Bobby, you come with me. The rest of you take a break. Don't worry, I won't charge you any extra time."

"You got your way, man," Terry punched Bobby in the arm as they were leaving the studio that evening.

"Yeah. Dinner's on me, guys," Bobby said, "As long as you don't eat too fucking much, Terry." They all laughed, spirits high with hope over a job well done.

Chapter 13

It was the end of March. Jules, having spent Spring Break in Florida with her parents, disliked going back to wearing sweaters and coats. It felt odd to be tan and cold. And she was tired of high school. She just wanted out. She just wanted to be free. In a matter of days she would be 18. She touched the points of the pretty pink-lined conch shell she had bought in a beach-side shop, hoping Bobby had gotten the anonymous postcard she had sneaked into the motel postal chute. He would know who it was from. She had signed it, "Whisper to me of the sea."

By the end of her first week back in school, she got a message from Bobby, via Gina. She was to listen to WMVD on Sunday afternoon at 3:00, alone. It was important.

Sunday afternoon, Jules sat at her desk, door closed, homework laid out, but unable to concentrate on it. What would she hear today? Gina had said Bobby was insistent. Maybe they had a record out. Jules tuned in early, before J.J. Dawes' show, just so she wouldn't miss anything, suffering through the Sunday afternoon Community Calendar. For all the waiting, still she felt startled when J.J.'s voice came through the speaker. "Hey, boys and girls, men and women, cats and dogs, it's your old friend J.J. Dawes, bringing you the newest and best from Kentucky and around the world, here on WMVD. Today we have a couple of very special guests, whose band has a new record out, and we'll be playing both sides of that for you. I'm talking, of course, about Midvale hipsters The Rooks Parliament. But before we get to that, here's the latest from Red and the Rovers. "

Jules' heart pounded. Her hands shook as she covered her mouth. She had never even heard them, never seen them play. The more she thought about that the angrier she got. It wasn't fair or right for her to be so excluded from his life.

Two more songs J.J. made her suffer through before he said, "For those of you who don't know, The Rooks Parliament rose from the ashes of The Deep See, one of Midvale's premier bands, who broke up last summer. You can catch them live every Thursday night at the Happen Inn."

That was news to her, too.

"They have a new single out, which hits the stores Tuesday, and you can pick yours up at Record Tree. Pick a hit at Record Tree. But we've got it here for you today. And here to tell us about it are singer and guitarist Terry Wallace and organist extraordinaire Bobby Lott."

They both said hello and Jules bit into the side of her finger.

"Now, Terry, you wrote the A-Side, 'Sidewalk Girl,' right?"

"Right."

"And what's it about?"

"About seeing a pretty girl on the sidewalk on your way to work every day, and even though you don't know her, you feel like you do, because she's there every day. So one day you decide to say hi to her." He laughed, "And she basically tells you to get lost."

She could hear Bobby laugh, as well, and oh, she missed that laugh. How long had it been since she'd heard him laugh? January 1st? There sure hadn't been any laughter the last time she'd seen him, shivering in the cold behind the school, without her coat, while Mark went off on his tryst.

"Well, let's play that side now."

The music came in sunny and hopeful with a perky beat and warm, fuzzed guitar, Terry's voice boyishly earnest, with just a touch of irony.

> Pretty girl on the street,
> Kinda girl you'd like to meet.
> See her on the corner every day.
>
> Waiting there, dressed so sweet,
> Lips just like a cherry treat.
> I've got to figure out just what to say.
>
> Sidewalk girl,
> Come and join my world.
> Sidewalk girl,
> Let me take you for a whirl.
>
> Morning comes, sun shines bright.
> She's waiting there in the light.
> Got to tell her how I feel today.
>
> Think about you every night.
> Come and make my world alright.
> She turns to me and tells me, "Go away."

> Sidewalk girl,
> Such a pretty pearl.
> Sidewalk girl
> She don't want me in her world.

It was a cute, catchy, understated song that promised to do well for them. It made Jules smile, but that short little keyboard break with the melancholy twist, played only once, after the first chorus, made her immediately want to hear it again, and not just because it was Bobby. And this, she knew, was the point, to leave the listener wanting it again.

"Now, Bobby, I understand you wrote the B-Side," J.J. said.

"That's right."

"Including the lyrics?"

"Yes."

"It's called 'All I Ever Seem To Do.' Do you want to tell us about that?"

"It's actually called 'All I Ever Seem To Do Is Make You Cry,' but they couldn't fit all that on the label. I wrote it for someone very special. She knows who she is. And this will probably make her cry, too," he laughed. "If it does, I'm sorry, baby. I love you."

"So, let's have a listen."

Jules had tears in her eyes already, before the drums ticked the beat and Bobby's rich, vibrato organ tones swelled in. That wasn't the Farfisa. That was a Hammond, and it sounded wonderful. Terry's guitar was almost clean, just a hint of distortion, playing sparse, sharp-edged rhythm chords at a slow pace. He sang the lyrics soulfully, and she clutched at every word, literally, her hand on the speaker.

> All I ever seem to do is make you cry.
> I see your tears and I just wanna die.
> I never meant to bring you such pain,
> But when I touch you,
> your tears fall like rain.
>
> Don't you see this is killing me too?
> I never dreamed I would love someone like you.
> I want to take you away tonight,
> Hold you tight,
> hold you tight.
>
> All I ever seem to do is make you cry.
> I just can't win, no matter how I try.

I never meant to tear us apart,
But when I kiss you,
I just break your heart.

Don't you see this is killing me too?
I never dreamed I could lose someone like you.
That I can take you away someday
Is all I pray,
all I pray.

Bobby's solo taking the song out was wild with pain, and more than a little anger, ending with a swish of his hands up and down the keys that ripped right through her.

"And there you have it," J.J. broke in, talking right over the sustain, and she kicked the foot of her desk with frustration. "The Rooks Parliament. My thanks to Terry and Bobby for dropping by, and remember, you can pick that up Tuesday at Record Tree. Pick a hit at Record Tree."

In Kentucky History class the next day, Tricia, on her way to her desk, dropped a manila folder on top of Jules' books. Jules didn't look up, ignoring the folder a few moments, then casually opening it in her lap. There was the 45, along with a black and white promotional photo of the band standing in an alley. Her heart pounded as she looked at the photo. Terry's hair was getting long and a bit wavy. She had never even known what Miles and Stephen looked like until now. Miles, wearing dark sunglasses, was tall and thin with straight hair down to his shoulders. Stephen was blond, hair parted on the side, with long bangs. He looked quite young. Bobby in a satin shirt and neck scarf, hand on his hip, was smiling that beautiful smile, and she ran the backs of her fingers lovingly over his image before closing the folder. She hastily scrawled a thank you note to Tricia, folded it up very small, and got up, walking to the back of the room to sharpen a pencil, tucking the note alongside Tricia's books as she passed. While Jules would have to hide the photo once she got it home, she could discreetly play the record. Her parents didn't know what The Rooks Parliament sounded like, or even who they were, so far as she knew. Shuffled in with her other 45s, no one would be the wiser.

Wednesday she was all nerves, dashing out to Gina's car at the final bell for their study session at Gina's house. As she pulled out of the parking lot, Gina squeezed Jules' hand. "Just relax."

"I can't." Jules looked at her watch.

"We've got time."

"That's the problem."

"You've got to at least try to act normal until we get to my room."

At Gina's house, they said hi to her mother and got snacks from the kitchen to take upstairs. They shut the door to Gina's room, sat on the carpet, turned the radio on low, and Gina kept her aqua princess phone nearby. They opened their books and laid them out before them.

"Breathe," Gina directed.

Then the phone rang, and Jules' whole body was jolted. Gina snatched up the receiver before her mother could get to it downstairs. "Hello?... She's here." Gina handed the phone to Jules.

"Hello?"

"Jules?"

"Baby?" Her hand shook, her voice quavered.

"I'm here, honey. Did you get to hear the radio show yesterday?"

"Yes. Oh, it's beautiful, your song. You guys sound so good."

"Did the record get to you yet?"

"Yes, Tricia gave it to me Monday, and the photo. You don't know how bad it's hurt, all this time never even having heard you guys, never getting to see you play, never–" She choked back tears.

"How do you think I've felt, not being able to share any of it with you? Writing all these songs, playing all these shows, knowing you're never there to hear them? It hurts so goddamn bad."

She sniffled. Gina stroked her back.

"Aw, honey, don't cry. Listen, I have to get back to work soon, and this is important. I hope it's good news. I don't know what we're going to do about this, but the band for your prom is us. It hasn't been announced officially yet, but it's confirmed."

Jules was stunned.

"You there?"

"I'm here. I– I just– I don't know what to say, what to think."

"It wasn't our idea, the dance committee approached us. We couldn't turn it down. I want you there, but I want you safe. I'll understand if you have to go with someone, but be careful. No big risks. And if you can't pull it off..."

"I'll be there. Somehow, I'll be there."

"And I know it's not till tomorrow, but happy birthday, baby. I love you."

"I love you too."

"And thanks for the postcard. I'll see you soon, sweetheart."

When they'd said goodbye, Jules set the receiver back in place. "Gina, we've got things to do."

Gina nodded. "I'm already working on some of it."

Jules' birthday started in sun and ended in darkness. She came home from work to a cake and presents, and the news of Martin Luther King, Jr.'s assassination. The world was truly going mad.

The Rooks Parliament had a double-sided hit on their hands. It rose quickly up the local charts, with both sides getting airplay, vying with each other for Number 1. Both sides made the Top 20 in Louisville and Lexington, with "Sidewalk Girl" charting as far away as Cincinnati, and even getting some airplay in Indianapolis. "Jerry, get it down to Knoxville," Bobby said. "Make sure they know the Deep See connection."

Terry proudly told Gina that they had played all the way up to Cincy and all the way down to Huntsville, Alabama. He didn't tell her that along the way they were unknowingly booked into a topless bar, where Jerry advised them, "Just enjoy the view, boys." Jerry thought it was time to look into cutting an album, something for which he considered Bruce's studio inadequate.

Bruce had his own proposal for Jerry and the band. "Why don't you give 'Stray Boy' to The Rebelles? I think they could do a good job with it and I want to get a single out by them. You'll get a percentage, of course." If they could help The Rebelles get a foot in the door professionally, Bobby and Terry were all for it. The girls had been out of the basement for several months now, and they were really getting good.

Jules and Gina were on the move, as well. Jules had found a date for the prom, a friend named Jeff, who was really taking his girlfriend, Audrey, but to help Jules, they were willing to participate in a charade.

Gina called Jules a week before the prom. "We have some important shopping to do, tomorrow after school. There's a cute little shop on Mary Street we need to check out, and a boutique on Freeman. None of the other stores were worth our while."

"Okay, sounds good," Jules said. "I need to order a boutonnière while we're out."

Jules had yet to wear the pretty grey dress and silver boots she'd bought in London, so she decided to wear them to the prom, with pale grey hose. Jeff, in a blue suit, came to pick Jules up, pinned a pretty corsage on her dress, and she affixed his boutonnière. They posed for Kate's camera. "Oh, you look so pretty, honey," Kate smiled, fussing over a flyaway strand of Jules' hair.

"You have her home by 10:30," Dan told Jeff. "And I expect you to behave like a gentleman towards her."

"Yes, sir," Jeff smiled. "You have my word on that."

"Good," Dan replied, and they shook hands.

They left in Jeff's car, Jules waving to her mom as they pulled away. Then they went to pick up Audrey. Jules lay down in the back seat and waited while poor Jeff went through the flowers and photos routine all over again.

"How did it go?" Audrey asked as they drove to Lee's Pagoda for dinner.

Jeff laughed. "It went fine. You can sit up now, Jules."

"I can't ever thank you enough for this," she told them. "I feel bad about being in your way."

"Don't worry about it," Audrey said. "We'll still have time after we take you home. Our curfew's not till 12 tonight."

Jules offered to sit at another table for dinner, but Jeff and Audrey wouldn't hear of it. She paid for her own meal, but when she tried to pay Jeff for her corsage he wouldn't let her. "And I don't need two of these," he smiled, giving her back the boutonnière he had removed at Audrey's house in order to receive hers. "It belongs on your real man, anyway."

When they arrived at the school gym, the stage was set up for the band, but they were not in sight. Jeff conspicuously escorted Jules through the archway constructed of balloons. Balloons and crepe paper streamers decorated the front of the stage and hung in exuberant clusters on the walls, and glitter was sprinkled on the floor. She spotted Gina near the refreshment table, which Mrs. Meeks, the school librarian, presided over to make sure no one spiked the punch. "Thanks, Jeff. You go get Audrey. I'll be waiting by the door when it's time to leave."

Gina saw her and met her halfway. "Look out, Mary Street," she grinned, pressing a key into Jules' hand. "I think we made the right choice."

"Oh, thank heavens," Jules sighed and gave Gina a hug. "Does he know? I haven't seen any of them."

"Yes, he knows. That's a seriously fab outfit, Jules. Those boots!"

Jules smiled. "This is the first I've worn any of it."

"Well, London girl, it's certainly drawn attention already," Gina grinned, tossing the end of the red feather boa Jules had given her over her shoulder.

Jules was quite aware of eyes on her, for a variety of reasons, she guessed. "Oh, God, Gina, I just want to see him," she pressed her palms together hard. "It's been two months. Two godforsaken months. Three and a half months since we– since the tea party."

"It will all be over soon," Gina soothed.

"Are they good? As good as The Deep See?"

"They're terrific. You're going to love them. Well, I mean, you already love one of them," she winked.

"So do you," Jules said.

"Yeah," Gina smiled. "I believe I do."

Dwitty escorted Tricia in. She was wearing a pretty avocado green crepe de Chine dress. Jules dared to go talk to them, to hug Tricia. "I don't care anymore," she said.

Most of the lights winked out above. Principal Sammons walked out on the stage and picked up a microphone. "Ladies and gentlemen, Class of '68, this is your night to dazzle. So grab your partners and get ready to dance to the music of four of our fine alumni, The Rooks Parliament!"

Jules grabbed Gina's hand and hurried toward the front as the band came out from behind the worn, navy velvet backdrop. Just as he reached his Farfisa, Bobby saw Jules. Their eyes met, and he smiled, and then Stephen started playing the beat.

Bobby had informed the band right from the start that the matching suits look was out. Everyone wore their own thing. Tonight Miles sported a red military coat with brass buttons and gold trim. Stephen's shirt was a wild dance of pink, yellow, and white swirls. Terry wore a long, tan shearling vest over a denim shirt and dark brown pants. Bobby wore a harvest gold Nehru jacket and ivory flares.

Jules was mesmerized. Their music had a dreamlike quality weaving through it, like a good high. Miles sang harmony to some of Terry's vocals. Terry spun out dizzying fuzzed guitar solos that overlapped and then gave way to Bobby's intricate, florid organ solos. Bobby often seemed to go off into his own world, sometimes closing his eyes, sometimes throwing his head back and gazing skyward, but during a sinuous, bluesy passage in a song they called "Sweet Amelia," he stared right into Jules' eyes, his gaze unwavering, like making love. She ached for him. "I love you," she mouthed. He closed his eyes and smiled.

Since it was a dance, they played some popular covers and the obligatory slow dance songs, but they gave them all their own feel, their own arrangements, rather than playing faithful copies.

When the band took a break, Jules and Gina went to the ladies' room. Jules was checking her hair and Gina refreshing her red lipstick when Melissa came in.

"What's up with your date?" Melissa asked Jules. "Why is he dancing with her?"

"He's not my date," she replied, and Gina chimed in with her, "He's just my ride." They both laughed.

"What do you mean?" Melissa puzzled.

"Wake up, Melissa," Gina said.

"I'm only here for one reason," Jules said, "for one man."

"But–"

"Don't you see? We never broke up. We've just been biding our time, seeing each other when we can. But all that's about to change."

The band launched the second set with "Sidewalk Girl," and cheers went up from the dance floor. Cast off high heel shoes began to litter the edges of the gym. As spirits soared higher, Jules and Gina danced in place, and Bobby smiled to see them having a good time. During "All I Ever Seem To Do," Bobby watched Jules all he could and she basked in his love, in his song, the tender, sad words he had written for her. She wasn't crying this time. There would be no tears tonight. His wild solo at the end was full of the promise of joy. As the song ended, Steven dropped the beat down slow.

"Last dance!" Terry announced. "And... I think we just lost our keyboard player."

Bobby had run to the edge of the stage and jumped off, taking Jules in his arms. As the band played without him, he danced with Jules, holding her close, kissing her hair. "I don't want to let you go," he said.

Near the end of the song, Terry deftly slipped in the words, "And her name is J-U-L-I-A-ay-ay-ay-ay-ay..." And with that they launched into a rousing rendition that sent the dance floor jumping and whooping and tossing flower petals and confetti. In the middle of it all Jules and Bobby kissed, and laughed, and kissed again. "It's all over now," she said, picking confetti out of his hair as she tucked the white rosebud boutonnière behind his ear. "It's all over. It's just down to us."

"Be careful, baby. Don't provoke him. I won't rest till you call."

When Jules got home, Kate was in her armchair, reading *Pride and Prejudice*. "Did you have a nice time?" she asked.

"I had a wonderful time."

Kate turned, parted the curtain and looked out. "Why didn't Jeff come in? Who's that other girl in the car?"

"Oh, he just offered to give someone a ride home. I don't mind."

"That's generous of you, dear."

"Well," she faked a yawn, "I'm tired. I think I'll head up to bed now, Mom."

"Goodnight, dear."

Jules got up early for a Saturday, unable and unwilling to sleep. She suffered a late breakfast with her parents, told them how the gym had been decorated for the prom, what dresses her girlfriends had worn. Very, very normal things, but inside the gears were turning, the spring was over-wound. *Get on with it. Go.*

Finally her dad set down his coffee cup with a thud and said, "Well, I better get out of here. I don't know how long I'll be. Depends on what shape those blueprints are in."

"And I've got to deliver all these Tupperware orders. Julia, be sure to check all the doors when you leave for work."

"Yes, Mom." Jules casually cleared her dishes from the table as her parents picked up their things and went out to work. When she was certain they were really gone, and weren't going to burst back in for something they had forgotten, she sprang into action. In the guise of cleaning up the house for her "date," she had already gathered all her records together and taken them to her room. Most other things she had strewn around were in her room now, as well. She sprinted up the stairs, pulled her suitcase out from under the bed, and began piling her clothes into it. She took it down to her car and put it in the trunk, taking out a few flattened cardboard boxes that would hold her books and personal effects. She knew she couldn't take everything. Not today, at least. There were old toys in the attic that still had sentimental value. Her rock and shell collections were out in the garage. She didn't want to be accused of stealing anything, either, so that meant leaving her bedroom furniture behind, and anything else of questionable ownership. A lump rose in her throat as she took down the magazine pin-ups from over her desk– The Beatles, The Monkees, Paul Revere and the Raiders. She shouldn't bother, she told herself. She shouldn't linger, but it was hard. Harder than she had thought it would be. Still, in less than an hour she had done more than she originally intended, with plenty of time to spare, she figured.

She was carrying the last thing down the stairs, her train case with her toiletries, when she heard the front door slam. Hard. She took a deep breath and raised her head high. With a step yet to descend she was eye level with Dan Greene. The first words out of his mouth were, "Where's your mother?"

"Still out."

"Why the hell aren't you at work?"

"I traded days," she said calmly.

She could see the rage building in his reddening face. "Oh, I heard all about what happened last night," he seethed, approaching her.

"I'm not surprised," she said coolly.

"Did you really think you could get away with it? Do you think I'm that big of a fool?"

"No," she said.

"That's 'no, sir,'" he said through his teeth. As she tried to walk past him, she saw his whole body turn, and his hand struck her cheek so hard it knocked her against the stairwell wall. He had never done anything like that before, and it was as if something in the air itself had snapped in two.

She straightened herself on wobbling knees, grabbing the handle of the case she had dropped, and looked for her father in the flustered face before her, looked in those clouded eyes for the man that, though strict and suspicious, she had still believed loved her and just wanted to keep her safe.

He looked at her face, then down at his hand, his open, shaking palm. She tasted salt. "I'm leaving now," she said quietly, and squeezed past him, not touching him, not being touched. He still stood at the bottom of the stairs, facing away from her. "There's an envelope on the table," she said. "It's the rest of what I owe you for the car." She gently closed the kitchen door behind her.

Chapter 14

"Where is she?" Kate Greene shouted at her husband, shaking the note Jules had left, saying she would call later to tell them where she was.

"I told you, I don't know! Probably ran off with *him*. And they can both go to the devil now. I wash my hands of her."

"Daniel Sutherland Greene, she is your daughter! This is all your doing. You drove them to this. You should have known you couldn't keep them apart. All you did was make them desperate."

"That's enough out of you," he shook a finger at her.

"If you'd left them alone, they'd be happily dating, planning a future, like normal kids. Hell, they might not have even stayed serious about each other. Jules was going to college. He had his music groups, and what now? We don't even know where she is!"

"I said that's enough!" He stood up and pounded his fist on the tabletop.

Kate picked up her jacket and snatched her keys off the table.

"Where are you going?"

"To look for my daughter," she said, slamming the door behind her.

"Yes?" Nora Lott answered her front door.

"Nora," Kate said, looking down, wringing her hands, "Do you know where my daughter is?"

"How should I know?" Nora put her hand on her hip.

"Do you know where Bobby is?"

"I assume he's at work."

"Do you know for certain?"

"What's all this about?"

"Julia was dancing with Bobby at the prom last night. Today she packed her things and left. We don't know where she went."

Nora heaved a sigh. "Alright, come in." She ushered Kate to a living room chair and dialed the phone. "Yes, may I speak to Bobby Lott, please? This is his mother." Kate looked up at Nora, who looked out the window at the driveway. "Okay, thank you." She hung up and looked at Kate. "They said he's left work already." Nora sat down in the nearest chair. "If they left this town, I can't blame them."

"Where's Rob?" Kate asked meekly.

"He took the car in to the shop, and no, I don't know which shop."

They sat in tense silence awhile, then Kate got up. "Perhaps I should go home and see if she's called. Thank you, Nora. If you hear anything–"

She nodded and rose to see her out. "And if you do–"

And then Bobby came through the door. They looked at him, and he looked at them, expressions of bewilderment passing between them.

"Bobby, honey," his mother spoke. "Do you know where Julia is?"

"No." He pulled off his tie and tossed it on the piano bench.

"Were you with her last night?" Nora asked.

"Yes."

"Did you know she was going to leave home?"

"Yes. I found out last night. I didn't know whether it would be today or not, just that it would be soon."

Kate clutched his arm. "Do you know where she was going?"

He nodded. "She got her own place."

"Where? Do you know?" Kate pleaded.

"I think," he said quietly, but firmly, "if she wanted you to know, she would have told you."

"No, please don't call him," Jules pleaded with Gina. "I'll just call him later like we planned."

"Jules, I think he needs to know." She wrung the dripping wash cloth out over the kitchen sink, then put fresh ice cubes in it and handed it back to Jules, who touched it to her swollen lip.

"He'll know later. I don't want to bother him with it at work. I'm okay."

"And what if your dad comes over here?"

"Then I don't want Bobby mixed up in it. If my dad comes over here, we don't let him in, and if he won't leave, we call the police."

"Jules, you're forgetting. Our phone isn't hooked up yet. How would we get to the pay phone?"

"Okay, maybe you're right. Maybe I should go call."

"Jules, I'd be lying if I said this didn't terrify me."

"When I looked in his eyes," she said, "it was like he had died."

"Shh– don't talk. Just keep that ice on. Let me get my purse and I'll come with you."

There was a loud knock at the door. Gina and Jules froze. "Jules, are you there? Jules, open up, baby, it's me."

They exhaled and slumped with relief. Gina got up and let Bobby in. He was still dressed in the suit he had worn to work.

"Oh, hey," he said to Gina. "Jules, your mom is at– Fuck! What happened?" He rushed to Jules. "Baby, your face." He took the ice pack from her and gently touched her cheek.

"It's okay," she said. "Just a fat lip."

"How?"

"He came home, just as I was leaving. He'd found out about last night."

She saw Bobby's nostrils flare, saw his chest rise and fall more quickly. "Your father did this to you?"

"Yeah." The thick, cold, numb mass of her lip quivered and she wanted to collapse from the stress.

"I swear to God, if he walks through that door I will fucking kill him."

"Bobby, honey," Gina said. "Take it easy, okay?"

"No one better lay a hand on her." He pulled her close and she laid the uninjured side of her face against his chest. He held her head against him, as though shielding her. "Baby," he said quietly, "Your mother is looking for you. She probably followed me here. I think she's pretty worried. What do you want to do?"

"If it's just Mom," she said, "it's okay."

Since Gina had moved under more favorable circumstances, and had an extra day, there were a few pieces of furniture. She had her bed and dresser from home, a desk, a couple of chairs. Terry had scared up a hand-me-down couch, and a decent mattress for Jules to use until she could get a proper bed in her room. The former tenants had left a thickly painted brown table in the kitchen.

Bobby took a disposable plastic cup from the box Gina had bought, and filled it with ice water. "Come and sit down," he said, leading Jules to the couch. He coaxed her to drink. Gina brought her another aspirin. Jules set the half empty cup on an upturned box positioned as a temporary coffee table, and had just settled back to rest under Bobby's arm when someone knocked. Bobby inflated like an angry cat. Gina held her hand up toward them like a stop signal and crept to the peep hole. She looked from one angle, then another, then slipped the dead bolt, leaving the chain attached.

"Gina, is Julia here?"

Gina looked at Jules and inclined her head toward the door.

"She alone?" Jules whispered.

Gina nodded. Jules closed her eyes and nodded in reply. Gina unfastened the chain and let Kate in.

"Oh, thank God, I was so wor–" Kate's hands flew up to cover her mouth. Gina closed the door and bolted it. "Oh my God, honey. What happened?"

"Your husband did this," Bobby stated.

"I'm okay, Mom," Jules hovered on the verge of tears.

"Yeah, she looks okay, doesn't she?" he sneered. "And, no, I didn't know while ago."

"Here, sit down, Mrs. Greene," Gina said, dragging up a chair for her.

"Thank you, no. No," she shook her head and went to Jules, sitting on the edge of the cushion beside her, on the opposite side from Bobby. "Let me see." She brushed back Jules' hair and examined the darkening red streaks across her left cheek. "Should we get you to a doctor?"

"She won't go," Gina said. "I tried."

"It's just a bruise," Jules said.

Kate looked up into Bobby's glare and shook her head. "He's never– no. He was strict, but he never harmed either of us."

"I didn't argue with him, Mom. I didn't raise my voice. I was on my way out. He must have found out at work about last night. Bobby and I danced. Just one dance. We just danced." She dissolved into tears.

"Shh– shh– I'm right here, baby," Bobby said softly and she hid her face in his shirt.

"Your mother told me something once," Kate said to Bobby. "She told me I needed to grow a backbone. I'm sorry it took something like this, but I'm sure as hell growing one now. I don't relish the thought of going back to my house tonight, but I know I have to. No, I won't tell him where you are, sweetheart," she stroked Jules' head. "But he's liable to find out eventually. Gina, is there a phone?"

"There's a phone booth across the street."

"I'm going to call your parents and tell them not to let Dan know where you are." She fished in her purse for a pencil and a store receipt. "Jules, honey, if you need me, call Janice, okay? Don't call home. Here's her number." She laid it on the box-table. Then she stuffed something into Bobby's shirt pocket. "It's all I've got with me right now. Take care of my girl."

When Kate had gone, Bobby gently sat Jules up. "Go pack a few things, baby. I'm taking you somewhere safer. Gina, I think you should go stay with your parents tonight."

She nodded.

"When are they coming to connect the phone?"

"Supposed to Monday."

"I don't think you girls should be here until they do."

Kate closed the kitchen door gently behind her. Dan sat with his elbow on the table, chin propped in his hand. She spoke barely above a whisper. "You miserable son of a bitch."

He hardened the set of his jaw, but didn't look at her.

"How in the name of God could you do that to our little girl?"

He began tapping the fingertips of his free hand on his place mat.

"I saw her, Dan. I saw what you did to her."

He dropped his hand from his chin and raised his eyes to meet hers. "I slapped her, is all. She had it coming."

"Slapped her?" She began pacing back and forth on her side of the table. "Slapped her with what?"

"Alright, so maybe I hit her a little harder than I intended." He rubbed his temple.

"A little?" Kate choked, tears burning her eyes. "Just a little?"

"Now, don't get hysterical. I'm sorry if I left a red mark. I'm sure it will be gone tomorrow. Anyway, where is she?"

"A red mark." She began to shake. "A red mark. She's got a swollen, bloody lip and her face is fucking purple!" She heaved the salt shaker across the room so hard it left a dent in the wall before crashing to the floor. "There's no way in hell I'm telling you where she is."

Bobby signed the motel register Martin Roberts. Martin was his middle name. He took the room key and parked in back of the building so his car wasn't visible from the street. He took Jules' suitcase out of the back and carried it into their room. "Stay here and rest, baby. I'm going across the road to get us something to eat. Keep the door locked. I'll take the key."

"Okay," she said, lying down on top of the covers.

It was easy enough to get food here, but finding something for Jules might not be so easy. The blow had cut the inside of her lip against her teeth. The motel didn't have a restaurant, so no room service. He passed up the burger joint and tried the diner. Luckily they offered a few take-out items. He got a burger, fries, and coffee for himself. For Jules he got a chocolate shake and the meatloaf dinner, figuring she should at least be able to handle the mashed potatoes and gravy. He sprinted back across the highway.

He hated to wake her. She hadn't even bothered to take her shoes off, she was so exhausted. "Come on, honey, you need to try to eat something."

She sat up groggily and scooted back to rest against the headboard. The night was growing chilly, so he turned up the heater. On the small black and white TV he found some old Western, and sat in the armchair to eat. The movie provided distraction, a small sense of normalcy. Jules made a valiant attempt at her meal, but he could see frustration and fatigue catching up to her.

When she'd eaten all she could manage, she got up, poured the little packets of salt into a glass of warm water and rinsed her mouth, then shut herself in the bathroom. Bobby squeezed a little of her toothpaste onto his fingertip and cleaned his teeth the best he could. He had nothing of his own with him but the clothes on his back and a sweater he'd tossed in the back seat a few days ago. He had felt it imperative to get Jules away quickly and to not stop by his house first. They'd had enough encounters for one night. He would make do.

He was toweling his face dry when she came out, carrying her clothes, dressed in a white flannel nightgown, subdued, quiet, beautiful despite the damage. She dropped her clothes into the open suitcase, turned down the covers, and got into bed, pulling her pale, small feet in. He turned off the vanity light, turned off the TV, hung the Do Not Disturb sign on the outer knob, and bolted the door. He stripped to his underwear and climbed in, facing her. She smelled softly of soap and steam. "You warm enough?" he asked.

"I will be in a minute," she said.

Nestling closer, he brushed back her bangs and kissed her forehead, damp strands of hair clinging to his fingers. "I love you," he said.

"I love you too," she whispered, managing a slight smile. She cupped her hand around his face a moment, then withdrew it, tucking her arms up against her chest and closing her eyes. He stroked her head until she fell asleep. Sleep wasn't going to come so easily for him. As he looked at her bruises, at what she had suffered just to be near him, it tore his heart. What had he ever done to deserve such faith? He sat up to snap off the lamp, leaned back against the headboard and cried.

Dan Greene sat alone in the church pew, the early light streaming through the simple squares of stained glass. Kate had refused to go with him. No one at church seemed to know anything had happened. When they asked about Kate, he just said she wasn't feeling well. He wasn't feeling very good himself, and the service was running long. He just wanted some kind of quick resolution, forgiveness, he supposed. He gave a restless sigh, his eyes wandering around the ceiling, the candle flames. The preacher was going on about gossip, raising his hand and bringing it down with each point, as if pounding the air. "Gossip," he proclaimed, "doesn't just harm your neighbor. Gossip will destroy *you*. It will harden your heart to good. It will make you look for evil where there is none. It will make you speak evil where there is none. It will make you hear evil where there is none. Gossip will make a person turn against their own friends. Gossip will turn a man against his wife, and a father against his children." Dan squirmed in his seat. His tie felt like a noose. He reached up to loosen it a little.

Bobby woke around 10. When he opened his eyes and turned to look at the clock, it took him a few seconds to realize where he was. His movements woke Jules. "Hi, baby," he smiled and smoothed back her hair.

"Hi," she smiled back.

"You're beautiful," he said.

"Oh, I'm sure," she laughed dryly. "How bad is it?"

"It's– colorful."

"Great."

He pulled her close. "Hell of a way to spend our first night together in a real bed."

"Yeah, not exactly how I'd imagined it would be."

"We'll have to make up for it."

"I'm sure we will."

"You hungry?" he asked.

"Yeah."

"You feel like going out, or you want me to just go get us something?"

"I want to go."

"Let me get a shower first, okay?"

"Sure. Wake me up when you get out."

Bobby stood with a towel wrapped around his waist, arranging his hand-washed underwear and socks on the heater vent to dry. "Is that what you're gonna wear?" her voice came from the bed.

"I'll have to wear a shirt and shoes with it," he deadpanned, "or they won't serve me." He turned to shake out yesterday's suit pants, and she was sitting up in bed, stretching. "Don't look," he grinned, untucking the end of his towel, knowing she would anyway. He let it drop, watching her eyes sweep down his body as he pulled on his pants and carefully zipped them.

"What are you doing?" she laughed.

"Unlike you," he replied, "I don't have another pair, and," he pulled a pair of lace panties from her suitcase and held them up, "I don't think these would fit me."

"I bet they'd look cute, though," she snickered. "So, you're just going without any."

"Don't have much choice, do I, until those dry? It's Sunday. All the stores are closed."

"You know I'll be thinking about that all day."

"Dirty girl," he teased. "Can I borrow your deodorant?"

"Borrow whatever you need, but I forgot my razor," she said, getting out of bed and going to the bathroom.

He was standing by the suitcase, putting on his shirt, when she came out and pulled her gown off over her head. His eyes followed the curves of her back. Bare except for pale pink panties, she turned to face him, and oh he wanted her. She walked toward the suitcase, but instead of reaching for her clothes, she reached for him, running her hand up the front of his pants. "I thought you wanted breakfast," he smiled.

"Let's make it lunch."

For once in their lives, they were secluded and anonymous, with all the time in the world. He wished it could last.

When hunger for food would no longer be denied, they dressed for the outside world. Jules leaned into the mirror, patting on extra make-up to try to dim the marks.

"I hope nobody thinks I did that to you," he said.

They walked across the two-lane highway to the diner. It eased him to see her eating scrambled eggs, carefully chewing small bites of ham. The swelling had started to go down and her spirits were starting to pick up. "Want to get out and do something today?" he asked. "We could try to find a movie theatre."

"I'd like that."

He looked at his watch. "Shit. I should call Terry."

Back at the room, he stretched his legs out on the bed and picked up the phone. Jules searched through the newspaper for the theatre listings. "Terry. Hey, it's Bobby."

"Where the hell are you, man? I called your house and your folks said you never came home. The guys are here waiting."

"Outside Elizabethtown. Just go on and practice without me, or call it off if you want. I can't be there."

"E-town? What the hell are you doing there?"

"Talk to Gina, and keep an eye out. She should be at her parents'. I had to get Jules away someplace safe."

"What do you mean 'safe?'"

He sighed. "Her old man had a go at her, hit her in the face. She'll be alright, but... "

"Holy Christ, man!"

"Listen, if you need to get ahold of me, here's the number." He read it off the phone dial. "We're in 116, under the name Martin Roberts. Just keep this quiet. Nobody knows where we are and I want to keep it that way."

"You can trust me, man. Christ, I'm so sorry."

Bobby hung up and put his arm around Jules' shoulder. "See anything good in there?"

"There's a 3:00 matinée at this place," she pointed to a listing. "*The Graduate*."

In the dark of the theatre, no one could stare at them and speculate. They could snuggle close and just rest and be entertained. Though they both enjoyed the film, as they stepped out hand in hand into the glare of daylight, Jules turned to him and said, "Geez, is there any such a thing as an uncomplicated romance?"

"I don't know, baby," he laughed. "I don't know. But rest assured I am not sleeping with your mom." Jules burst out laughing, and it did his heart good to see her amused.

They strolled up the street, window shopping, till they reached a park, where they enjoyed signs of spring. Small flowers in the slender grass, new leaves, mating birds, the smell of damp earth. They sat down on a bench and she hid the bruised side of her face against his shoulder, away from the gaze of the outside world. The low sun thinned by fine clouds turned from pale gold to soft orange as it sank behind the trees.

They dined in a small, dark restaurant where Jules could soften crusty bread in French onion soup and he could indulge in a steak. Custard pie and coffee topped it all off. He held her hand on the tabletop, and she twined her ankle around his. "I should go to work tomorrow," he said.

"Okay."

"I don't know where I should take you. I don't want you to be alone."

"School."

"Are you sure, baby?"

"I've got to go back sometime, and I don't want to get behind."

"One day won't matter, will it?"

165

"Maybe not, but I'll be surrounded by people there, by my friends. I'll be safe."

"We'll have to get a really early start."

Back at the room they made love again, tender, playful, lingering in the luxury of time. No need to be modest or quiet or watchful. Before sleep, they showered together, soft suds, warm water, warm, smooth skin. "You wear this in the shower?" she asked, slipping her finger under the slack of the bracelet she had given him, sliding her thumb across the word LOVE.

"I've never taken it off since you put it on me, not for anything."

With cautious fingers he washed her face. He so wanted to kiss her glistening mouth, but he didn't want to hurt her. Hesitantly he leaned down, just gently brushing his lips against hers. She didn't flinch, and as he bent toward her again, she reached up to sink her fingers in his wet hair. Between his lips he took her top lip, running the tip of his tongue across its contours. He felt her tongue move across his bottom lip, her mouth opening to invite him. Slowly, delicately he traced the edges of her teeth, tasted the awful tang of her wounds. She coaxed him deeper, a careful interlacing, her hands kneading the solicitous tension from his neck and shoulders. Deep peace flooded him.

That early alarm felt like a stab. He reached blindly to slap at the button to turn it off, squeezed his eyes shut hard before opening them in the still dark room. He stretched up to turn on the lamp, bracing himself against its rude brightness. He turned to Jules, squeezed her bare shoulder and kissed her cheek. "We gotta get up, baby, if you want to get to school."

The air was cool on their nakedness, the clock prodding, so they quickly dressed. Bobby's underwear was dry, but quite stiff. Instead of his shirt, he put on the sweater, buttoning it up. It was a little low on his chest, but it would have to do. He pulled on his suit pants and jacket, the sleeves tight with the sweater underneath. As Jules got ready for school, he dashed across the highway for paper cups of coffee. Though she hadn't asked, he picked up a sweet roll for Jules. He would have time to eat something at home, but she would be going straight to school and he didn't want her to go hungry.

Groggy, with his makeshift outfit and two days' growth of whiskers, Martin Roberts checked out looking decidedly less respectable than he had when he checked in. They were on the road before the sun had breached the horizon. Jules dozed. Bobby wished they could just go someplace else, someplace far away. Who knew what complications awaited them back home?

They stopped at her apartment just long enough to leave her suitcase and pick up her books. "You might be a little late," he said.

"It's okay."

With a quick kiss, he dropped her off in front of Midvale High, waited until she was inside the building, then drove home to get ready for work.

The halls had mostly emptied when Jules walked in, the bell for class having rung 10 minutes ago. She knew she was supposed to report to the office for a pass if she was this late, but she didn't want to waste the time, didn't want to go there. She walked into home room, clutching her books to her chest, head tilted so that her hair fell over her bruised cheek. She felt all eyes turning to her as she slipped into her seat and her hands began to tremble as she set down her books.

"Miss Greene, do you have a pass?" Mrs. Lewis asked.

"No, ma'am," she said quietly. When she looked up, her hair fell back. She heard someone quietly gasp. Someone else murmured.

Mrs. Lewis' mouth opened slightly and her eyes registered shock. "Miss Greene, may I have a word?" She held her hand out, indicating she wanted Jules to get up and follow her. Jules raised her head, mustering what dignity she could, and followed her teacher out of the room. Mrs. Lewis closed the door behind them. "What has happened, child? Have you been in an accident?"

Jules was tempted to say yes and just let it go at that, but no. Why should she lie to cover for him? She shook her head.

"Were you in a fight? Did a boy do this to you?"

Jules met her eyes. "No." She took a deep, shaky breath. "My dad."

Mrs. Lewis closed her eyes and shook her head. "Might I ask why?"

"I danced with Bobby Lott at the prom."

"He did this to you over a dance?"

She nodded. "I moved out Saturday."

"Wait here." Mrs. Lewis stepped back into the classroom, leaving the door open. "Tom, please monitor the class for me," she called a student up to sit at her desk. In a moment she came back out, bringing Jules her books. "Let's go to the office."

Her plight was laid out for Principal Sammons, her new address noted. She was to give her new number once her phone was connected.

Staff would be privately alerted to watch out for her. There was some debate between Mr. Sammons and Assistant Principal Dean as to whether her father should be confronted.

Mrs. Lewis took her to the school nurse, who confirmed contusions and a laceration of the bottom lip, but did not suspect any fractures and found no loosening of the teeth. "You were smart to ice it," Nurse Dunn said.

Mrs. Lewis escorted Jules back to home room, reclaimed authority from Tom, and picked up where she had left off. Jules tried to stoically endure the questioning glances.

Gina rushed to her at her locker after class. "You okay? I can't believe you actually came here today."

"I'm okay," Jules said, but she was fighting tears.

"Terry said y'all went to E-Town."

"Yeah. We drove back early this morning. Bobby needed to be at work today. I didn't really know where else to go but here, and anyway, I've got a Math test."

"I'm sure you could make that up."

Jules felt a gentle hand on her shoulder. She turned to see Dwitty, who blinked, puckered his lips and blew a silent whistle. "Wow. Terry told me to look after you. So," he smiled, "I am your devoted servant."

Jules smiled and Dwitty hugged her.

Word got around school quickly. Jules' friends rallied quietly around her. She insisted to Mr. Brown that she was indeed alright to take the Math test today. She felt frail, a little sick, tired of stares and questions, but she made it through the day. But as she walked to Gina's car, she heard a voice. "Julia."

Bitterness and fear mingled as she turned a sharp and wary eye, shook back her hair for him to see his handiwork. Dan Greene winced, then stepped forward. She stepped back. "Julia," he said gently, "I'm sorry." She didn't speak. "You don't need to be afraid of me. I won't bother you anymore. Go on and live your life."

She pressed her lips together and nodded, and suddenly Dwitty was at her shoulder, with Gina and Tricia fast on his heels.

"I'm going." Dan held up a dismissive hand at them, walked to his car, and drove away.

At the apartment on Mary Street the girls waited tensely as the man from the phone company tested the connection, put tools back in his canvas bag, and let himself out. "Should be all set now," he nodded to

Gina and left. Gina quickly bolted the door.

"Should I call Janice, have her tell Mom that I'm back?" Jules asked.

"I don't know. Maybe. She might be worried."

"I didn't call anyone while we were away. I don't know if she even knows I was gone anywhere."

"Your mom might not know that your dad was at the school."

"That's true. I'll call later. I think Janice works."

Gina took an Orange Crush out of the fridge. There was a gentle knock on the door. "Girls?" a woman's voice inquired. "Girls, are you there? It's Nora Lott."

Jules opened the door.

"Oh, child," Nora shook her head and reached a tender hand up to brush back Jules' hair and examine her face. "No wonder Bobby took you away."

"Come on in," Jules quietly invited.

Nora stooped to pick up a large paper bag. "I brought you girls some things," she said, carrying it in and setting it on the table.

"Thank you," Gina said.

"You should get some vinegar on that," Nora said to Jules. "It helps bruises go away faster. Do you have some?"

"No."

"Have Bobby bring you some. I assume he'll be by later."

"Yes."

"Just plain white vinegar. Dab it on with a cotton ball every night when you go to bed and again when you get up."

"Yes, ma'am. I will," Jules said meekly.

"I was worried, I won't lie, when Bobby didn't come home. Two nights. He should have called. He didn't have to say where you were."

"I'm sorry. He should have," Jules said. "He was just scared for me, I think."

"We wouldn't have given you away. Where are you staying tonight?"

"Here," Jules said. "Unless something happens to make me change my mind."

"Her dad was waiting after school," Gina said.

Nora's expression hardened.

"He said he won't bother me anymore," Jules said.

"Well I hope to God he doesn't," Nora declared. "Child," her voice softened and she stroked the top of Jules' head, "If you ever need a place to stay, you'll be safe with us, and you're very welcome."

"Thank you."

When Nora had left, Jules and Gina put away the generous bag of groceries she had brought, made a number of phone calls, including to Janice, and began preparing supper, trying to deal with limited kitchenware and a few missing ingredients, as well as lack of experience.

"You should have taken Home Ec," Gina said, stirring the spaghetti sauce.

"It will be fine. Just fish some of that burnt stuff out. I got distracted, is all."

"Well, sometimes I think Terry would eat anything that didn't move, and maybe some that did," Gina laughed.

Jules strained the pasta and poured it into a bowl while Gina tore up lettuce. There was a knock. "Vinegar delivery."

Jules let him in.

"Hey, baby," he smiled, a paper sack in one arm, a knapsack over his shoulder, and the other arm behind his back. "I brought your vinegar," he said, walking in and setting the bag on the table, letting the knapsack drop onto a chair. "And these." From behind his back he produced a bouquet of brightly colored zinnias. "I'm sorry they're not exploding and crawling around like the ones in England."

She laughed, putting her nose to one. "Thank you." She kissed him. "Let me put them in something."

"Oh, those are pretty," Gina said. "I like the purple ones."

Bobby began unpacking the bag – coffee, cream, a loaf of bread, a jar of peanut butter. Jules filled a tall glass with water and arranged the flowers in it. As she turned to set them in the middle of the table, he picked up the bottle of vinegar, twisted off the cap, and took a hearty swig. He shook his head vigorously and grinned, and she burst out laughing.

"What?" Gina turned, just as Bobby lunged after Jules, grabbing her around the waist.

"Kiss me," he growled, and she shrieked as he backed her up against the sink.

"Honestly, you two!" Gina laughed, snatching the salad out of harm's way as Bobby engaged Jules in a pungent kiss.

There was another knock, and Gina let Terry in. "I brought a contribution," he said, plunking a 6-pack of Black Label on the counter. "Jesus Christ," he said when he saw Jules.

"You should have seen it yesterday," Bobby said. "I'll take one of those now." He and Terry each opened up a can and sat down on the couch while the girls finished cooking and set the table.

"Fucked up bastard to do that," Terry said.

"Price of a dance with me."

"I can see why you got her out of here."

"I'm not budging from here tonight, I'll tell you that."

"Good. I didn't like the thought of Gina and her being alone. I thought about bringing Bruno over, but Gina said they can't have pets here."

"You can't stay?"

"I gotta be to work at 6."

"Gina coming to California?"

"She says no, she can't afford the time off work and she doesn't want to give up this place."

"That's too bad."

"Jules coming?"

"No way I'd leave her behind. She really wants to anyway. She's never been there either."

"Y'all deserve a vacation."

Jerry had a friend in Los Angeles who ran an independent recording studio and label out of the downstairs of his house. He had 4-track capability, whereas Bruce could only offer 2, and he was looking to sign hot, new bands. "I can get you some dates up and down the coast, too," Jerry told the band. "If we can break you out there and make it stick, you'll have it made." Of course, this would cost more money, and Bobby was hesitant about the band shouldering too much expense. His destitution in Cincinnati was still fresh in his mind. It was in their interest to keep expenses down, and to record quickly, so they strove to use the time leading up to the trip to write and rehearse, and make what extra money they could. Of course, whenever they played live, Jerry got a hefty cut, so a heavy schedule was fine with him.

As they sat down to supper, Jules and Gina each had a beer, leaving the last two for the guys. In mismatched chairs, eating off the surviving dishes of an old set Gina's mom was willing to part with, they chatted and laughed and relaxed. The girls felt safer with the phone working, and knowing they wouldn't be alone tonight. Jules tried to think of happy things, of her freedom, of having not just Bobby back, but her old friends. She tried not to think of that strange blank space in the center of her father's eyes.

The girls refused to do the dishes that night. Terry couldn't stay late, and Gina wasn't going to waste time in the kitchen that she could be spending with him. They put the radio on and lounged in the living room. Jules and Bobby retired to leave them alone, and to be alone. Jules washed her face for the night, then dabbed on vinegar, as Nora had instructed.

"You smell like a pickle," Bobby teased, and kissed her. "Taste like one, too."

"Does this really work?"

"It seems to. Mom's done that all our lives. She said it soaks in and thins the blood."

"The smell sure stings my eyes."

"Close them," he said softly, kissing her eyelids. He led her down onto the mattress with him, where they stretched out on top of the bedding. They began unbuttoning each other's shirts.

"Do you think they know what we're doing, my parents?" she asked.

"They know. And they know there's not a damn thing they can do about it." *Serves that miserable bastard right,* he thought. *Think about this tonight, Dan Greene, while you're lying in your bed. Think about me fucking your daughter all night. I wish I could see you sweating right now.*

When Gina came out, yawning, to the kitchen the next morning, Jules, in her aqua housecoat, had made a pot of coffee and was frying a couple eggs. "Where's Sunshine Superman?" Gina asked.

"He went home to put on his Clark Kent suit for work."

"You two should get married."

Jules plopped the eggs on a plate and took a piece of bread out of the wrapper. "You and I should get a toaster." She sat down at the table. "Things need to settle down a little first. I've got school to finish and we've got this trip to California coming up. Maybe when we get back. What about you? You two seem pretty cozy these days."

"Well," she shrugged, "he hasn't said anything."

"And if he did?"

Gina considered a moment. "I'd say yes."

"Son, hand me the wrench, will you?" Rob Lott reached out from under the depths of the kitchen sink cabinet. Bobby sat on the floor beside his father's hip, reaching in to hold a flashlight. Since he couldn't see what Rob was doing, or where the beam was directed, he felt the occasional adjustment of his hand. "Going out tonight?" Rob asked.

"Don't know yet."

"Planning to see Jules?"

"If she's got time. She and Gina are studying for some big test."

"Alright, I'll take that," he pulled the flashlight from Bobby's hand. "Turn the water on good and hard."

Bobby stood up and ran the faucet, waiting.

"Okay, that's good. Shut it off." Rob slid out, tossing a damp rag on the floor and wiping his brow with the back of his wrist. "Let's leave a bucket under that, just to be sure."

Bobby squatted down and began putting tools back in the toolbox, the routine of the years.

"Son," Rob said, "You're a man now, and I know you've got your reasons, but I want you to think about a couple of things."

Bobby took a slow breath. He could feel a lecture coming on.

"I know you were just doing what you thought best, but you had your mother worried. You should have called home over the weekend."

He closed the toolbox lid and latched it. "I'm sorry."

"You should apologize to her."

"I will."

Rob, still on the floor, looked past Bobby's shoulder through the doorway. "Sit down, son." Bobby sat down on the floor, facing his father, who picked up the rag and wiped his hands as he talked. "Let me put this plainly. You need to start sleeping at home. You're going to damage her reputation. That may not seem important to you. I know times are changing. But it counts for something in this town. You want people to respect her, don't you?"

"Yes."

"She's got her schoolwork to do. Don't distract her too much from that. And there's your little sister to think about. You should set a better example for her."

Bobby nodded.

"Don't fall behind on your practicing, either. You've got that tour coming up. You want to do your best for that, don't you?"

He nodded again.

Rob got to his feet and offered Bobby a hand. When Bobby was standing, Rob squeezed his hand and patted him on the shoulder with his free hand. "I am proud of you, son. I don't always agree with the things you do, but I guess we all have to sort things out for ourselves. Just be careful. Be good to her."

"I will," Bobby said.

Rob gave Bobby's hand a firm shake before releasing him. "And, Bobby," he said as Bobby turned to leave. Bobby stopped and looked back at his dad. "Might be time to think about marrying her."

Chapter 15

Friday night The Rebelles opened for The Rooks Parliament at the Happen Inn, a hip, new teen club that had opened in Midvale in an old storefront the previous fall. The club owner had decided to shift The Rooks from Thursdays to this prime slot to draw bigger crowds. Jules hadn't been to a rock show since she'd gotten back from England, and the only times she'd seen a band at all in that time were that unpleasant dance in the fall and the prom. She had yet to see The Rooks play their typical club show. They had played a show Wednesday night, but it was an invitation only fraternity dance, so Jules and Gina couldn't go.

The Happen Inn had a large dance floor, and the owner had sunk some money into good stage lighting and a loud, clear PA system. Midvale's teens rewarded his investment by turning up in droves, particularly on weekends, and the word spread to surrounding towns. Saturday nights he was able to bring in some bigger name talent from the cities and out of state.

As the band brought their gear in, the girls amused themselves, hitting the refreshment stand and chatting with friends. The guys came out to join them just before the show started, except Bobby. Jules figured he'd be along soon.

The club lights dimmed and all eyes turned to the dark stage as a slow "da-dum... da-dum" began on the bass. The stage lights rose on The Rebelles just as their voices in harmony sang, "He-e-e-e-e..."

"He told me that he loved me, and like a fool I believed him from the start," Alene crooned, changing the gender of the Monkees tune "She," slowly moving her hips to the beat. They were dressed in tight, black capri pants and shocking pink peasant blouses, and they certainly had everyone's attention. Gina looked at Jules. Jules looked at Terry, his mouth agape.

"They've been practicing," Gina remarked.

"I'll say."

"I bet they've got every guy in this place, um, you know..."

Jules laughed. "Including your boyfriend," she said in Gina's ear.

Then, at the bridge, the sound of an organ swooped in with a glissando and a light came up on Bobby, taking the solo on his Farfisa, playing with barely controlled fire and a smile on his face, the instrument swaying under the force of a series of staccato chords. Something told Jules the party was just getting started.

When the song was over, he was off the stage and she was in his arms, feeling heat and energy radiating from his chest. She turned to lean her back against him and watch the band. They went right into "(I'm Not Your) Steppin' Stone," and had the club rocking.

"We want to welcome back an old friend tonight," Carol said at the song's conclusion. "She's seen some hard times, but now she's back in the fold. Miss Julia Greene!" Jules was aware of brighter light suddenly upon her, and Bobby squeezed her tighter, then let her go as Carol extended a hand. "Come on up."

"Go," Bobby said in her ear. "Do it. Do it for me."

Do what?

Carol pulled her up on stage and led her to Alene, who said, "Let's sing your song, 'Harvest Moonlight.'"

Jules felt the blood drain out of her face. "No. No, I can't. Not for all these people."

"It's what your man wants. You can't let him down."

She glanced back at Bobby.

"Just share the mic with me. I'll sing it with you, okay?" Alene said.

Jules didn't have a chance to argue any further. Alene nodded to Nita and they started playing. She felt a little sheltered standing with Alene, rather than out in front on her own like she had been at the party. Her voice felt thin from lack of use, but Alene was there singing the first line along with her. After that, however, Alene took a harmony part. Jules relaxed as best she could, focused on keeping her lead part and not falling into unison with Alene. What she heard coming back to her through the PA was surprisingly pleasing, though the sound of her own voice was a shock, so different from how it sounded in her head. "I don't want any other. Don't dance with any other." She sang those lines straight to Bobby, to his soft smile.

When the song ended, Jules was surprised at the applause, actually felt embarrassed by it. Bobby lifted her down from the stage and kissed her as he set her feet back on the ground.

"This is our new single," Carol announced. "It's called 'Stray Boy.'"

Jules knew "Stray Boy" from the latter days of The Deep Sea. It had begun:

> If I follow you home, will you keep me?
> I'm a stray boy.
> Can I sleep on your floor, will you feed me?
> I'm a stray boy.

With The Rebelles at the helm it took on a whole new dimension, especially with Alene working a sexy growl in now and then, and the girls harmonizing the alternate lines and drawing out the word "boy." They had reworked the lyrics to give it a girl's perspective.

> He followed me home, Ma. Can I keep him?
> He's a stray boy.
> He can sleep on my floor, yeah, I'll feed him.

"I don't think she's talking about dog food," Jules elbowed Gina.

"You did great," Gina said. "I'm proud of you."

"I'm not cut out for the limelight."

"Nonsense. You did know he's recording the show, didn't you?"

"Who is?"

"I am," Bobby grinned.

"Tell me you're joking," Jules said.

"It's no joke, baby. I was going to tape our set anyway, but I thought I might as well get 'Stray Boy', too, so I just decided to do the whole thing. And now I'll have you singing your song, any time I want to listen."

"That's not fair," she said. "I don't have you singing."

"You've got me singing back-up," he reminded her.

"Big deal. I can barely hear you."

"That's because I like to actually sell records," he laughed, sliding his arms around her from behind, rocking her back and forth to the music.

When The Rebelles had finished their set, Bobby leaned down and said in Jules' ear, "I gotta go play." As she turned toward him, he kissed her full on the mouth before heading to the stage with Terry. She became aware that she and Gina were being assessed by a group of girls front and center. She tossed her hair back and enjoyed the jealous attention.

Neither the single nor the prom really prepared her for what she was about to see tonight. Here at the Happen Inn, the band played what they wanted to play, how they wanted to play it. They rarely played covers, and when they did, it was to suit themselves, not pacify dancers who wanted popular tunes. Their musicianship was of a higher caliber than The Deep See's, and they were tight and well-rehearsed, especially for so new a band. Bobby had quickly developed a reputation in the scene as being driven and uncompromising, a force to be reckoned with musically. Here their sound was less teen pop and more serious, more experimental. At times it took on dream-like qualities; other times it howled with raw emotion. They sounded like no one else in Midvale. "My God, Gina,"

Jules said between songs. "They sound incredible."

With a soft roll on the cymbal and a delicate, ringing riff on Terry's new Rickenbacker guitar, a sad melody began to take shape. Miles' gentle bass counter-balanced the flute-like tones of Bobby's organ. Terry began to sing in a quiet, unaffected voice. "Vanilla snow to wrap me in. A blanket blue for all our sin."

Jules' hand flew up to cover her mouth. With the other she grasped Gina's arm, her eyes clouding with tears. "You okay?" Gina asked.

"The words," Jules said, sliding her hand down to grasp her chin. "I wrote those words."

"Didn't you know about this song?"

She let go of Gina's arm.

"Oh, they didn't play it at the prom," Gina remembered. "But didn't he ever tell you?"

Jules slowly shook her head and covered her mouth again as Bobby looked down at her. Gina patted her gently between the shoulder blades.

People swayed in place. A few couples slow-danced. As the lyrics ended, the band took the song out with a long instrumental passage, Terry and Bobby weaving their separate melody lines around and through each other in a subtly shifting pattern that came back around to its original form at the conclusion.

When the applause died down, Bobby said into his mic, "Terry, I think I made someone cry."

"It's all you ever seem to do," Terry replied. Girls squealed.

"This is for you, baby." Bobby ripped into the intro. It definitely sounded thinner on the Farfisa, but took on an odd, haunting quality. Miles filled out the sound with an intricate bass line as Stephen built almost an R&B rhythm. Terry wailed, "All I ever seem to do is make you cry." The crowd was cheering louder than they had for "Sidewalk Girl." The little bunch of girls who had been watching Jules earlier were bouncing up and down, emitting occasional shrieks. Terry seemed to have a hard time keeping a straight face whenever he looked at them. He turned to Gina to sing, "I want to take you away tonight, hold you tight, hold you tight."

Stephen threw in an interesting, shuffling fill before the second verse.

"All I ever seem to do is make you cry." It was Bobby belting it out now for all he was worth!

The girls squealed. Jules grinned and moved to the music. He squeezed his eyes shut, reaching for the notes, and she pressed her hand to her heart. *He damn well better be rolling tape,* she thought.

Can't you see this is killing me too?
Ah, baby, I don't ever wanna lose you.
I'm gonna take you away someday,
Come what may,
Come what may.

Stephen kicked the bass drum for five hard beats and Bobby attacked the keys in a manic, swooping solo, fingers galloping up and down the board then stabbing at staccatos. He threw his head back for a screaming, sustained chord at the end. The crowd cheered and yelled and clapped, and Bobby, dripping sweat, surveyed the room with a wide smile.

"I'd say," Gina said to Jules, "that there are at least a dozen girls here who hate your guts right now."

Jules laughed. "And yours, too, I'll bet."

"Yeah, but Bobby really wears his heart on his sleeve for you."

The band caught their breath, had something to drink. As Terry tuned his guitar he asked the audience, "What do you want to hear?" People shouted various things, a jumble of suggestions. "What was that?" he asked a guy near the front. "'Time Tonight?'" He turned to Bobby. "What do you say? Give it a shot?"

"Yes!" Jules yelled.

Bobby laughed. "I think we better." There was a quick conference with Miles and Stephen.

"We'll try, but it's been a long time, and these two guys have never played it," Terry waved toward the rhythm section. They limped into it, with Bobby coaching, but caught on quickly. It took Jules back to the beginning, back to the park pavilion, their first dance, first kiss.

They played a couple more re-worked Deep See tunes and called it a night. Jules and Gina went for Cokes while the band consolidated their gear, which they would pack into the car just before they left. There was time for refreshments, to sign some autographs and talk with a few fans. Bobby put his arm around Jules. "What did you think?" he asked.

"It was beautiful," she said. "This whole night–" She was at a loss.

"Welcome to my world, baby," he said, pulling her tight to his side. "It's your world, too."

For the next few weeks, Jules and Bobby worked hard, she at final projects and exams, he at playing as many shows as the band could manage, as well as their regular jobs. She and Gina went along to see the band when they could, and Bobby and Terry spent what little spare time they had visiting the girls on Mary Street, occasionally staying overnight.

Jules, Gina, Tricia, and Dwitty could not have been happier to graduate. June 1st was sunny and hot. "Two weeks!" Tricia grinned, hand in hand with Dwitty as they joined their classmates assembling in the hallway, her modest diamond engagement ring catching the sunlight from the windows.

"I'm so, so excited for you," Jules smiled, and she and Gina took turns hugging her.

"She just can't wait to enslave me," Dwitty teased.

The gym was stuffy, despite the big box fans blowing from the sides. Principal Sammons, in his suit coat and snug tie, seemed to be melting in the stage lights, happy to turn the mic over to the other speakers and get a break in the wings.

Jules hadn't seen her family yet. She fought the urge to look around. She'd seen Bobby, and knew that Sissy and their parents were there. "Do you think he'll be here?" Bobby had asked.

"I don't know," she had replied.

When she walked up on the stage to take her diploma, she looked quickly out at the audience, but the lights were too bright in her eyes.

With the ceremony over, tossed caps retrieved, everyone left their alphabetical order to congratulate their friends and greet the cascade of guests coming out of their seats. Jules spotted her parents coming down from the stands. She waited, approaching them cautiously when they reached the bottom of the steps. Despite everyone around her, she felt exposed.

"Congratulations, honey," Kate smiled and gave Jules a hug and a kiss on the cheek.

"Thanks, Mom. " She squeezed her mother, trying to draw some strength from her.

When they stepped back from each other, Dan offered his hand. Her body tightened as she allowed his brief handshake, the first physical contact she had had with him since he had slapped her into the wall. The same hand, she realized. She shivered, despite the heat. "You managed to finish school, at least," he said.

"There was never any question," she defended.

"I'm surprised. You seem so bent on throwing your life away," he muttered, shoving his hands in his pockets.

"Dan," Kate laid her hand on his arm a moment, then took it away to pull an envelope from her pocketbook. "This is for you, honey," she handed it to Jules.

"Gramma and Grampa couldn't come?" Jules asked her mother.

"Your Grampa wasn't feeling well. I'm sorry, honey."

"Nothing serious, I hope."

"No, honey, just a stomach bug."

"I'll call them later."

"Why don't you let us take you out to dinner anyway?" Kate smiled.

"Thanks, Mom, but–" She saw Dan's eyes snap to glaring attention and felt a strong arm come to rest across her back.

"Congratulations, sweetheart," Bobby's voice said gently, and he kissed the top of her head, but she could feel the tension in his muscles, in the way his ribs inflated against her side. She couldn't see his eyes, but she could guess, judging by the cold steel of her father's.

"Hello, Bobby," Kate said.

"Mrs. Greene," he acknowledged her.

Jules looked to her mother, who took a deep breath and flashed a smile. "Well, honey, I guess we'd better be going now. Give me a call, okay?"

"I will."

Kate nudged Dan, twice, and they turned and walked away.

Back at the apartment, before changing clothes for a night of parties, Jules opened the envelope her mother had given her. Inside was a nice card, which her mother had signed as being from "Mom and Dad," having written that they were proud of her. It contained a $50 bill, a sum larger than Jules had expected, with a little note in her mother's handwriting that said, "You know better than I do what you need." Jules would put it, along with the money her grandparents and Aunt Nat had sent, in her bank account, resolving not to touch it, even for the California trip, unless she absolutely had to. She and Gina had paid the June rent, and she had already been setting money aside to pay Gina her share of July's before leaving town. If she was careful, she would have enough out of her remaining two paychecks to make up the difference and have some travel money. She had spoken for extra hours at Shearer's, covering for a co-worker who was going on vacation.

Dwitty and Tricia were married the morning of June 15th, the day before The Rooks Parliament were to leave for California. In her knee-length, white lace dress and white marabou-trimmed short veil, Tricia looked like a modern princess. With Terry as Best Man, and Tricia's sister Stella as Maid of Honor, Tricia and Dwitty took their vows quietly and solemnly, and sealed their new life with a kiss. "They're gonna have the cutest kids," Gina said to Jules.

At the reception, Tricia tossed her bouquet over her shoulder, but it flew straight to Jules as surely as if she had aimed it. "Ho! You know what *that* means, old man!" Terry shook his finger at Bobby, who was settling in at the piano.

"What makes you think she'd have me?" Bobby laughed, and began to play. He hadn't had time to memorize all the special pieces they wanted, so Jules laid her flowers on the piano and stood at his shoulder to turn pages for him. Talk and laughter rose and fell around the room. People walked by. But Jules focused on Bobby, enjoying his playing, listening for him to softly say, "Turn."

A lady brought them champagne punch and slices of cake, setting them on a little table beside the piano. Tony signaled Bobby to stop at the end of the song he was playing. Time for speeches, for toasts. Jules sat down to rest on the bench beside Bobby until he took her hand, kissed it, and said, "Back to work."

As Tricia danced with her father, Jules grew pensive, nearly missing Bobby's cue, then fumbling with the page corner. "Sorry," she whispered.

"It's okay," he said. "Just one more." At the end of that next song, he smiled up at her. "Thanks, baby. I know the rest."

Jules ate her cake and drank her punch, then went for a refill. She smiled at Tricia dancing with a small boy, at Gina dancing with Terry. As she neared the refreshment table, someone took her hand. "Hey, good lookin'," Dwitty grinned. "Come and dance."

She set her cup down and he led her out onto the floor. "I'm so happy for you two," she smiled. "Going anywhere for your honeymoon?"

"Well, we both have to be back at work Monday, but Tricia's never seen Mammoth Cave, so we're going down to Cave City tonight and we'll tour the cave tomorrow. In fact," he glanced at his watch, "we should probably leave before long. Depending on how things go, maybe we can go to England next year."

"We had such a good time there. I love your Gran."

"Yeah, I just wish, you know…"

"Yeah."

"Wherever he is, I hope he's okay. I hope he gets in touch someday."

Jules nodded, glanced at Bobby.

"But, hey," Dwitty brightened again, "maybe y'all could go with us."

When Bobby had played all he had been asked to, plus a couple extras, he left the piano to reclaim Jules and say goodbye to Tricia and Dwitty, who were preparing to leave. Tony stopped him halfway. "Here," he tried to hand Bobby an envelope.

"No, man, it's a gift," Bobby refused.

"Take it. I insist," he slipped it into Bobby's breast pocket.

"Thanks," Bobby said and shook Tony's hand.

"Good luck in California," Tony smiled and slapped Bobby's shoulder fondly.

Bobby joined his friends. As Jules, Gina, and Tricia shared a last little chat, he turned and said, "So, Dwitty, think you'll get some tonight?" Terry nearly spat his punch.

Chapter 16

Rob had helped Bobby tune up the Safari and make sure it was in good shape for the long trip ahead. Bobby was already in the habit of carrying extra belts, hoses, and fluids with him in case of a breakdown on a gig outing, and in the summer heat he'd be keeping a close eye on the temperature gauge.

He picked up Jules at dawn, putting her suitcase in the back on top of his, beside the Farfisa and a couple of rolled up sleeping bags, and they set out for San Francisco. Terry had bought an old trailer to pull behind his car, to carry the rest of the gear, and Miles and Stephen were traveling with him. Jerry would fly out to meet them.

Jules and Bobby had both been out West before on family vacations, she to Yellowstone, he to the Grand Canyon, but neither of them had seen California. "I've never seen the Pacific Ocean," Jules said, gazing out the window as Illinois became Missouri.

"Me neither," he said, arm resting on the open window, unbuttoned shirt ruffled by the hot wind. "I'm looking forward to it. You mind driving awhile?"

"Not as long as I know where to go. I'm not good with maps."

"We just stay on this road. You can wake me up when we're getting close to St. Louis." He found a place to pull over. She took the wheel and he lay down in the back seat, head on a pillow, knees up, to nap. He figured on four days to make the trip. He wasn't going to drive all night, like the others talked of doing, and didn't want to push Jules too hard. But he did plan to try to keep expenses down. They had brought sandwiches with them for lunch, a big Thermos of coffee, a bag of fruit to last the trip. Nora had washed out a milk carton, filled it with sweet tea, and frozen it, so that as it melted in the car, they would have iced tea to drink.

Jules wasn't comfortable driving in the cities, but an unbroken stretch of road through the countryside she didn't mind. If she could tune in a radio station, it helped keep her alert and pass the time. The heat was the main discomfort, with no air conditioning in the car, but the cold tea helped.

After supper at a diner in Kansas City, Bobby drove until dusk and pulled into a campground for the night. It was cheaper than a motel room, there was a bath house where they could shower, and the office had vending machines with drinks and snacks. He put the back seat down, stood the suitcases up, and shoved everything over so he could sleep beside them, giving him more room to stretch out. Jules slept in the front seat.

They were on the road early, on a quest for breakfast and coffee, which they found near Willow Brook. The Great Plains beckoned, but by midday, Jules' enthusiasm was beginning to wane. She was hot and tired and the seemingly endless flat, rural landscape became monotonous. They made it to Cheyenne that night, to another campground. Jules took a long shower to soothe her body and refresh her spirit, but the car seat seemed even less comfortable than the night before, and she didn't sleep well.

Wyoming seemed to go on forever, vast rolling plains. What saved Jules from fatigue was spotting pronghorn antelope among the cattle. When they finally reached Salt Lake City, they had a little time to spend at the Great Salt Lake. They walked along the shore, took photos, watched a ruby sunset across the water. As they sat on the hood of the car, watching the light fade, she leaned heavily against his side. "Can we please get a room tonight," she pleaded, "and sleep in a real bed? My back hurts. I'll pay for it."

"Okay, baby, we'll get a room, and no, you're not going to pay for it." He squeezed her tight against him.

In the morning, with a desolate drive ahead, they stopped at a store to load up on food and drinks. "Pray that this old car holds together," he said, popping the hood to check everything over. From the window of a worn diner, they looked out across the salt flats for breakfast.

Nevada was ruggedly beautiful, but the heat and dry air were beyond any Jules had experienced and it robbed her of strength and lowered her morale. She wasn't much help to Bobby, spending a large portion of the afternoon lying in the back seat, feeling too ill to eat lunch. "Keep drinking," Bobby urged. When he needed a stop, before resuming the journey he took off his shirt, soaked it with water, and laid it over her to help cool her.

As the sun grew low and the air began to cool, she began to feel better, but she was exhausted and dehydrated. When they reached Reno, Bobby got a clean shirt out of his suitcase to wear, and found a motel room. Cool showers, air conditioning, and ice water brought them much-needed relief and restored her appetite. The motel restaurant hadn't looked very clean or appetizing, however. Jules wanted to cry at the prospect of getting back into the car. Thankfully, they didn't have to go far to find a suitable place to get burgers.

Back at the room, they watched a little TV, then went to bed. Bobby rubbed some of Jules' hand lotion onto his left arm, sunburned from resting it on the car window frame. As they stretched out in the dark between the cool sheets, Jules quietly complained, "I wish I could just quit moving. I feel like I'm still in the car, like I can still feel the pavement under us. I felt that way all last night, too. I don't even want to think about getting back in the car tomorrow."

"It won't be so long a day tomorrow," he said, stroking her hair. "And we don't have to get up so early. Just get some sleep, baby, and try not to think about it."

The next day they arrived in San Francisco and found the house Jerry had arranged as their meeting place. Terry, Miles, and Stephen were already there. "Jerry's supposed to get in tonight," Terry said.

Bobby unloaded the car, and he and Jules set out for some sight-seeing on foot. He was glad of the chance to really stretch his legs, and the air, cooler than they had expected for summer, refreshed Jules and brightened her spirit. They walked down to Fisherman's Wharf and along the waterfront, laughing at the grunting sea lions on the piers, watching sailboats bob in a marina. With a late take-out lunch of fresh fried fish, they sat on a bench and looked out across the bay at the bridges, at Angel Island, and Alcatraz. "I want to go over the Golden Gate Bridge," she said.

"We'll have most of tomorrow free," he said. Jerry had sensibly built in an extra day on their arrival schedule, in case anyone got delayed on the trip, and to give them all a chance to rest.

As the sun lowered, strange clouds were gathering across the bay, a wall of murky mauve edged in white. "Fog," he realized, pointing it out to Jules. "That will move in here tonight."

He suggested they get back to the house. "I don't know if it's safe here after dark," he said, "and Jerry should be here by now, too." They took a cable car back up the hill, rattling between the tall, ornate buildings, and he smiled and laughed to see Jules enjoying herself so.

Jerry had indeed arrived at his friend Tom's house. "There you are, Lott," he said. "Tom was just talking arrangements. He said his sister will put half of us up. We were deciding who would stay where."

Bobby, Jules, and Terry would stay with the sister, Leah, and her family. She set her two young sons up with sleeping bags in the living room, allowing Jules and Bobby their room, two twin beds, and putting Terry in the guest room. Bobby joked with Jules about pushing the two beds together. "I won't have to fight with you over the covers," she remarked.

"You're the one who steals the covers," he replied.

"I'm just trying to get them back from you," she said. "Even if it's two beds, can you imagine people in Midvale putting us up in the same room?"

He laughed. "It's obviously a different world here, or at least among Jerry's friends."

That night the band, Jules, and Jerry shared dinner in Chinatown, choosing half of what they ordered based on how good it looked in the pictures, passing everything around the table. "Hell of a lot better than Lee's Pagoda," Miles commented.

They discussed the upcoming show, a small-time festival in Golden Gate Park, similar to the festival The Deep See had played in London, it would seem – a short set in the afternoon, with better known acts to follow, but unfortunately no nationally known groups. "Just our luck that the big names are all touring elsewhere," Terry said.

"All the more reason for folks here to come out to this," Jerry replied. "They've got nothing better to do."

"Apparently the Grateful Dead played last night," Stephen said. "I didn't find out till today."

Jerry would have more details the following evening regarding parking, set-up, and security. For now, they could just relax, finish their delicious meal, and swap stories about the trip.

Chinatown at night was lit with pretty, colorful lanterns hanging from the buildings and strung across the streets. Street musicians played strange music on even stranger instruments. The fog was moving in, making haze around the lights atop the tall buildings. Jules was glad she had brought a sweater, and even with it on, she was glad of the warmth of Bobby's side.

Back at their room, getting ready for bed, Bobby approached Jules from behind as she sorted through her suitcase, and slipped his arms around her. "Your place or mine?" he said at her ear.

The next day was bright, breezy, and pleasant. Bobby and Jules set out across the Golden Gate Bridge to the Marin Headlands and beaches north. The water was cold. They didn't go in above their ankles, and not often. On Muir Beach she found chunks of pretty, bluish green stone, hard and glassy, sea-colored. She put several nice pieces in her pocket. She would later learn it was called serpentine.

They drove the twisting coastal road on up to Stinson Beach, stopping along the way to look down into the surf from atop the rugged cliffs. They hated to tear themselves away and get back for the band meeting over supper that night.

Late the next morning, Jules and Bobby visited the fabled Haight district, to see what all the fuss was about and to pick up a picnic lunch. Hippies and freaks made for a colorful show outside shops peddling psychedelic wares, and music spilled out from tall Victorian houses. Jules snapped photos, as she had done everywhere interesting on the trip. While Bobby perused a used book shop, Jules ordered up a big sack of food in a nearby deli. As she walked out the door, a thin young woman with dark hair and sunken eyes approached her. "Got any bread?" she held out an empty palm.

"I've got some sandwiches here." Jules pulled one out to hand to the girl.

"I don't want that!" She knocked it out of Jules' hand, into the air. "I need money. I need a fix."

A man in ragged bell bottoms and a headband walked by, saw the sandwich land on the sidewalk, and his eyes widened. "A sandwich from God!" He picked it up, unwrapping it to eat as he walked away.

Jules, rattled, backed away from the woman, right into someone, which startled her further. It was Bobby, who caught her in his arms. "Hey, hey, it's alright," he said by her ear. "It's alright."

The woman sneered at them. "Stupid hillbillies," she muttered, and turned to beg from someone else.

"Come on, baby," he kept her close. "We need to go now anyway."

Golden Gate Park was a human kaleidoscope. Colors, beads, fringes, flowers, and lots of hair. A man played a wooden flute, and people with designs painted on their faces and limbs danced to it. A topless girl stood chatting with her friends. Jules reached up and turned Bobby's grinning face away from the sight and toward her.

"Maybe you should take yours off," he smiled.

"Later," she said.

"Why not now?" he teased suggestively.

"Because Terry's standing right over there," she replied.

"Good point," he conceded.

Terry turned to wave them over and Jules noticed a peace sign painted on his cheek. "I want something painted on me," Jules said to Terry.

"There's a girl right over there who will paint you," Terry nodded.

"Cool," she said, leaving Bobby and Terry to talk while she had a large daisy-like flower painted on the back of each hand, leafy stems twisting up her forearms. The artist was just finishing up when Bobby came to get Jules.

"Gotta go play, baby," he said. "We're on first. Seems we have the unenviable task of warming up a crowd who we have no idea what they like or what kind of thing is coming after us."

"I'll be right over here," she pointed to a space of lawn as they neared the stage. "Good luck."

"Thanks. See you soon."

She spread out the old blanket from the car and sat down on it, opening a bottle of orange juice, but deciding to wait to eat until Bobby returned.

When the band took the stage, Terry quickly had the crowd on his side simply by raising his hands, making peace signs. They got to play a longer set than The Deep See had in London, and they tried to play a variety of styles, in hopes of hitting on something pleasing to the audience, but they needn't have worried about that. The people gathered seemed open to whatever was on offer musically.

After their set was over, Jules waited, pulling tiny flowers out of the grass, tying them together by their stems into necklaces, as she and her friends had done with clover flowers as children. She put one on. The next band began playing, a folk combo with a violinist, featuring a female singer in a long dress. She sang of peace and rainbows, birds and love. Jules saw Bobby coming across the lawn.

"How did we sound, baby?" he smiled, sitting beside her on the blanket.

"Wonderful, of course." She handed him the orange juice and he took a drink.

"Would you tell me if we didn't sound wonderful?"

"I don't know. Would you ever not sound wonderful?" She offered him a sandwich.

He laughed and leaned to kiss her. When he raised up she put a flower necklace over his head.

They ate, relaxed. Bobby leaned back on his elbows and stretched out his legs. The folk band finished, followed by a sort of white Blues band who played long, rambling jams. Jules turned to get a muffin out of the bag for dessert and something unbelievable caught her eye. "Oh my God!" she laughed, covering her mouth.

"What?" Bobby wondered.

"There's people over there– doing it. Over by the bushes."

He raised up to look. "Shit, you're right," he laughed.

They couldn't resist watching. "I can't believe they're not even covered up," Jules said.

"I guess they just don't care," he said.

They didn't see Terry come up behind them. He tapped Bobby's shoulder and when Bobby turned, Terry held out a lit joint. Bobby took it, took a hit, and nodded toward the bushes. "Look over there."

Jules, realizing someone had joined them, turned, blushing, just as Terry said, "Holy crap!" and burst out laughing. Bobby handed the joint to Jules.

Terry sat down beside Bobby. "Man, you never know what the fuck you're gonna see next around here."

"Literally," Bobby laughed.

They finished the joint and Jules sank into the shimmer and peace. Bobby sat back on his elbows again and Jules lay on her back beside him, looking up into the blue depths of the sky as the music flowed around her like a bright stream. Bobby eased onto his side, smiling at her, toying with her hair. She ran her fingertip over his lips and he kissed it, pulled her close to kiss her mouth, lingering and gentle. They let go of everything but each other, peacefully floating together in sound.

After half a dozen groups, as darkness began creeping in, a band called Santana closed out the festivities with spirited, Latin jazz-infused rock, their young Mexican frontman, Carlos, playing bewitching Bluesy guitar riffs. Bobby and Jules were sitting up, arms around each other, Jules with a corner of the blanket pulled around her. "This guy's going places," Terry decided.

"Yeah, he's got a good sound," Bobby agreed.

The next morning The Rooks Parliament pulled out of town to continue their tour of California. They played down the coast – small clubs, beach dives, parks – a hippie audience one night, surf crowd the next, plenty of free time along the way. It went mostly well, but Bobby grew increasingly irritable with the band. There was too much partying going on before the shows to suit him. A couple drinks, a little grass was no big deal, but as the band got higher, the sets got looser, and that rankled him. This was supposed to be a chance not only to get favorable exposure, but to test out the new material for the album. He finally had it out with them one morning in a band meeting, without Jerry, before they hit the road.

"But being in a band should be fun," Stephen countered. "Partying's part of rock and roll."

"Yeah," Miles agreed. "Why do it if you can't have fun with it?"

"Fun is going out there and playing hard and playing well and coming off that stage knowing I gave the best performance I could up there," Bobby fumed. "And I can't do that, none of us can do that, if somebody else is too messed up to keep time or pay attention or remember their part or where they are in the song. Terry, you skipped a whole fucking second verse last night!"

"Don't start with me," Terry puffed up.

"What, you wanna have a go?" Bobby raised his chin. Terry cocked a fist.

"Enough, enough," Miles got between them. "Bobby, just take it easy, man. I understand how you feel and all, but it's okay if we're a little laid back sometimes. I mean, have you looked at the audiences? They're too stoned to know the difference, or care. Just enjoy the vibe, man."

"Enjoy the vibe, huh?" he nodded. "Okay, tonight I'll just enjoy the vibe."

It was a tense drive down to Pismo Beach. He tried to let the beauty of the coast soothe him. Jules in short shorts lounged with her knees against the dashboard, bare feet on the seat, arm out the window, the breeze flowing over her and through her loose, white blouse. He just wanted to get away somewhere with her, away from the others, away from any pressures. It was mid afternoon. They had plenty of time. He pulled off the highway and down a beach road. They walked in the sand, waded in the cool surf. Jules could never resist picking up shells. Her cheerfulness soothed him. She had put up with a lot the past few days, the band sleeping on couches or floors some nights, little comfort or privacy, though she did think it a neat trick when he zipped their two sleeping bags together into one big one. In Monterey there had been one bed available at the house where they stayed, and Jerry, in managerial status mode, claimed it, until Bobby took issue with his expecting a lady to sleep on the floor just to give him comfort. "Yeah, I know what you're after, Lott," he ribbed.

"Jerry, it's a single bed. She gets it to herself," Bobby said. Jerry capitulated and Jules got the bed.

Jules had been justifiably grumpy at times, but she'd weathered it and shaken it off, and they could look forward to a real room tonight. And that thought got him back on the road, to take her there and enjoy her before the show.

When they arrived at the club that night, the rest of the band was already there, and obviously enjoying "the vibe." Bobby was instantly annoyed. *Yeah, alright. Have some fun. Partying is part of rock and roll.* There seemed to be enough fun on offer. Why not try something different, even?

In the course of his chatting with people as the band set up, a perky girl in red offered to turn him on, in more ways than one. He behaved himself in the one respect, but he took her offer of a generous helping of cocaine. Yes, he was going to have fun tonight.

In the morning, Jerry called a meeting in his room. "What the hell was that?" he began, tossing his hands in the air, pacing the floor. "I seem to have made a mistake, because I had thought you guys were in the same band, playing the same songs at the same time! Instead Segrest's drunk off his ass, Peterson's off in space, and Lott's off to the fucking races! And you, Wallace, you were just– off!" Bobby got up and walked out. "Where the hell do you think you're going?"

He didn't reply, but kept walking, Jerry yelling after him. Jules was coming out of their room on a quest for a Coke. He took her hand, pulling her along. "Come on, baby," he said as he led her down the hall. "I need some peace."

He walked her down to the beach, let go of her hand, and sat down on the sand. "Can I ask what's the matter?" she ventured cautiously.

"I get fucking tired of being the one trying to hold things together all the time!" He picked up a handful of sand and threw it viciously, the wind quickly dissolving it to nothing. "And you see what happens when I don't! Stephen and Miles, maybe they just don't fucking know any better yet, but Terry does. I could kick his ass sometimes!" He ground his teeth as he tried to settle his breathing. "I'm sorry, baby, I need to–" He shook his head.

"I'll just go down by the water," she said.

He pulled his knees up to his chest and rested his forehead in the nest of his arms until he'd calmed a little, then stared at the waves, listening to their pulsing roar, trying to clear his head, letting them pull his thoughts away, replace them with wordless sound.

Jules had wandered a good ways up the beach and was slowly returning. He watched her wade in the surf, picking up shells. Her long, gauzy skirt, wet up to her thighs, stuck to her legs, making her a mermaid. She came to him with a handful of tiny shells, each one marked with rays of pastel sunset colors – peach, lavender, soft yellow.

"Come sit with me," he patted the ground beside him.

She scooped out a bowl-like depression in the sand beside her sandals, and laid her shells in it. "I'm going to get covered," she laughed, sand sticking thickly to her wet clothes as she sat down.

"You can rinse off before we leave."

"When do we need to leave by?"

"We need to check out in half an hour, but we're just going to Ventura. Couple hours to get there, Jerry said." He lay back on the sand and looked up at the sky.

"You're going to get sand all in your hair."

"I don't fucking care anymore," he huffed a little laugh. She lay down beside him and he snugged her up close to his side, the grit and wet fabric of her skirt plastered to his bare legs, dampness seeping into the side of his shorts. "I don't want to play tonight," he said quietly. "I don't even want to think about it. It would fucking serve them all right," his voice rose, "if I just didn't show up."

"Sh-hh–" She stroked his cheek. "Forget it for now. Let it go."

He turned to look at her, with the disconcerting feeling of sand creeping into the folds of his ear. "Baby, sometimes I think you're the only thing in this whole world that matters."

She smiled. "That's the sweetest thing anybody's ever said to me."

Chapter 17

The Ventura show was sober and accurate, if subdued.

Bobby and Jules had kicked back on the beach awhile that afternoon, watching the surfers, and he had tried to put his bitterness and apprehension aside. He let her drag him around for a little shopping before dinner. She bought a bikini; no one now could tell her she wasn't allowed to. Bobby certainly didn't disapprove. They kept to themselves, not running into anyone else from the band until they showed up at the club for set up.

As soon as he walked through the door, Bobby turned laconic and professional, keeping a lid on his emotions and opinions. Jerry fretted like a mother hen. "There you are! Thank God. I was beginning to wonder if you were even going to show up." Bobby just looked at him and didn't say a word.

After the show they packed up and drove to Santa Monica, to a yellow house on Euclid, the home and studio of Ezra Goldman. Ez-Press Records. His live-in girlfriend, a statuesque black lady with a voluminous Afro, greeted them at the front door. "Hey, babies," she beamed. "Come on in. I'm Freda, but call me Free." She ushered them into a tiny living room that had once been a foyer. Ezra had closed off the real living room and dining room as the studio. Free led them all into the kitchen.

"Hey, Jerry," Ezra called as he came down the stairs. "Long time!" They exchanged a brief, masculine, back-slapping hug and retired to the studio to chat, drink brandy, and smoke cigars.

"You in the band too, baby?" Free was asking Jules.

Jules was about to say no when Bobby, putting his arms around her from behind, said, "She's one of our songwriters." She leaned back into his chest and smiled.

"That's wonderful," Free replied. "Looks like she's maybe more than just a songwriter to you," she smiled at Bobby.

He gave a little laugh. "Yeah. A lot more."

"You married?"

"They might as well be," Terry commented.

"Well," Free asked, "Should I put you two in the same room, then?"

"If you don't, they'll end up that way anyway," Miles snickered. Bobby just rolled his eyes.

"Well, aren't you cheeky," Free addressed Miles. "There's drinks in the fridge," she announced, then took Jules' hand. "Come on with me, sugar. What's your name?"

"Julia, but call me Jules."

"Jules. Well, you somebody's jewel. I can see that," she smiled as she led her upstairs. "We got three guest rooms up here. I'll let you pick. There's these two," she showed her two rooms with two twin beds each, "and there's this one." It was a front corner room, a little bigger, and with a double bed.

"This one, I think," Jules said shyly.

"No need to blush, girl," Free smiled gently. "Love is a beautiful thing."

Free was an herbalist who worked in a shop called Earth Essence that sold natural remedies and perfumed oils and lotions. She cultivated an herb garden in her back yard, with not only medicinals, but a variety of cooking herbs. After breakfast, as the band settled into the studio, Jules helped Free clean up the kitchen. "Do you cook?" Free asked.

"A little. I'm still learning," Jules said. "Okay," she laughed, "I have a lot to learn."

"I can always use help in the kitchen," Free said. "Even if it's novice help, 'specially with all these hungry men we got around here now. I'm sure I can teach you something. Now, I'm usually here till after lunch and then I go work till 5 or 6. I like to start supper soon as I get home. Ez likes to eat by 7." She laughed. "I say 'likes to.' Sometimes I about have to pry that door open, though."

The studio was homey and comfortable, but clean and professional. The main recording room, which had once been the living room, was spacious, with a wood floor that bounced sound nicely, and a high ceiling, sound-proofed, as were the walls and covered windows. The dining room was divided into a small booth, primarily used for vocals, and the control room. Bobby, enamored of the Hammond B3 he had used on "All I Ever Seem To Do," had arranged to rent one. He began putting it through its paces, discovering its capabilities, deciding how he wanted to use it. He was also pleased to find a piano in the studio. While the upstairs rooms had a decidedly Bohemian aura and the kitchen had seen a lot of traffic, the plush environs of the studio, complemented by leather chairs in the control room, suggested that Ez had a bit of money to throw at his hobby turned business. While The Rooks would have the run of the studio most afternoons and evenings during their residence, Ez booked other bands in the mornings, usually to cut singles or for other short-term projects.

Once acquainted with the workings of the studio, the band set up their gear and worked to get it sounding the way they liked, rehearsing a few songs in the process, and then Stephen and Miles got right to work recording the first rhythm tracks.

Bobby took a break while they worked, to have a cup of coffee. He found Jules in their room, sitting on the floor in front of the purple book shelf, looking at a book, snickering.

"What have you got there?" he asked.

"This book. It was on the shelf here, next to the Bible, of all things. You've got to look at this," she grinned, her face a little red.

He squatted down beside her and she showed him a picture. He laughed. "What is this?"

"Some ancient Indian book." She showed him the cover. *The Kama Sutra*.

He sat down beside her and she showed him other pictures. "That looks awkward," he commented on one, sipping coffee, and took it from her for a closer look. "Hmm... we already do this," he said of the next page. "And this."

"We've never done that," she said of another.

"Interesting," he said, then turned and said softly against her ear, "Want to try it now?"

She turned and kissed him. "Shut the door."

L.A. offered good opportunities to see established groups as well as rising stars. The band and Jules all went to see Love perform, concerned that they might not be allowed into the club, but no one was checking I.D. The doorman, who barely looked legal himself, eyed Stephen suspiciously, but waved him on in. Stephen and Miles quickly went off on their own to chat up girls, while Terry stayed with Bobby and Jules. "Gina would love this," Terry said of the music.

"I wish she could have come," Jules said. "She would love this whole trip, and I wouldn't be the only girl."

"I'd be having more fun, too," Terry smirked.

The next morning at breakfast, Stephen introduced his sleepy-eyed new friend, Marla, a pretty, petite, mahogany-haired girl, who had apparently spent the night. She worked at a dress shop called The Celestial Body, and she and Jules became fast friends. Jules visited the shop, found its offerings to her liking, and bought more of the lightweight, ethnic clothes she had begun picking up on the trip.

Miles was with a different girl every night or two, and had made quite a few other friends. He seemed to be introducing someone to the rest of the band whenever they went out.

"I'm glad I'm rooming with Jerry, even if he does snore," Terry told Bobby. "Then I can just ignore whatever those other two end up getting into. And when Jerry leaves I'll have the room to myself."

But for all the ease and fun, the atmosphere in L.A. was strange and charged. It was just shy of a month since Robert Kennedy's assassination at the Ambassador Hotel. Media still crawled over the city. Jules felt the sadness. Terry picked up on the anger. "Anybody progressive gets any power," he said, "and they fucking shoot him. Buck the establishment, and you put your life on the line, but we have to buck the establishment." Early evenings, if he wasn't in the studio, found Terry parked in front of the TV in the small living room, watching the news.

Bobby spent much of his spare time at the piano or the Hammond, practicing, working on improvements to his song parts, keeping his fingers strong and nimble. It was obvious to Ez he was the most disciplined participant, and the most interested in the technology of the studio and the ways in which multiple tracks could be used to best advantage. He was the one most likely to want to continue work in the evenings, rather than just go out on the town, and he worked straight and sober more often than not. He took a keen interest in how the tracks would be mixed for the final product and made suggestions. "Too bad you don't live here," Ez told him. "I might hire you. You have a good ear."

On a grey, misty morning, Bobby and Jules sat on a housetop, near the peak of a steep roof, overlooking a town, the tops of trees. The air was cool and still. They were wearing their dark navy pea coats, sitting, arms around their knees, silent. Rooks began gathering, not the band, but birds, a few at first, huge and dark, dark as their coats. Then more. All around them, sitting. Watching them. A parliament of rooks, their voices scrapes and clicks and whirs. Deliberating. Considering.

He woke. The oscillating fan hummed and pushed warm air.

Dawn was a faint promise. It would be sunny again today, but for now the light was thin and colorless, tracing just the outlines in the room. He pulled Jules close. She mumbled something, not really waking, arms folded up against her as she nestled her face in his bare chest.

What did it mean? Those rooks. Did it even mean anything? They were good luck, weren't they? Weren't they? Why did they appear to judge? He submerged back into sleep, a dull nothing this time, an endless grey sea.

When Jules woke him, the sun was full on his face, the shape of the window stretched bright across the bed.

"What time is it?" he asked.

"Almost 1. Lunch is on the table." She wore a white sleeveless top and a thin, flowy skirt of lavender paisley that swirled airily when she turned.

He groaned and slowly sat up. He could hear banging in the kitchen below, voices, muted laughter. The smell of food woke his stomach. Jules was fussing with her hair in front of a small mirror that stood on the gaudily hand-painted old chest of drawers, a psychedelic, meandering design of loops and swirls and dots.

"Here, can you help me with this?" She brought a brush and a rubber band to the bed and sat down on the edge, her back to him. "It's hot. I want to put it back, just a loose braid."

He tried to remember how to braid. "Three strands?"

"Yes. Outer strand over and in between the other two. Alternate sides."

"I remember now." He drew the brush through her hair, sectioned it with his fingers, just enjoying the warm, satiny feel of it, the glints of gold and copper. Gently, loosely he twined it. It had grown long. Even braided it fell between her shoulder blades. Away from his job, in need of a trim even before he had left, his hair was beginning to grow shaggy and soft, ends flipping up here or there, the beginnings of loose waves. It was longer now than it had been even with The Knights. He liked the way it felt. Jules liked to sink her fingers into it, to stroke his face when he neglected to shave, which was fairly often these days. He considered growing a beard. Terry had quite a Fu Manchu mustache going. He hadn't cut his hair in over a year.

When he'd secured her hair with the rubber band, she thanked him with a kiss. "I'm going back downstairs now," she said. He got up, pulled on jeans and a denim vest, no shirt, washed his face and greeted the day, barefoot like Jules.

In the kitchen Terry and Miles were arguing politics over plates of pancakes. "Here, baby," Free said, handing Bobby a chipped, heaping plate of them.

"Thanks. Where's Jules?"

"She's out back with Marla," Free said.

He poured a cup of coffee and went out to sit with them in the shade on the small porch, beside a potted lemon tree. Marla was rolling a joint on the concrete. She lit it, took a toke, and passed it to Jules. Jules took a hit and passed it to Bobby. He declined. "I need to lay down some serious tracks today. I need to do it straight."

"Marla said I can string beads to sell at the shop. I want to go buy some today," Jules said.

"I make three times more than I pay for the loose beads," Marla said. "And it's easy and fun. You can sell them down on the beach, too."

"Sure, baby," he kissed the top of Jules' head. "But I don't know about you driving like that."

"It's just a few blocks," Marla said. "Over by where I work, so we're walking."

"Okay, just be careful, sweetheart."

The band went into the studio, and Jules went with Marla. "He seems pretty protective. Does he hold you back?"

"No," Jules smiled. "He just doesn't want anything bad to happen to me. We've been through some hard times."

"What sign is he?"

"Sign?"

"Zodiac sign."

"I'm not sure. Whatever February 2nd is."

"Ah. Aquarius. He likes to shake things up a bit, be different. An innovator. And very dedicated to what he does."

"That's certainly true."

"And what sign are you?" Marla asked.

"Aries."

"That's a sexy match. He likes to try new things and you like a bit of adventure."

Jules laughed, felt her cheeks flush.

"And I'm guessing you're not shy with him."

"I was a little, the first time I talked to him, but then I just wasn't anymore."

"You're both loyal. You said you'd been through troubles. That loyalty is what got you through. Here's the bead store. Come on back to the shop when you're done and I'll show you some things."

Marla returned to work. Jules went inside. The store smelled of incense. Bright floral fabrics covered the walls. Bins of beads stretched in a row before her, from packs of tiny seed beads to fancy swirled glass pendants. There were sparkly faceted beads, smooth plain beads, stone beads, wood beads. Just handling them was fun. The biggest problem was she wanted them all. She found tiny bells, even porcupine quills. It reminded her of trying to choose penny candy as a kid.

When she'd made her selections, and bought long, thin needles and strong thread, she took her purchases to The Celestial Body, where Marla showed her some special bead-weaving stitches when she wasn't waiting on customers, and Jules related the trials she and Bobby had endured. Before Jules knew it, it was time to close up shop and go back to the house.

On July 4th, Jules and Bobby sat on the beach, sharing a bottle of wine as they watched a distant fireworks display and a party of hippies dancing around a bonfire on the sand, singing "This Land Is Your Land." The recording was going well. Bobby was pleased to have a new palette of sounds, effects, and possibilities. Terry had written a new song, and they were working out an arrangement for it. Jules found her beaded jewelry sold quickly. At the beach, she had begun picking up shells with holes in them, rather than rejecting them, and she strung these onto necklaces and bracelets. She wrapped wire around stones or pieces of sea glass to create pendants.

"I wouldn't want to be in the way or anything," she said, "but I've never seen a recording session. I've never even been in a studio. Do you think it would be okay if I just watched one day?"

"Sure, baby. I'll show you around tomorrow, if you like. I'm sure Ez won't care if you sit in on a session. I'll ask the other guys. If it bothers them, you can just watch me work sometime if I'm recording on my own."

Jules got her chance the next afternoon. Terry and Miles were laying down the vocals on Terry's new song. From the control room, Jules could see them through the vocal booth window, sealed inside, wearing headphones, sharing a mic. "In the headphones," Bobby explained, "they can hear what's already on the tape without it going back through the microphone and getting picked up again."

Terry, eyes closed tight, was singing loud and strong, with conviction, Miles adding harmony on select phrases.

> The time has come to make a choice,
> to close your eyes or raise your voice.
> There's people dying in the war.
> What for?

Fly with me
to the inner sea.
Ride the frightened color shimmer waves.

Hold your breath.
Feel your inner death.
Swim out of your melting turquoise graves.

The time has come to save your soul,
to pull mankind out of this hole.
There's people crying up above
for love.

She stayed to hear the playback. Ez isolated each track for her, then played them all together, raising or lowering the volume of one or another to show how it could be adjusted in the mixing process. She found it all fascinating, and it made her feel more a part of Bobby's world.

The Doors played a Hollywood club the next night, and Jules and Bobby decided to go. They had no trouble getting in, and Bobby bought them each a drink from the bar. It was crowded and chaotic, but they found a place to sit at a table with two other couples, who struck up a friendly conversation with them, but appeared quite stoned and given to non sequiturs.

Jules and Bobby finished their drinks and settled in for the show, the crowd its own colorful spectacle, projectors throwing pulsing fluid images of color onto the ceiling and walls, and faces and bodies. The Doors were starting to fill arenas and large halls. They had just sold out the Hollywood Bowl. The days of being able to see them in a club, even a large club like this, had nearly come to an end.

Not far into the first song, "Break On Through," Bobby felt a familiar tingling in his skin. He nudged Jules. "I think we've been spiked."

"I know we have," she said, a grin growing on her face.

He was peaking when those familiar Vox strains introduced "Light My Fire." Captivated as most of the girls were by Jim, Jules, moving and swaying in the splashes of color seemed tuned right in to Ray, her every movement a reflection of what he was playing, her eyes, when open, usually on him, on his hands. When Jim would approach, growling and writhing, Bobby saw Jules, more than once, shrink back, avoid, a look in her eyes akin to mistrust, as though to say, "I'm not opening my soul to that."

Then it all slowed. "Take the highway to the end of the night," Jim sang. Vibrations of blue and white light shimmered like electric ripples, and it was Ray making them with the vibrato, Robby with tremolo. Bobby pulled Jules close in the shivering sound, feeling suddenly cold and anxious, as though he were in the bottom of a well, looking up. Something came over him. Cincinnati. The cold. No, the isolation. He was shaking, and with every shudder, blackness fell from his shoulders, then renewed, like liquid dropping down on him.

But here was Jules, leading him in a slow dream dance, sending pulses of warmth, an ember, but she kept fading from him.

When the song ended she let go. He shook his head hard, trying to clear himself, eyes wide.

"You okay, baby?" Jules asked, reaching up to touch his cheek.

He squeezed his eyes shut a moment, then blinked a few times. "Yeah," he decided.

But he wasn't. He was rattled. He barely made it through the set. "I need to go outside," he said. "Now."

In the hot, still air he leaned back against the front wall of the club, breathing, just breathing, taking some comfort in the relative simplicity of the pale vibrations of the street light. Jules was tracing the edges of bricks with fascinated fingertips. People trickled out of the club, talking, laughing, staggering around them.

"I'm in no shape to drive, baby," he said.

She shook her head. "Me neither."

He didn't know what to do. Maybe they could find a park, just a quiet place to sit until they came down a bit. Oh hell, he couldn't find his way out of a paper bag right now. He couldn't risk getting lost, not with Jules along. Was a park even safe? Once the people had gone, was it even safe here? He panicked.

"Hey, babies," a woman's voice said. A flowing swirl of Indian patterned fabric, all burgundies and browns. Straight, long, brown hair. It was Mary, one of Miles' new friends. She reached up to touch Bobby's face. "You need to mellow, baby. Come on over to our pad. It's just a few blocks." She took Bobby's hand to lead him. With his other, he grasped Jules' hand. Several other people joined them as they walked. The night seemed to stretch on forever like a gaudily lit tunnel that grew increasingly dimmer, even the stars collapsing in on themselves. He felt lost and afraid and helpless, tear tracks like ice down his cheeks.

Inside the house was all incense smell and patterns and big, soft pillows on the floor, like some fairytale sultan's tent. Several people lounged around, passing a joint, the smoke swirling, twining, elongating, like boneless fingers. Mary took a hit and considered it briefly. "Here," she handed it to Bobby.

He shook his head. He wanted down right now, not further up.

"Take it," she urged. "It's real mellow stuff. It will help." He complied. Jules took a hit too, and led him across the room to a vacant place to sit. There was music. Sitars. Not loud, thankfully. His ears, his whole head needed a rest. He tucked his knees up to his chest, hugging himself, just wanting it all to stop.

Gradually his nerves began to calm. Everything softened. He felt warm again. Jules was beautiful, examining a strand of beads someone had draped around her neck. What color were they? Every time he thought he knew, they changed.

He became aware that someone else was stroking his hair, soothing, tender. He lay back against a soft bosom, closing his eyes, drifting...

"Love is meant to be shared," a woman's voice was saying, somewhere in the middle of the room. "It should be free. We should all be free." He opened his eyes to find a beautiful girl on either side of him. One of them was topless.

A long-haired, bearded man had Jules by the hands, leading her in a slow, giggling dance, around and around. "Don't be stingy," he was saying to anyone who was listening. "Don't lock it up. Spread the love around. Spread it over the whole world. Make the whole world free."

"Free," Jules said dreamily.

Was that man leading her away? The two women flanking Bobby were stroking up his body, stroking his face, turning his head, kissing him, sinking him deeper into the pillows. Someone turned up the music, sinuous, twisting psychedelic jams.

It was early when he sat up sharp. Soft light filtered in, despite the tapestries over half the windows. The two girls were asleep, entwined naked beside him. The bearded man, shirtless, in white pants, sat in lotus position in a corner. A few scattered people lay asleep or passed out, but Bobby didn't see Jules. He fumbled hurriedly for his clothes and pulled them on.

"Where is she?" he demanded of the sitting man. "Where's Jules?"

"Sh-hh." The man didn't open his eyes. "I'm meditating." He began to quietly chant.

Bobby shoved the man's shoulder. "I said, where is she?"

"How should I know? Little girl freaked out and ran away," he shrugged.

"Ran away? What do you mean 'ran away'? Ran away where?" His rising voice woke someone, who groaned.

"Relax," Mary said from the kitchen doorway, a dusting of flour across the front of her dress, that same burgundy dress from last night. "I found her wandering around the yard. I tried to get her to come in and crash here, but she kept saying she wanted to go home, so I drove her home."

He dashed out the front door, head still fogged, and tried to get his bearings. That tree. He remembered that tree. And that red sign. He rushed up the street, asked someone on the corner where the club was, and managed to find the car.

When he got back to the yellow house, he found Jules in the kitchen, barefoot in a loose, blue floral dress, drawing a glass of water from the tap. The house was quiet. "Oh, thank God," he breathed. She took a drink with her back to him, set the glass on the counter.

Then she wheeled to face him. "How could you do it? How *could* you?" She pounded her fists against his chest, frustrated, angry tears clouding her eyes.

He let her get a few blows in before grabbing her wrists. "I was high. And what about you? You went off with *him*. You wanted to give free love a try."

"No. I didn't. And when I figured out what was happening, I ran. I didn't want him. I didn't even want him touching me. God, Bobby, how could you even think that? But you!" She struggled against him, trying to hit him again, but he held on.

"Jules, I'm sorry. I really am. If it's any comfort, not a whole lot happened. Those girls were more interested in each other than they were in me anyway."

"A comfort? 'Not a whole lot'? You were naked with two girls! God, do you know how disgusting that is?" She shoved against his hands and turned her head away. "And how do I know you didn't– catch something?"

"Baby, I didn't do it with them," he said quietly, trying to calm her. "I didn't do it with anybody. I just crashed out. Honest to God, I couldn't stay awake." He rubbed her wrists with his thumbs. "Oh God, Jules, I am sorry," he said. "I love you so much."

"Damn it, Bobby, love *isn't* free, and I don't want to share you!" She had stopped fighting and was sobbing now instead.

He dropped her wrists and pulled her tight against him, but she tucked her arms up between his chest and hers.

"You always said I was your only girl."

He winced. The guilt sliced right through his stomach. "And you said I was your only man. Goddamn it, Jules, I don't want to share you either! I wanted to strangle that creep."

"Then why didn't you come and get me?"

"I thought you wanted to be free," he said quietly. "You just kept saying 'free'." He laid his face against the top of her head and let his tears flow into her hair. "Baby, I was so fucking high I couldn't think, and I didn't choose that any more than you did. When I woke up and couldn't find you, it scared me to death. Jesus, why the hell didn't we think to just get a cab?" She clutched at his shirt and he rocked her back and forth, back and forth, choking on pain and regret, and anger at those arrogant, stupid people trying to force their drugs and ideals on others, heedless of the damage, thinking that was going to somehow save the world.

At length he laid his hands on her shoulders and held her back to look into her wet, swollen eyes. "Baby, please, let's put this behind us. I think we both just need to go home, get out of this crazy place. Just a few more days, honey, and we can do that. Hell, I'll quit and we can leave tomorrow, if you want."

"Bobby," she said plainly, looking down, "I think I might be pregnant."

He hadn't expected that. "How?"

"The usual way, you idiot."

"No, I mean, aren't you still taking The Pill?"

"With everything that's been going on, I guess I missed a few." Her eyes began filling again.

He took her head in his hands and lifted her face, to kiss her. "Marry me," he said.

"You don't have to. It's my own fault."

"I want to." He kissed her again. "Don't you want to?"

"I've wanted to for a long time."

"Is that a yes?"

She took a deep, shaky breath, searched his eyes. "Yes," she whispered.

He smiled. "Let's go."

"Where?"

"To get married."

"Right now?"

"Why not? Grab your shoes. If we start now, we can get there by mid-afternoon, I think."

"But– what if I'm not? What if it's a false alarm?"

"Then we'll have more time to get settled."

"You wouldn't feel like I–"

"Jules, this isn't just about that. Baby, I'd been going to ask you anyway."

"You had?"

"I was just waiting for the right moment. Then all that shit happened." He looked away, then back to her eyes. "In a few days we'll be going home. What do you think it's going to be like there? We can't live there like we live here, and I don't want to live here."

"Neither do I," she shook her head, "and I don't want to go back to living like we were."

"Is it important to you, a big wedding back home?" he asked.

She shook her head, gave a bitter laugh. "It's not like Dad's going to walk me down the aisle."

His smile broadened. "Let's go."

"Where the hell have you been?" demanded Jerry when they returned to the yellow house the next day.

"Jules and I took a little side trip yesterday," Bobby said.

"You missed a band meeting, a rehearsal, *and* a session. You'd better have a damn good excuse."

He hugged Jules to his side and said softly, "We got married."

"You what?"

"We got married. Yesterday," he said.

"Oh, for fuck's sake."

"In a manner of speaking." Bobby tried to twist down a smile, then he and Jules burst out laughing.

Bobby got right to work, joining the session in progress. "Shit, where you been, man?" Terry asked.

"We could hear y'all fighting or something yesterday," Stephen said. "Woke me up."

"Fuckin' early," Miles grumbled.

Bobby just held up his left hand to show them his wedding ring.

"Holy God!" Terry laughed.

"Yeah, well, don't tell anybody back home, alright? We want to do that ourselves when we get back."

"Understood," Terry said.

Jules sat on the back porch, back to the wall, bare legs stretched out in the sun, wearing the red shorts and tie-dyed t-shirt she'd grabbed on their way out the previous day. She turned her hand in the light. A white gold band, and snug against it, another that cradled a tiny diamond on either side of a lustrous white pearl. "From the sea," he had smiled. "From my soul."

It hadn't quite sunk in yet. The golden slant of yesterday's early sun shining in on her in the car, while her head ached from sleeplessness, lingering drug traces, and so much crying. Waking later to the rustling sounds of Bobby fumbling with a map. Hamburgers in the car for lunch. A ceremony that took a third the time it took to buy rings for it. And then, in a plain, inexpensive room a delicious nap in the air conditioning, clothed, exhausted, sleeping face to face, hand in hand. Later, looking out at the desert dusk, a quiet dinner. Too quiet. Too lingering. Putting off what they had never put off before. Nightfall, stars, a walk, wondering aloud what the others were thinking. Facing each other beside the bed, the time it took to meet each other's eyes. "Can you forgive me?" he had asked quietly, taking her hand.

"I already have, or else I wouldn't have married you. That doesn't mean I've forgotten."

"No, of course not," he'd looked down. "We can just–" he'd shrugged, "sleep."

"That's a hell of a thing to tell a girl on her wedding night."

He'd given a little laugh, looked at her sheepishly.

She'd stepped closer to him, said softly, "Help me forget."

Then he'd kissed her, held her tight, and it was balm. "You've got me nervous, baby," he'd said. "Nervous as our first time."

"You were nervous?"

"Of course I was."

She smiled, ran the smooth, cool surface of the pearl across the bow of her top lip. Free would be home any minute. It would be time to start supper, time to give her the news.

Jerry flew home to Midvale the next day, back to his law practice. The band worked in earnest in the studio, and Jules occupied her time weeding Free's herb garden and stringing the rest of her beads – some for herself, a necklace for Gina, a few last items for the shop. When Bobby came out of the studio and up to their room, she gave him a necklace she had made for him with a particularly nice piece of green sea glass, and mother-of-pearl beads alternating with pale aqua pony beads. "It's beautiful," he smiled, holding the glass up to the light to look through its sand-worn translucence before fastening it around his neck. The pendant fell just below his collarbone, the cool glass warming against his skin.

As they all gathered for supper, Marla presented Bobby and Jules with her wedding gifts, a long string of white beads for each of them, each necklace culminating in a pair of pewter pendants impressed with their zodiac signs. After the meal, Free pulled them aside more privately. "I brought you a little something, too," she said. "My own signature love blend." She handed Jules a brown glass apothecary bottle filled with oil. "It smells good, it tastes good, and it will make you glide," she smiled.

After lunch the next day, Free went to work and Jules went to The Celestial Body to take in the rest of the jewelry she'd made. Ezra tromped into the kitchen. "Where's Miles?" he demanded, looking at his watch.

"At the doctor's," Stephen replied.

"The doctor's? What the hell's wrong with him?"

"Apparently one of his ladies has been spreading more than love," Terry smirked.

"Oh, Christ," Ez shook his head.

"Yeah," Terry grinned, "I guess he woke up this morning feeling crabby."

Bobby nearly spat his coffee, covering his mouth to keep it in until he was able to swallow. "God, Terry, that almost came out my nose," he laughed.

"He asked me what to do about them, and I said hell if I know, I'm smarter than that," Terry snickered.

"Well, shit, Terry, I'm impressed," Bobby said. "I didn't think you were smarter than anybody."

Terry shoved him, he shoved back, and pretty soon they were laughing and scrapping across the table, then out of their chairs.

"I give up," Ez tossed his hands in the air. "I give up! When you guys are ready to get some work done..."

"Yeah, alright," Bobby said, and they stopped. Until Terry shoved his head and they started in all over again.

Then Miles walked in, turning from ash to crimson. "Right," Ezra said. "Let's get to work." They started walking toward the studio door, but Ezra stopped Miles. "Eh-eh... first you go get those sheets off the bed and out in the trash."

Jules returned, having taken her jewelry profits to a record store, and was about to take her purchases up to their room, when Bobby came out of the studio door. "Ah, there you are," he smiled. "I need you." With a hand on her back, he guided her into the studio and shut the door.

"What's up?" she wondered.

"We're recording 'Vanilla Snow.' It really needs a woman's voice on the harmony. I want you to sing it."

"Me? On the record?" She blinked, shook her head.

"Yes, you. You can do this. Don't be afraid. We'll send Miles and Stephen out, if you want."

She took a deep, slow breath to steady herself. "I'll try, I guess, but I don't promise."

"Let's go listen through the track. Terry will coach you through your parts." Bobby kissed her cheek. "You'll do fine. Trust me."

It was beautiful what they'd done with it. Terry had paired the Rickenbacker with an acoustic guitar. The drums and bass were gentle, and rather than organ, Bobby had played piano. She learned her part from Terry, practiced it with him until she got it right. "Relax," he told her. "Don't tighten up your throat, just let it flow."

"But what if I mess up when we record it?" she worried.

"Then we just redo it. It's just you and me on this track. It won't hurt anything else."

When Terry told Ezra they were ready to tape, Jules adjusted her headphones and looked nervously out the booth window at Bobby. "I love you," he mouthed. She closed her eyes and focused on the task at hand. They kept the third take.

Jules still wasn't used to hearing her own voice as others heard it, and she felt flushed and embarrassed during the playback, attuned to every tiny thing she wished she could do better, but Bobby, Terry, and Ez were all pleased. Terry even gave her a supportive hug, and Bobby teased him about trying to steal his wife.

Bobby and Jules had grown wary since the Doors show, and resolved to avoid clubs or parties. They mostly stayed at the house. That evening as Jules and Free stood at the kitchen counter, working from a basket of beautiful fresh produce to make a nice supper for whoever would be around that night, Bobby wandered into the kitchen. Ez, Stephen, and Miles were locked in the studio. Terry had gone out to buy cigarettes and whiskey. On the stove, Free's special seasoned rice and beans were cooking. "That smells terrific," Bobby smiled. "Anything I can do to help?"

"You could work on the salad," Jules suggested.

He washed the lettuce and tore it up into a big bowl. He washed and sliced tomatoes. Free showed him how to scrape carrots. He peeled and sliced a cucumber. Free went out to the porch to pick lemons from the potted tree and basil from her herb garden. Jules was making garlic butter for the bread and Bobby was trying to pit an avocado when he suddenly said, "Shit!" He slapped the knife down on the counter and rushed to the sink, holding his right palm under his left hand. He turned the water on. "Ah, fuck!" he grimaced and kicked the sink cabinet.

"What is it, honey?" Jules rushed over. Drops of blood dotted the counter and the edge of the sink, a red stream of blood and water swirling down the drain. "Oh my God, Bobby, what did you do?"

"I don't think a Band-aid is gonna fix this," he said.

She looked at his left index finger, laid open under the water, and saw bone. Her body convulsed with a gag.

"Hold on, baby," he said. "Don't look. Just hand me a dish towel or something."

She was shaking, dizzy. "Free!" she called at the top of her lungs. She grabbed a clean dish towel out of the drawer, handed it to Bobby, and leaned out the back door. "Free!"

"What is it, baby?" Free called from amidst the herbs.

"Quick, where's the hospital?"

"Hospital?" Free came running.

"Bobby cut himself. Bad. I've got to get him to a hospital."

"Whoa, baby, you look pretty bad yourself." She hurried in after Jules. Bobby had a corner of the dish towel wrapped tight around his finger. It was already bleeding through. "Come on, I'll take you," she said, grabbing her keys off the hook by the door. "I can get you there faster than I can tell you how, and your lady here looks too green to be driving." Free turned off the stove, ushered them out to Ezra's car and they sped off.

Terry returned just as things were wrapping up in the studio. He paid little attention to the half-prepared meal on the counter, only noting that it smelled and looked pretty good from the table as he set his purchases down. Ez sauntered into the kitchen with the others in tow. "I want you guys to take a listen, see if you can do something around this. Where's Bobby?"

"I don't know," Terry said. "I just came in."

"Free!" Ez called out. "Free! Where the hell is everybody?"

Terry went to the cupboard for a glass. "Shit, this doesn't look good," he said. "Somebody's had an accident here." He pointed out the blood to the others.

"Son of a bitch," Ez said. He went to the front door and looked out. "My car's gone."

"They must have gone to the hospital," Miles said.

Terry took a shot of whiskey and lit up a cigarette while Ez paced up and down the kitchen. Stephen looked curiously into the pot. "That looks good."

"We might as well have some," Miles said. "Who knows when they'll be back."

Terry surveyed the scene. No blood on the food. He grabbed a towel and wiped up the blood trail, rinsed out the sink. The phone rang. Ez snatched up the receiver. "Hello? Free, where the hell are you? What happened?" The others turned to listen. "How bad?... Shit. Son of a bitch... Alright, alright... Yeah." He slammed the phone back on the hook. "Don't any of you touch a knife! I mean it!"

"What's happened?" Terry asked.

"Apparently Mr. Domestic Bliss doesn't think he needs fingers to play keyboards."

"He cut one off?" Stephen looked horrified.

"No, thank God, but I guess he did a number on it."

It was late when the three returned. Terry was in the living room reading the newspaper. "God, I hate emergency rooms," Bobby muttered. Jules looked pale and drawn.

"How bad is it?" Terry asked.

"We're home!" Free announced to the house.

Bobby held up his left hand, a thick wrapping of gauze swaddling his index finger, and pointed along it with his right. "I sliced it pretty good, but I managed to miss the joint."

Ez burst in.

Bobby continued, subdued. "Five stitches. I cut it to the bone."

Terry winced. "Ew."

"I didn't even really feel it when I did it, but I sure as fuck feel it now."

The next morning Ez called a meeting of the band, Jules, Free, and Marla. "You guys, I don't want any of you messing around in the kitchen, do you understand? No cooking! That's what your old ladies are for."

"Excuse me?" Free butted in, hand on her hip. "That's what us 'old ladies' are for? You lucky you even got an 'old lady,' with an attitude like that."

"Alright, alright!" he held up his hands in surrender. "That's what the non-musicians are for. Okay? Okay?" He turned to Free, who huffed grudging appeasement. "No musicians in the kitchen, except to eat. I don't even want to see you with a butter knife!"

Bobby was at the piano after breakfast, working out how to play, holding his bandaged finger up away from the keys. It stung. The stitches pulled as he stretched his hand, but he could compensate, for the most part. If he wrapped it thinner, he could fill in the necessary notes in the chords. Right now the dressing sometimes pushed the adjacent keys. Years of dogged practice were paying off. His hands were limber enough, his fingers strong enough that he could shift from normal fingering without too much trouble, only mental obstacles, overcoming habit. He worked, and worked, an hour, two hours. Jules brought him coffee, urged him to take a break. His hand ached. He took a couple aspirin.

In the studio he and Terry worked around the rhythm track that Stephen and Miles had laid down. The tune emerged. Bobby worked, concentrated, fought for it. "Take it slow, man," Terry said. "Don't wear yourself out."

"If we're going to use this, we've got to get it done."

"We've got time. It's the last song, and we've got tomorrow."

After lunch, having re-wrapped his finger to better suit him, he laid his tracks down and called it a day. Unless someone had a last minute idea, he was done recording.

That night he took Jules to the beach. He needed rest, craved the sound of the surf, the way it smoothed out his thoughts, lulled him. He took his tape recorder with him. "What are you doing?" Jules had asked when he put it in the car.

"I want to tape the sound of the waves," he said, "so we can listen to it while we sleep."

Chapter 18

"Nora, you better come here," Rob said. "Bobby's brought home another stray." He engulfed Jules in a fatherly hug. "Welcome to our family. Not that you weren't welcome before."

"Ah, you're back," Nora hurried in, holding out her arms to her son.

He kissed her cheek and hugged her. "Mom," he said by her ear, "We got married."

She held him back at arm's length. "You did?"

"We did," he smiled and held up his ring.

She laughed happy astonishment and pulled his head down to kiss his cheek. "I guess I shouldn't be surprised." She pulled Jules into a hug and kissed her cheek, as well. "Come in and sit down. You must be exhausted. I'll fix you something to eat." They all went to the kitchen. Nora gave Jules a Coke, started the coffee pot for Bobby and Rob, wanted to see Jules' ring and hear about California as she cut peach pie for everyone.

"How did things go out there, son?" Rob asked Bobby. "The recording go well?"

"I think it went very well. Even got Jules to sing on it," he reached over to squeeze her shoulder.

"Bobby, what on earth did you do to your finger?" Nora caught sight of the stitches.

"I had an argument with a knife over an avocado."

"Scared me to death," Jules said. "He cut it to the bone."

Nora winced and reached for his hand, to examine it.

"I've lost some feeling in it. Some of it may come back over time. I can play just fine."

"Well, you just be careful, you hear?" Nora said.

"But," he turned back to Rob, "I lost my drummer."

"Lost him how?"

"He didn't come back. He likes it out there, found a girl and wants to live there. I don't know what's going to happen now. I'd kinda counted on some income from playing around here until I can find a job and get us a place. And Jules needs to move out of her apartment. Gina's got a new roommate waiting."

"Maybe you can find someone to just fill in," Nora offered.

"Maybe," Bobby shrugged. "If he could learn the songs fast enough."

"Call Dwitty," Jules said.

"He's got work and night school."

"Maybe he could just play at the Happen Inn on Friday nights."

"I'll ask him, but I'm not going to pressure him if he doesn't want to do it. He'd need time to rehearse with us, too."

"Son, if you haven't found a place before Jules needs to move, the two of you can stay here in the meantime."

"Thanks, Dad." He turned to Jules, "Whatcha say, baby?"

"That's fine with me," she said, then turned to Nora, "if you're sure you don't mind."

"We don't mind," Nora smiled, reached for Jules' hand and squeezed it.

When Bobby had had his second cup of coffee, he said, "We just dropped our things at the apartment and came right here. Jules' family doesn't even know yet." He looked to Jules. "What do you want to do? Do you want to just stop by?" he questioned gently.

She thought a moment. "I think I'd rather call first."

He nodded. "Go ahead."

"Do you mind?" she asked Nora, nodding toward the phone.

"Heavens no, child."

"I'll call Maggie tonight," Bobby said.

"You'd better call your grandparents, too," Nora said. "I'm sure they'd rather hear it from you than from us."

Jules stood up and went to the wall phone, put the receiver to her ear, dialed, waited, heard it ring, steeled herself.

"Hello?" It was Dan.

"Hi, Daddy," she said. "Is Mom there?"

"Your mother is out," he said. There was no warmth in his tone.

"Have her call me later, please, at the apartment. Tell her we're back safe." She couldn't conceal her happiness as she said, "Tell her we got married."

Click.

"Daddy?"

Dial tone.

She put the hand set back and just stood facing the wall.

"Baby?" Bobby questioned softly.

Slowly she turned to him, shaking her head, color drained from her face. "He hung up," she said quietly, too numb for tears as she walked slowly toward the table. Bobby reached for her, pulled her into his lap, held her as she hid her face in the side of his neck. "He fucking hung up," she muttered, too dazed to mind her language in front of his parents.

She felt him shake his head slightly. "No, Mom, it's okay," he said.

Jules closed her eyes, heard Rob's quiet voice. "Come on, dear."

Chairs scraped against the floor and she heard Nora's voice fading through the doorway, "Lord God. What kind of a man would do that to..."

Bobby smoothed Jules' hair. "You okay?"

"I don't know if he'll even tell her I called," she said.

"If you don't hear from her, call that friend, Janice."

"Yeah," she sighed.

"I'm so sorry."

"It's okay."

"No," he said. "It's really not okay. It's hurting you."

"I guess it's just the way it is, though."

He hugged her tight, rocking her ever so slightly, and she tried to quiet her mind and rest her heart. She remembered how Free had told her to breathe in slowly and deeply, to hold, then release twice as slowly. *I am at peace. I am at peace.*

Just as she stood up, they heard Sissy burst into the living room. "Hey, I'm back. I'm so thirsty. I need a Coke."

"Sissy, wait," Nora said.

"It's okay," Bobby called out.

"Oh my God, you're back!" she rushed in. "How was it? How was it?"

Bobby laughed. He took Jules' hand. "We got married."

"Oh!" Sissy covered her mouth, her eyes wide. "You eloped? That's so romantic."

Jules and Bobby laughed and he hugged her against his side.

"Did you get married on the beach?"

"No, we got married in Las Vegas, in a little chapel."

"Going to the chapel of love," she sang, from the Dixie Cups song. "Did you go gambling?" she asked excitedly.

He laughed. "Can't do that without money. I needed mine for these," he took Jules' hand and held it up for Sissy to see her rings.

"Oh, that's so pretty!" She leaned closer and took Jules' finger to have a good look. "Oh, you two are so perfect for each other. I always knew you'd get married."

"Bobby, honey," Nora leaned in the doorway, "Why don't you two stay for supper?"

"Thanks, Mom, but we need to get back to the apartment in case her mom calls."

"How about tomorrow night, then?"

"What do you say, baby?" he asked Jules.

"That would be nice," she smiled.

They hadn't been back at the apartment long, and were sitting on the couch eating cheese sandwiches when Gina and Terry came in. "Oh!" Gina squealed, "The Magnets are back!" Jules set her plate on the coffee table to go meet Gina's outstretched arms.

"I think you'll find they're more than magnets now," Terry chuckled.

"What do you mean?" Gina asked as she and Jules embraced.

Jules laughed, drew back from her, and held up her rings.

"No!" Gina grinned.

"Yes," Jules nodded.

"Okay, tell me everything," Gina said. "Well, not *everything*," she snickered.

Kate called late. Terry and Gina had gone out again. "Your father's in bed, finally. I wanted to wait so we could talk without him interfering."

"He hung up on me."

Kate exhaled forcefully through her nose. "I'm not surprised. He's not happy. You didn't really expect him to be, did you?"

"I thought maybe he would at least accept things now. We're married. Isn't that enough?"

"Julia, he's never going to accept Bobby. He just isn't. The way you went about things doesn't help."

"What about you?" she ventured quietly. "Aren't you happy for us?"

"Honey, I'm not quite sure yet how I feel," Kate sighed. "I'm relieved that you're back safe. I was worried about you the whole time you were gone."

"We were fine, Mom. Didn't you get my postcards?"

"Yes, I got the cards, but you could have sent a card one minute and been... dead the next."

"Oh, Mom. We could get the bomb dropped on us any minute, too."

"Have some respect. You wait. When you have kids you'll see how it feels."

"When does Bobby get some respect?" She waited for a response.

"Julia, it's late," Kate said some moments later. "I need to go. We'll talk more tomorrow. Good night, dear."

"Good night."

Jules hung up, tired, distraught, frustrated. Bobby got up from the couch and went to her, taking her into his arms. "Come on, honey, let's get some sleep."

"I just– just–" She clenched her fists against his back.

"Sh-hh... Let it go for tonight. You're worn out and so am I."

She heaved a sigh, tried to relax, uncurled her hands and let them slip down to hold his waist.

"I know it's not the same," he soothed, "but you're part of my family now, and they love you. They'll be good to you. They're happy for us."

Natalie thought it only right to celebrate Jules and Bobby's wedding with some sort of reception. By the skin of their teeth, Kate managed to secure the park pavilion for a couple hours on Saturday, because someone else had canceled a reservation. Kate ordered a cake, made punch and finger foods, consulted Jules about the guest list. They kept it small, manageable, the most important people. Nora insisted on helping with the food and with setting things up. They laid out a pretty spread, and as the guests arrived, gifts accumulated on the cake table. Tricia and Dwitty were there. Melissa had come, but without Chip. "He had to work," she claimed. Miles sauntered in with a girl he had sometimes dated. The Rebelles had all come, poised to sing their own a capella rendition of "Here Comes the Bride" as a surprise. Sissy had met Sonya and struck up a chat.

When Bobby and Jules crossed the parking lot, they paused near the walkway behind the stage, remembering. "You were such a wolf," she said.

"I was," he admitted. "And you were a flirt."

"Saw something I wanted," she smiled. "It worked, didn't it?"

"And then you put me off!"

"You ended up getting what you wanted."

"Got more than I bargained for," he grinned, pulling her into a kiss. Someone thumped his head with a flicked finger, and he looked up to see Terry innocently walking past with Gina. "I guess we should go in."

As they stepped through the doorway, cheers rose up from the gathering and The Rebelles sang, trying not to laugh.

> Here comes the bride
> who wouldn't be denied.

That's quite a catch
that she's got by her side!

Here comes the groom.
Hand him a broom,
'cause she'll be the boss
of the household soon.

Jules wore her blue batik dress, her actual wedding dress. Rather than the t-shirt and jeans he had been wearing on that day, Bobby wore his ivory pants and a pink paisley shirt. They both wore the white bead necklaces Marla had given them, and sandals.

"I remember when pink and blue were the other way around," Natalie laughed to Kate.

"I remember when a lot of things were the other way around," Kate grumbled.

"It's a different world, Kate. They have to find their own path through it."

Maggie and Bill came. Jules had never met them. Maggie was tall, dark-haired, and resembled Bobby, though she looked more like Nora than he did. She was quiet and reserved, but amiable, as was Bill, a respectable-looking, rather ordinary man, an insurance salesman. They seemed placid and content in each other's company.

Jules' grandparents were there, all soft hugs and kisses and doting, pleased to meet Bobby, seemingly disposed to accept anyone Jules thought good enough for herself.

Rob's widowed mother, a bent, fragile woman, had come on a rare outing with her daughter Dorothy, whom Jules barely remembered from the Christmas party at Bobby's house that seemed so long ago. Grandma Bonnie reached out a cool, shaky hand to caress Jules' cheek. "Such a pretty little thing," she smiled, then jabbed Bobby in the ribs. "You be good to her, you big galoot," she frowned, then dissolved in laughter, and Bobby gave his grandma a gentle hug and a kiss on the cheek.

Since Jules and Bobby both knew everyone else there, they split up to socialize.

When he approached her and Kate, Natalie gave Bobby a big hug. When she let him go, she leaned back, reached up and gently pinched his cheek. "You look a lot better than the last time I saw you."

He laughed. "I feel a lot better. I finally feel like I've gotten the cold out of my bones."

"You've got more meat on those bones, too."

"You've met?" Kate puzzled.

Natalie smiled. "Oh yes, we've met. How was California?"

"Sunny and weird," he laughed. "It's like a different world out there, maybe a little much for us. We had fun, but it's good to be back."

Jules and Gina stood some distance away, cackling about something, trying not to spill their punch. Bobby looked at them, shook his head and grinned. Terry came up behind Gina and put his arms around her waist. "Maybe you're next, old man!" Bobby shouted to him.

"Shi-i-i-it..." he smirked. Gina reached up and playfully smacked his jaw.

Bobby looked around at his family, his friends, their smiles and laughter, but there was a hole, an empty place, by the table, in his heart. Tyler should be here. *But, damn you, Tyler, you don't even know what I've suffered because of you, the misery you caused Jules and me. Bad enough to lose you, but you nearly cost me everything.*

Kate took Natalie aside, out of earshot of Bobby or Jules. "When did you meet Bobby?"

"When Jules came up last winter. When he was starving and freezing his butt off with no heat, trying to do right by your daughter."

Kate shot her a perplexed look.

"Yes, they saw each other. I took him out with us, fed him, let him sleep by the fire, gave him money, loaned him a heater and some clothes. He was trying so hard to make it on his own."

"You went behind our backs like that?"

"Yes, I did."

"Why?"

"Why? Because Dan was being an ass, and because I never forgot what love is."

"Natalie, you didn't have that right."

"Dan Greene's rules don't apply to me. I didn't marry him, you did. God knows why." She gestured toward Bobby and Jules, smiling, lit with reflected sun, arms around each other as Jules showed Sonya her ring. "Look how happy they are. How could anyone deny them that?"

"I just worry. The way they ran off and got married, I have to wonder if she's– you know."

"Expecting?"

"Dan seems sure of it. She hasn't told us anything."

"If she is, she is, and Bobby's done right by her."

"They're so young for that yet."

"You were just turned 20 when she was born. She's 18, and if she is expecting, she's not far enough along to show. She'd be getting close to

218

19. That's not so big a difference, is it?"

Kate heaved an irritated sigh. "You're so blithe about this. What if it was Sonya?"

"I've done my best to raise her to be smart, and in the end that's all I can do. Of course I want her to make good decisions, but she's becoming a woman. I'll have to let go soon, just like mom had to let go of us. He's a good boy, Kate. She could do a hell of a lot worse."

Rob and Nora came to meet Natalie and thank Kate for setting up the reception. "Dan's not coming?" Rob asked.

Kate shook her head. "No, and perhaps that's best. I'm sorry for the trouble he's caused everyone."

Nora squeezed Kate's shoulder supportively. "I wish things had been different, but I'm glad they got through it alright. They do love each other so. Bobby will take good care of her, rest assured, and so will we. We love her too."

Before she and Sonya left, Natalie hugged Jules one more time. "I can't believe your father wouldn't come today," she grumbled as she let her go.

"Actually, I'm relieved he didn't."

"Are things that bad between you now?"

"Aunt Nat," Jules said, looking down at her hands, turning her engagement ring around her finger. "You don't know, do you, what he did the day I moved out?"

"No, honey."

"Ask Mom."

When everyone else had left, Terry and Gina approached Bobby and Jules and handed them a card. "A little something for the happy couple," Terry said with a sly smile. "We'd be more than happy to join you."

Gina giggled.

Bobby tore open the envelope and pulled out the card. "Congratulations on your wedding," he read aloud, and opened it. "May every happiness be yours this day and always." Under it Terry had written, "Here's two tickets for your honeymoon trip." Enclosed were two festive looking squares of blotter acid. Bobby's smile dissolved.

"We're partaking in a few minutes," Terry grinned. "It'll be Gina's first."

Gina took Jules' hand. "I'd like it if you did it with me. I'm a little nervous," she confided.

"I–" Bobby bit his bottom lip. "I don't know, man," he said to

Terry.

"Somebody spiked us at that Doors show," Jules said. "Bobby had a bad trip."

"Shit, I'm not surprised," Terry said. "That's some dark stuff. Sorry, man. Set and setting. That's what somebody told me. If your mind is in the wrong place, or the place is too much..."

"Yeah," Bobby nodded.

"But, hey, the park is beautiful and peaceful, the sun is out, we can go where nobody will bother us, and we can all crash at the apartment. Your last night there. What do you say?" Terry pitched.

"Baby, I'd like to trip with Gina," Jules said. "But you don't have to. You can just hang out." She added with a laugh, "And be our daddy."

That made Gina laugh.

Bobby took a deep breath, looked out at the trees, looked at his friends, his sunny wife. Then he tore the squares apart and popped one in his mouth. "No Doors music, and no naked hippie parties," he said.

"Naked hippie parties?" Gina raised her eyebrows.

"Don't ask," Jules said.

Late that night on Mary Street, well past their peak, but still high, Terry was still pulling out clover leaves Gina had stuffed in his shirt pockets at the park, and she, still giggling, strewed them around the living room like confetti. Terry put on the first Love album. "It's so, so cool that you saw them," Gina said. "Oh, I wish I had gone."

"I'll take you there someday," Terry said.

Jules and Bobby lay on the mattress in her room, the music bleeding through the wall and slipping in under the door. Bobby was smiling, gazing at the ceiling, relaxed. He watched the bubbles of blown plaster ripple and froth like sea foam.

"We danced to this record at Carol's party, way back when," Jules said. "Remember? That seems so long ago."

"The first night you sang for me," he said. "All pink and shimmery."

"And terrified," she laughed.

"I was impressed, and proud." He turned on his side to face her. "I felt honored."

"Don't dance with any other," she whispered, fingering the top button of his shirt. "Never, ever."

"Jules," he kissed her gently, the soft pillow of her bottom lip radiating warmth and comfort through his whole being. "You are my only girl. You'll always be my only girl. I've never, ever meant to hurt you. Or make you cry."

"A few times," she said, "they were happy tears."

In the morning, Jules woke from shallow sleep and squinted at the clock on the floor across the room. 11:00. Bobby slept close at her back, his knees tucked up behind hers, his arm limp across her ribs, the bracelet she had given him still encircling his wrist. She reached behind her to squeeze his bare butt. He groaned, nestled closer. "We should get up and get dressed," she said. "Mom's coming over to help me pack."

"Mmm… yeah, okay," he said groggily and kissed her ear before rolling onto his back. "Nice to think, though," he smiled, "that it doesn't matter anymore."

"Mom would be embarrassed," she laughed.

"She'd get over it." He stretched his arms above his head, whacking his knuckles on the wall.

The house was quiet. Terry and Gina had gone off somewhere. Jules, on her way to the kitchen, laughed at the wilted clovers on the rug and picked a few of them up. They'd had a beautiful time, Gina amazed and amused by everything, Jules laughing with her, showing her pretty things, while Terry philosophized ridiculously and Bobby sat placidly leaning against a tree, watching the sparkling, gurgling creek flow by. "Terry, shut the fuck up," he'd say every once in a while.

Jules scrounged up a late breakfast to share with Bobby before he went out to run errands. On the table sat their wedding presents. Terry and Gina had given them a toaster and a cookbook, humor and practicality rolled into one. Jules' mom had given them a set of nesting Tupperware containers, with $50 tucked inside the innermost one. Sissy had given them a pretty flower vase. Bobby's parents had given them a blanket and two sets of sheets, which Bobby seemed to find amusing. Various relatives had given or sent money. Miles gave them a set of coffee mugs. Dwitty and Tricia gave them a photo album containing copies of many of their pictures from England, assorted snapshots of the band, a few pictures of Bobby and Jules from Dwitty and Tricia's wedding reception, and a note promising pictures from Bobby and Jules' reception.

Soon after Bobby left, Kate arrived and she and Jules set to work.

"Julia," Kate asked, taking a blouse off a hanger and neatly folding it, "If you don't mind too much my asking… I've been reading some things, women's books, some studies. You're married now. I just wondered–" Kate shrugged.

"Wondered what, Mom?" Jules shifted the books in the box to try to fit one more in.

"When Bobby– makes love to you– do you–"

Jules stopped, looked at Kate with raised eyebrows.

"Do you have orgasms?"

"Mom!"

"No, I'm serious. I don't mean to embarrass you, but–" Kate's face flushed.

"Well, yes. Why?"

"Is it… as wonderful as they say?"

Jules' heart sank. "Oh, Mom, you mean…"

"I've never had one, honey."

"It is, Mom, every bit as wonderful as they say." She reached out and took her mother's hands.

Kate squeezed her daughter's hands and looked at her with a sad smile. "I'm glad for you."

"Maybe Dad just needs to, you know, take a little more time with you."

Kate huffed, let go of Jules' hands and took down another shirt.

Jules didn't know what to say, returned to shuffling books around. She picked up *The Canterbury Tales.* "I bought this in Canterbury. It was so pretty there." A snapshot fell out, one Tricia had taken of Jules and Bobby on the cathedral steps, arms around each other's waists. "Look," she showed her mother.

"I've never seen that one," Kate commented.

"I kept it hidden. I hid a lot of pictures."

Kate sighed. "I know you went through some hard times, and I'm sorry for that. I also know you went behind our backs."

Jules laughed, "Yeah, Aunt Nat let the cat out, didn't she?"

"I'm guessing there were other times. I had my suspicions. Just because I didn't say anything doesn't mean I approved. I felt like you were growing up way too fast and I didn't know what to do about it. You'll have kids of your own one day and you'll see what that feels like. There wasn't anything I could point to to call you on. You were good in school, did your homework, you didn't miss work, you never broke curfew, you seemed to always be where you were supposed to be when you were supposed to be. But I just had this feeling. You'd be sitting up in your room, reading, playing records…"

"Plotting," she admitted with a laugh.

"Yes." She gave her a stern look. "You and Gina. God knows what you two got up to. I'd really rather not. When you moved out, that was bad enough. Then when you ran off with him to California, well… Everyone was talking, of course." She patted down the shirt she had just folded and shook her head. "God, your father's been miserable to live with."

"I'm sorry, Mom," she whispered.

Kate looked up, straight into Jules' eyes. "You had to pick trouble, didn't you?"

Jules boldly held her gaze. "I had to pick love."

"Love," she shook her head. "Well, I hope it lasts. I hope you can make a good life together."

"Thanks, Mom."

"Have you found a place to live?"

"We're going up Wednesday to start looking, and look for jobs."

"Up? Up where?"

"Louisville."

Kate looked puzzled.

"I took the scholarship to U of L."

"You're going to college?"

"I wasn't sure I could at first, but with the scholarship, Bobby thinks we can make it alright. I want to try, at least."

"I just figured... I mean, I thought maybe you were–" She looked at Jules' abdomen.

Jules laughed. "I'm not pregnant, Mom, if that's what you mean."

Kate grasped Jules' upper arm. "Good. Take your time. Don't rush your life."

"We take life as it comes," she said softly. While she'd been relieved to discover she wasn't pregnant, she'd also felt a little disappointed.

Kate dropped her hold and turned back toward the closet. "Jules, honey, I'm divorcing your father."

Jules' eyes widened in shock. "Why?"

"I don't love him anymore, and I don't think he loves me. I don't think we've really loved each other for a long time, but it's been so gradual. One day you just realize you're not happy and you're not going to be happy if you stay. I don't like what he's done to me. He would allow me just enough, grudgingly, but just enough to make me think I had some independence, some worth of my own. He tolerated me selling Tupperware, but he wouldn't let me get a real job. He insisted it would make him look bad, like he couldn't provide for us. He tolerated the Women's Circle, barely. He'd get mad sometimes, call us 'a bunch of women's libbers.' He gave me just enough to make me think he wasn't holding me down, and I tried to be a good wife and a good mother to you. I hope I was."

"Of course you were, Mom." Jules hugged her.

"But, honey, what he did to you," she choked on emotion, held

Jules back to look at her. "When he hit you like that, when I saw what he'd done, I just couldn't love him anymore. I couldn't love someone who would do that. I didn't want to." Tears spilled from her eyes and she fished a hankie out of her skirt pocket. "I know a lot of men treat their kids worse. A lot of women put up with worse than I have, but why should they? Why should I? Why should we always have some kind of threat hanging over us, holding us down in 'our place', as they say? Why should we have to live half starved?"

"Oh, Mom." Jules rubbed her mother's back.

"I'm not so old, am I? I want to be loved. I want someone I can love. I want someone who will let me be myself. I'll never have that if I stay with him. Hell, I don't even know who myself is anymore."

"Shh– it's okay, Mom."

There was a quick knock, and as Jules and Kate stepped into the living room, Bobby pushed open the door, nearly obscured by cardboard. "I got some boxes from the grocery store," he said, dropping them in the kitchen and taking a newspaper from under his arm. "And I picked up a Louisville paper."

Kate quickly dabbed her eyes and stuffed the hankie back in her pocket.

"Everything okay?" he said more quietly.

Jules nodded. "Mom, come and sit down, take a break. Do you want some coffee?"

"Yes, thank you, dear," she sniffled.

"I know *you* do," she poked Bobby in the ribs. He grabbed her and gave her a kiss.

"Anything I can do?" he asked softly.

She shook her head.

Kate sat down in a chair. Bobby sank into the sagging couch, pulled the want ads out of the paper and laid the rest on the coffee table. "Hi, Mama G."

"Hi, Bobby." She tried to smile.

"Something wrong?"

She smoothed her lap, then looked up into his eyes. "I'm leaving Dan."

He blinked, stroked one of his jaw-length sideburns. "Where will you go?"

"Natalie's finding me a place up there. I want out of this town."

Bobby nodded, took a deep breath.

"Jules, honey," she turned toward the kitchen, "There are still some things of yours at the house. If you want them, you need to come and get them."

"When? I mean..."
"He'll be at work tomorrow."
Jules looked at Bobby. "I'll come with you," he said.

They loaded her things, and their wedding presents, into the back of the Safari and she drove the Dart behind him to his house. He stacked her boxes along one wall of his room, and used the leftover empty boxes to begin packing his own things. Jules was back to living out of a suitcase, which Scraggs quickly decided was a bed.

"I'm going to miss this old piano," Bobby said, sitting down to play it after supper, with Jules beside him on the bench. "Have to save up to buy my own, I guess. I can't keep up my playing the way I'd like to without one."

"We'll make it a priority," Jules said.

"Yeah," he said. "If there's anything left over to save."

Late that night, after a leisurely walk around the neighborhood with Lady, they retired to Bobby's room and got ready for bed. Door closed, lights off, they climbed between the sheets.

"Ever since the first day you showed me this room," Jules said, "I've wanted to make love here in your bed, with your music hanging above us on the walls. I used to lie in my bed, thinking of you lying here."

"And I would lie here thinking about you, wanting you." She nestled tighter up against him. "Let's make your wish come true," he whispered against her lips.

Touching, kissing, they worked each other's night clothes off, stroking up desire into need. He rolled her onto her back, moving in her slow and deep. Suddenly, he laughed, leaned hard to one side, and Jules heard a thud on the floor. "Cat climbed up my back," he explained, and she laughed too. They resumed, faster, and the headboard began knocking against the wall. "Shit!" he whispered. She tried not to giggle. He grabbed his t-shirt off the floor and stuffed it between the headboard and the wall. "We'll be lucky if the damn bed doesn't collapse," he grumbled. The furniture sufficiently quieted, they could concentrate on each other again. Though she tried, in her pleasure, Jules couldn't be silent. "Sh-hh," Bobby breathed, trying not to laugh, "Sh-hh." She closed her mouth, but soft moans escaped through her nose, and he lost himself in the feel of her, tight around him, quivering, clutching at his shoulders and hair.

He slid back on his heels to rest, his head upon her breast. She massaged his shoulders and stroked his hair until they'd caught their breath, then he stretched out beside her. "Ah, Jules, you're a good, good woman," he said softly. "No man could ask for better." They sank into the soft-worn mattress, into gentle sleep.

They slept till noon, oblivious to any activity in the house. Rob had gone to work. Sissy was outside with a neighbor friend. After a quick shower, not bothering to shave, Bobby turned the bathroom over to Jules. He stripped the bed and crept to the laundry room with the sheets. He was just stuffing them in the washer when Nora walked in. "Good morning, Mom," he said casually. "Or afternoon."

"I can take care of that, honey," she offered.

"No, it's okay." He busied himself, trying not to betray his embarrassment.

"I'll put some extras in your room," she said in her pleasant, practical tone.

After lunch, Bobby drove Jules to her former house. At Kate's direction, he brought a step ladder in from the garage and used it to get into the attic access in the upstairs hallway. Jules went up after him and pointed out which boxes were hers. He brought them down and took them out to pack into the car, pausing to glance into Jules' old room, at her white bed and dresser. He had never seen them before.

Kate and Jules went ahead to the garage to find Jules' possessions there. "Do you two have anything to start out with, in the way of furniture, I mean?" Kate asked her.

"Bobby's desk," Jules laughed. "Maybe his chest of drawers."

"No bed?"

"Not yet. We thought we might see if we could buy that mattress from Terry."

"You need something better than that. Who knows that thing's history? And it doesn't even have box springs."

"It's in good shape. It would do in the short term."

"How are you getting everything up there?"

"Terry's going to drive up with us with his trailer."

"Then take your bed and dresser. I may have some other things you can take, too. Call me when you're ready for them."

Wednesday morning after Rob left for work, Bobby sat at the table drinking his coffee, looking at a map, waiting for Jules, who was getting ready for their first excursion to Louisville. Nora sat down across from her son, with her own cup of coffee, breakfast finished, dishes cleared. He folded the map so that a portion of the city showed, and stacked it with newspaper pages, listings circled in red pen.

"Good luck today," she said. "I hope you find a nice place."
"Thanks, Mom."
She fought a smile. "One with good, thick walls."
He covered his face, sputtered, and they burst out laughing.

Chapter 19

The ground floor apartment was small and a bit shabby, but had a strip of yard, and they were allowed to have Scraggs and Lady. As he and Terry set up the bed frame, Bobby was amused by the tiny stickers and decals on one of the headboard posts – a flower, a peace sign, a heart barely containing the word Love. A schoolgirl's dreams. They could be any girl's dreams. But these were his girl's dreams, his wife's dreams.

Bobby had already started work a few days before, as the bookkeeper and shipping clerk at an auto parts and repair shop, making the long commute between Midvale and Louisville. Once Jules had registered for her classes and gotten her schedule, she planned to find part time work, as well.

In the kitchen, Jules unpacked assorted dishes and cookware from their wrappings of dish towels, bath towels, an apron, a couple of table cloths for which there was, as yet, no table, all things her mother had collected from around the house that she neither planned to take with her nor leave for Dan. "He's damn lucky I'm leaving him anything," Kate had remarked. She had given them Jules' bedding, a lamp, the rocking chair in which she had rocked Jules when she was a baby.

As they'd left the Lotts' house that morning, Nora had tucked a rolled up $5 bill into Jules' hand. "I know it's not much, but you can't have an empty fridge."

Rob had gone out to the Safari as Bobby was about to close the tailgate, praying it would clear the end of his desk, and handed him an old toolbox. "Grandpa's tools?" Bobby questioned.

"And a few extras. Go ahead and take them now. Why should you have to wait till I'm dead? I know you can use them."

When Terry left the new apartment, Bobby tried to pay him for his help, but Terry refused. "You need it a lot worse than I do," he said. "Maybe I'll need a favor from you someday."

"Thanks, man," Bobby said, and they exchanged a brotherly hug.

"See you Friday night," Terry replied.

Bobby and Jules waved goodbye to him as he pulled away, then locked up the apartment and went to the grocery store. They bought the basics, and Jules was thankful Free had taught her how to stretch a dollar in the kitchen and still eat well. For tonight, ham sandwiches and store

228

brand macaroni and cheese, only 20 cents a box, seemed an easy choice for a first meal in their new home.

As Bobby turned the key in the front door lock, Lady let out a low, "Woof." *Good. I know she's old and lazy, but no one else would*, he thought. He pushed the door open and was about to walk past the dog, when he stopped.

"Wait," he said. He set his bag of groceries inside and reached for the one Jules held. "Don't move." She looked puzzled as he set the other sack inside. "We're forgetting something."

"What?"

"This," he smiled, lifting her up in his arms to carry her over the threshold. He kicked the door shut behind them and carried her into the bedroom, laying her on the bed, pushing Scraggs out of the way to make room for himself. He pulled Jules close and kissed her. "We're on our own now, baby. For better or worse."

"It seems strange. It's not someone else's place, no roommates..."

"Except furry ones," he laughed.

"I'm happy to have the furry ones."

He ran his fingertips down her cheek, kissed her again, pressing his body tight against hers as he reached down to run his hand up her thigh.

"I think we'd better stop here for now," she said against his lips. "Unless you want to give the neighbors a show."

He turned to look at the window, and laughed. There were no curtains. "I guess we need to put the food away anyway."

Before they went to bed that night, Jules took the larger of the two table cloths and pinned it up over the bedroom window. "Shall we hang this up over the bed?" She held up her old Raiders centerfold.

"Is that where you had it in your room?" he smirked.

"No, actually it was over my desk."

"And what have they got that I don't?"

She laughed. "Tights!"

"And money," he conceded as she folded it and put it back in the box. "Thank God I don't have to drive an hour and a half to get to work tomorrow," he said, setting his alarm. Before settling in with Jules between the sheets, he switched on his tape deck, turned low, and the sound of the surf washed gently over them.

Dwitty had agreed to play one show, Friday night at the Happen Inn. He could only manage two rehearsals to try to learn the songs, but Miles would coach and cue him through the set. They were billing it as a farewell performance, and Rob had run off some nice flyers at work. Tricia and Gina put them up around town.

Kate had gone to visit Natalie and had found an apartment. She would be in Midvale for the weekend, to pick up the rest of her things and sign some papers at the bank. "Mom," Jules said on the phone, "You've got to come to the show. Bobby's parents will be there, and Sissy, and I really want you to see the guys play. You may not get another chance."

"I'll think about it, dear. Let's see how things go that day."

"It would mean a lot to me," Jules said, "and we'd get some time together. Bobby and I will be spending the night. Maybe you and I could go shopping Saturday or something."

Nora invited Kate over for supper at their house before the show, and she accepted. Sitting at the warm, life-scarred, wooden table with Rob and Nora, Sissy, Bobby and Jules, Kate felt comfort. The Lotts were refreshingly unpretentious, open-hearted, their fondness for Jules obvious. It saddened Kate that Jules' own family had come apart. "Your Aunt Nat has a boyfriend," she told Jules. "Frankie."

"Really?" Jules smiled. "That's great! What's he like?"

"Oh, he's kind of short. Brown hair, brown eyes. He's an art teacher at Sonya's school."

"What does Sonya think about it?" Jules asked.

"It's a little embarrassing for her, I think, having her mom dating one of her teachers," Kate laughed. "But she likes him."

At the Happen Inn, Jules stood with their parents, even though it meant not being up front. Gina and Tricia joined her. "This meeting of the Band Women's Club will now come to order," Tricia joked.

"Honorary members!" Gina announced, taking Nora and Kate by the hand, and they all laughed. Spirits were high, smiles infectious.

"I'm sure you noticed," Terry said into his mic as the band assembled on stage, "that we're calling this a farewell show." He was met with a chorus of nos and boos. "We hope it's just a farewell for now show. Life's brought us a lot of changes recently. We just recorded an album out in California, which should be out soon." Cheers from the audience. "You may have noticed our old friend Dwitty back here on the drums." Loud cheers. Dwitty stood up to take a quick bow. "He's filling in tonight, because Stephen has decided to live in L.A." More boos. "So, bear with him. He's barely had time to learn our songs. Miles is about to start college in Lexington, and Bobby just moved to Louisville, so things are a bit complicated right now, but we'll see what happens. In the meantime—"

he raised his hand in the air, Dwitty clicked his sticks together to count off, and the band struck a ferocious chord, going into their reworking of "Mean Girl," both for nostalgia and because Dwitty was more comfortable starting out with something he knew well. The crowd certainly approved.

The band interspersed a few old favorites with the newer material, familiar to many in the audience from shows leading up to the California trip. Dwitty handled the new songs just fine, keeping it simple when he needed to. His style was different from Stephen's, but Terry and Bobby knew what to expect from him, and Miles was adaptable.

"Here's a new one," Terry announced deep into the set. "It's called 'The Inner Sea.'" It was the song for which Jules had watched them record the vocals, never dreaming in that moment that she would be in that booth herself just a few days later. It sounded good live, rich and moody, fuzzed out Telecaster over sinuous Farfisa, Terry's voice a dark, but melodic warning. He had the crowd in the palm of his hand, and Jules had felt that magic turn of mood come over the room that always happened here at their shows, when the lighthearted party evolved into a powerful, mesmerizing groove, when the audience locked in on the music, and the band, in turn, soared even higher.

Terry left the stage and Bobby leaned into his mic. "Drop it down, Dwitty. Nice and slow. We're gonna give Terry a break here." Dwitty and Miles set a stripped down Blues backing. Bobby tapped in a few chords to set the tone, leaving a measure of space between his sentences, as he would between lines when he sang the lyrics. "In church they talk about testifying. Well, I'm gonna do a little testifying tonight about the power of love."

A boy in the crowd yelled, "Amen, brother!" People laughed. Bobby flashed a smile.

"I wrote this song for my baby," he continued. "Some of you know our story, some of you don't, but it's all in here." He nodded to his bandmates.

Jules could hear Miles, off mic, slowly count, "1-2-3-4- hit it!" Dwitty accented the spare rhythm with power and snap, and Bobby began to sing, with a gentle tension that built in intensity with each stanza. It was a song Jules had never heard.

> When you first came
> into my world,
> thought you were just
> another girl,

but you taught me love
I never knew,
and so I fell
in love with you.

Take me in your arms and hold me
oh so tight.
Give me all your wild, sweet loving
all through the night.

And so I took you,
and made you mine,
drank your loving
sweet as wine.

Then the storm hit,
and the rain.
They tried to tell us
not to see each other ever again…

He drew that last word out a full pulsing twelve beats as Dwitty and Miles built up the volume, and he ripped into an organ solo of tortured sustains, rapid-fire staccato passages, and full-blown Gospel, his fingers rippling the keys, then wringing out wailing chords. The keyboard shivered and swayed with the force of his playing as he grimaced, shaking his head with the beat, eyes closed, or threw his head back, biting hard on his bottom lip as he sometimes did when making love. Jules, flushed, enrapt, had dropped Gina's hand after squeezing it so hard Gina protested. She clasped her own hands tight into a double fist and pressed them against her heart. His parents, her mother were standing right behind her, and here he was singing and playing this sensual song in such a bold, naked way.

We met in secret,
loved in fear.
On dark, dark nights
we slept in tears.

They tried to tear us
both apart,
but they can't kill
what's in our hearts.

Take me in your arms and hold me
oh so tight.
Tell me that you'll still love me
through this black night.

We broke free!
chased the sun,
and in the desert
became one
one
one

Dwitty threw in a passionate fill, then dropped back quiet.

And so I took you,
and I made you mine,
my only girl
till the end of time.

Take me in your arms and hold me
oh so tight.
Tell me that you'll always love me
all through this life

all through this life

all through this life.

He took it out soft and easy, dropping in the Beatles' line right at the end, "All you need is love. Love is all you need."

As the last notes faded, the crowd burst into applause. "Go, son!" Rob shouted, and Tricia laughed.

Bobby wiped sweat from his eyes and shook his damp hair back, grinning at the crowd.

"My God, Rob," Nora gushed. "I didn't know he could play like that."

Jules glanced back at her mom. Were those tears glistening in Kate's eyes?

"Come on up here, baby," Bobby held out his arm and walked to the front of the stage.

She went to him and he lifted her up. "God, Bobby, that was

amazing," she breathed, and he smiled as he kissed her. "When did you write that?"

"Last week, jamming in practice. We're gonna do 'Vanilla Snow' now. I want you to sing back-up on it, just like you did on the record."

"You know how nervous this makes me," she protested.

"You'll do fine, honey. You can take my mic and stand back here with me."

"Okay," she consented as he walked her over to his keyboard. How could she say no after the performance he'd just given her?

"That's my girl," he smiled. He kept a hand around her waist as he pulled his mic from its stand. "Some of you may know her," he said to the audience, "as Miss Julia Greene."

Gina, Tricia, and The Rebelles cheered and enticed applause.

"But now she's Mrs. Bobby Lott," he beamed, and the applause grew louder, though Jules noted with pride the group of girls in front of the stage muttering among themselves, barely putting their hands together. "She wrote the lyrics to this next song. And somebody tell Terry he can come out of the bathroom now, I'm done singing," he joked.

Terry came laughing onto the stage and strapped on his Rickenbacker.

It really came home to Kate, the other life her daughter had been living, the intensity of passion between Jules and Bobby, and just how forceful and talented an artist he was. And Jules! Kate had no idea she wrote lyrics, or sang. It was hard to reconcile this Jules with the quiet, studious, obsequious girl who had been hiding so much at home. No wonder she had bolted when she had the chance. As uncertain as she might be about some of Jules' lifestyle choices, she was glad Dan hadn't succeeded in breaking her spirit and turning her into some restrictive man's dutiful wife. She understood now why Natalie had reached out to support them, despite the rules and reasons to the contrary. Kate had seen Bobby's strength and resolve in the way he protected Jules after her father's abuse, but she'd only ever seen a hint of his passion smoldering underneath his quiet nature, until tonight. Even in his youth Dan had never blazed like that.

Kate and Dan barely spoke now. If she was at the house, he would leave. She had been sleeping in Jules' bed, but with it gone now, she was sleeping in Janice's guest room. Thank God he wasn't contesting the divorce. He just seemed to be washing his hands of her the way he'd washed his hands of Jules. At least Jules had Bobby. What did Kate have? She might have been the only person in the room, she felt so alone. She sniffled, dabbed at her nose discreetly with her finger, and then she felt

Nora's arm around her.

When the song ended, Bobby lifted Jules down off the stage and she went back to family and friends. "Oh, honey, I didn't know you could sing like that," Kate put her arms around her. "That was so pretty, and you wrote that?"

"The words. Bobby and Terry wrote the music. It's on the album, and I sing on it. We'll get one to you."

"Terry," Bobby said into his mic, "I think I'm losing my touch."

"Marriage will do that to you," Terry quipped.

"I didn't make her cry."

"I thought that was all you ever seemed to do."

The girls in front squealed.

"Maybe not anymore," Bobby smiled, and with a stroke of his hand up the keys into the opening chord, they were into the song, to the audience's delight.

"I've heard this," Kate realized. "You've played this," she said to Jules. "But, no, I've heard it on the radio, too."

Jules grinned. "It's a hit here, Mom. It went to #1. It charted in four states. Bobby wrote it for me last winter. The A-side charted in five states. 'Sidewalk Girl.' They'll play it last."

And Kate recognized it, too. "I never really realized, sweetheart," she told her daughter, "and I know you were in no position to tell me at the time."

"See why I wanted you to come tonight? I wanted you to see all this. I wanted you to know."

And then Jules' girlfriends were bouncing around her, all laughter and smiles, good wishes and goodbye hugs. "It's not like we'll be that far away," Jules said, "or that we won't be back often."

Late, the house quiet, Bobby turned to Jules as she sat on the bed in his nearly empty old room. The walls, stripped bare of music and mementos, would get a fresh coat of paint tomorrow, as Bobby had promised his mother. Lady slept on the rug. Scraggs, who disliked car rides, remained at home in Louisville, safe inside with large bowls of cat food and water. "Sorry I didn't have time to wrap it." Bobby placed a large, flat box in Jules' hands. She lifted the lid to find a fat reel of tape. "I figured you might want tonight's show."

A smile spread wide across her lips. "Your song," she said softly, closing the box and holding it protectively. "Thank you."

The night before Jules was to start classes, Bobby called her to his side on the clearance sale green couch, where he had settled in to watch *The Smothers Brothers* on the used black and white TV he had bought, the TV on which they had witnessed the horrific violence raging outside the Democratic National Convention in Chicago. Riots seemed to spring up like weeds all across the country. Campuses had become hotbeds of radical unrest, and demonstrations were met with increasing brutality by the authorities.

"Come here, baby," he said softly, hugging her close. "I know this is important to you, but I'd be lying if I said it didn't scare me. Things are just so crazy, and you don't even have to be involved to get hurt. Please promise me that if you ever sense anything brewing at all you'll come straight home. Please."

"I promise," she said. "I'll keep my eyes open and I'll be careful."

Chapter 20

"You, of all people, I would have expected to know about these guys," Terry said, standing at the foot of the stage, waiting for the show to begin. "This cat they've got playing keyboards is supposed to really be something else."

"Well, I've been a little busy," Bobby smiled. Propelled by the October release of "The Inner Sea" as a single, edited down to three minutes, The Rooks Parliament's self titled album was doing well in the regional market, with a few pockets of interest in California. "Vanilla Snow" was slated for release in two weeks, mid-March. Jerry was pushing for some sort of summer tour, but it seemed unlikely. Terry and Bobby had other concerns, and no one had seen Stephen, much less played with him, since they had left Los Angeles. He had called Miles to say he was playing with a band out there, emphasizing that it was "just a side project." With the band in disarray, Bobby had used his clout, and his ability to read standard notation, to get work as a session musician, and his reputation for excellence and flexibility of style was growing. It wasn't as gratifying as playing in a band, but it paid better and he was meeting other talented musicians. He was content for the time being, though doing this in addition to his bookkeeping job meant less time with Jules. She was working, too, as a clerk in the campus bookstore. They were soon going to need all the money they could get.

Gina squeezed Jules' hands. "How far along are you?"

"Three and a half months."

"Are you having morning sickness or anything?"

"Yeah, some. It was kinda bad for a while. Bobby's mom said to have a cup of black tea and a piece of dry toast first thing in the morning. You throw it up, but then you're fine the rest of the day. I figured she should know. It does seem to work."

"You excited? Scared?"

"Both. Bobby's excited. And Mom, of course. She can't believe she's going to be a grandmother. And his parents are thrilled. It's odd, this little person growing inside me, half Bobby and half me." She laid her hand on her abdomen. "I can't wait to see it, to hold it."

"Are you hoping for a boy or a girl?"

"Oh, it doesn't matter. One day I hope it's a boy, the next day I want a girl," she laughed. "So, how are your plans going?"

"We've booked St. Basil's for June 14th. We can have the reception in the parish hall. Let me know when you can come down and look at dresses with me."

"Oh, Gina, I just don't know…"

"Come on, you can't back out on me."

"Gina, I'll be out to here!" she held her hands well in front of her belly.

"It will be fine. I won't make you wear anything stupid looking. You'll be beautiful, you and Bobby up there together with us."

"These guys got banned from the Albert Hall for burning an American flag on stage," Terry excitedly told Bobby, "and they're English. The world is watching America, Bobby. I think it's time we took more of a stand. We should join the revolution, re-form as a protest band."

"I don't know, man," Bobby shook his head. "I'm not really into doing that."

"Music is your vehicle, man."

"Yeah. Yeah, it is, and I want to keep it pure. I don't want to mix politics with it. What the hell, really, do I know about politics anyway? I see stuff happening, but I don't know what to think about a lot of it. My music is about the love of music. It's not about dividing people or choosing sides. It's for anyone who wants it.'

"Yeah, well, look at you. You're safe, for now anyway, family man. But what about Tyler?" He grasped Bobby's upper arm. "Don't you care about him, about others like him?"

"Of course I fucking care!" He shook off Terry's hand. "He was my best friend."

"Well, shouldn't you do something then, for your best friend?"

"We don't know what happened to Tyler. Maybe he dodged the draft, or maybe he ran off with a girl, or maybe he just didn't want to go back to fucking Midvale! All we've got is speculations. Unless you know something and you've been holding out."

"I always figured *you* were."

Bobby's head dropped as he shook it. "No, man. I don't know a goddamn thing. I knew something was bugging him, but he wouldn't tell me." He pushed his wallet deeper into his pocket. It still held that scrap of note, that little piece of Tyler he could never let go of, that tiny little ragged hope. *Take care, brother. Maybe someday–* He'd never shown it to anyone, not even Jules.

And then his head snapped up and his chest inflated. He clenched his hand just short of grabbing Terry's collar. "But don't you ever, ever insinuate that my wife or my child are a draft dodge. I married her because I love her, and I believe in love. I believe in saying it and I believe in living it. Our child is made of love, and nothing else. Yes, I want freedom, and peace, and equality for all of us. Who in their right mind doesn't? But I don't pretend to have the answers. This country's gone fucking crazy. We're killing our own on our own soil. Things are going to get worse, you mark my words. And I've got a family to try to keep out of harm's way."

Terry was mustering up a retort when Gina stepped between them and backed him off. "Leave him be, Terry. We can't all always walk the same road. Y'all are supposed to be friends, remember?"

Bobby pulled Jules close to his side, still staring Terry down. "It's okay, baby," she said softly.

Terry lowered his eyes, reached his hand out to Bobby. "I'm sorry, man. You do what you think is right."

Bobby nodded and gave him a brother handshake.

"That's more like it," Gina smiled. "Now, let's just have some fun!"

"Right on!" Jules grinned and slapped Gina's palm.

When The Nice walked out on stage, they looked like just another hippie band, with one notable difference; they didn't have a guitarist. "They used to have one," Terry puzzled. It would soon become obvious they didn't need one.

The keyboardist, a thin man, with brown hair and bangs, just a few years older than Bobby, had in his arsenal two Hammond organs, a C3 and an L100, three Leslie rotating speaker cabinets, and a grand piano. Bobby could not have guessed just how these instruments were about to be used. In a fringed leather jacket, tight jeans, and tall boots, this fellow approached the L100. He played a chord, and while holding it, began to flip the power switch off and on, making the tones fall and rise, fall and rise. He began to tip the organ back with his knee and let it fall back into place, creating a crashing sound by jolting the internal reverb spring. Back and forth, back and forth, crashing, building speed, approximating the sound of a train, grinning maniacally as he prepared to take the audience on the ride of their lives. The bassist and drummer commenced a galloping rhythm foundation and the organist, his instrument distorted by a fuzz box, began playing Bach. Another round of noise, and he was into a rollicking version of Brubeck's "Blue Rondo a la Turk," but in 4/4 time, giving it a rock feel, and a lot of flair. Having played through the song flamboyantly, he began to improvise, then vaulted right over the organ, leaning it against himself and reaching over it to play Bach, back to front! Bobby glanced at Jules, whose mouth was agape. It was a fairly common audience reaction just then.

When the song came to its grinding, noisy conclusion, the bassist introduced, "Mr. Keith Emerson." Bobby wasn't likely to forget this name.

The bassist, Lee Jackson, was also the vocalist, and after raspily singing a couple of poppier psychedelic numbers, introduced a longer piece, "Ars Longa Vita Brevis," a strange amalgamation of rock, classical, and jazz elements that saw him drawing a bow across his bass strings, featured the drummer, Brian Davison, playing an assortment of small gongs and blowing a whistle, and Keith moving mid-song from the C3 to the piano, which he not only played in normal fashion, but also reached inside to pluck the strings.

They even bent Bob Dylan songs to their purposes. And Jean Sibelius. Tim Hardin's "Hang on to a Dream" became mellifluous piano jazz.

To cap off the performance, Keith grabbed the L100 and dragged it violently around the stage, all 350 pounds of it, yanking and twisting it to create feedback, then played an instrumental that deftly combined Bernstein's "America" with Dvorak's "New World Symphony." At the song's climax, he produced daggers from under his belt, which he dramatically stabbed between the keys, but not without purpose. "Do you see what he's doing?" Bobby turned to Jules. "They're holding the notes for him." He played along with the interval created by the daggers, manipulating the power switch to make the organ moan and wail like a banshee. Then he pulled out the knives and hurled them into one of the rotating speaker cabinets, and proceeded to climb on top of the instrument, feet straddling the lower keyboard. As he pulled up on the back of the cabinet with one hand and flexed his feet and knees, the instrument rocked and crept across the stage. He was actually riding it! It teetered menacingly at the edge of the stage, and Bobby pulled Jules protectively close.

Keith dismounted and dragged the organ back, then grabbed a drumstick, reached inside the open back of the organ and began bashing on its innards as Lee recited, "America is pregnant with promise and anticipation, but is murdered by the hand of the inevitable."

Bobby stood dazed. He'd certainly never seen or heard anything like that. But this man wasn't just stepping over musical boundaries, he was, albeit violently, interacting in new ways with the technology of his instruments, and that impressed Bobby as much as the music.

"That," Jules said, "was seriously sexy."

"Stiff competition, eh, Bobby?" Terry punched his arm.

"Look at him!" Gina laughed. "He looks like he's just seen God."

"I think what I've just seen," Bobby said, "is the future."

www.ingramcontent.com/pod-product-compliance
Lightning Source LLC
Chambersburg PA
CBHW030409020726
47493CB00003B/1001